IN THIS SMALL SPOT

BOOKS BY CAREN J. WERLINGER

Currently available:
Looking Through Windows
Miserere
In This Small Spot

Coming soon:
Year of the Monsoon
Neither Present Time
She Sings of Old, Unhappy, Far-off Things

7 July 2017

in this small spot

To Leana,

Blessings to you.

Pax,
Caren Werlinger

caren j. werlinger

In This Small Spot
By Caren J. Werlinger

Copyright © 2007, 2013 by Caren J. Werlinger. All rights reserved.
Published by Corgyn Publishing, LLC.

eBook ISBN: 978-0-9886501-4-5
Print ISBN: 978-0-9886501-5-2

Scripture readings are taken from the Jerusalem Bible, copyright 1966 by Darton, Longman and Todd Ltd., & Doubleday and Company Inc. Used by permission.

Cover photograph by José Luís Mieza

Cover design by Patty G. Henderson
www.boulevardphotografica.yolasite.com

Book design by Maureen Cutajar
www.gopublished.com

E-mail: cjwerlingerbooks@yahoo.com

This work is copyrighted and is licensed only for use by the original purchaser and can be copied to the original purchaser's electronic device and its memory card for your personal use. Modifying or making copies of this work or distributing it to any unauthorized person by any means, without limit, including by email, CD, DVD, memory cards, file transfer, paper printout or any other method, constitutes a violation of International copyright law and subjects the violator to severe fines or imprisonment. Please purchase only authorized electronic editions.

This is a work of fiction. Names, characters, places, and incidents are the product of the author's imagination or are used fictitiously, and any resemblance to actual persons, living or dead, businesses, companies, events, or locales is entirely coincidental.

Dedication

For Beth
nunc et ad infinitum

Acknowledgements

The acknowledgements for this book go back more than thirty-five years: to my aunts who were nuns in a medical order, to the nuns in our local parish and the nuns of various other convents here in the U.S. and in England who met with me and wrote to me, all of them replying to my neverending questions as I searched for my path in life. I eventually found it, and discovered that it did not lie within convent walls, though a part of me is still drawn toward a life of contemplation.

And though that part of me has always wondered "what if?", I cannot now imagine my life without my partner, Beth. For over twenty years, she has been by my side, my most perfect other – and often better – half.

As always, I must thank the people who read my early drafts of this novel and offered their feedback and encouragement: Beth, as well as Marty, Marge, Susan and Debbie. I am indebted to all of them.

I was still having difficulty finding the right title for this book, even after it was mostly written, when I heard a beautifully spare piano composition by Windham Hill artist Tim Story, titled In This Small Spot. The piece itself was so haunting, so contemplative, that it became part of my soundtrack (in addition to LOTS of Gregorian chant) as I worked on the subsequent edits of this novel. The title just worked wonderfully for this book, so I owe a tremendous thank-you to Mr. Story.

And to my readers, thank you. I would probably keep putting my little stories out there, even if you didn't read them, but it sure makes it more gratifying when you do!

in this small spot

Typical Daily Schedule at St. Bridget's Abbey

4:30 a.m.	rise
5:00 a.m.	Lauds
6:00 a.m.	Prime
6:15 a.m.	breakfast (Silence ends)
7:30 a.m.	Terce
7:45 a.m.	Mass
9:00 a.m.	work
11:15 a.m.	Sext
11:30 a.m.	lunch
	Recreation
1:15 p.m.	None
1:30 p.m.	work
4:00 p.m.	Vespers
4:30 p.m.	Rest, reading, study
5:30 p.m.	supper
6:30 p.m.	Compline
7:00 p.m.	Lectio Divina
8:00 p.m.	Matins
9:00 p.m.	retire (Silence begins)

Chapter 1

A few drops of water, unable to cling to the fly line as it was whipped off the stream, hung suspended for a split second, miniature prisms in the morning sunlight. The fly and line landed softly above a small eddy in the current. There was a sudden splash as the fly drifted over the eddy, and a fat rainbow trout was rushing upstream, accompanied by the singing of the reel and Mickey's whooping laughter as she held the rod.

In an effort not to lose the fish, she worked her way upstream also, slipping on mossy rocks while trying to keep the rod up with tension on the line. The trout gradually tired, and she was able to reel it closer. After a few more minutes, she was kneeling in the shallows near the bank with the tired trout lying placidly in the water between her knees. She unhooked it with her forceps, and gave it a gentle nudge back into deeper water. At the realization that it was free, the trout flipped its tail, splashing water all over Mickey's face. Laughing again, she wiped her face with her sleeve and said, "Thank you, mister trout, for a memory that will last me the rest of my life."

As if on cue, a deep-toned bell began to ring in the distance. Sighing, she looked around. Still kneeling in the water, she listened to the noise of the stream as the water roiled over rocks in the streambed. She watched robins and chickadees hopping from tree branch to ground and back up again. The trees were just beginning to bud on this April morning in the Adirondacks. Small pockets of snow remained on the ground on the north side of the trees, hidden from the weak spring sunlight. Green shoots were pushing up through the fallen leaves littering the ground, and small bunches of crocus bravely bloomed. She heard the hollow clunk of a hoof striking a rock, and looked the other way to see a curious Angus cow looking over a nearby fence at her. A small black calf peeked from behind its mother, not sure what to make of this creature in the water.

Mickey picked up her rod and got to her feet, sending the calf skittering away across the field. She climbed up the bank and started along a trail through the woods. The trail eventually diverted from the stream, and the water sounds grew fainter as she continued down the mountain. After a half hour's walk, she came to her four wheel drive vehicle. She quickly broke down her fly rod and pulled off her wet waders and boots. Slipping into dry shoes, she hopped into the driver's seat and began to drive carefully down the rutted dirt road. Another thirty minutes and she was pulling into the drive of a small white clapboard farmhouse with a sturdy red barn adjacent. The white door of the barn slid open as she got out of the SUV.

"Hey, Mickey," yawned the man emerging from the barn, rubbing his hands through his red hair, so that it stood up at odd angles. "How was the fishing?"

"It was great. Ten or twelve fish." She looked at his blood-shot eyes. "Have you been working all night?"

"Yup," he grinned. "When the muse is with you... Want to see?"

Accompanying him back into the barn, Mickey saw a larger-than-life clay sculpture of a nude woman holding an infant.

"Oh, Jamie," she breathed, "it's exquisite." Circling the sculpture bathed in the soft light coming from the south-facing windows, she took in the gentle play of light and shadow on the clay's contours. "I don't think Michelangelo could have done a better job with the anatomy."

"Thanks," he murmured modestly, but his face shone with pride as he looked over his work. "I think it's one of my best."

Mickey put an arm around his shoulders and said, "C'mon. Let's get some breakfast."

They walked over to the house where Jamie made coffee while Mickey fried eggs and bacon at the seventies-era avocado green stove. A little while later, as they sat at the table over empty plates, sipping a second cup of coffee, Jamie broke the silence.

"Mick?" He looked up into blue eyes almost identical to his own. "Are you sure about doing this?"

She looked out the window for several seconds before answering. "I've asked myself that question a million times. I honestly don't know. Maybe it won't work out. Maybe I'll leave in a few months, or be asked to leave. Who knows? But I have to try." She took a deep breath and carried her plate to the sink. "I'd better get ready."

Jamie did the dishes while she went upstairs to shower. Back in her room, she dressed slowly in a grey flannel skirt, white blouse and grey sweater. Lacing up plain, black shoes over thick black hose, she stood to study her reflection in the mirror. She couldn't help but laugh at herself. She tucked one last book into the trunk at the foot of her bed. Hesitating a second, she put a black leather bag inside also and closed the lid with a snap of the brass latches.

When she came back into the kitchen, Jamie looked up and gagged on his coffee, spraying some on the newspaper he was reading.

"What?" she scowled. "You've seen me in a skirt before."

"Yeah," he laughed, wiping coffee off his chin with his sleeve, "when we were five! Oh, I wish Mom could see this."

"Leave her out of this." Gesturing back up the stairs, she asked, "Are you sure the other boxes won't be in your way? I wasn't ready to get rid of everything, you know, just in case."

"They won't be in the way at all," he smiled. "That room will be yours anytime you need it."

"Jamie," she began, but her voice cracked. He came to her and gave her a hug. "I don't know what I would have done without you these last couple of years."

"I know," he whispered. "You would have done the same for me." They both wiped their eyes and went upstairs to get the trunk and her one suitcase.

When everything was loaded into the SUV, Mickey handed Jamie an envelope. "This is the registration to the truck, and a copy of my will, you know..."

"Just in case," he finished.

They got in and drove. Jamie tried to keep casual conversation going, but after receiving nothing but monosyllabic responses from Mickey, he gave up. After about twenty minutes, a tall stone bell tower came into view over the trees. As they drew nearer, a sprawling complex of buildings, mostly stone, became visible behind a tall cast-iron fence. "St. Bridget's Abbey", in large bronze letters formed an arch over the entry to the long drive.

Jamie followed the drive up to the largest of the buildings, and stopped the car in front of a pair of tall oak doors. When Mickey just sat there, her hand gripping the door handle with white knuckles, he asked, "Want me to drive away before anyone comes?"

She laughed sheepishly and got out. Bracing herself, she raised the brass knocker and rapped twice. In a moment, one of the heavy doors was opened by a diminutive nun in a full-length black habit.

"Hello, Sister Lucille," said Mickey nervously, "I'm Mick- uh, Michele Stewart."

"Of course, my dear," replied the nun with a smile which made her eyes crinkle. "I almost didn't recognize you. Do you have any baggage to bring in?"

You have no idea, Mickey thought wryly as she reached to take her suitcase from Jamie. Together, they carried the trunk over the threshold. Turning to Jamie, she gave him a hug.

"Call me if you need anything," he murmured. He gave her a kiss on the cheek, and went back to the SUV. Mickey heard him pull away as Sister Lucille swung the oak door shut.

"Mother Theodora asked to see you when you arrived. Follow me, dear. Your trunk and suitcase will be taken to the postulants' dormitory."

Sister Lucille led Mickey on a familiar path through a maze of marble-tiled halls, passing many heavy oak doors spaced at regular intervals in the plaster walls which were painted a creamy white. As always, Mickey felt like she was making a lot of noise as her footsteps echoed in the corridors, while Sister Lucille didn't seem to make any sound other than the soft wooden click of the rosary she wore at her waist. At last, Sister Lucille stopped and knocked on a door at the end of a hall.

"*Venite,*" said a voice from within.

Sister Lucille opened the door, and replied, "*Pax tecum.*"

"*Et cum spiritu tuo.*"

"Mother, Michele Stewart has arrived," Sister Lucille announced as she stepped aside to allow Mickey in.

"Thank you, Sister," Mickey said as Sister Lucille pulled the door shut.

"I wasn't sure you would come," said Mother Theodora as she stood to greet Mickey. She was not an especially tall woman, but she exuded a calm authority that, from the beginning, had made her seem imposing. Mickey had always felt that Mother Theodora's piercing dark eyes could see right through her. In all their talks over the past two years, she had been brutally honest with Mother Theodora, simply because it had seemed futile to be anything but.

"To tell you the truth, I wasn't sure either until I actually knocked on the door."

"You look, uh, different." Mother Theodora smiled.

Mickey laughed, an infectious, self-deprecating laugh. "I suppose I do."

"Please, sit down," Mother Theodora said, indicating one of the chairs in front of her desk. She sat in the other, the folds of her black habit falling into place around her.

Mickey had spent many hours in this office, situated in a round tower on the southeast corner of the abbey. Large windows looked out on the grounds, and the sunlight streaming in highlighted the grain in the wide wooden floorboards. The circular walls were lined with bookcases, built to match the curve of the stone walls.

"You will join the others in a few minutes," Mother Theodora began, "but I wanted a chance to speak with you privately beforehand."

Mickey shifted uncomfortably in her chair. Surely Mother Theodora hadn't changed her mind at this late date?

"I have decided not to share our conversations with Sister Rosaria, your postulant mistress. Being a postulant can be difficult enough without added scrutiny."

Mickey met her gaze unflinchingly. "Thank you, Mother. I know there are many who would feel you are making a mistake. I won't betray your trust."

Several seconds passed as Mother Theodora searched Mickey's eyes. "I know you mean that, Mickey. But remember that an abbey is not a place where you can run from yourself. Quite the contrary. Having stripped away the disguises and distractions of the outside world: clothes, career, material possessions, the true you is most often magnified, for better or for worse."

Smiling suddenly, she stood and pressed a button on her desk. "I may not have a chance to speak with you later, so I'll take this opportunity to welcome you to St. Bridget's."

Mickey stood to receive an embrace from Mother Theodora. Sister Lucille knocked and escorted Mickey through an unfamiliar series of halls to a sparsely furnished room where four other young women waited, all dressed in similar fashion with simple clothing in shades of grey, black and white. She murmured a hello which was shyly returned by the others. She could see they all felt as nervous as she. It was obvious that, at 36, she was much older than the others.

A door on the other side of the room opened, and a matronly nun entered. "Hello, girls. I'm Sister Rosaria. I will be your postulant mistress. Welcome to St. Bridget's." She looked around, appraising them. "This can be a difficult time, adjusting to abbey life. If any of you have problems, please know that you can come to me anytime."

She bustled over to a table where lay a pile of neatly folded white linens. Picking one up, she said, "I will pin your veils on before we go into the Chapel."

One by one, Sister Rosaria refolded the short white veils and placed them on the heads of each of the postulants, using bobby pins to hold them in place.

"Now, are you all ready? You will be presented to the community following the Eucharist."

She opened the door through which she had entered, and led the five postulants to the main Chapel. The east end of the Chapel was highlighted by a magnificent stained-glass window depicting Jesus greeting Mary Magdalene after his resurrection. Below the window was the altar, a plain, massive slab of granite, embellished only by a beautiful altar cloth. A couple of steps down from the altar dais were the nuns' stalls, arranged in tiers on either side of the Chapel so that they faced each other. Each wooden stall contained a narrow wooden kneeler and a hinged seat which flipped up to reveal a small storage space for prayer books. At the west end of the Chapel, separated from the nuns' stalls by a floor to ceiling grille, was the public area where visitors and locals could come to hear Mass on Sundays and holidays. Above this small chapel was the organ loft, with a forest of pipes reaching up to the vaulted stone ceiling which was supported by a series of stone arches and pillars.

As Mickey and the others took their places in the stalls indicated by Sister Rosaria, there were some covert glances from the other nuns. Outright curiosity was unmonastic - a term all of the postulants would become familiar with over the days and weeks to come - but for most of the nuns, this was their first glance at the incoming postulants, "our first chance to size them up." They knew from experience that fewer than half any incoming cohort of postulants typically made it to final vows, though no one said that to the postulants. "Well," the nuns would have said pragmatically, "it is a hard life, and not all are suited."

Looking through the grille separating the nuns' stalls from the public sanctuary, Mickey remembered how many hours she had spent in those pews wondering where she was being led. Now at last, on this side of the grate, she wondered if she would be up to the journey.

Chapter 2

"Alice? Where are you?" Mickey dropped her keys and overstuffed briefcase in the Stickley chair beside the door.

"I'm in the kitchen," Alice called out, offering a cheek for Mickey's kiss, but keeping her eye on the sauce she was stirring. "This should be just about ready..."

"Ummm, smells wonderful," Mickey sniffed as she got dishes out of the cupboard.

Mickey set the table as the last bits of the cooking ritual were concluded. She smiled as Alice carefully spooned the sauce over a large bowl of pasta.

"Not that I'm complaining," Mickey said as she uncorked a bottle of wine, "but you must be tired. Why did you go to so much trouble?"

"Because I know you," Alice smiled. "If I didn't cook, we would be eating Cheerios."

Mickey laughed. "You're right." She poured two glasses of wine and brought them to the table while Alice carried the bowl of pasta.

"How was your day?" Mickey asked as she stabbed at her salad.

Alice gave her a wry look over the top of her glasses. "Today was our field trip to the Natural History Museum. They had a reproduction of some large meat-eating dinosaur, complete with sound effects." She took a bite of her pasta. "One roar and we had forty second-graders screaming and running in different directions." Mickey tried not to laugh. "By the time we caught them, they had all started crying." Mickey couldn't hold it in anymore, and Alice laughed with her, shaking her head. "It was a disaster. We'll probably get calls from every parent tomorrow asking why their kid had nightmares about dinosaurs." She took a sip of wine, then asked, "So how was your day?"

Mickey swallowed before answering. "Mrs. Wallace died today. Her family was with her. It was time. I'm so glad she finally felt like she could let go." Mickey paused to take a drink from her water glass. "Had to do a biopsy on Danielle Wilson's leg today. We'll probably have to remove it." She stared down at her plate, pushing the pasta around with her fork. "Her dog got hit and killed by a car yesterday. She's only ten." Her voice trailed off.

Alice reached out and took Mickey's hand. Mickey stared down at their intertwined fingers, her eyes filling.

"I really love you," she said, looking up into Alice's gentle, dark eyes.

"I know." Alice smiled, kissing Mickey's hand. "Do you want to go to the shelter tonight and see if we can find Danielle a puppy?"

Mickey brushed a tear from her cheek. "Could we? I already asked her parents if they'd mind."

"Are you going to sneak it in to her in the hospital?" Alice asked, though she already knew the answer.

Mickey grinned. "Of course."

Chapter 3

Four-thirty a.m. Sister Rosaria's small silver bell tinkled in the darkness. Mickey groaned, but was instantly awake, old training kicking in automatically. Sitting on the side of her bed, she could hear the other postulants stirring. A large round tower room on the third floor, two stories above Mother Theodora's office, the dormitory was furnished with a dozen beds set at intervals around the circular wall – "but we haven't had that many postulants for decades," Sister Rosaria had told them. With one shared bathroom, Mickey was grateful they were only five, though she knew that was a luxury the rest of the community didn't enjoy. Hanging curtains separated the beds and provided privacy. In the low light from the wall sconces, the postulants silently dressed and made their beds. Mickey still had difficulty getting her short white veil properly positioned, as there were no mirrors.

By five o'clock, all the nuns were in their stalls in Chapel. Above them, the bell rang for Lauds. The organ sounded a single lingering note, and with one voice the entire community began the daily ritual of praise, the ancient Gregorian chant rising in waves to the vaulted ceiling above.

Mickey and the others were still learning how to keep their place in the Divine Office, the Book of the Hours. "We keep the Office in its full Solemnity," Sister Rosaria told them. "Most other communities have gone to an abbreviated version." She paused with a slight sniff. "While that alteration allows more work to get done, we embrace the Office as our *opus Dei*."

Each evening, Sister Rosaria helped them mark their prayer books for the next day, smiling patiently at the postulants' sighs of exasperation. "But it changes every day!" they exclaimed in frustration. Sister Rosaria nodded. "Of course it does. How boring it would be if we sang the same thing every day. You will learn." The days were divided into eight hours, though "why do they call it an hour? Some of them are only ten minutes long?" Lauds was the first hour of the day, followed by a short period of silent prayer. Then the bell for Prime was rung, and following Prime the community gathered in the refectory for breakfast.

Standing at their places as Mother Theodora led them in singing grace, the nuns gave thanks prior to eating. Breakfast was the first time each day when conversation was permitted. During much of the day and all through the night, Silence was observed, to be broken only for urgent matters. The quiet created a more reflective atmosphere. "If you're talking, you're not praying," Sister Rosaria reminded the postulants repeatedly. They quickly found that, even when conversation was tolerated, frivolous babble was not. "Speak only when you have something edifying to say." 'Edifying' was another favorite word of the nuns. Learning to curb their tongues was the first and greatest stumbling block for most of the postulants. "Even words matter here," Mickey wrote in her first letter to Jamie, "as if they are a resource not to be squandered meaninglessly."

Over their first few weeks together, the five postulants got to know one another, sharing bits of their backgrounds – "or more than a bit," Mickey would have sighed. The other four were all in their twenties. Abigail Morgan was the youngest at twenty-one. She blithely told them, more than once, that she had always known she would be a nun. She chattered endlessly about the various convents she had visited before deciding on St. Bridget's. "Even my name led me here," she laughed, although she was never called Abby by the senior nuns who believed nicknames were inappropriate. "She is so twenty-one," Mickey wrote to Jamie. "I often find myself longing to slap her."

One of the biggest surprises for Mickey was how easily irritated she was by little things. She had to force herself again and again to swallow the sarcastic remarks which seemed to jump onto her tongue. She had never considered herself a mean person, but "can't you *ever* be quiet?" she snapped at Abigail one afternoon, earning herself a reprimand from Sister Rosaria. Here, with so much focus on self-control and intellectual pursuits, with no workouts, no hours of concentration in the OR, no rushing about from place to place, no outlet for all of her pent-up energy, Mickey felt the meanness gathering under the surface like a boil, getting ready to erupt, "and one of these days, it's going to blow and all this nastiness is going to escape," she would have said if she had felt she could say such things aloud. If she had, she would have quickly realized she wasn't alone.

Tanya Petersen, a postulant who had come to St. Bridget's from Minnesota, was normally very quiet and even-tempered. One afternoon as the postulants were on their hands and knees cleaning the marble floor of the main corridor of the cloister, Sister Fiona came by to inspect their work. Sister Fiona was from Ireland, and was very particular about the cleaning of the abbey.

"Hmmm," she said, leaning over and swiping a finger over the tiles. "Again, please."

"But, Sister," Tanya protested, "we've already scrubbed the floor twice."

Sister Fiona simply looked down at her with a questioning expression.

"Yes, Sister," Tanya said.

As Sister Fiona's black skirts disappeared around the corner, Tanya threw her brush into the bucket, splashing herself and the floor with dirty water. Sputtering and blinking the water out of her eyes, her pale Swedish complexion went a peculiar blotchy pink as she fought to keep from swearing.

"I baptize you in the name of Sister Fiona," Mickey intoned in a deep voice, tossing Tanya a clean rag to wipe her face. In a moment, all five were giggling uncontrollably.

Wendy Barnes was the second oldest postulant at twenty-eight.

She had taught in a Catholic school in Philadelphia with nuns whose order she had entered and left after three years, saying, "I needed an order with more discipline." Indeed, she seemed to embrace their new routine with scrupulous adherence to detail and discipline, leaving the others often feeling hopelessly undisciplined.

"I guess she likes rules," Mickey shrugged to Jessica Thomas, the last postulant in this year's group. Jessica was "round. It's the only word I can think of to describe her," Mickey wrote to Jamie. "Her body is round, her face is round, her eyes always look big and frightened and round behind her round glasses, even her mouth when she sings looks like those tacky porcelain angels Mom had on the mantel when we were growing up." But Jessica's roundness extended to her personality. She was unflappable, rolling with whatever came her way. She knew a little bit about everything, and was always ready with a response if asked, even if she never volunteered an answer. Mickey quickly came to respect the intellect behind Jessica's perpetually hesitant façade, adding, "She's probably the most intelligent one in the group."

Mickey remained vague about her background. It had never occurred to her that her relationship with Mother Theodora might be unique or unusual, but none of the others had such a connection. Jessica's family had known of the abbey for years, coming from a nearby town for Christmas and Easter since she was a child. The others had had most of their correspondence with Sister Ignatius, the nun in charge of answering aspirants' letters, helping them through the entrance process, as she had Mickey when at last Mickey had decided to enter. And, though her letters were full of advice and encouragement, Sister Ignatius also used that contact to size up the suitability of the aspirants. "This one will do," or "I have some reservations about this one; she seems better suited to an active order," she reported to the Council as they decided whom to admit. "They asked me to wait a year," Abigail told the others, "Finish my degree. But I begged them to let me come now. I didn't want to be put off."

Mickey had no idea if Mother had influenced the Council to accept her, but sensed that her relationship with Mother, if known, would set her apart from the other postulants even more than her age and profession. "I worked in a hospital," was all Mickey had said when asked what she did prior to entering St. Bridget's. *Let's hope that's all that ever has to be said of that,* she thought.

Following breakfast was the hour of Terce and then Mass. Father Andrew was the priest assigned to St. Bridget's from St. Dominic's, the monks' abbey near Palmyra. Mickey guessed him to be in his mid-fifties, his salt and pepper hair cropped short with a tonsure. As he sang the Mass in Latin, his beautiful baritone provided counterpoint to the nuns' voices as they alternated responses. Sometimes, Mickey got so caught up in listening that she forgot to sing. A soft clearing of the throat from Sister Rosaria snapped her back to attention as she scrambled to find her place. Invariably, a sigh would follow from Sister Rosaria's direction.

After Mass another bell signaled one of two work periods built into the day. Bells for everything. In those first days, "I felt lost," Mickey would recall later, trying to remember what came next, but gradually, she began to recognize the voices of the different bells: Lauds, Prime, breakfast, Terce, Mass, work, Sext, lunch – and she began to feel the flow of the days.

☩ ☩ ☩

"*Ubi caritas et amor, Deus ibi est. Simil quoque cum beatis videamus...*"

"Where charity and love are, there God is. Just as the saints see –"

"No!" came a sharp rebuke from Sister Stephen.

Work for the postulants was divided between classes and helping in various parts of the abbey. The postulants' classes initially focused on Latin – "which should still be taught in schools," Sister Stephen often lamented. "It would make our work so much easier."

Sister Stephen was a stern teacher, holding the postulants to strict pronunciation and grammar. To Tanya now, she said, "'*Beatis*' is the object of the preposition '*cum*', and '*videamus*' is first person plural, 'we see', not 'they see'."

Mickey, who had taken Latin – "a million years ago" – had a

shaky leg up on the other four, but still struggled to turn it into the living language of the Office. As beautiful as the plainchant was, it meant much more when she understood what she was singing, but she, along with the others, was intimidated by Sister Stephen who "must be a hundred years old," Abigail had whispered during one of their first classes.

"Not quite," Sister Stephen said drily as Abigail quailed at being overheard. "Fortunately, my hearing still works fine. But when you can ask me in Latin, I'll tell you how old I am. For now, back to Aquinas."

As much as Mickey found herself enjoying the challenge of learning Latin, their other class, Church history, was another matter. She and Mother Theodora had talked at length about how to distinguish one's faith in God from one's feelings about the Church and some of the things it had committed or permitted in the past.

"How do you reconcile yourself with that?" Mickey had asked in frustration during one of their early conversations.

Mother Theodora thought for a while. "I assume you were born in the United States?" Mickey nodded. "Why do you stay?"

"What do you mean?"

"Well, the United States government has committed unimaginable atrocities against the native people who occupied this land before us. It sanctioned Jim Crow laws and other forms of discrimination against blacks, and still sanctions discrimination against homosexuals today. Why don't you leave? How do you reconcile yourself with being a citizen of a country that could do those things?"

"Believe me," said Mickey ruefully, "I've thought about moving to Canada more than once."

Mother smiled. "Neither of us can change the history of the world we are a part of. And as angry and ashamed as we may be by aspects of those histories, what we can offer now is a commitment to work for justice and to see that those atrocities are never allowed to happen again."

"What about your vows?" Mickey challenged.

"What about them?"

"Don't your vows mean you're supposed to consider the Church infallible?"

Mother shook her head. "No vow can compel us to accept anything we truly feel is against our conscience. I am bound to a certain level of obedience to my superiors," she said, "but I feel a greater obligation to work to right the wrongs that have been committed in the name of righteousness."

After months of reflection and prayer on that conversation, Mickey had decided that she would not allow her philosophic disagreement with the Church's politics and history to dissuade her from testing her vocation. What was testing her vocation was Sister Renatta, the nun who taught Church history. Part of Mickey's irritation was triggered by Sister Renatta herself. She was very thin, with hollowed-out cheeks and large eyes, made even larger when framed by her wimple and veil. Her face often bore an expression akin to a trance as her eyes would fill with tears in response to some vision only she could see. She looked as if she had stepped out of the pages of one of the illuminated medieval texts in the library, and she spoke in bland platitudes that gave Mickey the distinct impression that she could easily have been quoting from a twelfth century manuscript. Mickey doubted that Sister Renatta had ever questioned anything in her life, placidly doing and believing as she was told. Mickey thought perhaps she was alone in her impatience with Sister Renatta until one morning when Sister Renatta had kept them past her allotted time, pretending she hadn't noticed Sister Stephen pacing impatiently at the back of the classroom while she breathlessly concluded her lesson on the life of St. Thérèse of Lisieux. Mickey heard Sister Stephen mutter to Sister Rosaria, "One foot already in heaven, that one."

Chapter 4

Spring came in a rush of color as flowers and trees and bushes within the high stone walls of the abbey gardens all burst into bloom at once. The nuns, even those who weren't gardeners, reveled in the color as they wandered the enclosure during Recreation. Selected cuttings were used to bring spare bits of color into the Chapel and the common room. "We don't want to be garish," Sister Rosaria said, as Mickey smiled at the thought of the nuns being garish. But, "in a sea of black and white, more than a little color can seem like too much," Sister Rosaria insisted seriously, with a reproving glance in Mickey's direction.

As the weather warmed, the postulants and five novices - three first years and two second years, wearing their black habits with short white veils - were recruited to help on the abbey's farm. The abbey kept a small dairy herd, chickens and a few requisite barn cats to keep the mouse population under control. The cats were all spayed or neutered, courtesy of the local veterinarian who cared for the occasional sick cow or helped with difficult births. In addition to the animals, the abbey raised hay to feed the cows through the winter months and kept an apple and peach orchard plus a large vegetable garden. A total of a hundred acres was enclosed within the abbey's outer fences.

Sister Regina directed the juniors as they planted the vegetable seedlings she had tenderly nurtured in the abbey's small greenhouse.

Wearing work aprons and sleeves, they planted the young plants in the rows Sister Regina had prepared in the garden.

This work, the first physical outdoor work Mickey had done in weeks, was like a tonic to her. Her cheeks were flushed and she felt like she had extra energy. By the time they got to the refectory for lunch after a couple of hours spent working in the garden, she was famished. Mickey hadn't been sure what to expect from convent food – "funny how worried we all were about that," she wrote to Jamie – but she was pleasantly surprised at the heartiness of the meals. She considered it fortunate that she preferred plain food, but she never left the table hungry. Second helpings weren't frowned upon, but leaving food on the plate was. Sister Rosaria only needed to admonish them once about that. "Being hungry isn't a sin; being wasteful is."

Tanya, Jessica and Abigail all seemed to be as hungry as Mickey was after their morning's work in the garden, but Wendy took only a tiny helping of food. "She's starting to look like Sister Renatta," Tanya murmured. Looking at her more closely, Mickey realized Wendy had lost a good bit of weight. Sister Rosaria obviously noticed as well. "Believe me, abbey life will provide you with all the suffering you think you need," Sister Rosaria reproved Wendy when she saw the meager portion she had taken. Mickey hid a smile. Sister Rosaria had been postulant mistress for a long time. "Picking you up after you faint is more suffering than I need. Eat," she said sagely.

Wendy's exaggerated strictness had quickly become an irritant to Mickey, but "it's none of your business," she told herself repeatedly. Still, "I can't pretend I didn't enjoy hearing her scolded for a change," Mickey confided to Jessica who smiled in agreement.

In June, when the first hay was ready for mowing, Sister Regina started up St. Jude, the abbey's ancient tractor, named for the patron saint of lost causes. Each time she started the tractor, Sister Regina murmured a prayer asking St. Jude to intercede. It worked every time. Of course, it helped that Sister Regina kept the tractor immaculately clean, oiled and lubricated with generous amounts of grease. Then the two of them pulled the mower through the fields, leaving the hay to dry for a few days. Whether it was luck, or divine intervention, no one knew, but it never rained while the abbey's hay was drying. All the other farmers in the region would mow also as word got around that "St. Jude is cutting." When it was time to bale the hay, three farmers who had square balers would come over to the abbey's field. The square bales were loaded onto a flat trailer pulled by St. Jude. This was where the postulants and novices helped, dividing themselves into ground crew and trailer crew, throwing the bales onto the trailer where they were stacked up. When the trailer was fully loaded, the bales were taken to the barn where they were hoisted into the loft with ropes. Generally, the abbey got three hay cuttings in over the course of the summer, which gave the cows plenty of feed to keep them producing milk all winter long.

It took two days to get the first hay crop into the barn. Mickey was on the ground crew, and quickly learned to use momentum to swing the bales up onto the trailer. Even so, she and the others were so sore they could barely move the next morning. As they were working the second day, the trailer was only half full on its second load when the bell rang for Sext.

"Why are we stopping?" Wendy asked as St. Jude halted. She wiped her sweaty face with her sleeve, then scowled as little bits of hay stuck to her face. "Let's stay and get this over with."

Sister Regina's eyebrows raised slightly. "Did you hear the bell?" Wendy nodded. "We're here to pray, not to make hay or anything else," a sentiment echoed by Sister Rosaria who reminded them often, "Praying is our work. All the rest is meaningless without that. When the bell rings to signal an hour, you must stop what you're doing – no matter how frustrating that may be – and attend to our real work."

To Mickey's surprise, prayer was work, but she came to realize that she had never prayed for any length of time before. Saying the rosary was probably the longest period she had ever spent praying – "those days when I was praying for a miracle," she would have said – and even for that brief time, it was difficult not to let her mind wander. In the abbey, in between the set times for the Divine Office, there were periods of silent meditation, often spent praying for people or situations known to the nuns personally, or perhaps taken from the prayer board where prayer requests sent to the abbey were posted, sometimes lines snipped from a letter, or perhaps a worrisome headline clipped from one of the newspapers the abbey subscribed to.

"People often think we withdraw from the world to isolate ourselves and forget about what goes on out there," Sister Rosaria told them, "but it is our duty to keep abreast of the happenings of the world. How can you pray for it if you don't know what is happening?"

Prayer requests came from everywhere. "Please ask God to bring Tribble home to me," wrote a little girl in Buffalo, including a photo of her lost kitten.

Some of the requests were heartwrenching. There was a letter from a young father of three whose wife was dying from a brain tumor. His despair and fear were almost palpable. Most of the nuns prayed for the family; Mickey prayed for the doctors and nurses caring for the wife.

"You've got to be kidding," had been the initial reaction of Mickey's three male partners when she had told them of her plans. When they realized she was serious, the next question was, "Why are you going to waste your skills as a surgeon?" This had been the almost universal reaction as Mickey had gradually informed friends and co-workers of her decision. "At least go into a medical or missionary order," they said, but "I'd be accomplishing no more than I do now. Maybe saving a life, maybe not. It's not enough. I want to do more," was all she could say to most. To only a few close friends, "I need to try and do something for their souls; that's what really matters." Prayer wasn't dependent upon the skill of the person offering the prayer; it wasn't limited geographically or physically; it wasn't even limited by reality or any of the laws of science. To no one but herself, she had admitted, "I will never again have to tell someone there's nothing I can do."

She had arranged a one-year sabbatical from teaching at Johns Hopkins, as well as a leave from the practice, with a buyout price negotiated in the event she didn't return. When her partners disputed the dollar amount of her share of the practice, she had reminded them, "Religious life requires a vow of poverty, not of stupidity!"

☩☩☩

"Michele," Sister Rosaria gestured to Mickey as she got in line for lunch. "Could you take this tray to the chaplain's residence, please?"

She passed a heavily-laden tray with several stacked, covered dishes on it into Mickey's hands.

"Quickly, while it's hot," said the nun in the kitchen, leaning down to peer through the low pass-through.

Mickey nodded and hurried through the refectory, out into the enclosure. A hot summer breeze was blowing and she had to hold tightly to the tray as she walked across the park to a wooden door set in the stone wall. Backing through it, she followed a flagstone walk to Father Andrew's small house. The tray was too heavy to hold with one hand to knock, so she balanced on one foot and tapped the door with the other. It was opened in a moment by an old nun.

"There you are," she said brusquely. "Come in, come in," she said, stepping back to let Mickey enter.

Mickey carried the tray inside and set it on the dining table. The old nun hurried over and began laying out the covered dishes.

"Don't just stand there," she ordered.

Mickey quickly helped remove the covers, her stomach growling as aromatic steam rose from each dish. "This is a lot of food for one person," she observed.

"It's not for one person," the nun said, placing serving spoons in the dishes. "Father Andrew has a guest." She placed the covers on the tray and rearranged the dishes and bowls on the table until she was satisfied that everything was as it should be. "Take that to the kitchen," she said, flapping a hand. Mickey carried the tray to the small kitchen while the nun called out that lunch was ready.

Father Andrew entered the dining room with another elderly man in a secular black suit with a white collar.

"Andrew," said the other man, looking strangely out of place next to Father Andrew in his habit and the nun in hers, "they spoil you. I can see why you love it here."

Father Andrew smiled. "Thank you, Sister Linus. This looks wonderful."

She gave an arthritic bow. "You're welcome, Father. I'll be back to take care of the dishes." She went to the kitchen and gestured to Mickey, taking her by the arm and walking her to the front door. "You can go now," she said.

Mickey turned to ask if she was needed to come back and collect the tray when Sister Linus shut the door in her face. "You're welcome," she muttered.

She hurried back through the enclosure to get her own lunch.

"Michele!"

Gritting her teeth, Mickey turned to see Sister Lucille waving at her. "Could you please take this to the vestment room for me?" she huffed, holding a paper-wrapped package nearly as tall as she was. "They brought it to the front door by mistake." Mickey opened her mouth to ask if this couldn't be done later, but Sister Lucille was already walking back to her office.

With an exasperated sigh, Mickey turned. "Where is the vestment room?" she asked aloud to no one as the community was all in the refectory. She knew a bit about it - "we have a waiting list of nearly two years," Sister Rosaria had told them proudly. "Our orders come from all over the world - and not just Catholic churches and monasteries, but other denominations and even synagogues." But none of the postulants had been there, as only the nuns specially trained for that work were assigned there.

Frowning, Mickey remembered seeing a "Deliveries" sign on one of the outside walls of a wing of the monastery. She let herself back out into the enclosure, through the wooden door again, past Father Andrew's house to the far end of the abbey's main building where she saw a concrete parking pad and a door. Struggling to hold the roll as the stiff breeze tugged on it, she turned the knob on the door. The wind grabbed the door and flung it wide open.

There was an angry exclamation as she stepped inside.

"Close that door!"

Mickey reached back and wrenched the door shut. Inside, all was chaos. Swathes of cloth had been blown off tables, and spindles of thread were rolling across the floor. Mickey could see the twinkling of sunlight off the motes of dust and dirt that had blown in with her.

One nun was scrambling about picking up pieces of material.

"Look what you've done!" she exclaimed.

"I'm sorry," Mickey gasped, dropping her wrapped roll and reaching for one of the large sheets of cloth lying crumpled on the floor.

"Stop!"

Mickey froze. The nun hurried over to her.

"Look at your hands," she commanded. Mickey looked down to see that her hands were smudged with dirt from the paper wrapping on the roll she had been carrying. "You cannot touch silk with hands like that." She groaned as she laid out a length of embroidered scarlet cloth on one of the worktables. "It will take us days to get these clean."

"I'm sorry," Mickey repeated.

"Why did you come in that door?" the nun asked crossly.

"Sister Lucille asked me to bring this," Mickey said, pointing to the roll. "I didn't know any other way here."

The nun took a deep breath, controlling her irritation with great effort. "I will take care of this mess. You may go."

Mickey nodded and reached for the door through which she had entered.

"No!"

Mickey turned.

"That way." The nun pointed to a wooden stair Mickey hadn't noticed in the excitement.

"Yes, Sister," Mickey said. Behind her, she could hear the other nun grumbling. "You're welcome, too," Mickey said under her breath.

She climbed the steep wooden stairs, glancing back at the nun who now had a small brush and was carefully whisking the scarlet cloth. Exiting the vestment room, Mickey found herself in an unfamiliar set of corridors. After a few minutes' wandering, and a couple of wrong turns, she began to recognize where she was and hurried back toward the refectory which was now empty except for Jessica who was waiting with a plate.

"Oh, thank you," Mickey said gratefully as she bowed her head for a quick grace and sat to eat.

"What happened?" Jessica asked. "Where have you been?"

Quickly, in between bites, Mickey told her.

"I wondered," said Jessica.

"What?"

"About Father Andrew. Whether he ever had visitors," Jessica said. "It must be so lonely for him. At least we have each other."

"Well, that old nun, Sister Linus, is certainly protective of him," Mickey said. "But she's nothing compared to the other one, the one in the vestment room."

"Sister Anselma," Jessica said, nodding.

"How do you know these things?" Mickey asked her.

Jessica shrugged. "I just listen. The other sisters say she's like some kind of genius in there, with the weaving and artwork, but... difficult," she said tactfully.

Mickey snorted. "That was very edifyingly said."

Chapter 5

Mickey stirred in the early morning light. She rolled over in bed, and heard the shower in the bathroom next door. Closing her eyes, she drifted off to sleep again until, "Wake up, sleepy," she heard in her ear.

Smiling, she said, "Mmmm, you smell good." She could feel Alice's soft lips on her forehead, her cheeks, her mouth.

"Come on," Alice murmured. "Time to get up."

"Oh," Mickey groaned. "Do I have to? I didn't get home until two."

"I know," Alice said sympathetically. "But Christopher is counting on us. We're in charge of the cookies after Mass today."

"Oh," Mickey groaned again. "I'm sorry. I was supposed to help you bake them."

Alice yanked the covers away. "Luckily, I figured you wouldn't get home in time to help, so I baked six dozen."

"Ummm, not anymore," Mickey said, sitting up on the edge of the bed, her hair sticking up in a bad case of bedhead. "I ate three oatmeal cookies when I got home last night."

"That was probably your dinner," Alice said.

"Yeah. It was. Thanks."

Thirty minutes later, Alice was loading Tupperware containers full of cookies into Mickey's hands to carry out to the car. When they got to St. Matthew's, the side door to the rectory was standing open.

"Good morning," beamed the large, burly man standing there.

"Hey, Christopher," Mickey returned. Without asking, she popped open the lid on the container holding the peanut butter cookies.

Looking around guiltily, Christopher took two, popping one whole cookie into his mouth. "To keep my energy levels up, you know."

Mickey grinned. "I know and God knows, but you'd better wipe those crumbs out of your beard."

He quickly combed through the thick dark hair with his fingers. "I don't know what I'd do without you," he said.

"Without Alice, you mean," Mickey corrected.

"No," he said sincerely. "I meant both of you. Your donation to the PFLAG group was very generous."

"What's generous is your letting them meet here," Alice said, coming from around the car with another armful of cookie containers. "I'm guessing you didn't ask the bishop."

Christopher shrugged and laughed. "Better to ask forgiveness than permission."

"See?" Mickey said indignantly, turning to Alice with her arms outstretched. "How come that doesn't work when I say it?"

Alice looked at her, one eyebrow raised slightly. "It's his church. And he doesn't have to live with you."

Chapter 6

"Mother, I was angry at being asked to do an extra task in the kitchen. I broke two plates because I wasn't paying attention."

Each week, the community held a Chapter of Faults before Mass. Mother Theodora would call the names of five nuns to come forward, one at a time, kneel before the community and confess any transgressions against abbey rules or other sisters.

"Most convents have done away with the Chapter of Faults," Sister Rosaria told the postulants when she had first explained the process, "but in a cloistered community where we can't get away from each other, even little things can fester and grow with time. Better to clear the air while they are little."

Mother Theodora would assign each a penance in accordance with the severity of her infraction. To the nun who had confessed the breaking of the plates, "You will ask the forgiveness of the Sister you were angry with, and you will assist her with her work in addition to your own for one day."

Mickey had discovered that Mother Theodora's brand of penance was powerful. Requiring personal forgiveness rather than simply assigning menial, unsavory tasks as penance had the effect of drawing the community closer together. "Sister Stephen is much less intimidating after she has had to ask your forgiveness for losing her temper with you three times last week," Mickey had written to Jamie who thought this was a barbaric practice when he learned of it, but "no one can hold a grudge under those circumstances," Mickey insisted and usually the penitent would only be permitted to perform a token task by the other sister.

Usually, but not always. Twice, Mickey had confessed to losing her temper and swearing – both times at Wendy. *There's just something about her*, Mickey often thought in frustration, but… it was impossible for her to put it into concrete terms. It wasn't anything Wendy said or did overtly – "but she isn't overt, that's part of the problem," Mickey would have said if she could have voiced these thoughts aloud. Wendy was still scrupulous in her observance of the rules – when Sister Rosaria was looking. But Mickey had noticed how often Wendy seemed to disappear when there was work to be done, only to reappear just in time for the work to be inspected. Her comments often contained subtle double-entendres, *but why am I the only one who reads the nastier meaning into them?* Mickey wondered. None of the senior nuns seemed to notice these things; in fact, they seemed to delight in the ease with which Wendy had adapted to the discipline of monastic life, treating her like a sort of pet.

"It must be me," Mickey said with a shake of her head. And yet… just the week before, Wendy had taken full advantage of Mickey's penance, letting her scrub an entire floor by herself before returning and feigning that she only meant for Mickey to start on it before she took over. But there was something else. Wendy had said she got caught by one of the senior nuns and couldn't get back any sooner, but later, Tanya had mentioned seeing Wendy reading in the library. It was one thing to not want to scrub yet another floor, but to actually lie….

"Does anyone else wish to speak?" Mother Theodora asked, her voice cutting through Mickey's thoughts, when the last of the five had finished. Mother expected only those who felt they had committed serious infractions to come forward if their names weren't called. "Otherwise, we'll be here all day," she often said.

Mickey kept her eyes downcast, knowing she should probably confess everything she had just been thinking. "You're being uncharitable," she told herself sternly for the hundredth time.

☨ ☨ ☨

The air throughout the orchard was heavy with the smell of apples and there was an autumn bite in the air. The peach harvest was long over, the preserves sold to local markets.

"Can't we keep more of them?" Tanya had asked mournfully, as peaches were her favorite. "Only a dozen or so jars stay with us," Sister Regina said. "The ones that discolored and don't look as appealing. The rest must go to raise money for the abbey," just as the apple butter would soon, as well as the cheese the abbey made from the cows' milk. "I don't mind selling that," Jessica said with a wrinkled nose. "It stinks."

As the days cooled and shortened, as the plants in the enclosure garden died and were pruned back, Mickey's mood – "and my temper," she would have admitted remorsefully – darkened also. She had expected it; this time of year was always like this now. "Would it be any easier," she asked herself, "if it had happened in the spring when everything was blooming and coming to life?" She knew it had nothing to do with the time of year and everything to do with her memories....

The juniors were called upon again to help harvest the apples from the orchard. Mickey set her ladder against a tree farther down the row, separated from the others. She could hear their conversation and laughter as she filled the canvas bag hanging from her shoulder. She tried to maintain a polite demeanor with the others, but just that morning, "Michele!" Sister Rosaria had reprimanded her when she snapped at Abigail for, "for being Abigail," Mickey said to herself now as she moved her ladder around the tree. She knew the others found her prickliness tiresome, and were content to leave her by herself. From what she could hear, Wendy was once again comparing St. Bridget's with her former convent, and it was all Mickey could do, even from a distance, not to tell her to shut up.

At Recreation, she had taken to wandering restlessly off to isolated parts of the enclosure or back to her stall in Chapel. She tried writing to Jamie, but gave up in exasperation, the unfinished letter lying folded on her bedside table in their dormitory.

In wandering the enclosure paths, she had discovered the monastery's cemetery, a few stone benches providing places among the gravestones for prayer and reflection. Set on a slight hill, the cemetery provided a view down toward the abbey and the lower garden where figures walked about, all dressed alike in black and white.

Mickey heard a rustling and looked around to see that Jessica had carried her ladder over and set it up in the next apple tree. Abigail's voice carried to them. With a roll of her eyes, Jessica climbed her ladder and began picking, "and my immediate reaction," Mickey would admit shamefacedly later, "was to be pissed. I almost gathered up and left. I'm glad I didn't." Jessica understood, as few did, Mickey realized, the comfort of simply being near, without any need to fill the silence. Side by side, they picked through the afternoon work period until the bell rang for None. They carried their picking bags and ladders back to the tractor, and then headed to Chapel, following behind the others.

It was early October before the picking was done and the apple butter was made and bottled.

"Michele," Sister Rosaria said, catching Mickey at the end of Vespers one afternoon, "Mother Theodora would like to see you, please."

Mickey had seen Mother nearly daily for the past seven months, in the Chapel and during the talks she sometimes gave for the juniors, but other than casual greetings during Recreation, there had been no direct contact. If she were to be honest, this had been one of the most unexpectedly difficult things about entering St. Bridget's.

I knew it would be different, Mickey thought as she made her way through halls that no longer seemed a maze, *but I had grown to rely on our talks – even I didn't know how much until they couldn't happen anymore.*

She understood. "No favorites." How many times had Sister Rosaria told them that that was one of the greatest dangers of community life? Mickey was astute enough to have realized that her relationship with Mother could hardly be unique – "You have no idea the people who come to consult our dear Mother," Sister Lucille could have told her. "I often wonder how she gets anything done," but, somehow, Mother did. "What must be done, is," Mother Theodora would have said simply. Mickey had never considered before that her visits and talks might have taken Mother away from other things – "more important things," Mickey was coming to realize – but Mother had never, not once, made her feel an imposition.

Knocking, she heard Mother Theodora's voice call, "*Venite.*"

"*Pax tecum*," Mickey responded as she entered and closed the door behind her.

"*Et cum spiritu tuo*," Mother Theodora answered as she rose. "Sit down, Mickey." Mickey realized how accustomed she had become to being called Michele. It sounded comforting to be addressed by her nickname, and she suspected Mother Theodora did it to set her at ease.

"How have things been going?" Mother Theodora asked conversationally.

Mickey smiled. "It's definitely been an adjustment from my old schedule. And it's been quite a while since I sat in a class. I'm afraid Sister Stephen is convinced at times that I am hopeless."

Mother Theodora laughed. "Sister Stephen has thought that about many generations of us." Her expression became more serious. "How are you getting along with the other postulants?"

Mickey's heart jumped a little. Was her dislike of Wendy obvious? "The age difference between us seems a chasm at times, but for the most part, we all get along well. And Sister Rosaria is very patient and kind."

"Actually, Sister Rosaria is the one who asked me to speak with you."

Mickey's heartbeat increased again as she tried to keep a neutral expression. "Is there a problem, Mother?"

"Only that she has noticed a distance in you lately. She says that for the last few weeks, you've isolated yourself from the group and she is concerned. She said you wouldn't talk to her about it."

Mickey's jaw tensed and her eyes focused on the wood grain of the floor.

"If I remember correctly," Mother Theodora continued, watching Mickey's face, "this is a difficult time of year for you."

Mickey glanced up. "I didn't expect you to remember," and even she could hear the note of accusation in her voice.

"I remember," only Mother didn't say it aloud. Her face had such a knowing, chiding expression that Mickey instantly understood that Mother remembered every word of their conversations as much as she herself did.

"I should have known better," Mickey said as her face flushed.

She rose suddenly from her seat and went to the window, her hands tightly clenched together. When she turned to look at Mother Theodora, there were tears in her eyes. "There are times when I miss her so much it's a physical pain, like an amputation. I've been praying that it will pass, and I know it will. It always does." She turned back to the window. "But I can't tell Sister Rosaria why I'm so distracted. I haven't meant to draw attention to myself."

She remained standing at the window, waiting for Mother Theodora to speak.

"Mickey, all of us go through periods of struggle. At times, it may be a personal grief, or sometimes a dry period in your spiritual growth, or a time of questioning your vocation. In such a small community, any difference in behavior will be noticed, but we try to respect each other's privacy. Sometimes it's hard to know how to offer support without intruding. I don't think you've tried to draw attention to yourself. I think your efforts to isolate yourself and not be noticed have had the unintended effect of drawing the notice of Sister Rosaria, who is, after all, very experienced in watching and observing."

She came around her desk to stand next to Mickey, laying a gentle hand on her shoulder. "It's natural to grieve, Mickey. And it's important not to try and wall off your grief. God uses these times of vulnerability and frailty to touch us in ways he can't when we are feeling strong and in control."

Mickey nodded and wiped a tear from her cheek. "I like strong and in control better, though."

Chapter 7

Mickey woke at the usual time on Thanksgiving morning, even though the community had been given permission to sleep in until six, with Mass beginning the day at six-thirty. She dressed silently and tip-toed from the dormitory. Once in the hallway, she hurried to the cloakroom to get her heavy cloak. She opened the door to the enclosure garden and gasped. Three or four inches of snow covered everything, and the snow was still falling in large, feathery flakes. She stepped out from the covered stone walk and lifted her face, letting the heavy flakes tickle her skin. The snow created an even deeper hush than normal.

Mickey felt a childish desire to dive into the snow and make a snow angel, but she suspected the senior nuns might feel that was inappropriate, angel or not. She settled for scooping up snow and packing it tight, then hurling her snowball at one of the trees. The snowball splattered against the dark trunk, leaving a telltale white lump on the bark. She made and threw several more snowballs, her breath forming clouds of steam that hung in the cold, damp air. She had another snowball packed, her arm drawn back and her foot up like a big-league pitcher when she was startled by the sound of the door opening behind her.

Turning, she saw another nun entering the courtyard. Sheepishly, she held the snowball while the other nun approached. As she drew near, Mickey recognized Sister Anselma in the dim grey light. Sister Anselma stood with her hands tucked into her sleeves, her long, black veil and cloak giving her a very dignified air. Mickey was suddenly aware of how ridiculous she must look. Her short veil had slipped, and the snowball was melting into her frozen fingers. She opened her mouth to speak, but remembered she couldn't break Silence. Finally, she closed her mouth, tossed the snowball over her shoulder and walked back inside shaking her head.

Sister Anselma watched her go with a bemused expression.

By the time the nuns were assembled in their stalls, the public pews had filled nearly to capacity. As the bell rang to signal the start of Mass, there was no sign of Father Andrew. The peals of the bell faded away and still no priest. A very faint rustle of unrest had begun to move through the community when, suddenly, he appeared in the door of the sacristy, straightening his chasuble as he walked to the altar. Mickey tried to keep her eyes on her prayer book, but there was an audible tremor in his voice as he began the Introit. She stole a glance toward the altar and was shocked at the dark circles visible under his eyes, even from a distance. As the nuns sang their responses, there were slight lapses where Father Andrew seemed to struggle to find his place. Mother Theodora subtly altered the tempo of the responses to give him more time, and the community followed her lead. During the consecration of the Eucharist, Mickey could see his hands shaking as they held the host.

"Poor thing, he must be sick," the nuns murmured sympathetically as they made their way to the refectory for a late breakfast following Mass.

The normal work schedule was suspended for the Thanksgiving holiday. Instead, the community used the time to make preparations for Advent which marked the beginning of the church year and came with a feeling of anticipation leading up to Christmas. "It's like being a little kid again," Abigail said gleefully, and even Mickey had to admit that the excitement was contagious. During the four weeks of Advent, an Advent wreath was lit in the Chapel with a smaller one in the refectory during each evening meal as a reader read a passage from various meditations on Advent and Christmas as they ate.

The juniors spent Recreation each day rehearsing their traditional Christmas concert for the rest of the community under the direction of Sister Margaret, the precentrix. "This is a heavy load on her," the novices warned the postulants. "She still has the Christmas choir to rehearse also." They also helped with the Chapel decorations. Sister Teresa, the sacristan, was in charge of putting out the chalices and plates for Communion each day, and for the cleaning and decorating of the Chapel. There was a lot of extra work involved in preparing the Chapel for Christmas. The novices had helped with these tasks before, and directed the postulants as they hung evergreen garlands from the stone arches and pillars. Mickey was up on a ladder accepting garland strands from Sister Helen, one of the second year novices, and attaching them with wire to the small hooks set in the stone. As Sister Helen climbed back down to get another strand, she mis-judged the rungs and fell a couple of feet to the floor. Mickey came down off the ladder quickly, asking her if she was okay.

"It's my knee," Sister Helen responded, grimacing.

Without thinking, Mickey began palpating and moving her knee carefully. "It seems to be just a sprain," she pronounced. She realized the others were all gathered around them. Suddenly feeling very self-conscious, she helped Sister Helen to her feet and said, "You should get some ice on that. Why don't we get you to the infirmary?"

Sister Helen put one arm over Mickey's shoulders as Mickey put her arm around Sister Helen's waist. Gingerly, Sister Helen limped out of the Chapel. Once in the infirmary, Mickey left her with Sister Mary David, the nun in charge there, and hurried back to the Chapel. Wendy seemed to be waiting for her, because she came over as soon as Mickey returned.

"How is she?" she asked casually.

"Fine." Mickey was on guard. She squatted down to get more garland.

"It's a good thing you were here."

Mickey was starting to get annoyed. "It wasn't a serious injury."

"Maybe," Wendy shrugged. "But it was bad enough for you to almost carry her to the infirmary."

"What is your point?" Mickey asked in a low voice, straightening up to face Wendy.

Wendy shrugged again. "Nothing... it just must have felt good, to be able to help, I mean."

Mickey bit back the words that leapt to her tongue. Clenching her jaw, she turned her back on Wendy and carried her garland back up the ladder.

☩ ☩ ☩

Over the next few weeks leading up to Christmas, Mickey kept her distance from Wendy, but she could feel Wendy's gaze whenever Sister Helen spoke to Mickey during their rehearsals at Recreation. To Mickey's chagrin, Sister Helen was friendlier after the knee sprain, and did seek opportunities to speak with Mickey whenever she had a chance.

She's just being nice, Mickey kept telling herself. *Don't let Wendy make you question yourself.*

When Sister Margaret asked Mickey to sing a duet of *The Cherry Tree Carol* with Sister Helen, Mickey was uncomfortably aware that Wendy was listening.

"You have a good voice," Sister Helen said appreciatively.

"No, just loud," Mickey grinned, blushing. Sister Helen easily had the best voice among them, a soaring soprano that often gave Mickey goosebumps when it reached into the upper octaves.

"Your alto will provide perfect counterpoint if we transpose the harmony to a lower octave," Sister Helen insisted, getting excited about the project.

In spite of her nagging worry about Wendy, Mickey found herself enjoying the rehearsals with Sister Helen who was also an excellent pianist and provided the accompaniment. Patiently, she coached Mickey through the harmony whenever Mickey's voice would slip back into the melody. The first time they made it completely through with no mistakes, Sister Helen laughed and gave Mickey a hug.

"We make a good pair," she said, looking at Mickey with an intensity that chilled Mickey's heart. No matter how much she wanted to dismiss Wendy's jealousy, she could no longer pretend Sister Helen was just being friendly.

When she was teaching, Mickey had often had medical students of both genders develop crushes on her. Occasionally, a crush crossed the line into infatuation. In the beginning, Mickey had tried to gently discourage the attention, but "you do realize how much more elusive and attractive that makes you," Alice would point out drolly, amused at Mickey's consternation when that approach didn't work. Mickey had discovered that a little public humiliation in the form of one or two biting, sarcastic comments was much more effective, although "I feel horrible," she always said afterward. What made this situation especially difficult was Mickey's suspicion that Sister Helen would have been mortified at the suggestion that she had a crush on Mickey. She kept remembering what Mother Theodora had said about abbey life magnifying the real her. "You wanted this to happen," she could hear Wendy saying, and she couldn't help wondering if she was, in fact subconsciously doing something to invite this attention. In an atmosphere of women who had foresworn physical intimacy, touch was incredibly powerful, even touch as simple and innocent as examining an injured knee. She appreciated as never before the delicate balancing act of living in a small, cohesive community and still maintaining enough personal space to stay true to monastic life.

Sister Helen had become curious about Mickey's past and what brought her to St. Bridget's. She began interrupting their rehearsals to talk.

"Are you trying to be mysterious?" Sister Helen asked with a smile as Mickey evaded her questions.

Mickey could see that this tactic was not working. Hardening herself, she replied coldly, "What I'm trying to do is tell you that my past is none of your damned business."

Sister Helen looked as if she had been slapped. Her cheeks reddened and she blinked back tears. "I'm sorry," she said in a quavering voice.

"Let's pick this up tomorrow," Mickey said curtly as she got up and left. Stalking away, staring at the floor, Mickey rounded a corner and ran heavily into Wendy, almost knocking her over.

"Sorry," Mickey muttered before hurrying along, cursing under her breath.

Wendy was staring after her retreating form when Sister Helen emerged from the music room. Startled, she saw Wendy and reversed direction, but not before Wendy saw the tears streaming down her cheeks.

✠ ✠ ✠

Christmas came to the abbey with a fresh blanket of snow. The juniors had outdone themselves, and the Chapel looked magnificent. There were evergreen garlands everywhere, now adorned with brilliant red clusters of holly and nandina berries. There were extra candle sconces inserted into the stone pillars behind the nuns' choir stalls and flanking the grille that separated the choir from the public pews. The dancing light from the extra candles seemed festive while simultaneously creating deeper shadows which lent an increased air of austerity to the Office in the dark winter days leading up to Christmas.

There was an almost palpable feeling of anticipation among the nuns as Christmas drew closer, as this was one of the few times during the year when families were permitted to enter the enclosure for a reception after Mass on Christmas Day.

"We do not forbid visits from family in those first months," Sister Ignatius had told all of the postulants during the admission process, "but we find it helps new postulants settle in better if family holds off visiting until Christmas."

Jamie had written that he would be coming. Mickey hadn't seen him since the day he had brought her to St. Bridget's. She had never written as many letters in her life as she probably had in the last nine months - mostly to Jamie, but also to friends and former colleagues in Baltimore. In keeping with its adherence to traditions such as the full habit and singing the Office in Latin, St. Bridget's had avoided bringing in computers and the internet. "But a lot of religious orders have web sites and they say that much of their outreach to this younger generation happens via computer," some of the more progressive nuns argued, while others reasoned, "Part of our role, part of what calls women to us, is the simplicity of the life we have chosen. We do not wish to remove ourselves entirely from the world, but we don't have to invite it inside our walls on the internet." Writing was the most economical way of communicating with people outside the abbey. Telephone calls could be made, with permission, if something needed more immediate attention. Mickey had had to re-learn the art of written description, something which was very unlike the terse, concise notes she had used in medical charts and the neverending e-mails she had had to respond to.

On December 24th, the afternoon work session was cancelled so that the nuns could have an early dinner and retire to their cells for some rest before rising again for a late Matins and a period of reflection before midnight Mass.

Mickey was just leaving the refectory after supper when Sister Lucille came to her, telling her that she had visitors in one of the parlours. Wondering who in the world could be here, she walked quickly to the abbey's entryway, where there were four parlours for receiving visitors. Peeking into the first, she found it empty. She heard voices coming from the second and walked into it to see Jamie and their mother sitting there. She stood there in shock. Jamie leapt up and came to her with a big smile and a hug.

"What are you doing here?" she asked as she held him tightly. "I wasn't expecting you until tomorrow – and I wasn't expecting this," she added in an undertone.

"Thought we'd surprise you," he answered with that look she knew so well, partly because she'd used it so often herself, the one that said, "I knew you'd be mad if I told you about this ahead of time, so I'm springing this on you now."

Turning to her mother, Mickey guardedly said, "Hello, Mom."

Natalie Stewart did not come over to embrace her daughter. She sat stiffly in her chair, her blue eyes pale and icy, her bony, arthritic hands tightly clasping the purse in her lap. She looked Mickey from head to toe and said, "I never thought I'd see you in a skirt again."

Turning back to Jamie with an amused expression, Mickey said, "Well, you surprised me."

He grinned apologetically as they sat.

"So, Mom, how long are you up here for?" Mickey forced herself to make polite conversation.

"I'm not sure," Natalie replied, looking around the parlour with an expression of distaste. "Probably a week, and then I'll go back to Florida."

Mickey gave Jamie a pitying look.

"So, do you really intend to pursue this convent thing?" Natalie asked.

"I'm here, aren't I?" Mickey warily replied.

"Do they know about... you?" Natalie continued. "I wouldn't think they would want people like you in here."

Closing her eyes and praying for patience, Mickey said, "The Abbess and I had many honest conversations prior to my entering St. Bridget's."

"And you're willing to give up everything? For this?" Natalie gestured around the parlour with its clean but plain furnishings. "Your house? Your money?"

Mickey smiled pityingly. "Those things mean nothing by themselves. I would have thought you would have come to understand that these past ten years."

Natalie's eyes narrowed angrily. "Don't you dare compare yourself and your, your... to what your father and I had. He wanted me to be well taken care of –"

"So, Jamie," Mickey interrupted, turning to her brother, "how is your work going?"

Natalie furiously clamped her mouth shut.

"It's going really well," Jamie said, jumping into the ensuing silence. "I've got three commissions, one of them for a gallery in New York."

"Good for you," Mickey said proudly.

"How are things going here?" he asked.

"Surprisingly well," she admitted. "I'm settling in better than I thought I would. I'll be asking to enter the Novitiate in April."

"How long does that last?"

"Two years. After that, if I'm accepted, I'll take my simple vows which can last up to five years before taking final vows."

"Wow." Jamie's eyebrows raised in surprise. "I didn't realize it was such a long process."

"They want us to be really sure before we make a lifetime commitment."

A bell rang, and Mickey looked up.

"We should go," Jamie said, standing. "We'll be back for Mass tomorrow."

Mickey gave him another quick hug. "Thanks for coming... I think," she whispered in his ear.

He chuckled and let her go.

"See you tomorrow, Mom."

Natalie Stewart didn't reply as she walked stiffly out of the parlour.

Chapter 8

After Christmas, the abbey returned to a more normal schedule. Mickey had held her breath, feeling she would breathe a little easier once her mother was back in Florida, but, to her surprise, Natalie had behaved herself on Christmas day and had been civil if not friendly. Jamie, of course, had been very charming, and he and Mother Theodora had hit it off as if they were old friends. Tanya's parents came to visit all the way from Minnesota. Mickey smiled remembering how nervous and wide-eyed Jessica's younger sister had been – she looked exactly like Jessica. Wendy, she'd noticed with a touch of curiosity, was the only one of the postulants who hadn't had any family there for Christmas.

The postulants were re-assigned to help in different areas of the abbey. Mickey and Abigail were assigned to the kitchen. It was hard work, and required missing some of the hours of the Office in order to have each meal ready on time. Never much of a chef, Mickey was quickly relegated to clean-up or chopping of ingredients, but "no cooking for you," Sister Cecilia commanded after tasting Mickey's first unsavory attempt at mixing a simple stock for soup.

Sister Cecilia was in charge of the kitchen. She was a large, no-nonsense woman, and Mickey privately thought she would have done well in the Army. Sister Cecilia made up all the menus, ordered all the food and personally did most of the cooking. It was a huge responsibility.

Far from complaining, Mickey actually enjoyed the mindless nature of washing pots and pans; it gave her time to think, "woolgathering," Alice would have said with a knowing shake of her head. The only cloud over her Christmas recollections was Sister Helen's coldness. After Mickey's rebuke, their remaining rehearsals had been peremptory, and once the juniors' concert was concluded, Sister Helen had had nothing more to do with Mickey. Even now, on those occasions when Mickey happened to be at the kitchen pass-through, collecting dirty dishes, Sister Helen would not meet her eyes, would not speak. As much as Mickey wished she could apologize, "it's better this way."

Over the next few weeks, Mickey and Abigail adjusted to the routine of the kitchen. Mickey found to her surprise that Abigail's youthful bravado disappeared when she was around the senior nuns. She was very receptive to instruction, and humbly accepted Sister Cecilia's criticism as she was allowed to help with the preparation of the ingredients for the hearty, warm soups and stews Sister Cecilia made during these dark, cold months of winter. Sister Cecilia seemed to be making a special effort to teach Abigail, and Mickey grudgingly had to admit to herself that Abigail was thriving under the attention.

"Michele," said Sister Cecilia one afternoon, "please take this tray to the chaplain's house."

"Oh, Sister," Mickey protested. "Please, no. The last time I did that, Sister Linus practically threw me out."

Lowering her voice, Sister Cecilia said, "Yesterday, Sister Linus slipped in the snow and dropped an entire dinner tray. She's getting on a bit, but... I know you will be tactful enough to realize that when she snaps at you – and she will – well... you won't take it personally."

With a resigned sigh, Mickey picked up the tray, covered with a clean kitchen towel and ferried it across the snowy enclosure to Father Andrew's residence. As before, Sister Linus answered the door and impatiently beckoned Mickey inside.

"I'll do this," she said, taking the tray from Mickey and laying the lunch dishes out on the table.

Mickey, who hadn't had the chance to put on a cloak, stood there, shivering. "Would you like me to wait to take the tray back, Sister?"

"No," Sister Linus said. "You can come back later." She glanced at Mickey, whose shoes and stockings were wet and snowy. "Go in the kitchen first and get some hot tea before you catch cold."

Mickey found a hot kettle on the stove and a tin of teabags on the counter. Pouring the steaming water into a mug, she could hear Sister Linus calling to Father Andrew. A moment later, she joined Mickey in the kitchen.

"Would you like some tea, Sister?" Mickey asked.

Sister Linus peered up at her, her bright eyes looking out from a wizened face. "All right, then."

Mickey poured another mug of boiling water and let the teabag steep while she handed the first to Sister Linus.

"How long have you been taking care of things here?" Mickey asked, cradling the second mug in her cold hands.

"Over thirty years," Sister Linus said. "Through five chaplains."

"That's a long time to be doing one thing," Mickey said in surprise. She knew that most of the positions within the monastery were rotated, with the exception of a few positions like Sister Regina on the farm and Sister Margaret in charge of the music, and even then, "None of us is irreplaceable." How many times had Sister Rosaria said that?

"The Fathers won't have anyone else," Sister Linus said proudly.

"No," Mickey smiled as she took a sip of her tea. "I can see that they wouldn't." She drank a bit more of her tea as Sister Linus went to check on Father Andrew.

"I'll be back later for the tray," she said when Sister Linus returned to the kitchen. "I'll let myself out."

Ferrying the meal tray three times a day became a regular part of Mickey's responsibilities after that. "I'm not sure," she confided to Sister Cecilia, "but I think Sister Linus might actually be relieved not to have to do this." She still wasn't exactly friendly, but "she doesn't throw me out of the house anymore," Mickey laughed.

February arrived with a cold snap that put a hard freeze on all the plants, turning the clinging snow to crystal so that everything looked as if it were encrusted with diamonds in the winter sunlight. Mickey returned to the kitchen after having delivered the lunch tray, shivering and bringing the empty breakfast tray back when she saw Sister Cecilia holding Abigail who was white as a sheet, clutching a towel to her hand.

"She cut herself," Sister Cecilia said. "I'm taking her to the infirmary."

"I'll take her, Sister," Mickey volunteered, wrapping an arm around Abigail's shoulders.

"Yes, of course, thank you," Sister Cecilia replied distractedly, already cleaning up and disinfecting the cutting board where Abigail's blood had dripped.

When they arrived at the infirmary, Sister Mary David came over immediately to inspect Abigail's hand, unwrapping the bloody towel. "Oh, dear," she said, "this is definitely going to need stitches."

"May I?" Mickey asked, pulling on a pair of gloves.

"Yes," Sister Mary David said, stepping back with a frown. Mickey gently pulled the edges of the cut apart and had Abigail bend her finger.

"Can you do stitches, Sister?" Abigail asked in a quavering voice.

"No, I'm afraid I can't," replied Sister Mary David with a worried expression as Mickey reapplied the pressure of the towel. "We'll either have to call the doctor out here or take you to the hospital in Millvale. Either way it will take over an hour."

Mickey spoke, but it felt to her as if the words were issuing from someone else's mouth. "Would you both please wait here a moment? I'll be right back."

Having made up her mind, she walked quickly to Mother Theodora's office before she could reconsider.

"*Venite,*" came the answer to Mickey's knock.

"*Pax tecum,*" said Mickey as she entered to find Mother speaking with another nun whom she didn't know.

"*Et cum spiritu tuo,*" Mother Theodora said, looking up from the papers they were studying.

"I'm sorry, Mother," Mickey said. "I didn't mean to interrupt."

"I'll give you a moment," the other nun said, getting up to leave.

"Yes, Michele?" said Mother Theodora.

"Mother, Abigail has cut her finger rather badly. She needs stitches. We could take her to the hospital, or..." she looked down at the floor, "I could do it, with your permission."

Mother Theodora put her pen down and sat back in her chair. "What supplies would you use? I doubt our infirmary has what you would need."

"I took the liberty of packing a bag of emergency supplies just in case they were needed. I know how far we are from town."

"Then, my next question is, are you prepared to open this door to your former life?"

Mickey met her gaze with a small smile. "No," she admitted, "but that's a selfish impulse. There's no reason to incur the time and expense of an ER visit when I can take care of this here."

Mother Theodora looked at Mickey approvingly. "Very well. Thank you for doing this."

Mickey went to the postulants' dormitory and opened the trunk at the foot of her bed. Inside, she found her black medical bag. She closed the trunk and hurried back to the infirmary.

Sister Mary David had Abigail lying down with a cool compress in her forehead. "She was becoming faint," she explained as she came over to the table where Mickey was laying out a suture kit and gloves.

"Sister, I can take care of the stitches here, with your permission, of course," she added, deferring to Sister Mary David's authority in the infirmary.

"Of course." Sister Mary David's eyebrows went up. "Then we'll talk."

Sister Mary David stood by, calming Abigail, as Mickey swabbed Abigail's finger with Betadine and then injected enough Lidocaine to numb it.

"Are you okay?" Mickey asked Abigail as she picked up the suture needle with a very fine thread attached.

Abigail nodded. She suddenly looked very young.

"You really won't feel this," Mickey assured her gently.

A few minutes later, she snipped the suture at the end of a line of tiny, neat stitches. She wrapped Abigail's finger with sterile gauze and said, "You shouldn't get this wet for about a week."

"I'll speak to Sister Cecilia," Sister Mary David said, handing Abigail a pain medication and some water. "Do you feel well enough to go to Chapel? It's almost time for Vespers."

After Abigail had gone, Sister Mary David came over to where Mickey was cleaning up. "Michele," she began, "I assume you are not a nurse. Are you a physician assistant?"

"No," Mickey replied, glancing up. "I was a surgeon."

Sister Mary David just stared at her for a moment. "But why wasn't I told before now? There have been so many times we could have used you..."

"Sister," Mickey straightened up. "I didn't enter the abbey to be the in-house physician. My being here is completely separate from my previous profession. I'm going to ask you not to say anything about this. If there's an emergency, then of course I want you to come get me, but otherwise, I'm not here to practice medicine." She smiled apologetically. "And I still have an awful lot to learn about being a nun."

Sister Mary David blushed. "Forgive me, Michele. That was... I understand."

A short time later, Mickey was seated in her stall in Chapel. That was the first time in nearly a year that she had treated a patient. Granted, it had been a minor injury, but she was a little surprised at how easily she had slipped back into that role – surprised and chagrined. The organ startled her. She hadn't heard the Chapel filling. Looking around at the faces of these women, faces that were becoming so familiar, she had the peculiar feeling that something had shifted today. *This is where I belong*, she thought, closing her eyes. *This is what's real.*

Chapter 9

"This is Dr. Stewart," Mickey said, rubbing her eyes tiredly as she answered the page.

"Hey," came Alice's voice over the phone. "You were supposed to be home three hours ago."

"Oh, hon, I am so sorry." Mickey looked at her watch. "I got called in on one of Tucker's surgeries. The idiot removed a twelve-year-old kid's scapula before he did a lung biopsy. The entire left lung was full of tumors. I removed the lung, but he's got to have chemo and radiation, and now he can't use his left arm. He probably won't make it," she finished quietly.

Mickey pressed her fingers to the bridge of her nose as she listened to the silence on the other end of the phone. "I should have called," she said. "But he was already on the table..."

"The car is packed," Alice said at last. "Can you leave if I come by to pick you up?"

"Yes. I'll be waiting for you."

As Mickey hurriedly changed out of her scrubs in the locker room, she whispered a prayer of thanks as she had done a thousand times before over the past ten years. It would have sounded trite if she had tried to explain it to anyone else, but she literally felt that Alice was God's gift to her. She resolved to focus all of her attention on Alice over the next few days as they traveled to their weekend house on the Chesapeake Bay.

"I'm sorry," Mickey said again as she got into the car. "You have every right to be angry."

Alice wove through the hospital parking lot. "I was," she admitted after a moment. "But how can I measure a weekend at the Bay against a twelve-year-old boy's life?"

"I truly don't deserve you," Mickey said, taking Alice's hand and squeezing it.

"I know." Alice grinned at her. "And I'll remind you of that if you complain about the new couch I bought today."

Chapter 10

"In a month, you will have been here a year," Sister Rosaria told the postulants in March. "It is time for you to prepare for the decision as to whether or not you will be entering the Novitiate." As part of that process, the postulants were required to make a seven day retreat. "This retreat will be conducted in complete silence, except for the daily session each of you will have with the senior nun assigned to be your spiritual advisor," Sister Rosaria explained. "You will move from the dormitory to cells for private sleeping quarters. Your meals will be taken in a small room off the refectory. You will not participate in the Office, although you may listen to it, and you will not be doing any work, since the focus of the week is to be prayer and reflection."

During her meeting explaining the retreat to the five postulants, Sister Rosaria told them who their spiritual advisors were. To Mickey's mortification, hers was Sister Anselma. The seniors serving as advisors had all received intense training in guiding the retreat process. "Our task is to listen," they would have said – listen to the retreatant, and listen for God's whispers pointing the way to a meaningful experience. The advisors were also very much aware that the retreat process could bring up intense emotional issues. Things easily suppressed under the busy-ness of daily life often surfaced in the stillness and silence. The retreat process could have a profound impact, not only on someone's psychological state, but also on a shaky vocation. "More than one woman had left the abbey after a difficult retreat," Sister Rosaria warned them. "This is nothing to be ashamed of. Monastic life is not for everyone. Even those with a true vocation may find that this retreat simply points them down another path."

"Don't fool yourselves into thinking you deserve God's attention as a reward for entering religious life," Sister Renatta advised them in her last lecture - "even if the retreat goes badly, that's something to be grateful for," Mickey joked in an undertone to Tanya who immediately coughed to cover her laugh. Sister Renatta's eyes got misty as she continued, "Saint Teresa of Ávila went through a dry period of nearly twenty years without any sense that God was listening. Her perseverance was eventually rewarded with a state of grace and communion with our Lord that most of you will probably never experience. I myself have experienced several moments of grace, and I can assure you they are most stirring. Remember that you are beginners on this journey."

The day before the retreat was to begin, the postulants were all packing up their clothes and few belongings in preparation for the move to their cells. Loudly enough for Mickey to hear, Wendy said to Tanya, "Yeah, I've done this two or three times. The most important thing is who your spiritual advisor is. I'm so glad I didn't get Sister Anselma, or I should say Sister Absentia. I've heard she's like some kind of ice queen - the perfect nun with no emotions."

Wendy, in her snide way, had been even more aggressive and challenging to Mickey ever since Abigail's accident with the knife. Mickey had forced herself to bite her tongue and remain quiet, but finally, "Whoever you got," she said as she picked up the other end of Jessica's trunk to help her carry it to her cell, "I hope she's smart enough to see through your bullshit."

Mickey's cell was at the end of the corridor, next to Jessica's. They were all furnished alike, with a bed, a small wardrobe and a writing desk with a bookshelf on top. Mostly what Mickey had brought with her were books. She set her trunk at the foot of her bed, and then sat at the desk to write Jamie an overdue letter. "I don't know how busy all this prayer will keep me," she wrote, "but seven days feels like a very long time."

The next day, they met with their spiritual advisors for the first time right after Mass. Mickey was greeted by Sister Anselma and shown into a small study near the library. Mickey waited for Sister Anselma to sit before she took an adjacent chair.

"The first thing I want you to know is that anything we discuss is as confidential as the confessional," Sister Anselma began. "I would only repeat our conversations to Mother if I felt it was absolutely necessary, and then only with your permission."

Mickey was watching her grey eyes intently as she spoke. This was the first time Mickey had had a chance to really study her face, and she was startled to realize that Sister Anselma was probably no older than she was. She knew the nuns didn't measure age chronologically, but she was still surprised that someone so young would carry so much responsibility within the abbey.

Sister Anselma continued, "In order for me to guide you to the best of my ability, it would be helpful to know a little about you and what brought you here."

Mickey quickly considered how much to tell her. It had taken a long time before she opened up completely with Mother Theodora. "I was drawn to religious life as a teenager and almost entered a convent right after high school," she began sheepishly, "but I decided to go to college, and there, I became interested in medicine and pursued medical school. I had been teaching at Johns Hopkins, and was a partner in a surgical practice in Baltimore." Mickey paused. Sister Anselma's expression hadn't changed, and her eyes were still fixed on Mickey's face. "After... a few years ago, I guess I just reached the point of feeling I needed to do something more. I found the abbey by accident one day, and then met Mother. It was through my conversations with her that I eventually decided to enter."

Sister Anselma's face softened. "I wonder if she knows how many of us she's brought here." She held out a small book and pen. "You will use this journal to write down the Scripture passages I give you to pray with each day. Try to spend an hour with each passage, and then write down your feelings, thoughts, any words or phrases that speak to you. Begin each session with a prayer asking to be open to what God wishes to say to you. Have you ever prayed like this before, Michele?"

Mickey shook her head.

"Try to relax and not force your prayer in any specific direction." She flipped through the Bible on her lap, and gave Mickey three Scripture readings to start with. "We'll meet here each day at the start of Recreation." She stood, and the folds of her habit fell gracefully into place. She looked down at Mickey and added, "I believe there is still enough snow left outside for another snowball fight with the trees if you are so moved."

╬ ╬ ╬

The first five days of Mickey's retreat passed calmly enough. The passages that she had been asked to pray with had been taken from all over: Lamentations, Isaiah, Psalms, the Gospels, Paul's letters. The common thread which seemed to be emerging was Mickey's difficulty trusting and believing that she could be an instrument of God's will. This was the hardest thing she had done at St. Bridget's, maybe the hardest thing she had ever done.

She had glimpses of the others at meals, and occasionally, out on the abbey grounds. They seemed to be struggling also. She saw Tanya and Jessica in tears at different times.

Meeting with Sister Anselma the afternoon of the fifth day, Mickey was looking forward to the end of this retreat and was about to say so when, "Michele," Sister Anselma began with a small frown, "I am not sure why or what exactly, but I sense a block of some kind, keeping you from getting where you need to be."

Mickey stared at her. "I don't feel that way. I'm not sure what is supposed to happen on these retreats, but I feel like there have been moments of real clarity and insight that weren't there before."

Sister Anselma's sharp eyes searched hers for a long moment. Finally she nodded and said, "Very well. I could be wrong about this."

Opening her Bible, she began picking the next set of readings for Mickey to pray with. She looked up and saw that Mickey had stopped writing and that the color had drained from her face. "Michele?"

"Why did you choose that passage from Wisdom?" Mickey asked, looking down at her journal.

Sister Anselma's eyebrows raised a little. "I don't know. I told you I pray for guidance each time we meet. Why?"

Mickey paused. "That reading is connected to a… a difficult time in my life. I'd rather not pray with that one."

Gently, Sister Anselma said, "Maybe that's why I was prompted to give it to you. Please try."

Mickey nodded and closed her journal.

※ ※ ※

The virtuous woman, though she die before her time, will find rest.

"Tell me," was all Sister Anselma said the next day. She noticed, but didn't comment on, the dark circles under Mickey's eyes. She suspected Mickey had not slept at all.

Length of days is not what makes age honourable,
Nor number of years the true measure of life.

Mickey stared at the pen in her hands, pushing the cap off with her thumb and clicking it back on, over and over. "I'm afraid I didn't really get anywhere with the readings you gave me yesterday," she said in a low voice.

"Why not?"

She has sought to please God, so God has loved her.

Mickey frowned and rubbed her forehead. "I don't know," she said irritably. "I just couldn't seem to settle my mind."

Sister Anselma sat silently for a long time, until Mickey finally looked up at her.

"Michele," she said, her expression neutral, "I would like your permission to speak with Mother. I believe we should extend your retreat."

Mickey's heart sank. "How long?"

"A full thirty days."

After the seventh day, Mickey ate alone in the room off the refectory. The others returned to the normal routine of abbey life. Sister Anselma didn't give Mickey different Scriptures to pray with. She kept asking Mickey to stay with the ones she was stuck on. Not until the tenth day did Mickey begin to open up even a little.

"The reading from Wisdom, with some gender changes, was one of the passages used in the funeral of my partner, Alice," she finally told Sister Anselma that afternoon.

"How long were you together?" Sister Anselma asked quietly.

"Twelve years. We met while I was in medical school." Mickey's eyes stared, unfocused, at the wall.

"Tell me about her."

For the first time in days, Mickey's face softened a little. "She was everything to me," she said in a voice barely above a whisper. "She was the gentlest soul I have ever known. She always knew what I needed – whether it was just to listen when I needed to vent, or hold me when a patient died, or make me laugh when I was taking myself too seriously."

Mickey was surprised when Sister Anselma didn't ask any more questions. She finally gave Mickey three new Scriptures. When Mickey sat down to pray with them, they were joyful passages – Psalms 138 and 139, the Song of Songs. A front of unseasonably warm air had moved into the region, and she was able to go outside to spend the hours praying with those passages, immersed in memories of the love and happiness Alice had brought to her life. She felt tremendously relieved that she was through the worst of this retreat. She slept better that night, and felt more prepared to face Sister Anselma the next day.

To her disappointment, Sister Anselma didn't ask any questions about those prayer sessions.

"What kind of surgeon were you?" Sister Anselma asked unexpectedly.

"I'm sorry?" Mickey asked, not sure how to interpret the question.

"What kind of surgeon were you?" Sister Anselma repeated, refusing to clarify.

"I was a general surgeon, but my specialty was oncological cases – removing cancerous tissues," Mickey opted to answer.

Sister Anselma was looking at her intently. "Were you a good doctor?"

Mickey could feel her face burn. "I don't know how to answer that," she responded honestly.

Sister Anselma simply nodded and continued watching Mickey. "Tell me how Alice died."

Mickey was unprepared for this. She felt her face get hotter, and her heartbeat quicken. "She was complaining of back pain. But she taught second grade; she was always having to bend and stoop." She had to stop to try and breathe. "By the time an MRI was done, her cancer was everywhere. She opted not to have chemo. We used the time we had left to travel, visit family and friends."

"How long?" Sister Anselma's voice was gentle, but her expression was inscrutable.

Mickey tried to answer, but had to clear her throat twice before sound would come out. "Eight weeks."

Sister Anselma looked away at last, and began turning the pages of her Bible. She gave Mickey four new Scriptures to pray with, and then she said, "If you need me, Michele, at any hour, I want you to come and get me. My cell is 130."

Mickey went out to the garden enclosure as the rest of the community gathered in the Chapel for None. She sat on a bench under a gnarled cherry tree and opened her Bible to the first of the passages. After just a couple of minutes, she snapped the Bible closed, too restless to concentrate. The warm wind beckoned. She left the stone confines of the abbey enclosure, and went out to the orchard. None of the trees was in bloom yet, but buds were beginning to swell and the air smelled of spring. She stood on a hill, facing to the west, eyes closed, breathing deeply.

Later that afternoon, Sister Anselma went out to the enclosure following Vespers. There, she found Mickey's Bible and journal sitting on a bench, pages fluttering wildly in the mounting wind as a storm blew in with roiling black clouds. She gathered the books up as the first raindrops began to fall.

✥ ✥ ✥

"Where was she?" Mother asked. "What happened?"

"I don't know," Sister Anselma said. "I couldn't find her all afternoon or evening. I was keeping an eye out for her. I… I believe her retreat is coming to a crisis point. Jessica helped me look for her. When we finally found her in the organ loft, she was like this."

Mickey sat hunched on the side of her bed, a blanket wrapped around her shoulders, her face flushed and feverish, her clothing and hair soaking wet and ice cold. Outside the rain slashed at the windows and the wind whistled as it rattled the old windows of Mickey's cell.

"In here, Sister," Jessica said, leading Sister Mary David in.

Sister Mary David knelt and laid a hand on Mickey's cheek and forehead. "She's burning up." She slid a thermometer into Mickey's mouth. "Michele? Michele?" When she received no response, she glanced questioning up toward Mother and Sister Anselma.

"This is how she's been," Sister Anselma said. "She doesn't respond."

Jessica backed out, closing the door.

Sister Mary David peered at the thermometer. "Hundred two point six. Let's get her to the infirmary."

"Wait." Sister Anselma looked from Mother Theodora to Sister Mary David. "Could you care for her here? Or could I help?"

Sister Mary David was puzzled. "Why in the world would you not want her in the infirmary?"

Sister Anselma's gaze shifted to Mother Theodora. "I realize what I'm asking seems drastic, but I truly believe Michele's retreat should continue. I'm afraid she will lose all that she's gained if we stop now."

Sister Mary David was looking at her as if she were suggesting torture. "Can't she do that in the infirmary?" she demanded.

Sister Anselma considered her answer. "It isn't only the normal commotion of the infirmary's comings and goings; I'm also concerned for Michele's privacy. I'm not sure what may come up, especially while she's in this fevered condition, but I'm fairly certain it shouldn't happen where others can overhear."

Mother Theodora thought about this. She looked at Sister Mary David. "Can you physically care for her here? Is there special equipment needed that requires she be in the infirmary?"

"I suppose not," Sister Mary David admitted. "With a fever this high, she'll need someone with her constantly until it breaks."

"I know you're very busy, Sister," Sister Anselma acknowledged. "I don't mean to inconvenience you."

"I believe the three of us should be the only ones to watch over her for now," Mother Theodora said.

"Mother, you can't! There are so many demands on you as it is," Sister Anselma protested.

Mother's gaze met Sister Anselma's directly as she said, "I believe you are correct about issues that may rise to the surface at this stage of her retreat, and I do not wish to compromise Michele's privacy any more than this situation requires."

Sister Anselma nodded in acknowledgment of what lay unspoken between them.

"If I may ask the two of you to get her out of those wet clothes and into bed, I am going to get a cot for us to use."

By the time Mother Theodora returned with a folding cot, Mickey was in a dry nightgown and under several blankets. Sister Mary David went to get medications and other supplies she thought they might need. She also brought water and juice.

"I'll stay with her first," Mother Theodora said in a tone which cut off any protests. "Sister Mary David, please come to relieve me in the morning. Sister Anselma will relieve you after lunch. We'll rotate until her fever breaks."

Mother Theodora got up every hour for the rest of the night. Mickey's fever actually climbed higher. She took a few sips of the liquids Mother gently coaxed her with. She seemed to sleep fitfully, but when she was awake, her eyes were focused on something only she could see. She didn't respond to her name or to questions.

At four a.m., there was a soft knock on the door, and Sister Mary David came in. Mother gave her an update on Mickey's temperature readings and went to get some sleep until it was time for Mass. Sister

Mary David continued to rotate the cold compresses on Mickey's forehead and kept trying to get her to drink. Mickey's shivering continued. She alternately grasped the blankets to hold them more tightly around her, and then tried pushing them all off. Sister Mary David gently, but firmly, kept covering her up.

When Sister Anselma got there, Mickey was sleeping. "Has she said anything?"

"Nothing." Sister Mary David gathered up empty juice containers. "I'll come back before dinner to check on both of you."

Sister Anselma pulled a chair up next to the bed. She took Mickey's Bible off the desk and quietly read out loud the passages she had given Mickey to pray with. Mickey's fever remained constant at just over a hundred and three throughout that day. Not until that night did it start to come down even a little. Sister Mary David and Mother Theodora had both rotated through shifts. Sister Anselma was with Mickey again when she spoke for the first time.

"Alice?" Mickey's voice startled Sister Anselma who was dozing on the cot. She got up and came over to the chair. She reached out to change the compress on Mickey's head, but Mickey grabbed her hand and held it tightly.

"I am so sorry," Mickey whispered, tears running out of the corners of her eyes.

"Sorry for what?" Sister Anselma asked, but Mickey drifted off again, still holding to Sister Anselma's hand and whispering "sorry" every now and again.

A couple of hours later, Mickey's temperature was down a bit more. Her eyes focused on Sister Anselma's for the first time.

"What happened?" she asked weakly.

"We're not sure. We found you soaking wet in the organ loft, delirious with a very high fever."

"I remember going out to the orchard – I just needed to walk." Mickey stared at the ceiling for a long time before saying, "Did you know our property butts up against a schoolyard?"

"No," said Sister Anselma, watching Mickey closely.

"I sat there all afternoon, listening to the children's voices,"

Mickey said. "I got caught in the storm. I don't remember much after that. How long ago was that?"

"Over twenty-four hours," Sister Anselma replied as she placed a fresh cold compress on Mickey's forehead.

Mickey seemed to just realize where she was. She noticed the cot. "You haven't been here the whole time, have you?" she asked, aghast.

"Mother, Sister Mary David and I have been with you in shifts. Your fever got to nearly one hundred and four. We were afraid we might have to call an ambulance."

"I am so sorry. I never meant to cause so much trouble." Mickey looked stricken. "You are all so busy…"

"Nonsense," Sister Anselma said firmly. "But 'sorry' seems to be on your mind a great deal. The only things you've said are to call Alice's name and keep repeating that you are sorry. Sorry for what, Michele?"

Mickey's face was still flushed and hot with her fever. Her eyes looked at Sister Anselma as if haunted. Sister Anselma's image began to swim as Mickey's eyes filled with tears. She closed her eyes and the tears spilled over.

"I should have seen," Mickey whispered.

Understanding dawned on Sister Anselma's face. "You blame yourself for her death?" she asked softly. "You think you should have been able to save her?"

"I should have paid more attention, should have caught it earlier," Mickey's voice cracked as her throat tightened. "If she'd been a patient… I always saw things others missed, diagnosed things no one else saw. But… with Alice… I didn't pay enough attention."

"Could anyone have seen what was happening?"

Mickey didn't answer, but she almost seemed to convulse with the effort of holding back her sobs.

"Let it go," Sister Anselma murmured.

And the anguish broke forth in waves. Mickey's whole body was racked with the depth of her sobbing. Each time it started to quiet, new waves came.

As she sat there, knowing Mickey needed to work through this,

Sister Anselma's face changed – her features relaxed, softened, "melted," Sister Mary David would say later.

Mickey cried until she cried herself to sleep. Watching her curled up on her side, her eyelashes and cheeks still damp, Sister Anselma reached out and laid her hand gently on Mickey's head. To her surprise, Mickey actually felt cooler. She wasn't sure why, but she let her hand linger, not wanting to break contact.

☊ ☊ ☊

When Mickey awakened the next morning, the fever was completely gone, and Mother Theodora was with her. Mickey sat up, feeling disoriented.

"Was Sister Anselma here last night, or was that a dream?" she asked, rubbing her forehead.

Mother Theodora smiled. "It was no dream, although I don't doubt you've had some bizarre ones. Being ill always does that to me."

Mickey felt her own face. "I think my fever broke."

"I don't think that's all that broke last night," Mother Theodora said cryptically.

Mickey didn't seem to hear. "Mother? Not that I mind, but why wasn't I taken to the infirmary?"

"It was Sister Anselma's idea," Mother Theodora replied as she handed Mickey a glass of orange juice. "Drink. She felt it was important for your retreat to continue and that it should probably do so in a more private location than the infirmary." She watched Mickey's face as she asked, "What do you remember of last night?"

Mickey delayed answering by drinking more of her juice. "I'm pretty sure I remember everything, although it seems distorted. I woke to find Sister Anselma here. It took me a minute to realize where I was. She told me I had been calling Alice's name and saying I was sorry." She looked down at her glass as her eyes filled with tears again.

"It's all right," Mother Theodora said quietly. "I just wanted to be sure you recalled what happened. I think it will be important as you continue your retreat. Do you think you could eat something?"

Mickey nodded.

"Good. I'll give you time to wash up and change nightgowns. I'll return in a little while with some breakfast."

Sister Mary David was with Mother Theodora when she returned. She insisted on taking Mickey's temperature again. "Almost normal," she pronounced.

"We'll leave you now," said Mother. "Sister Anselma will be by later, and the two of you may decide the best schedule for the remainder of your retreat. I think it would be wise for your meals to be brought to you for the next few days, until you are fully well."

With that, Mickey was left alone and in silence once again. "Well, in silence maybe," Mickey would have said, "but certainly not alone," as memories long pushed to the recesses of her mind kept surging into the present.

Chapter 11

Mickey stopped outside the classroom door, balancing three pans of cupcakes in one hand while she opened the door with the other. One of the more distractible students who hadn't been paying attention anyway saw her and gasped. Immediately, the whole class was watching her as she quickly put her finger to her lips, signaling silence. She glanced at Alice who was writing on the board with her back to the class. Quickly lighting a candle on one of the cupcakes, she signaled the class and they all started singing Happy Birthday.

Alice jumped, dropping the marker, and turned with a big smile.

"Make a wish, Miss Worthington!" the children shouted, squirming in their seats. Several of them blew with her as she made a wish with her eyes scrunched tight and blew out the candle.

Alice's fingers intertwined with Mickey's briefly as she took the cupcake from her. Mickey went to pass out the rest of the cupcakes with one of the second graders clinging to her waist.

"Thank you, Dr. Mickey," each child said as he or she was given a cupcake.

"You know you totally disrupted my lesson plan," Alice said as Mickey unwrapped her own cupcake.

"You bet. You're not supposed to work on your birthday. Wait till you see what else I brought!"

She retrieved her backpack which looked suspiciously full. She pulled out a box of gloves, paper surgical gowns and masks. Soon twenty-three midget surgeons were running around, flapping their too-large gloves and tripping over the gowns.

A few faces appeared at the classroom door as other teachers and one of the assistant principals came by, laughing and pointing as the children milled around. Mickey waved them in, passing out more cupcakes.

"Well, it's a cinch I'm not going to get any more work done today," Alice said, giving up and dropping into a vacant chair with a second cupcake.

Mickey sat down beside her as they laughed at the little ones. "I love you, Miss Worthington," she whispered in Alice's ear.

Chapter 12

Mickey was finally approaching the end of the longest thirty days of her life. If she had thought the worst was over with the fever, "boy, was I wrong," she admitted later. Sister Anselma had been relentless, asking Mickey to dig ever deeper, going places she didn't really want to go. Never much of a crier, it seemed a lifetime's worth of tears had been released and Mickey seemed powerless to stop them.

"I sense such strong regrets from you," Sister Anselma said one day. "Do you regret the choices and decisions you made?"

Mickey considered. "I regret having had to make choices between Alice and my work. I know she didn't blame me, but it all felt so pointless after she was gone." Her throat tightened painfully as she said, "We spent so much time planning and dreaming about what we would do after we retired. I kept telling myself, every time I let her down or cancelled our plans to be at the hospital, that I'd make it up to her someday." Here, tears began to fall again. Mickey tore more toilet paper from the roll she had taken to carrying with her to blow her nose. "I let so many opportunities to be with her pass me by, thinking there would be time later, but..."

Mickey spent long hours walking outside as she prayed, enjoying the orchard, now in full bloom, but "please don't wander too far," Sister Anselma pleaded. "You are not fully recovered and Sister

Mary David will never forgive me if you get ill again."

All around Mickey, the abbey moved in its unalterable rhythm. "Even in the midst of a crisis," Sister Rosaria had told the postulants, "the death of an abbess, for instance, the work of the monastery, the Office, all must go on. This transcends all else." She had seen other members of the community, of course, and they acknowledged her with silent nods, leaving her to her prayer. Twice, small nosegays of spring flowers had been left in her stall in Chapel with little notes. One note was inscribed with part of Psalm 46, *"Be still and know that I am God."* Mickey tucked it in her pocket and carried it with her everywhere. She could feel the community lifting her, supporting her, even if they didn't know the specifics of her struggle. "We don't need to know the details; we are with you," they would have told her.

As the voices carried from the Chapel, singing the hour of Vespers, Mickey sat on the bench she had adopted under the cherry tree, now bursting with pink blossoms, enjoying the late afternoon sunshine as she read from Jeremiah, *"I have loved you with an everlasting love, so I am constant in my affection for you."*

"What is it?" Sister Anselma prodded the next day.

"How do you keep coming up with these?" Mickey asked in frustration. "Aren't we done yet?"

Sister Anselma looked at her with a bemused expression that clearly said, "Apparently not."

Mickey expelled a pent-up breath. "I told you I almost entered a convent after high school. I was," she held up a thumb and forefinger a hair's breadth apart, "this close to entering. They would have sent me to college, probably nursing or teaching, but something held me back. Cold feet, I guess." She fingered the cover of her journal, tracing a pattern with a finger as she continued, "All through college, I had a kind of guilty feeling that I was ignoring that call. And then, when I met Alice, and was so incredibly happy with her, I absolutely did not want to consider the possibility of a vocation."

Here, Mickey had to pause and take a drink of water. Sister Anselma waited patiently until she was able to continue.

"I'm realizing... part of my struggle since she died, and this all started again – entering St. Bridget's – should I have just gone when I was eighteen? Did Alice have to die for me to wake up and listen?"

Mickey's eyes filled with tears again as Sister Anselma leaned forward. "Listen to Jeremiah," she said. "You may have been chosen long ago, but that doesn't mean the work you did, the life you lived wasn't part of that call – and that includes your love for Alice. We'll never understand why loved ones are taken from us, not while we're here on earth anyway. Maybe we'll understand one day. But God's love doesn't work like that. His love is everlasting and his time is not our time. Everything comes together as it is meant to."

Mickey looked at her through red-rimmed eyes. "You really believe that?"

Sister Anselma sat back. "With my whole heart."

Inevitably, in the fourth week of the retreat, Sister Anselma said, "You told me in one of our early sessions that you didn't know how to answer when I asked you if you were a good physician. If you can exclude Alice from that question, how would you answer?"

"I guess I'd say I was a good doctor," Mickey replied hesitantly.

"I'm sure you've been asked this many times," Sister Anselma's eyes probed Mickey's, "but why abandon something you were gifted at? Are you running away from the responsibilities and inevitable failures of practicing medicine? Are you turning your back on an entire way of life out of anger? Or are you truly feeling called to a life of prayer?"

Mickey stared at her without answering.

"I want you to ask yourself those questions as you pray with these Scriptures."

☩ ☩ ☩

Finally, the last day. Rather than giving Mickey new readings to pray with, Sister Anselma had asked Mickey to read back through her journal and see if particular entries stood out.

"The whole period around the fever stands out in my mind,"

Mickey told her when they met, "but it's almost non-existent in the journal. I feel like I was being held to a flame – parts of me burned away in the heat, other parts became translucent, and yet other parts weren't even touched, like wet leaves on a bonfire." She shook her head. "I don't believe that fever was caused by any bacteria or virus," she looked at Sister Anselma suspiciously, "and I wouldn't be surprised if you arranged it."

To Mickey's surprise, Sister Anselma actually laughed. Mickey had never even seen her smile.

"Believe me, Michele, I don't have that much influence." Her expression became more serious. "How do you feel about requesting entrance to the Novitiate? Do you feel that you are being called to continue on this path?"

"Yes, I do," Mickey responded. Then she grinned, "At least until the path forks again." She looked down at her hands. "I want you to know that I am fully aware of how much trouble I've been. I'm sure you had no idea of what you were letting yourself in for when you agreed to direct my retreat. I don't know how to thank you."

Sister Anselma was so quiet that Mickey raised her eyes. Sister Anselma's face wore a peculiar expression, "melting again," Sister Mary David would have said with some amusement.

"Michele," she faltered, the first time Mickey had seen her at a loss for words, "for more reasons than you could know, I consider myself privileged and blessed to have been chosen as your guide and confidante." She paused. "I think it is just possible that I will take even more away from this experience than you."

Mickey emerged from the solitude of her retreat like someone stepping from a dark cave into sunlight. It was difficult to focus, there was so much commotion as she resumed a normal schedule. She had to smile at the thought that the abbey seemed noisy, especially during the somber season of Lent.

Back among the postulants, Mickey was warmly welcomed by Tanya and Jessica. Sister Anselma had told Mickey about Jessica's help searching for her the night of the storm, and Mickey was certain that Jessica must have heard some of what occurred while she was ill, since her cell was next door, but as far as she could tell, Jessica had said nothing to anyone else. Jessica did seem to be slightly in awe of Sister Anselma. "She talks to me now," she whispered to Mickey during Recreation. "She never did that before."

Mickey felt as if she had lost a lot of time in their classes. "What's up with her?" Mickey asked, indicating Wendy who was sniffing and red-eyed as they came into Sister Stephen's classroom for Latin on her second day back in the regular routine.

Tanya rolled her eyes. "She's been like that ever since we were told your retreat was being extended, saying hers was so hard and so painful. She'll never say what exactly – that, apparently, is personal, but she doesn't seem to mind being a public snot factory."

Mickey choked with laughter.

"The thing that worries me," Jessica continued in a low voice, "is that Abby is getting all wrapped up in the drama."

She was right. Mickey watched from a distance as Abigail stuck near to Wendy, solicitous and concerned as Wendy seemed to be constantly weeping. "You of all people have no right to criticize that, after this past month," Mickey told herself sternly, but still... Wendy's displays seemed so... ostentatious.

A few days later, Mickey was summoned to Mother Theodora's office. She was standing, looking out the window when Mickey entered. "Sit down, Mickey."

Mickey took one of the chairs and waited for Mother Theodora to speak. They hadn't had any contact since the morning Mickey's fever broke. At last, Mother Theodora turned from the window.

"You look thin, child. I've been worried about you."

Mickey gave her a wan smile. "I've been worried about me, too. I can honestly say I hope never to go through anything like that again."

Mother Theodora came to sit in the chair next to her. "When Sister Anselma came to ask me about extending your retreat, I wasn't sure it was the right thing to do. I was afraid that much of what might surface would be beyond her ability to help you with."

"She was incredibly patient and understanding. I'm sure that month was exhausting for her."

Mother Theodora smiled. "Perhaps, but I think in many ways, it turned out to be as beneficial for her as I hope it ultimately was for you."

Mickey looked puzzled. "She said something to that effect on our last day, but I'm afraid I don't understand."

Mother Theodora looked at Mickey for several seconds before speaking. "Let's just say that Sister Anselma has maintained a certain... aloofness from the rest of the community. She is highly respected for her work, but not especially loved. Her experience with you has had the unintended side effect of putting a small chink in her armor."

Mickey looked worried. "Mother, I'm sorry if I've upset the balance of things in any way."

"Mickey," Mother Theodora said thoughtfully, "I have a feeling we've only seen a glimpse of how you will affect the balance of life at St. Bridget's."

Chapter 13

Tanya paced as Mickey sat with her elbows resting on her knees, staring at the floor. Abigail's foot jiggled in an agitated rhythm while Wendy drummed her fingers nervously on the windowsill as she stared out at the grounds. Only Jessica waited placidly.

"Before you are accepted for your Clothing," Sister Rosaria had told them at the beginning of Holy Week, "the community will vote on each of you. If any of you receives ten percent or more negative votes, you will be asked to leave."

"But," Tanya sputtered, "that's only seven votes!"

Mickey's gut clenched as she considered the possibility of being asked to leave. *Not now,* she thought. *Not after everything I've been through,* but, as if to make the unthinkable more real, she'd received a packet that week from her surgical practice. She didn't need to open it. Her year's leave of absence was nearly at an end. Inside, she knew, was the buyout contract, waiting for her signature. It sat, still unopened, on her desk.

Tomorrow, Holy Thursday, would begin the solemn ceremonies culminating in Simple Vows for Sister Helen and Sister Stephanie and the receiving of the habit for the five postulants, but "will there still be five of us?" Mickey asked herself as they waited.

One by one, they were called to meet with the Council and hear the results of the vote. Besides Mother Theodora, the Council was made up of six other sisters, including the prioress, the Abbess's second in command. Sister Scholastica was the current prioress. The other five were elected by the community to serve staggered terms of five years each so that there were never any more than two new Council members, with the possible exception that if the Abbess died, her successor might be new to the Council.

None of the others returned to the room where they were waiting, so that after what seemed a long time, only Jessica and Mickey remained. When Jessica's name was called, she gave Mickey an encouraging smile and then Mickey was left alone. She understood that the women in this community took the voting process very seriously, and would not vote no on the basis of petty grievances, but still – there was Sister Helen, and she was sure she must have irritated some of the others as well. How many times had Sister Rosaria and Sister Stephen had to rebuke and correct her? And she knew she hadn't hidden her irritation with Wendy very well, but "is that enough to make them question my suitability for monastic life?" she wondered.

When at last Mickey was called in to the Council room, she found the members seated around a long table with Mother Theodora at the head.

"Sit down, Michele," Mother Theodora invited, indicating the empty chair at the table. Mickey nervously sat.

Sister Scholastica apparently was in charge of this process as she was the one who spoke next, saying, "We are pleased to tell you, Michele, that you have been accepted into the Novitiate. Even though you will not be under vows, you will be expected to contribute and live as a full member of this community. If you desire to leave, you may do so at any time, but it is our fervent prayer that your vocation will lead you to stay with us at St. Bridget's."

It took a moment for the words to sink in, so prepared had Mickey been to hear a "We're sorry," speech. Mickey bit her lip and swallowed the lump in her throat. "Thank you," she said simply.

When she got back to her cell, she took the buyout contract from the envelope and read it over. Now, the final decision was solely in her own hands, needing only her signature to complete the last step of walking away from her old life, "from everything you worked for, everything you built," said a stubborn voice in her head. She stuffed the contract back into its envelope.

Thursday evening was the Mass commemorating the Last Supper. Following the reading of the Gospel, Mother Theodora donned an apron and washed the feet of twelve members of the community - "which always includes the novices taking their vows and the postulants moving to the Novitiate," Sister Rosaria had said, overriding their protests by reminding them, "part of humility is learning to receive graciously."

At the end of the Mass, the altar was draped in a black cloth as Father Andrew placed the remaining Communion bread in a small side chapel where the nuns would maintain a constant vigil, rotating half-hour prayer shifts through the solemnity of Good Friday, remembering the anguish of the crucifixion - the long, hushed hours afterward when all must have seemed dark and lost.

I know that lost feeling, Mickey thought as she knelt through her shift, allowing herself to feel the despair and anguish that she remembered only too well....

╬ ╬ ╬

> "Magnificat anima mea Dominum,
> et exultavit spiritus meus in Deo salvatore meo,
> quia respexit humilitatem ancillae suae.
> Ecce enim ex hoc beatam me dicent omnes generationes..."

Mickey and the other four, wearing simple white robes, their heads uncovered and hair uncut for the last time, processed behind Sister Helen and Sister Stephanie who sang the Magnificat. Behind them, the public chapel was full to bursting - "we haven't had this many new entrants in years," the nuns had murmured appreciatively when it became known that all would be moving on to the Novitiate. Mickey felt goosebumps erupt as she listened to Sister Helen's soaring voice and her throat tightened painfully. "For He that is mighty hath done great things to me and holy is His Name…"

The community took up the last two stanzas as Sisters Helen and Stephanie prostrated themselves on the floor, their foreheads resting on their hands. The sunlight filtered in through the stained glass window above the altar so that the two women lay in a pool of reds and greens and blues spilling over the flagstones where Mother Theodora and Father Andrew stood with Bishop Marcus who had come to preside over the celebration, looking like one of the magi, with his regal bearing and dark complexion, accentuated by brilliant white robes richly embroidered with gold. He stepped forward.

"Sister Helen Bennington, are you prepared to make your vows before this community, to God and to your Abbess, to live in poverty, renouncing material and worldly possessions; to live chastely, renouncing human love in favor of the love of our Lord; and to live in obedience to the Abbess who stands in Christ's place as the head of the community?"

"I am," Sister Helen replied.

"Then rise, and receive this ring as a token of your commitment," he said, sliding a plain silver band onto her left hand. Sister Helen then moved to Mother Theodora who handed her a pen with which to sign her vow agreement. The process was repeated for Sister Stephanie, and then both of them disappeared into the sacristy where their short white veils were exchanged for long, black ones. They took their seats in the choir as the postulants now prostrated themselves on the cool stone floor.

"What do you ask?" Bishop Marcus asked each in turn. Their reply, "To enter the Novitiate of St. Bridget's Abbey and try my vocation here."

"My heart was pounding so hard," Mickey would tell Jamie later, "I didn't think I was going to be able to speak. I saw myself lying there, gasping for air like a netted fish."

As they rose to go to the sacristy, Mickey was so light-headed, she thought she might pass out. Inside, Sisters Teresa and Fiona waited for them. They took off the white robes, and had their hair cut short. Mickey's had grown longer over the past year than it had ever been, but the others all had much longer hair. They were then all helped to change into the habit with its full-length robe, then the yoke which hung front to back, girded with a rope belt through which was hung a wooden rosary. The white, starched wimple was placed on their heads, framing their faces with the laces in the back pulled snug. Then the white novice's veils were pinned into place.

All of the senior nuns remembered those milestone moments, and many had happily shared their reminiscences with the postulants recently. "You should have seen my gown," several of the older ones recalled, as before Vatican II, full wedding gowns were the norm for the Clothing. "We were real brides of Christ back then," they said fondly. "Not like now, where there is no formality and the young ones act as if they are just 'buddies' with our Lord," they added, not so fondly.

Mickey and the others were grateful there were no longer wedding gowns - "I would have had to wear a tuxedo," Mickey joked.

"But nothing we wore before compares to this," the older nuns all also said, running their hands affectionately over the sleeves of their habits. "Just wait. It will fit," - "or it won't," a few could have said.

Back in the Chapel, the five stood before Mother Theodora who said to them, "Receive the habit, a symbol of your commitment to a life of poverty and simplicity, girded with a rosary so that prayer will be your constant companion. Receive also your new names in Christ. Jessica Thomas, you will now be known as Sister Jessica. Tanya Peterson, you will now be known as Sister Tanya. Abigail Morgan, you will now be known as Sister Abigail. Wendy Barnes, you will now be known as Sister Wendy. Michele Stewart, you will now be known as Sister Michele." As she addressed them in turn, she laid a hand on each head and blessed them.

Following Mass, the nuns formed a line in the corridor connecting the Chapel to the cloister so that the two newly professed nuns and five new novices could be welcomed by each member of the community. Most offered small whispers of encouragement along with an embrace. When Mickey got to Sister Anselma, there were no words, but an especially tight embrace and one of Sister Anselma's rare smiles.

Last in line was Mother Theodora. When Mickey was standing in front of her, she held Mickey at arms' length, looking at her for several seconds before embracing her. "It suits you," she said approvingly.

"Wow," said Jamie a little while later, fingering the sleeve of Mickey's habit. The community and visiting family members of the seven women celebrating the day – "nope, not seven families, only six," Mickey muttered to Jamie when she noticed Wendy again had no family present – had gathered in the refectory for a small reception.

"This is a big deal," he said, looking around.

Mickey smiled. "It's a very big deal." The wimple felt stiff and tight under her jaw. "I'm not sure how they work in these," she said, sliding a finger under it and tugging on the starched fabric, "but I guess I'll get used to it."

"Should I take a picture for Mom?" he grinned, pulling out his phone.

"Oh, shut up," she grumbled.

"Is that any way for a nun to talk?" he teased.

Back in her cell that evening, Mickey signed the contract ending her partnership in the surgical practice.

Chapter 14

A warm night breeze blowing off the bay evaporated the light sweat covering Alice and Mickey's naked bodies. They were enjoying a rare weekend alone with no friends or family joining them. Mickey lay with her head resting on Alice's shoulder, an arm and leg draped over Alice's body, sifting Alice's silky dark hair through her fingers.

"That was amazing," she said, still breathing heavily. "You know exactly how to read me and give me what I want."

Alice traced a fingertip along Mickey's earlobe. "We've learned together, and it's only gotten better with time."

Mickey sat up to pour them both more wine. "The best things really do get better with some age on them," she said as she handed Alice her glass.

"Are you sure?" Alice asked, propping up against the pillows.

"What do you mean?"

"Well, I feel silly admitting it," Alice said softly, "but, I still get afraid sometimes that one of those beautiful, adoring young medical students will catch your eye, and you'll take off for a new life with fewer obligations and better sex."

Mickey shook her head. "No one is more beautiful to me than you are," Mickey murmured, running her fingers over Alice's stomach. "I love our life just as it is." She tilted her head, looking down at

Alice. "Besides, why in the world would I want to start over having to break in someone new? It's taken me ten years to get you trained."

"If this were white wine and I didn't have to worry about stains, you would be wearing it about now," Alice said wryly.

Mickey laughed and leaned down for a kiss. She drained her wine glass and lay back down beside Alice on the day bed they had put on the porch outside their bedroom. "I'm so glad we had this porch screened in."

Alice smiled in the dark. "I know. We wouldn't want your delicate freckled skin to get mosquito bites in sensitive spots."

Mickey rolled on top of Alice and grinned. "You're the only one allowed to bite my sensitive spots."

Chapter 15

"It's about time," Sister Linus said as she opened the door to let Mickey in with a breakfast tray.

Almost as soon as Mickey had ended her retreat, Sister Cecilia had called upon her to resume bringing the food trays to the chaplain's residence.

"I don't know how you did it," Sister Cecilia said, "but you're the only one whose head Sister Linus hasn't bitten off. It's like pulling teeth to get anyone else to do this."

Even once Mickey was in the Novitiate and her duties were supposed to have changed, Sister Cecilia had pleaded with the Novice mistress, Sister Josephine, "Please, give Sister Michele leave to keep doing this."

"I don't mind," Mickey said in response to Sister Josephine's questioning glance.

Sister Linus had, in fact, seemed to have missed her. "I saw you," she said now as she laid out the dishes on the table. "When you were on your retreat. Under the cherry tree. That tree was planted the year I entered. Seventy-six years ago."

"Really?" Mickey said in surprise. "So, you're...?"

"Ninety-four," Sister Linus chuckled. "Back then, we entered at eighteen. But I think some of the seniors had bets on whether I'd last." Her smile turned to a scowl. "But now, they think I can't do anything. 'You should rest,' they say. 'You've earned your retirement.' Want to sit me in a corner, let me darn torn sheets until I just stop one day."

She looked at Mickey shrewdly. "Your retreat, it looked like it was hard."

Mickey felt her cheeks grow hot. She just nodded.

"Good," Sister Linus said approvingly. "If they're easy, there's no point. God isn't easy."

Neither was the Novitiate, as the new novices were finding out. While they continued studying Latin, they began studying the history of St. Bridget's which had been founded in 1820 by a group of Scottish nuns trying to escape the persecution of Catholics by Protestants determined to make Great Britain entirely Protestant. "And to think, if we'd waited just nine wee years, we could have stayed in Scotland," Sister Josephine joked in her Scottish burr which had softened after twenty years in the States, but was still present. If Sister Rosaria had been like an elderly maiden aunt, strict and stodgy, Sister Josephine was the younger, roguish aunt – one who had probably gotten into plenty of trouble herself, with laughing green eyes and a ready sense of humor. Mickey suspected there was red hair under that wimple.

"Our vows are not just some promise we make to then lay them aside," she told the five new novices and the two second-years. "They must become part of the fabric of who we are."

She invited debate and argument as they began reading and discussing books and papers on religious vows and monastic life in general.

"None of us is a completely open book," she told them, "but keeping secrets is a form of pride, a reliance on self instead of community, and it's one of the most dangerous things to a cohesive community." She scanned the group quizzically. "How do you deal with pride?"

"I pray for humility," said Sister Miranda, one of the second-years.

"Ah, and how will you know if you get it?" Sister Josephine asked.

Sister Miranda looked puzzled.

"Praying for humility can be a bit tricky," Sister Josephine warned them. "It tends to come to us through humiliation which is not usually what we have in mind when we ask for humility."

Mickey smiled, remembering several instances where she had learned that painful lesson.

"The other thing about humility that makes it unique is that if you ever realize you've attained it, you just lost it."

"But then," Tanya frowned, "how are we to become humble?"

"Good question," Sister Josephine replied, and dismissed them.

Though the novices were not yet under vows, they were expected to begin living as if they were, and poverty was one of the first things Sister Josephine tackled as they were required to make their first inventory of their belongings, something they would henceforth do yearly. "It should be simple," Mickey wrote to Jamie, "all we have to wear are two habits and two nightgowns and our underwear," but "you will be surprised how difficult it is to give up other things," Sister Josephine warned them. "Five books may not seem like many, until you realize you started with three and then it grows to eight and soon you will be hoarding. You may keep three books," she said to Jessica, "and the others will be available from the library when you want to read them." Mickey had laughed at the thought that any of them could be accused of hoarding until, "how many pens do you need, Sister Michele?" asked Sister Josephine as she looked Mickey's list over. Beautiful pens had been the one thing that Mickey had collected. "I can't help myself," she said to Alice so many times when she came home from an antique shop with another fountain pen, but the four she hadn't been able to part with had been gifts. The memories associated with each – one from Alice for the completion of her residency, one from Jamie, one had been her father's, one from a patient – made them all precious to her, but "you may keep two," Sister Josephine said gently, "so you have one as a back-up," she added chidingly, and Mickey knew she was being eased into the mindset of true poverty. "The poor don't have even one of these things," they had heard over and over, "but somehow it doesn't make it any easier to give things up," Mickey wrote with her father's pen.

☩ ☩ ☩

Mickey lay in bed in her cell, listening to the wind whistling through her window. *Come on,* she thought as she tossed restlessly. *You should be exhausted.*

The novices and this year's three new postulants, who had entered after Easter, had spent the work periods over the past several days helping Sister Regina get the abbey's large vegetable garden planted for the year. As she typically did, Sister Regina had started most of the plants weeks earlier in the greenhouse, as New York's spring could be unpredictable. The weather had remained cool and blustery, and Sister Regina had watched the weather forecast fretfully, but "we can't wait any longer to get these plants in the ground," she said at last.

Once furrows were dug and all was planted, everything had to be covered with firmly anchored netting to protect the tender young plants from the deer and rabbits who knew they had a safe haven on the abbey grounds.

"They know we won't shoot them," Sister Regina grumbled, "but we can at least make them work for whatever they manage to steal."

Despite Sister Regina's complaints, Mickey noticed that she kept salt blocks and piles of surplus corn near the edge of the wooded portion of the abbey's land.

Over the couple of weeks it took them to get everything dug and planted, Mickey noticed that Wendy and Abigail usually managed to be off by themselves in some corner of the garden far removed from the others. More than once, Tanya caught her eye with a questioning nod in their direction.

Finally, as they finished planting in late May, the weather began to break with a strong, warm wind blowing from the south. Mickey stood in the garden facing into the wind, feeling something restless stirring within her.

Mickey listened to the wind now, tossing in her bed until after midnight, trying to make herself go to sleep. Giving up, she dressed and exited the abbey as quietly as possible. Outside, in the enclosure, the wind whipped her veil. Overwhelmed by the need to stretch her body, she let herself through the enclosure gate, picked up her skirts and ran to a small hill in the orchard. She hadn't been out this far since the day she got caught in the storm. Exhilarated by the exercise, she stood breathing in the wind, tasting it, letting it fill her. She wasn't sure there was a specific rule against it, but she felt distinctly unmonastic as she unpinned her veil and removed her wimple. The wind felt wonderful as it blew through her hair, "or what's left of it." Carefully placing the veil and wimple in the crook of an old apple tree, she took off running again.

A half-moon lit her way as she ran between the rows of trees. At last, winded and jubilant, she slowed to a walk and circled back toward the abbey. She became aware of a different moan from the wind. Puzzled, she stopped and listened. Someone was crying. She moved quietly toward the source. In the light from the moon, she saw a nun leaning against a tree, her hands covering her face. Remembering what Mother Theodora had told her about respecting each other's privacy, Mickey had turned to leave when suddenly the other nun grabbed a broken tree branch lying on the ground and began hitting it against the trunk of the tree, over and over. Startled, Mickey just stood and watched.

"Damn you!" It was Sister Anselma. As suddenly as she had started, she dropped the branch and fell to her knees. "Forgive me," she sobbed, covering her face with her hands again.

Mickey stood, torn. She didn't want to intrude on a scene she was sure Sister Anselma hadn't intended anyone to witness, but the anguish in her voice was so powerful....

"Sister?" she said softly, walking nearer. Sister Anselma started and gasped.

"I'm so sorry to intrude," Mickey began, kneeling beside her. "I was out here, and heard you crying. I'll leave if you wish, only...are you all right?" She laid a tentative hand on Sister Anselma's shoulder.

To her surprise, Sister Anselma sat in the grass and began to laugh. Not sure what to do, Mickey sat beside her and waited.

"Michele," she said at last, wiping tears from her face, "what are you doing out here?"

"I couldn't sleep. I needed to run and feel the wind –" she suddenly remembered and reached up to her hair. "Oh my gosh, I left my veil in a tree!"

Sister Anselma started laughing again, and Mickey couldn't help laughing along. *If I'm going to make an idiot of myself,* she thought, *at least it's with someone who already knows some of my most unflattering secrets.*

When the laughter faded, there was only the sound of the wind and the creaking of the tree branches. Mickey waited.

"I got a letter today," Sister Anselma said at last, looking up at the moon. "My mother died last week."

Mickey sat in disbelief. "Why didn't someone let you know sooner?"

"Probably because my mother told them not to. Everyone does as my mother says… said," she corrected the tense.

"I don't understand," Mickey prompted softly.

"I come from a very dysfunctional family," Sister Anselma explained. "Very wealthy and very troubled. My mother used her money to manipulate everyone: my father, my sister and brother. And me for a while." She looked out at the apple trees around them. "Finally, when I was eighteen, I'd had enough. I left home and took whatever jobs I could find to put myself through college. She was furious that cutting me off didn't bring me crawling back to her."

"I think it's very admirable that you were strong enough to stand on your own two feet," Mickey offered.

Turning to Mickey, Sister Anselma said, "There was nothing admirable about the anger and spite that drove me then." She hesitated, plucking a blade of grass and twisting it in her fingers. "While I was in college, I got pregnant. I didn't want the baby, but I didn't want my mother to get her hands on it, either. I knew no adoption would be safe from her attorneys and bribes. I had an abortion solely to keep my mother from getting my baby." She bowed her head, pressing her fists against her forehead. "I'll never be able to atone for that," she finished softly.

Mickey sat in stunned silence at this revelation.

"No one but Mother Theodora knows about that," Sister Anselma added after a long pause.

"How long has it been since you last had any contact with your family?"

"Since before I entered," Sister Anselma answered in a low voice. "Mother encouraged me to write, and I did a few times, with no response." She was quiet for a long time. "Fifteen years of religious life, and I still let her make me that angry." She looked down at her hands. "I'm sorry you had to see that."

"Please don't apologize to me," Mickey insisted. "That's a long time to live with so many unresolved issues, and now there can be no opportunity to get any resolution. I know I couldn't pray hard enough to make that bearable."

Sister Anselma closed her eyes for a moment. "I thought I could."

Taking a deep breath, she got to her feet. "Come. We should get back. We've broken at least a dozen rules tonight. Go get your veil."

╬╬╬

Predictably, Sister Anselma's name was called during the Chapter of Faults the week after the "orchard incident," as Mickey had come to think of it, but "I would have had to confess even if my name weren't called," she knew Sister Anselma would have said.

"Mother, I broke Silence, cursed and lost my temper."

"Was any of this directed toward another person?"

"No, Mother. Toward a tree in the orchard."

Mother Theodora's eyebrows went up. "I see. You will assist Sister Regina in pruning the orchard for one week."

"Does anyone else wish to speak?" Mother Theodora asked when the five had finished.

Mickey had gone back and forth over whether she should speak up. Finally, she rose and knelt. "Mother, I broke Silence and ran."

Mother Theodora stared at her for a few seconds. "At the same time?"

"No... I... felt restless one night, so I went outside and ran. Breaking Silence was separate."

Mother Theodora's mouth twitched as she tried not to smile. "Well then, since you seem to need more physical activity, you will attend only Mass, Compline and Matins for the next week, and you will assist Mr. Henderson in replacing the abbey's fences."

After the second day with Mr. Henderson, the abbey's caretaker and maintenance man, Mickey was dead tired. *This penance is working,* she thought as she yawned over her dinner. Old fence posts had to be dug up so they could re-use the holes; new posts had to be sunk and tamped into place, and then new wire had to be stretched and fastened to the posts. Even with gloves, Mickey's hands were cut and blistered from the work.

On the evening of the fourth day at this, Mickey was in the library for the period between Compline and Matins. Several of her blisters had ripped open and bled that day. She'd had to go to Sister Mary David to have them dressed with antibiotic ointment and gauze. Sitting at the library table, she fell asleep on one of Thomas Merton's books they were supposed to be reading for Sister Josephine. She started awake when she felt a hand on her shoulder. It was Sister Anselma; the bell for Matins was ringing. Sister Anselma's gaze flicked to the blood-tinged bandages on Mickey's hands and back to her face. Mickey quickly closed her book and tucked her hands into the sleeves of her habit.

"Thank you," Mickey mouthed silently, grinning sheepishly.

The next morning, Mother Theodora caught her as she was leaving the enclosure to join Mr. Henderson again. She took Mickey's hands in hers, looking at the bandages. "You are done with this penance, Sister," Mother said firmly. "I only wanted to tire you, not scar you for life."

Chapter 16

Grunting under a heavy load of wet sheets, Mickey and Tanya transferred them to the large dryers in the abbey's laundry room. Here in the laundry, personal items as well as linens had to be washed, dried, folded and placed in bins for pickup. Each member of the community was assigned a number, and small embroidered tags were sewn into each garment.

Mickey had found it a little disconcerting at first to have strangers washing her underwear, but it really was a very efficient system, much more so than if each nun did her own washing. In fact, that model applied throughout the abbey. There were a few nuns whose special knowledge or skills were needed in a specific area - such as Sister Regina on the farm or Sister Mary David in the infirmary - but most of the others functioned "like a community of ants," Mickey had described to Jamie when she first entered. "It never feels rushed, that would be unmonastic, but a tremendous amount of work gets done by sharing the labor."

Each member of the community was also given a kit containing needles, scissors, black thread and white thread. With these, they could make small repairs in their habits and undergarments, and keep their hair trimmed. Mickey had already had to make several small repairs of tears in her habit - "it's a good thing I'm good with stitches," she grumbled, but, "how *do* you manage to do so much damage?" Sister Josephine asked in frustration. "What are you doing? Crawling around on your hands and knees?"

"As a matter of fact, I am," but Mickey didn't say it. Sister Linus, just the day before, had pulled Mickey into the chaplain's house when she arrived with the breakfast tray.

"Help me," she said.

In the sitting room, Father Andrew sat sprawled in a chair, his hair and clothing disheveled, reeking of alcohol.

"He's got to say Mass in an hour," Sister Linus said, taking one of his arms. Mickey took the other, and together, they got him to his feet. Sister Linus steered them down the hall to the bathroom.

"I am not undressing him," Mickey said firmly as they pushed him into the shower.

"Don't worry," said Sister Linus. "He'll come to. He always does." She turned on the cold water and stepped back as he yelled and flailed. "Go pour him some coffee."

Mickey returned in a moment to find him sitting in the bottom of the tub, soaking wet, looking up at her blearily. Sister Linus handed him the coffee and said, "You drink this and get cleaned up, Father. Then come and eat some breakfast."

"I don't understand," Mickey said as she and Sister Linus went back out to the sitting room. "Where did he get alcohol?"

"Those men," Sister Linus said scathingly. "The ones who come to visit him. They bring bottles as thank-you gifts. Idiots. I try to get rid of them - the bottles, not the men - but sometimes he hides one from me." She pointed to the sofa. "I think there's a bottle under there."

Mickey got down on her hands and knees, groping under the couch until she could feel the cold smoothness of glass. As she pulled out an empty brandy bottle, the sleeve of her habit snagged on a nail under the sofa. Sister Linus took the bottle to the kitchen trash can and dropped the bag on the floor until the bottle broke. Then, she stomped on it, breaking the glass into smaller pieces.

"This can't go in recycling," Sister Linus said, handing the bag to Mickey. "Take it straight to the trash."

"We do not throw away anything that can be recycled, reused or composted," Sister Rosaria had told the postulants over and over whenever she saw them about to throw something in the trash that didn't belong.

"But Sister," Mickey protested as Sister Linus shoved the trash bag into her hands. "He needs help. We can't -"

"In the trash," Sister Linus insisted. "And you will not tell anyone about this. Do you understand?"

"But -"

"Please, Sister," said Sister Linus more gently. "It would humiliate him no end if this got out."

Mickey sighed. "Yes, Sister."

Mickey carried the bag to the trash bin. As she walked back through the enclosure gate, fingering the tear in her sleeve, she became aware of agitated whispers. Abigail appeared without warning from behind a vine-covered trellis on the other side of the garden and entered the cloister without noticing Mickey. Mickey paused, knowing Wendy must still be there, staying out of sight. For a moment, she contemplated staying to see how long Wendy would hide, but "whatever," she muttered with a shake of her head, following Abigail inside.

☩☩☩

"Trust," said Mother Theodora, "is integral to all that we do, all that we are."

Mother gave monthly conferences for the novices, "a gift I hope you fully appreciate," Sister Josephine had said to them, "as our Mother is so very busy. But she feels it is a priority to become better acquainted with you."

"Our trust in God is what makes faith possible," Mother continued. "There are those who think us fools, praying to a God no one can see and whose existence we cannot prove. But we trust that our faith is not misplaced. Living as we do, in a community where we depend on one another, we absolutely must trust each sister to do her duty, to behave honorably and prayerfully…"

Mickey looked down. She had kept her word to Sister Linus not to say anything about Father Andrew's drinking. His occasional bouts of tremors and tardiness made sense now, and she found herself scrutinizing his physical appearance, but there had been no further episodes of drinking that she could tell. Neither he nor Sister Linus had said anything more to her about that morning.

"*I won't betray your trust.*"

"That's what you told Mother the day you entered," said Mickey to Mickey. "And now look at you."

"But this isn't hurting anyone else," Mickey argued with herself.

"It isn't helping, either."

As if Mother could read her thoughts, she was saying, "Trust must be mutual. It is an aspect of faithfulness, of pledging to stand with one another through good times and bad, through trials and times of stress. Our vows and our common pledge to live a life of prayer give us the ability to be one community despite our many differences in culture and age and background. We must all strive to uphold that trust."

Mickey slept fitfully that night, Mother's words pricking the edge of her consciousness – "and my conscience," Mickey would have admitted – so that when a soft knock tapped on her door in the middle of the night, she was immediately awake. She opened her door to find Sister Helen standing there.

"Sister Mary David asked me to come for you," Sister Helen whispered.

Mickey didn't ask questions. She nodded and turned to put on her robe and the old short postulant's veil as it wasn't proper to walk through the abbey with her head uncovered.

Apparently Sister Helen was now working with Sister Mary David in the infirmary. When they got there, Mickey saw Sister Mary David leaning over one of the beds where a frail, elderly sister lay.

"It's Sister Francis Marie. She's been here in the infirmary for a few months," Sister Mary David explained. "Her breathing became labored this afternoon. I've been watching over her. I think it's time, but... I just wanted someone else to confirm that we shouldn't do anything. I hope you don't mind."

Mickey squeezed her arm as she knelt beside the bed. "Of course I don't mind." She took a stethoscope and listened to Sister Francis Marie's heart and lungs. Sitting back on her heels, she said, "You're right. It's time. Let's just be with her."

Mickey realized this was the first death at the abbey since she entered.

"Should we call Father Andrew?" she asked.

"She asked him to give her Last Rites a few months ago." Sister Mary David smiled. "She said there was no sense waiting until she was really old."

Mickey chuckled. "What about Mother?"

"I'll go," Sister Helen offered.

They pulled a few more chairs around the bed. When Mother Theodora arrived, she and the others knelt beside the bed, praying the rosary as Mother held Sister Francis Marie's hand. Somewhere in the middle of the rosary, Sister Francis Marie stopped breathing.

"She was my novice mistress," Mother Theodora said, wiping a tear from her cheek.

Mickey had been through this many times. Sometimes it was hard, especially with a child, other times - like this - it was so peaceful. Even as painful as Alice's death had been personally, she had always felt blessed to be witness to this moment of passing.

Sister Helen was upset, trying not to cry. All the prior difficulties between them forgotten, Mickey went to her. "You were present for a very special moment," she said softly. Sister Helen nodded, blinking back tears.

It was about three a.m. when Mickey went back to her cell. Coming around the corner into the corridor where her cell was, she saw movement in the dim light. It was Wendy, silently closing one door and disappearing through another. When Mickey got closer, she saw that it was Abigail's cell she had come from. She stood there a moment, stunned in her anger and disbelief. It was one thing to flirt, to develop an emotional attachment, but this? She briefly considered barging into Wendy's room, but, "no," she told herself firmly. "You know your temper too well. Think about this."

In her cell, she paced angrily. "How could they?" she whispered. "How could they violate Mother's trust –?"

She stopped abruptly. "It's only a matter of degree," she realized.

She took off her robe and veil and got back into bed, her mind made up to do what she should have done from the start.

☩ ☩ ☩

Mother Theodora announced Sister Francis Marie's passing to the community following Lauds that morning. The funeral was held during Mass the next day, followed by a procession up to the cemetery where Mr. Henderson and one of his sons had dug a grave. Sister Francis Marie's plain wooden casket was easily carried by six of the nuns. It was a beautiful summer day with a gentle breeze blowing.

"*Requiem aeternam dona ei, Domine, et lux perpetua luceat ei. Requiescat in pace...*"

The voices of the nuns as they sang the prayers for the dead were peaceful, celebratory. As Father Andrew summed up Sister Francis Marie's life, Mickey learned she had been eighty-five, eighteen when she entered, like Sister Linus. Like Mother, many of the older nuns had fond memories of being novices under her guidance, and several of them were sniffling and puffy-eyed.

Mickey walked part way back down the hill, and then stopped, waiting.

"I need to speak with you," she said to Father Andrew as he drew near.

They walked off to an isolated part of the garden where Mickey said, "I can't do this. I won't do this." She peered into his eyes, clear of any alcoholic haze, but troubled now as he gave a resigned nod.

"I know," he said heavily. "It's not right to ask it of you. I'm sorry." He took a deep breath as he looked up at the brilliant blue sky above them. "To tell you the truth, I'm relieved. The always wondering who and how and when someone will find out. I'll talk to Mother."

Mickey's eyes narrowed. She hadn't had a lot of experience with alcoholics, but the little she'd had prompted her to ask, "When?"

"Today," he said, smiling grimly. "Now." And, to her surprise, he turned and called to Mother who was on her way back from the cemetery.

☩ ☩ ☩

"So what is the point of the vow of chastity?" Sister Josephine asked a few days after Sister Francis Marie's funeral as the novices met for one of their regular sessions to study vows.

"It frees us from other attachments that would distract us from following God's will," offered Sister Christine, the other second-year.

"There are a lot of ministers and missionaries out there who have spouses and children, and are doing God's work," challenged Sister Josephine. "They would argue that they are still following God's will." One of the things Mickey had come to appreciate about her was her lack of dogmatic insistence that Catholicism was the only or best faith - "something Sister Renatta never could have done," Mickey had commented to Jessica. Sister Josephine challenged them constantly to think in broader terms.

"It is your responsibility to be aware of what is happening in the world," Sister Rosaria had reminded them frequently, something now echoed by Sister Josephine in her talks with them. "We chose to cloister ourselves so that we could concentrate on our work without the petty distractions of the everyday world, but it does not remove us from the concerns of the outside world," she said. "Read the newspapers we subscribe to or listen to the news on the radio during Recreation. After all, it is your job now to pray for the world. If you're going to ask for our Lord's attention, you had better know what you are talking about."

"Personally, I think it's unfair to the families," Tanya responded now to Sister Josephine's challenge. "It's one thing to decide for yourself to answer God's call; it's another to take your family with you, especially if you're doing mission work in a dangerous part of the world."

This sparked a lively debate on the pros and cons of families involved in missionary work, which led circularly back to Sister Josephine's original question about celibacy.

"Well, there's tons of discussion about whether Catholic religious should be required to be celibate, but if you look at most contemplative traditions - Buddhist monks and nuns, for example - chastity or celibacy is an element in most of them." Jessica surprised everyone by offering this observation. "So for us, in a contemplative order, chastity would seem to be a necessary component even if it weren't required as Catholics."

Sister Josephine beamed. She loved it when the group engaged in an energetic dialogue rather than passively waiting for her to lecture to them. "What about the distinction between chastity and celibacy, since you brought them both up," she pushed. "Is there a difference? Anyone?" she prompted when no one replied right away.

"Well," ventured Sister Christine, "I think of celibacy as only abstaining from sex. Chastity includes emotional attachments. Kind of like the difference between the letter of the law and the spirit of the law."

Mickey glanced over at Abigail who hadn't said anything and was looking at the floor. The day after the funeral, Mickey had pulled Wendy and Abigail into the novices' classroom at the start of Recreation.

Closing the door, she turned to them and said, "This is going to stop."

Wendy and Abigail looked quickly at each other. Abigail burned a deep red, but Wendy's face took on a mulish expression. "What are you -" she started.

"Don't," Mickey cut in, her voice assuming its most authoritative tone. "Don't even play that game with me. I'm going to make this simple. You have three choices. One - if you want to be together, just leave. We're not under vows; you can leave right now. Two - if you decide to stay, this stops. Mother, Sister Josephine and Sister Rosaria do not deserve to have this happening under their noses."

Wendy's cheeks were a blotchy pink. "And what's the third choice?" she asked contentiously.

Mickey looked her straight in the eye. "I go to Mother."

"You wouldn't have the guts," Wendy sneered.

"Watch me," Mickey replied coldly. "I'll give you one week to talk and make up your minds." And she left.

Now, Sister Josephine responded to Christine. "Is it really as clear as that?" She looked around the room with a shrewd expression. "How do you define sex? Is it just intercourse, or is it broader than that?" – "I can't imagine having that conversation with Sister Rosaria," Tanya would whisper later – Without waiting for an answer, Sister Josephine continued, "And what about the emotional part? We cannot live in a vacuum with no emotional connections to anyone, no friends. When does that become a problem?"

"When it becomes exclusive," Mickey volunteered. "When you don't want anyone else around while you're with someone, warning bells should go off." She deliberately avoided looking at Abigail or Wendy, but Abigail suddenly got up and left the room.

Two days later, word spread through the abbey that two of the novices had opted to leave. All that was said formally was that they had realized their vocations did not fit with life at St. Bridget's, but Mickey suspected there was a lot of private speculation as to why these two novices decided to leave at the same time.

There was almost a collective sigh of relief, though, among the other novices. The others may not have known why exactly, but Wendy and Abigail had been generating a tremendous undercurrent of tension. With the two of them gone, "it's so much easier to talk now," Sister Miranda observed innocently.

Mickey hadn't really known how much Sister Josephine had seen or noticed until one day about a week after Wendy and Abigail had left. Mickey was the last one to leave the classroom when Sister Josephine said casually, "There's been an enormous change in the dynamics of this group recently. I can't help but wonder if Wendy and Abigail had help in making their decision?"

Mickey looked into Sister Josephine's green eyes. With the tiniest hint of a smile, she answered, "Good question."

Chapter 17

Snow was falling in sparse flakes from a leaden Christmas Eve sky as Mickey and Alice drove from their house in Baltimore to spend Christmas with Alice's family in central Virginia. Holiday music played on the car stereo, and Alice's hand rested on Mickey's thigh as Mickey drove. Near Warrenton, they passed an intersection of two rural highways with a flea-market site on one corner. During nice weather, this flea-market was very busy, filled with buyers and sellers exchanging money and re-cycled treasures. Today it was deserted except for one woman with her for-sale items set up on one of the tables. She had no coat, just an old men's sweater wrapped tightly around her.

Mickey looked questioningly over at Alice who smiled and nodded. Mickey quickly turned into the flea-market and parked near the woman's stand. There was an old station wagon parked there also, with three children inside who pressed their faces against the window to watch. Mickey and Alice got out, zipping their jackets against the penetrating cold.

"Hi," Mickey said, smiling.

"Hello," the woman answered, looking at them hopefully. She was thin, and as Mickey got closer, she saw that the woman was probably only in her thirties, although she had initially seemed much older. Spread out on the table before her was an assortment of kitchen pans and utensils, Tupperware containers and knickknacks. All of them were clean, but clearly well-used.

"I'm so glad you're here," Mickey chattered. "We really need a few more gifts for a niece who is moving to her own apartment, and we were sure we wouldn't find any stores open. She could use a lot of what you have here." She picked through the items, taking some of the most worn things, and asked, "How much for these?"

The woman looked at the pots and utensils Mickey had picked up, and said, "Fifteen dollars?"

"Oh," Mickey said, frowning. "I'm sure that's a fair price, but..." she reached into her jeans pocket, "all I can afford is ten." She looked up at the woman. "Would you consider a trade? Ten and my jacket? It's old, but it's still in pretty good shape."

"I don't know," the woman replied, looking out at the highway where the few cars passing sped by, showing no sign the drivers even noticed her.

"Please?" Mickey pressed. "I can't afford to give my niece new stuff, and she really could use these things."

The woman looked back at the car where the children were still watching everything. "All right," she said finally.

"Oh, thank you so much," Mickey smiled, taking off her jacket and handing it and the ten dollars to the woman.

"Merry Christmas," Alice said as they gathered up their purchases and took them to their SUV.

Waiting until they were back on the road, Alice asked, "How much was in the jacket?"

Mickey smiled sheepishly. "I'm not sure. Two or three hundred." Pointing to the back of the vehicle, she said, "I'm not sure what to do with the things we bought."

Alice smiled back. "I'm sure the women's shelter can use them for someone who actually is setting up a new apartment." She reached out and took Mickey's hand in hers. "I love you so much."

"Why?" Mickey asked, smiling over at her tenderly.

"Because you're you."

Chapter 18

The heat soared into the nineties, unusual for this region of New York. The stone architecture of the abbey kept it cool for the most part. A few areas within the abbey had been updated with the luxury of air conditioning: the kitchen, the laundry, the library and the vestment room. Mickey still hadn't figured out how most of the older nuns managed to look perfectly comfortable in the habit when she was sweating ceaselessly, and she was very grateful she was still assigned to the laundry.

Fortunately, the last hay cutting had been baled and stored in the barn before the heat hit. Those nuns who did opt to go outdoors during Recreation tended to stay in the deep shade of the enclosure's stone walkways and trees, only a few intrepid souls venturing out to water and tend the poor plants which were suffering in the heat. Mickey stepped outside, the heat hitting her like a wall. There, on the bench under the cherry tree, sat Sister Linus.

"You don't need to bring the meal trays anymore," Sister Cecilia had said to Mickey the day after Father Andrew's talk with Mother. "I was told that he will be eating here in the refectory with us from now on."

He was accompanied by another monk, an elderly man introduced to the community as Father Raymond, "who will be using our library in his research for a book he is writing," they were told.

The nuns didn't gossip, but there was still a kind of telepathy vibrating through the community that told them something had been amiss, even if they didn't know the details. "Small ripples get noticed in a small pond," Mickey wrote to Jamie as she confided her guilt at being the one to bring the chaplain's house of cards crashing down. "And speaking of houses," she added, "the postulants are now tasked with cleaning his house weekly. I'm guessing that's so there is no more hiding bottles."

"What does this mean for Sister Linus?" Mickey had asked even more guiltily, but no one would answer that question.

"That is not an appropriate question for a junior to ask," she was told by Sister Josephine, who added more gently, "She has been in religious life longer than we have been alive. She will understand."

Since then, Mickey had hoped for an opportunity to speak with her, but "how can she disappear in a community of only seventy-five women?" Mickey asked in frustration when day after day went by with no sign of her.

Now, spying her under the tree, Mickey debated whether to go to her. Screwing up her courage, she sat down next to Sister Linus.

There was only silence for long minutes.

"Brrr," Mickey said, shivering. "I might have to step back out into the sun to warm up."

Sister Linus turned away.

"I hope you'll forgive me," Mickey said sincerely. "I felt like I was lying to Mother, and I just couldn't do it any longer."

Sister Linus remained silent for several seconds, then said, "I should be asking your forgiveness, Sister. I... I became so prideful of the secrets I knew, things only I knew, that I lost sight of my duty to my Abbess. That is the danger of secrets. They become power, and I... I liked it," she admitted softly.

"What are you doing now?" Mickey asked.

Sister Linus barked a bitter laugh. "I have been retired."

"Really?" Mickey asked in surprise. "You weren't offered another duty?"

"I was offered the laundry," Sister Linus sniffed dismissively.

"Oh," Mickey nodded. "I'm working in the laundry." She looked around at the garden. "But I can see how demeaning that would be after taking care of the abbey's chaplains."

Sister Linus opened her mouth to retort, and then closed it. "Mother Felicita warned me that pride would always be my downfall," she said contritely. "The faults that enter with you never truly go away. Excuse me. I must go speak with Mother."

The next day, as Mickey arrived in the laundry, she smiled to see Sister Linus already there, folding some sheets. "Would you like me to take the other end, Sister?"

After that, Sister Linus was in the laundry every day, cheerfully waiting for Mickey. "How does she have so much energy in her nineties?" Tanya asked with a shake of her head as Sister Linus stuffed numbered bins with folded piles of laundry.

It was here, folding a large pile of linens with Sister Linus, that Sister Lucille found Mickey one morning. "Sister Michele? You have a visitor."

"I'm not expecting anyone," Mickey said in surprise. "Do you know who it is?"

"She said she was your little sister," Sister Lucille smiled.

Puzzled, Mickey followed Sister Lucille to the visitors' parlours. Entering the one Sister Lucille indicated, Mickey went white.

"Mickey? Is it okay that I came?"

Mickey had to sit before answering. "Jennifer, I'm sorry. It's just... for a second, it was like Alice was standing there."

Thirteen years Alice's junior, Jennifer was the youngest of Alice's seven siblings. "I know. No one can tell our pictures apart," she said with a resigned sigh. "I'm not even sure Mom really knows the difference when she looks at old photos." She sat next to Mickey on the sofa. "I should have called or written."

"Don't be silly," Mickey insisted, recovering enough to give Jennifer a hug. "You look wonderful!"

Jennifer looked Mickey up and down. "You look... different," she laughed.

Mickey grinned. "I'm sure I do. Fill me in on what's been going on with you and your family."

"Well, I finished my Master's in art history this past May," she beamed. "And I just got hired as the assistant to the curator of textile art at the Mannheim in New York. Since I was so close, I decided to come out and see you." Jennifer caught her up on all the family news. "I'm sorry I haven't written more. I was so busy in school."

"You don't have to apologize," Mickey assured her. "I remember what it was like in school."

Jennifer looked deeply into Mickey's eyes, and took Mickey's hand like she used to when she was younger. "I've really missed you," she said softly. "I feel like I've lost two sisters." Her eyes filled with tears.

"Shhhh," Mickey whispered, putting an arm around Jennifer's shoulders.

"Nothing's been the same since Alice died," Jennifer sniffed. "I don't think I realized how much she held our family together."

Mickey sighed. "I sure came unglued without her."

Jennifer wiped her cheeks. "Is that why... this?" she asked, plucking at Mickey's sleeve.

Mickey laughed. "No. They don't let you in to have a breakdown. They're not that desperate. I had to work through the worst of it on my own before I felt I could ask to enter. But it still catches me off-guard sometimes. I'll see something she loved and I'm flooded with memories. I can't believe how much I miss her."

"I still don't understand why you're doing this," Jennifer insisted, and suddenly Mickey could clearly see her as a stubborn ten-year-old.

Smiling, Mickey admitted, "I guess it does seem like a strange choice. It's actually something I almost did right after high school, but I decided to try college first, and then I met your sister, and..." She sighed again. "I felt so utterly lost after she was gone. I buried myself in work for a while, but it got to the point where I couldn't stand going to the hospital. I started coming up to my brother's just to get away. I literally got lost one day and found the abbey by accident." Mickey smiled as she pictured Mother saying, "Or perhaps not by accident."

"It's hard to explain, but it felt like I was coming back to a place I used to know."

Jennifer frowned. "But don't you miss being with someone?"

Mickey looked into those dark eyes so like Alice's. "Whether I was here or not, I don't think I'd be with anyone else."

"Are you allowed to leave?" Jennifer asked, looking at the windows as if she expected to see bars.

Mickey laughed again. "We choose not to, except for the nuns who do the abbey's shopping, or for doctor's appointments, things like that." The bell for Sext began ringing.

"Is it okay if I come out to see you sometimes? Or do you not want reminders of your old life?" Jennifer asked timidly.

Mickey placed her hands on Jennifer's shoulders. "You are family. Past, present and future. I would be very disappointed and sad not to have you in my life. I'd love for you to come out whenever you can." She hesitated a second. "It probably sounds corny, but I keep you and your family in my prayers."

"I don't think it sounds corny at all," Jennifer said solemnly.

Mickey walked her to the door and hugged her tightly. "Thank you so much for coming," she murmured.

As she watched Jennifer drive away, Mickey felt an awareness that life was not linear, but moved in slow-moving circles, like an eddy in a stream, a current inexorably pulling people back into her life.

╬ ╬ ╬

August 15 was the Feast of the Assumption, one of the "Mary Feasts", as Mickey used to call them. "Probably the only reason I'm still Catholic," she used to tease Christopher, "is that they had the sense to keep Mary in a place of prominence in all this Father, Son and Holy Maleness." Christopher, unperturbed, would nod and say, "You're right. But I don't think the Creator really cares what gender we assign it. Calling it Father just made it something we could understand, that's all."

The scientist in Mickey cast a seed of doubt in the belief that Mary's earthly body was actually taken to heaven, and she read with some skepticism the accounts of St. Bernadette and the many others to whom Mary had allegedly appeared, but "I want to believe in those things," she admitted to Sister Josephine. "Then do," said Sister Josephine.

"Just like that?" asked Mickey. "You make it sound so simple."

Sister Josephine smiled. "Belief is simple. It is doubt that is hard. We can't prove any of this in ways that our puny minds or science or medicine can understand. If we try to rationalize it, we'll drive ourselves crazy."

"But," Mickey frowned, "it feels so childish and naïve to just believe because I'm told to believe. Isn't that what the church has done to people for centuries? 'Believe in what we tell you because we know better than you? Believe the earth is flat. Believe the sun revolves around the earth.' I'm afraid my trust doesn't extend that far."

Sister Josephine considered. "Trust your heart. That's what Bernadette did, in spite of the reprimands and threats of the local church authorities – all male, I might add – she defied them and did what she knew was right and she trusted her heart. That simple act of trust made all the difference for those of us who look to her for inspiration."

"Excuse me, Sister Josephine?" Sister Lucille opened the door to the novices' classroom. "I'm sorry to interrupt, but Mother asked to see Sister Michele at once."

Mickey accompanied Sister Lucille out of the classroom and went straight to Mother Theodora's office. The door was ajar when Mickey got there. She knocked and was startled to hear Mother skip the standard greeting and say instead, "Come in, Mickey, and close the door behind you."

Mother Theodora came from behind her desk, and held a letter out to Mickey. Mickey couldn't decipher the expression on her face as she accepted the letter and read it.

It was from an attorney, alleging that Wendy Barnes and Abigail Morgan had fled St. Bridget's owing to sexual harassment by Michele Stewart, a known lesbian. It went on to say that, at different times, she had cornered each of them, fondling and kissing them and trying to demand sexual contact in return. It further alleged that

Michele's behavior was noticed and ignored by Sister Rosaria, Sister Josephine and other nuns. The letter requested a meeting to discuss a settlement for the emotional distress suffered by Abigail and Wendy. A copy had gone to the Cardinal's office as well.

Mickey's hands were trembling in anger by the time she finished. Her face was red and hot. She looked at Mother Theodora in disbelief.

"Sit, Mickey," Mother Theodora said calmly. Taking the other chair herself, she said, "I don't believe one word of that letter, but I have to ask if any part of it is true?"

Mickey looked Mother Theodora in the eye and replied, "No." She was too shocked to elaborate.

Mother nodded. "I think they, and their lawyer, are trying to take advantage of the Church's recent embarrassment with regard to all the years of looking the other way in the priest sex-abuse scandals." She frowned. "But why you?"

Mickey's jaw clenched. "Wendy and I have clashed from the beginning. But after our retreats, she and Abigail had become much closer. The night Sister Francis Marie died, I saw Wendy leaving Abigail's cell. I confronted them a few days later. They didn't deny that they were together. I told them they either had to stop or leave, or I'd come to you."

Mother sat stunned for a few seconds. "Why didn't you go to Sister Josephine and let her handle this?"

Mickey slumped back in her chair. "Maybe I should have, but I had no proof, only a gut feeling. I seemed to be the only one who didn't like or trust Wendy. All the senior nuns thought she was wonderful, but she is one of the sneakiest, most manipulative people I have ever known. I didn't think anyone would believe me." She looked down at the letter in her hands. "Wendy doing this doesn't surprise me that much, but Abigail…"

They both sat staring at the floor for long minutes.

"What's going to happen?" Mickey asked at last.

"I don't know," Mother replied quietly. "I would imagine the diocese will send someone to investigate the validity of the claim."

"Surely they won't consider offering a settlement?" Mickey asked, horrified.

Mother Theodora shook her head. "I honestly don't know." She looked at Mickey. "This could get very uncomfortable for you. I'm sure questions will be raised about your past."

"What about you?" Mickey asked. "Will this affect their confidence in your leadership? You won't face sanctions because of this, will you?"

Mother Theodora didn't answer.

Chapter 19

Still listening to Christmas carols as they drove home to Baltimore, Alice was driving while Mickey played with the new flyfishing reel she had received from Alice's parents. As they approached the flea-market intersection, Alice gasped. Mickey glanced up and did a double-take. There, at the same stand, was the woman they had bought things from a few days ago. Flapping from a hanger tacked to the wooden stand was Mickey's jacket.

Mickey stared with an open mouth as Alice slowed for the red light. Alice didn't say anything, trying not to laugh. When the light changed and they were moving again, Mickey put her head in her hand and groaned, "I am such a sucker."

"Someone has to be," Alice said.

"Gee, that makes me feel loads better."

"No," Alice clarified, reaching over for Mickey's hand, "I didn't mean it that way." She squeezed Mickey's hand, making her look up. "You trust everyone. You chose to do something good and generous for someone who seemed to be in need when no one else even saw her. You can't control what she does with your gift and whatever she does with it does nothing to diminish your goodness in giving it. I love you for that," she said with a smile that made Mickey's heart melt.

Mickey twisted in her seat for one more look. "Damn, I really liked that jacket." She turned to Alice suddenly and said, "Hey, you don't suppose we could –"

"No!"

Chapter 20

The diocese wasted no time in reacting. Mother Theodora received a telephone call telling her a diocesan attorney would be at St. Bridget's Tuesday next, accompanied by Bishop Marcus. They wanted to interview Mickey, of course, as well as Sisters Rosaria and Josephine, and all of the postulants and novices who had been with Mickey plus anyone else with pertinent information.

Mother Theodora asked Mickey how she wanted to handle this with the community at large.

"Even here, rumors will circulate," Mickey sighed. "Better to give everyone the facts as we know them rather than let them speculate as to what all the fuss is about."

So Mother Theodora called a meeting of the entire community. A tense silence filled the room as they waited for her to speak. "Sisters, we are in the midst of an unfortunate situation, one which is likely to shake our very foundation," she began. "The diocese and the abbey have received a letter from an attorney representing Wendy Barnes and Abigail Morgan, the two novices who left us recently." Mickey noticed she did not refer to them as Sister. "They are accusing Sister Michele of harassing them, physically and sexually." As expected, there was an immediate low ripple of voices reacting to this news. Mother Theodora continued in an assertive voice, "I do not for one second believe any of these charges, but with recent events across the country, the diocese cannot ignore accusations of this nature."

Mickey could feel how red her face was; she couldn't help it. She didn't know where to look. If she looked people directly in the eye, would it be seen as a declaration of innocence or as intimidation? If she kept her eyes lowered, would that be viewed as humility or as guilty shame? She felt trapped.

"As we resolve this issue, I ask all of you to pray." Mother Theodora's voice broke into Mickey's thoughts. "Pray for Sister Michele whom I believe has been unjustly accused. Pray for St. Bridget's, that we do not become a house divided. But most of all, pray for Abigail and Wendy, that they will realize the error of making these false allegations in what I believe is a misguided attempt to redress some perceived wrong."

Mickey sat in shock at this last part, not because she couldn't believe Mother had asked them to pray for Wendy and Abigail, but because *it didn't even occur to me to do so*. Even after all this time, she didn't turn to prayer as her foremost means of dealing with things beyond her control. Her first impulse was to keep searching, keep trying to find some way of altering the outcome herself, rather than turning it over and saying, in essence, "I need your help. I'm not strong enough to deal with this on my own."

It was one of those moments, like Sister Anselma's melting during Mickey's retreat, when "I felt like God prodded my soul with that realization," Mickey would try to explain to Sister Anselma much later. "It was so much more intimate than just the mental awareness of something. For the first time in my life, I knew with absolute certainty, that I am never alone."

That moment of grace would be called upon many times as the interviews began.

Father Thomas Applegate arrived at St. Bridget's the following Tuesday in the midst of a cold, grey drizzle, accompanied by Bishop Marcus. Father Thomas came with his own agenda. He carried the burden of having unsuccessfully defended the diocese in two of the priest sex abuse cases, and the diocese had been ordered to pay millions to the victims. He knew his superiors didn't hold him responsible for those losses, but he was determined not to be in that position again.

In contrast to Bishop Marcus's dark beauty and calm demeanor, Father Thomas was short and squat, his face permanently scarred by acne. He reminded Mickey of a fat ferret, his small eyes darting about nervously behind thick eyeglasses. He had the irritating habit of constantly rotating the ostentatious ring he wore on his left hand by turning it with his thumb and little finger. The more agitated he became, the faster he twirled the ring.

The interviews started with Mickey. She sat in a chair in the middle of three tables arranged in a U, with Bishop Marcus and Father Thomas seated with Mother Theodora at the middle table, and members of the abbey's Council seated on either side. Father Thomas wasted no time in delving into Mickey's past. He asked a few standard questions about where she lived prior to entering and how long she had been at St. Bridget's.

"Have you ever been involved sexually with another woman?" he asked unexpectedly.

Mickey hadn't been prepared for this to be his approach. She tried to keep her eyes on him, but she was painfully aware of the stares of the Council members on either side of her.

"I was in a long-term lesbian relationship prior to entering St. Bridget's," she said, trying to keep her voice even.

Father Thomas's eyes popped at such a candid admission. "You... you admit you're a lesbian?" he asked incredulously. In his excitement, he forgot to twirl his ring.

Clenching her fists tightly, Mickey was grateful for the concealing design of her habit's sleeves.

"Yes."

Mother Theodora interrupted. "Sister Michele was candid with me about her past. Her partner died four years ago. It was a faithful, monogamous relationship. I saw no reason why Michele should not be treated the same as any of the other widows who have sought entrance to St. Bridget's in the past. Assuming we are all honoring our vows, someone's past relationships are not necessarily reason to deny entrance."

Mickey scanned the faces of the Council members. Most were neutral or sympathetic, but Sister Scholastica's expression caught Mickey by surprise. It was "triumphant," Mickey would realize later when trying to digest everything that happened.

"Yes, but to admit a known lesbian to an abbey of nuns," Father Thomas sputtered, clearly feeling that he had an airtight case now.

"Father Thomas," Mickey spoke up, getting angry. "I gave up an extremely lucrative medical practice to enter St. Bridget's." She had forgotten only three members of the community knew about that - *oh well, too late now.* "I also taught at one of the nation's leading medical schools. I've had dozens of students and patients become infatuated with me over the years. If I had wanted casual sex, I could have had my fill, without forcing anyone - male or female or both at the same time." *Might as well shock them all at this point.* "And I could have had it without the deprivations and inconveniences of living in a monastery." She thought she saw Mother Theodora cover a smile. "Now, might I suggest that our time would be better spent addressing the specific allegations of which I am accused."

"I am inclined to agree," Bishop Marcus spoke for the first time.

Father Thomas jerked his head in an impression of a nod toward the Bishop as if someone else were manipulating his movements. "Very well. What is your response to the allegations?"

"They are completely false."

The expression on his face clearly said he had expected her to deny the charges and didn't believe her. After all, he'd heard similar denials before, only to have them proven to be lies. Proven in front of a judge and jury, leaving him standing there looking like a... He gave his head a minute shake. "You never..." he struggled to find the right word, "approached either of them?"

"Absolutely not."

"Can you prove that?"

Mickey stared at him. "Is that how this is going to work? I'm guilty of these ridiculous charges unless I can somehow prove I didn't do these things?"

Some of the Council members shifted uneasily in their seats.

"No," Bishop Marcus spoke again, "that is not how this is going to work. You have given us your response, Sister. At this point, I believe we should call in any others who may have pertinent information to offer."

"Very well," Father Thomas acquiesced again to the Bishop's authority. "Sister Michele, you are dismissed, for now."

Mickey quickly looked to Mother Theodora who immediately protested. "Father, I believe Sister Michele has the right to hear anything anyone else has to say so that she can rebut if necessary."

"But what if her presence intimidates them?" he argued.

"We are not dealing with children," Mother insisted. "If anyone wishes to substantiate these allegations, they must do so in Sister Michele's presence."

Tanya and Jessica were brought in first, one at a time, as they had been part of that postulant class. Both supported Mickey's claim that they never witnessed any inappropriate contact from Mickey toward either Wendy or Abigail, nor had Mickey ever approached either of them in the manner of which she was accused. During their testimony, Sister Scholastica gave a couple of impatient sighs as if she were itching to ask her own questions.

Next, the novices who had had contact with Mickey testified, giving the same account as Jessica and Tanya. Mickey felt her heart drop when Sister Helen was called in.

When asked the standard questions about any inappropriate contact, Sister Helen responded, "No, but..."

Sister Scholastica and Father Thomas leaned forward as one. "But what?" he pressed.

Sister Helen's face reddened and there was an audible tremor in her voice as she said, "Last Christmas, when Sister Michele and I were rehearsing for the Christmas concert, I..."

"Yes?" Father Thomas said, a little impatiently.

"I developed an attachment to Sister Michele," she said softly.

"Did she encourage this?" Sister Scholastica asked eagerly.

Sister Helen shook her head, blinking back tears. "Just the opposite. She tried to keep me focused on our rehearsals, avoided answering questions about herself until one day..." she paused, looking so humiliated Mickey couldn't help but feel sorry for her.

"What did she do?" Father Thomas prodded.

"One day, I guess I was being more insistent, trying to learn more about her, when she chastised me."

"Chastised how?" Sister Scholastica asked sharply. "Did she touch you?"

Sister Helen shook her head again. "She told me her past was none of my business and she walked out." She sat up a little straighter. "It took me a long time to understand that she had hurt my feelings deliberately to make me angry with her." She glanced at Mickey for the first time. "It worked, and it was the appropriate thing to do."

Mickey's relief at Sister Helen's honesty was immediately dampened by an audible tskk of disbelief. She glanced over at Sister Scholastica who was shaking her head as she bent over the table, jotting notes on a piece of paper.

After Sister Helen's testimony, the proceedings were adjourned until the next day when Sister Rosaria and Sister Josephine were called. Sister Rosaria bustled indignantly at the suggestion that anything like this could have happened under her nose, but Sister Josephine wasn't so certain.

"I never was aware of anything but tension and animosity between Sister Michele and Wendy, but I had noticed that Wendy and Abigail were becoming overly attached to one another," she said.

"What?" Father Thomas exclaimed, looking up from his notes.

"I was considering how to deal with it when they announced they were leaving." She looked at Mickey. "I suspected they had help in making that decision."

All eyes turned to Mickey.

"Sister," Mother Theodora said, "I think you'd better tell them what you told me."

Mickey nodded and recounted what she had seen and said with regard to Wendy and Abigail.

"Why didn't you tell us this before?" Father Thomas demanded, scribbling furiously.

Mickey looked at him. "I didn't feel that making counteraccusations was necessary. Their relationship has no direct bearing on these accusations against me. I question whether Abigail is even a willing participant in all this. This is about Wendy's resentment of me." She glanced at Sister Scholastica. "Their relationship was inappropriate in here, even though they weren't yet under vows, but it didn't seem necessary to cast stones at them in order to clear myself."

An awkward silence filled the room.

"Father Thomas," said Bishop Marcus, "do you wish to call anyone else? Or do you need further information from anyone who has already spoken?"

"No," Father Thomas said smugly. "I believe I have everything I need."

Mickey's heart sank.

"Sister Michele," Bishop Marcus turned to her, "I am deeply sorry about this entire matter." He looked to the Council members before he spoke next. "You have had to publicly reveal more about your past than most of us would be comfortable doing. It is my sincere hope that the confidentiality of these proceedings will be honored, and that you can return to life as normal within the abbey while this matter is deliberated."

╬ ╬ ╬

Returning to life as normal was not as easy as Bishop Marcus had hoped. Even though it seemed ludicrous that Wendy and Abigail's claim could have any legal merit, no official confirmation had yet been received regarding a possible settlement. In the meantime, Mickey felt as if a spotlight were on her all the time, a perception intensified by the fact that no one seemed to stay near her for very long. She honestly didn't know if she was just being overly sensitive, but "I feel like a mouse living under a hawk nest," she said to Jamie who had come to the abbey at her request. It didn't help that every time she looked around, Sister Scholastica seemed to be watching her.

Jamie was furious when he learned of the accusations and the aftermath. "God, Mickey, these are supposed to be forgiving, prayerful people," he said indignantly.

"They're also just people," she sighed. "And they're scared. They're scared of what they don't understand. They're scared they'll be accused also by associating with me. The whole thing has taken on the feeling of a witch hunt."

And it had.

"You managed to stir up more trouble than I did."

Mickey turned to find Father Andrew a few feet from her in the enclosure garden, pruning some of the rose bushes.

He held up the pruners in response to her questioning look. "I've found it helps to keep busy. Idleness is not good for me." He looked around at the nuns roaming the garden paths. "Listen." Mickey frowned as she listened.

"What?"

"Exactly," he said. "No laughter, little conversation. Look at how stiff and formal they are with each other. They don't know where the boundaries are anymore. I've heard a few of them say Sister Scholastica has called some of the sisters in to ask about relationships," he said, "but I don't know if I believe that. We've been through this before," he said as he resumed snipping rose branches.

"Really?" Mickey asked.

Father Andrew shrugged. "We're human. Things happen. And then for a while, there's this hypervigilance. For us, it was Brother Wilhelm. He actually did call people in. It can tear a community apart."

Mickey remembered Mother asking them all to pray for St. Bridget's.

"But this will pass," he assured her.

"You think so?"

"Yes," he smiled. "Nothing really happened. But your reputation is forever sullied."

Mickey looked at him shrewdly. "So much for the confidentiality of the inquisition."

He chuckled. "Yup."

Mickey walked on and heard her name.

"Come and join me," Sister Linus said, inviting Mickey to sit with her on her bench.

"Aren't you afraid to be seen talking to me?" Mickey asked as she sat.

Sister Linus chortled. "I'm too old for you to try any hanky panky with me."

"Hanky panky?" Mickey laughed.

"Do they still call it that?" Sister Linus asked. "Not that I ever got any. Except that time George Hennessy kissed me at the county fair. But I knew that wasn't for me."

Mickey smiled.

Sister Linus peered at her, her sharp eyes probing Mickey's face. "How long ago did she die?"

Mickey blinked. One thing this whole legal mess had done was distract her from what time of year it was. "It will be four years next week," she said in mild surprise.

Sister Linus nodded.

"I knew some sisters who entered after losing a husband," she observed. "Don't know any who came after losing a wife, but our generation didn't talk about things like that. Can't be that different. I'm sorry."

Mickey's throat was painfully tight as she nodded. Sister Linus took her hand, patting it.

"This will blow over," she said, echoing Father Andrew. "You'll see."

Maybe's she right, Mickey thought later that evening. The juniors were all working in the orchard again, helping to get the apple harvest in. That afternoon, Jessica and Tanya had followed Mickey down a row, setting their ladders in trees adjacent to hers. Mickey glanced from one to the other.

"What are you doing?" she asked, as she dropped a handful of apples into the bag hanging from her shoulder.

"We've decided this foolishness has gone on long enough," Jessica announced.

"Are you sure it's safe to be associating with me?"

"Uh, let's see," Tanya furrowed her brow as if deep in thought, "be associated with you or let that bitch ruin the dynamics of our group?" Mickey wasn't sure if the bitch in question was Wendy or Sister Scholastica, but as she felt the same about both of them, she didn't ask.

"Sister!" Jessica exclaimed from inside her apple tree as she stretched to reach an apple. "Your language!"

"Shit. Now I'll have to go to confession," Tanya grumbled.

Mickey laughed, the first time she had actually laughed in weeks. They talked as they picked. Sister Regina came by to check on their progress, but rather than shushing them as she would normally have done, she simply nodded at the amount they had harvested and moved on.

When the bell rang for Vespers and they had deposited their ladders and picking bags on the trailer, Jessica and Tanya each linked an arm through Mickey's and walked together back to the enclosure.

Jessica did shock Mickey by saying, "Maybe Sister Scholastica will think we're having a three-some."

They took their places in their stalls, and, when Vespers was over, the three of them headed for the library to read an assignment for Sister Josephine. Sister Anselma intercepted them.

"Sisters," she greeted them as she neared. "Sister Michele, may I have a word please?"

Tanya and Jessica went on to the library as Mickey followed Sister Anselma.

"I should have come to find you long ago," Sister Anselma said, steering them toward a quiet corner of the cloister. "I kept hoping I'd run into you..." She stopped walking and looked at Mickey. "I wanted to tell you how sorry I am, and how angry, that you were put through that whole experience. I know how difficult it was for you to open up to me. I can only imagine the type of questions you must have had to answer, and what it must have been like to have your life dissected and exposed in that setting. You have handled this with more grace and goodness than I could muster."

She looked down at the black and white marble tiles on which they were standing. "I've never known anyone quite like you. If any good comes of this, I believe it will be that we will learn by your example."

Mickey stood there for a few seconds, not sure what to say. "I don't think I realized until today how much I needed to hear some expression of support." And all at once, the weight of everything she'd been dealing with came pressing down, and she could feel herself on the verge of tears.

In a move that stunned Mickey even more than what she had said, Sister Anselma embraced her and said, "I'm so sorry you've felt so alone in this."

Mickey held her tightly for a few seconds and released her reluctantly. She went on to the library, her heart buoyed so that she felt lighter than she had since before Mother showed her that damned letter. *No matter what happens,* she thought, *I will get through this.*

Chapter 21

Mickey's second Advent at St. Bridget's was fast approaching. Just before Thanksgiving, Mother Theodora sent for her again. *What now?* she wondered as she made her to Mother's office.

"*Venite.*"

"*Pax tecum.*"

"*Et cum spiritu tuo,*" said Mother, gesturing Mickey to one of the chairs. In her hand fluttered another letter. "This one is good news," she smiled when she saw the look on Mickey's face. "At least I hope it is."

"What do you mean?" Mickey asked, her heart lifting a little.

"Well, I wrote to the superior of the community Wendy had entered prior to coming here," said Mother. "I don't know why it didn't occur to me to do so before. It might have saved us all a great deal of worry and aggravation, but... I must admit, I've never had to deal with anything like this before. In going back through Wendy's file, I realized that none of her letters of reference was from anyone affiliated with that community, which, now, strikes me as odd. Obviously, we didn't catch that prior to her entering. I had to..." She cleared her throat. "... describe in some detail why Wendy left St. Bridget's and the legal matter we're embroiled in, and I asked their superior whether she could provide any information as to why Wendy had left their community. It seems she is repeating her prior pattern." Mother held the letter out for Mickey to read. "It wasn't known until after Wendy left, but one of the young sisters there confessed to a sexual relationship with her."

Mickey looked up. "So, does this mean the diocese will tell them to go to -" She blushed. "Sorry, Mother."

"I quite understand, and I would probably phrase it the same way myself," Mother said wryly. "I don't know. I have forwarded copies of this letter to the Bishop and to Father Thomas as well as to Wendy's attorney. I may get my hands slapped for that, but I'm not convinced Father Thomas wants you to be found innocent, and I didn't know how promptly he might act on this, so..."

"Better to ask forgiveness than permission?" Mickey grinned.

"Exactly."

☩ ☩ ☩

"Any response yet?" Jamie asked when he came out for a Thanksgiving Day visit.

"Not yet," Mickey sighed.

"How are things here?"

"Better. The atmosphere doesn't feel quite as paranoid as it did," Mickey said. "But I still catch Sister Scholastica watching me. I'm not sure what exactly she thinks she might see me do in the middle of seventy-five nuns during the day, but it's clear she still thinks I'm guilty of something."

"Um, maybe being a lesbian?" he offered.

Mickey snorted. "Probably. If she'd been the abbess, there's no way I would have been admitted."

"On another note," Jamie said, "Have you written Mom?"

"No," she laughed. "Why in the world would I do that?"

"Mick -"

"Jamie," she cut in, "she didn't even come to Alice's funeral. You heard her last year. She has never accepted me as I am."

"She's not getting any younger," he gently insisted. "Someday it'll be too late to even try making this better."

Mickey couldn't help but think of Sister Anselma in the orchard that night.

"I'll think about it," she said grudgingly.

All the juniors' spare time for the next several days was taken with decorating the Chapel, so that it wasn't until late November, during a cold, rainy afternoon when everyone was inside for Recreation, that Mickey had a chance to seek out Sister Anselma.

"Could I speak with you for a moment?" she asked. "Privately?"

Sister Anselma nodded and ushered her to the same conference room they had used for Mickey's retreat. Somehow, within the confines of this room where so much of Mickey's soul had been laid bare, it was easier to delve into this topic.

"My relationship with my mother is almost as dysfunctional as yours was," she began. "My brother is encouraging me to make amends while I can, and I couldn't help but think of your situation." She paused. "If it's not too difficult for you to discuss, I was wondering how you're feeling about... everything now that you've had a few months for it all to sink in. Do you wish you'd done more to reestablish communication with your mother when you could?"

Sister Anselma looked at Mickey in that unsettling way she had of seeming to see deep inside Mickey's heart. "What is the basis of your difficulties with your mother?" she asked, and Mickey felt like she was back in her retreat.

"Well, being gay definitely didn't help, but it started way before that." She frowned, trying to recall. "It always seemed, as far back as I can remember, that she favored my twin brother, Jamie, and my father favored me."

"Can you think of any reasons why that was so?"

Mickey thought again. "My father was a chemist, and I was always fascinated by what he did. Jamie is an artist, a sculptor, and he and dad never connected in that way."

Sister Anselma tilted her head. "Could your mother have been jealous?"

Mickey had such a comical look of surprise on her face that Sister Anselma smiled.

"Maybe that is the root of your conflict with your mother," Sister Anselma suggested. "If you and your father shared a common interest, a passion, that your mother and brother didn't - perhaps your mother felt threatened by that bond. What does your father have to say about this tension between you? Does he see it?"

"He died over ten years ago," Mickey replied. "And Mom has been more and more bitter and angry since then. She surrounds herself with all the material things his life insurance and will provided for her, but it doesn't make her any happier. Or nicer."

"And your brother is encouraging you to keep trying to bridge the gap?"

Mickey smiled. "Jamie is such a good guy. He has always been the peacekeeper." The smile faded. "My mother never acknowledged Alice. It made me angry, but Alice always said the best way to change her attitude was for us to just keep loving one another. If it were up to me, I'd probably never see her again, but I think Jamie is concerned that I'll regret it if Mom dies, and I haven't at least tried."

"He's right." Sister Anselma frowned at the floor a few seconds before continuing. "I told you I wrote my mother a couple of times when I first entered because Mother Theodora urged me to do so. But when I didn't get any response, I stopped."

"That sounds reasonable."

"What I didn't understand then was that Mother didn't ask me to write to make my mother feel better; she asked me to write for myself." She looked intently at Mickey again. "You have no control over what people do with what you offer. All you can control are your own actions. Do you give unconditionally, and keep giving even if your gift is refused or abused or misconstrued somehow? Or do you stop because the offering didn't elicit the response you wanted?"

Suddenly, Mickey was back in the car with Alice, watching her jacket flap in the wind.

"Are you all right?" Sister Anselma asked.

"I... yes..." Mickey stuttered, "It's just that Alice said almost the exact same thing to me once."

"Then she must have been an extraordinarily intelligent, insightful woman."

Mickey stared at her. "Was that a joke?"

Sister Anselma looked at her with a perfectly straight face. "I never joke."

☩ ☩ ☩

Jamie wrote Mickey a card excitedly telling her that he and their mother would be out for a visit Christmas Eve afternoon.

"Merry Christmas, Mom," Mickey greeted her, forcing herself to initiate a hug which was stiffly returned by Natalie.

"Thank you," Jamie whispered as he held her tightly.

"I hope I'm not intruding," Mother Theodora said as she came unexpectedly to the visitors' parlour, "but I heard you were visiting, Mrs. Stewart, and I wanted to thank you personally for the cases of oranges and grapefruits you sent us. We are inundated with sweets this time of year, but it is such a delight to have fresh fruit. It was so kind of you."

Mickey hid a smile as her mother stuttered that it was nothing. Even Natalie Stewart could not resist Mother Theodora Horrigan's charm, and she was pouring it on.

"And James," Mother said, turning to Jamie, "I understand you are a very accomplished sculptor. If you are returning tomorrow, perhaps you could bring some photos to show me?"

Jamie blushed furiously, but promised to bring them.

Later that night, voices rang out during the Midnight Mass, singing the timeless words of the angel to the shepherds, "*Gloria in excelsis Deo et in terra pax homnibus bonae voluntatis...*"

For Mickey it felt even more spectacular with her mother and Jamie there, and everyone getting along for the first time in ages.

The Christmas Day schedule was a day of free time after breakfast, with Mass scheduled for eleven and the family reception immediately following. Sister Lucille found Mickey in the common room where someone was at the piano, playing *Winter Wonderland*.

Beckoning Mickey over, she said, "Sister? You have visitors. I thought they were relatives and invited them to come back for Mass and the reception, but they asked to see you now if possible."

"Did you get a name?" Mickey asked as she followed Sister Lucille toward the entry.

"The Wilsons."

Mickey stopped. It couldn't be. She finally forced her feet to keep moving. When she got to the entryway, there stood Danielle Wilson and her parents.

"Danielle?" Mickey exclaimed. "Look at you! You're all grown up!" She gave Danielle a tight hug.

Danielle looked shocked at the sight of Mickey in a habit. Mickey laughed. "A little different than the last time you saw me, huh?" She turned to Danielle's parents and greeted them also, inviting them all into one of the parlours.

"How old are you now?" Mickey asked once they were all seated.

"I'm sixteen," Danielle answered. As she sat, Mickey noticed a prosthetic foot sticking out from her pants leg, a result of the amputation Mickey had performed when Danielle was ten.

"How in the world did you find me?" Mickey asked.

"I'm afraid Danielle made a pest of herself at your office until they gave her your address just to get rid of her," Mrs. Wilson explained apologetically.

"Well, what brings you all the way up here?" Mickey turned back to Danielle, puzzled.

"Well," Danielle said shyly, "I wanted to give you this." And she held out a photo of herself with a scruffy terrier mix. "That's Mickey, the puppy you brought me."

"Mickey?" Mickey laughed.

Danielle grinned and shrugged.

"Well, thank you, but I'm sure there's some other reason you came to see me."

The room got very quiet.

"I've decided I want to be a doctor, a surgeon like you," Danielle said.

"Danielle, that's wonderful –"

"But my cancer has come back."

Mickey felt like a dagger had been plunged into her heart. "Where?" she asked quietly.

"My lungs and spine."

From long practice, Mickey kept her face neutral. "Is your oncologist recommending chemotherapy or radiation?"

"Both, and probably surgery. That's why I came to see you. To see if you would do my surgery." Danielle's blue eyes bored into Mickey's.

Mickey was not expecting this. "Danielle..."

"We tried to tell her it was impossible." Mr. Wilson spoke for the first time.

"You always told me anything was possible," Danielle insisted.

"And it is. You have to believe that," Mickey assured her. "But I don't practice medicine anymore, Danielle."

"But you could," Danielle said stubbornly. "You could operate and make me well like you did last time."

Mickey reached a hand out to Danielle's shoulder. "I want you to listen to me. One thing I've learned being here is that I didn't make you well – I was only an instrument God used then. Now, you need to trust your new doctors and I will pray non-stop for you. I'll ask everyone here to pray for you."

"But it's not the same," Danielle said with tears in her eyes.

"It's better. I can be of more use to you here than I can in an operating room," Mickey told her gently. Just then, a bell tolled. "It's time for Christmas Mass. Come to the Chapel and then come talk to some of the sisters afterwards, please?"

Mickey showed the Wilsons to the Chapel, and took her seat in the choir. Father Andrew and Father Raymond co-celebrated the Mass, Father Raymond's reedy voice straining breathlessly while Father Andrew sustained the chant in rhythm with the nuns' responses. The music was glorious, but Mickey's heart felt weighed down. Danielle's cancer had been serious the first time; they had been lucky to catch it early and seemingly get it under control. But now, with new tumors in her lungs and spine, it was doubtful medical intervention would work this time, *so something else must*, she thought as she prayed.

After Mass, Mickey introduced Danielle and her parents to Jamie and Natalie, and then began introducing her to some of the other nuns. As Danielle was engaged in conversation, Mickey slipped away, watching from a distance. Sister Anselma came over to her as she watched Danielle laughing with Jessica and Tanya.

"A friend of yours?" Sister Anselma asked.

Mickey nodded. "A former patient also. She tracked me down, like a terrier," she said with a small smile. The smile faded. "Her cancer has returned. She came to ask me to operate on her again."

Sister Anselma searched Mickey's face. "She must have a lot of faith in you, to come all this way to find you."

"I guess she does," Mickey said softly.

"What did you tell her?"

"What could I tell her?" Mickey said in a low voice. "I told her I'd pray, that we'd all pray, but... her cancer is very likely terminal."

Sister Anselma's eyebrows raised in mild reproof. "Where is your faith? Isn't this why you chose a life of prayer over a life practicing medicine?"

Mickey looked at her. "You're right," she admitted, abashed. "She had that much faith in me; now I just have to find a way to match it."

Chapter 22

"Come in," Mickey called out in response to the knock on the door.

"Hi, there," Alice said softly as she peeked around the door.

"Hi," Mickey smiled as she got up from her desk. She pushed her office door shut and gave Alice a long, slow kiss.

"What was that for?" Alice asked when they came up for breath.

"Just because," Mickey said tenderly, brushing her fingertips over Alice's cheek. She took Alice by the hand and led her to the couch along the wall. "So what brings you downtown?"

"I finally made that appointment to see David about the back pain I've been having," Alice answered. "He wants me to have physical therapy. He thinks it may be arthritis."

Mickey frowned a little. "I know we're not kids anymore, but I doubt if it's arthritis. Did he order any scans or x-rays?"

"Not yet. He said he will if PT doesn't help." She changed the subject. "Can you get away for dinner?"

Mickey noticed Alice's tactic, but let it slide. "I could be here all night, but being with you sounds like a lot more fun. Let me just finish this outline for tomorrow's lecture." She went to her desk and stood leaning over to type the last bits of the lecture outline.

"Your butt looks so good in scrubs," Alice said as if commenting on the weather.

Mickey looked over at her, one eyebrow raised. "What kind of mood are you in?"

"What kind do you think – after that kiss?" Alice grinned.

Mickey laughed. "Let me turn the computer off, and then I'll feed you so you'll have plenty of stamina for all the love-making we're going to do tonight."

"I can't wait," Alice laughed. She started to rise from the sofa and caught her breath as a sharp pain hit her unexpectedly, but by the time Mickey turned from the computer, it had passed and she was smiling again.

Chapter 23

Abbey life continued, flowing seamlessly from one season to another, but "It doesn't matter what season it is, we're still the cleaning crew," Tanya complained as the juniors took down all the decorations they had put up in the Chapel for Christmas.

"Think of it as the gift of youth," said Sister Teresa unsympathetically.

Mickey grinned as she carried the extra candle sconces to the sacristy where they were stored. She stopped as she saw Father Andrew sitting in the chair there. She couldn't help glancing toward the cabinet where the communion wine was kept in a locked cabinet, the key one of many dangling from Sister Teresa's belt.

"Don't worry," he said when he saw her. "No matter how bad it gets, I've never touched that."

Mickey squatted down, carefully placing the sconces in a waiting box. "Are you okay?"

He nodded, leaning forward to rest his elbows on his knees. "I just had to get out of that house. Some days are just - shaky ground. You know what I mean? And Ray is driving me crazy," he admitted.

"Is he here permanently?" Mickey asked.

"Oh yes," Father Andrew said bitterly. "If not him, someone else. I will never live alone again." He looked down at his hands which were tremoring slightly. "But that's probably a good thing."

Mickey noticed the tremor as well. "There's nothing – I mean, you didn't receive any Christmas bottles of anything –?"

"No," he said. "All visitors and gifts now have to be approved by Mother Theodora and my abbot, and I'm sure they are warning people not to bring any libations." His tone was light, but there was a tightness about his mouth as he spoke.

She gestured out toward the Chapel. "We could use some help if you're bored," she suggested.

He exhaled. "Why not?"

He spent the remainder of the morning work period helping clean and undecorate the Chapel, and seemed to be in lighter spirits by the time the bell rang.

"Thank you," he murmured to Mickey as she headed toward her stall.

January passed into February, and before the nuns knew it, Ash Wednesday and Lent were upon them. The season of Lent was always a time of greater introspection and prayer for the nuns. They fasted – "in the old days, we really fasted," sniffed the older nuns. "One meal a day, not two like we do now," but "much of our work is too physical for us to get by on one meal a day and not fall ill," Mother Theodora reasoned. "Two meals a day is enough of a sacrifice."

In addition, they were permitted to make additional Lenten sacrifices. "Small ones," Sister Rosaria always warned the postulants. "You may give up coffee, or music during Recreation, but we already live such stringent lives that anything in excess is ostentatious. A nun who creates a spectacle of her piety is not nearly as pleasing to our Lord as the one who goes about her business, perfectly cheerfully, so that no one notices her at all."

Mickey felt as if she were doing this for the first time – "well," Jessica said when she mentioned this aloud, "last year, you spent almost all of Lent on your retreat, didn't you?" *Was that just a year ago?* Mickey wondered as she watched the postulants wandering the enclosure in prayer as they began their own retreats. It was like one of Sister Anselma's vestments, each woman adding a different color thread to the piece, but the whole making a fabric held together by the flow of the Church year and the Divine Office and the daily work of the abbey.

For Mickey, the dark winter days were brightened considerably when Mother Theodora at last sent for her to tell her that the legal charges were being dropped.

"Really?" Mickey asked, feeling as if spring had come early.

"It has been an extremely drawn-out process, but, yes," said Mother.

"Thank goodness we're done with them, once and for all," Mickey said with a heartfelt sigh.

She went straight to her stall and knelt, offering a prayer of thanks, and then continued with prayers for Danielle, who was in the middle of a horrible round of combined radiation and chemotherapy. Mickey had kept a prayer card up on the board, and knew that a number of the sisters wrote to the Wilsons regularly, as she herself had done. "Please spare her," she prayed fervently. "She has so much to offer, so much to do; don't take her from her parents."

Easter came and went, with Sisters Christine and Miranda now under simple vows and no longer in the Novitiate. Mickey, Tanya and Jessica, as second-year novices, were getting to know the newly Clothed first-years: Sister Kathleen Dawson, Sister Nancy Seaton and Sister Alison Youmens. Mickey quickly grew to like all three of them, but Tanya, for some reason, did not.

She scoffed sarcastically during one of their discussions of the vow of obedience, when Sister Nancy commented that she thought this was the hardest vow of all. "I agree with her," Mickey said, ignoring Tanya's surly expression. Obedience, the vow most expected to be the easiest, was often the greatest stumbling block, "at least it is for me," Mickey admitted.

"I could have predicted that," Jamie said later when Mickey discussed this with him.

"What?" she asked.

"What?" he repeated in astonishment. "You never did anything without an argument! I could get my chores done five times over and you would still be trying to bargain with Mom that you would do yours later, after whatever else you were all wrapped up in."

"It's not enough to simply do what is asked of you," Sister Josephine had told them often, "you must do it cheerfully, completely, without holding back or resenting it," and, "there's the rub," Mickey could have said. It took a tremendous amount of discipline to stop what she was doing and immediately respond to a request from a superior, "without grumbling or sighing or muttering under your breath," Sister Josephine with one slightly raised eyebrow and a half-glance toward Mickey.

Just a couple of days previously, Mickey had been working with the other juniors, helping to clean the classroom, "from top to bottom," said Sister Stephen enthusiastically. "Move desks and tables and chairs, take down curtains and blinds, wash the windows." Mickey was up on a ladder, wearing a work apron and sleeves over her habit as she reached for cobwebs "no one else can even see," she grumbled, when Sister Josephine came to the classroom and called up to her.

"Sister Michele, weren't you supposed to be in the infirmary five minutes ago to schedule your check-up?"

"But I'm almost done –" Mickey protested, glancing down and seeing the look on Sister Josephine's face. With an exasperated sigh, she climbed down from the ladder, shaking her head and grumbling to herself.

"Obedience is way harder than celibacy," Mickey admitted now to Sister Josephine who gave her a droll smile.

"Speak for yourself," Tanya grumbled, but so quietly that only Mickey and Jessica heard. Mickey looked at Jessica quizzically, but Jessica just shrugged, equally puzzled by Tanya's bad temper.

It seemed the theme of spring cleaning had spread from one area of the abbey to another, "and we're cleaning again," Jessica sighed as, one Saturday afternoon in late April, the juniors were cleaning the library. The books, some of them very old, needed dusting, as did the shelves. Mickey was once again on a ladder, handing a stack of books down to Sister Alison when Sister Mary David ran into the library, her face white.

"Sister Michele, will you come?" she asked, gasping for breath.

Without wasting time asking questions, Mickey climbed down

immediately, nearly knocking Father Raymond off his feet as he tottered by with an enormous book in his hands. Nuns never ran, but they were running now, Sister Mary David trying to explain between gasps for air.

"Mother Theodora... has been sick... bad ear infection... wouldn't stay in bed... went to vestment room... got dizzy..."

When they got to the vestment room, Mickey saw in a glance that Mother Theodora lay in a heap at the base of the stairs. Sister Anselma, Sister Catherine and Sister Paula were all kneeling around her.

Mickey rushed down the steps to Mother's limp body. She felt for a pulse and found it weak and rapid. Taking off Mother Theodora's veil, she said, "We've got to get her turned over." She quickly palpated for fractures as she straightened Mother's arms and legs. "I'll take her head," she said as she positioned herself. "Everyone else get on either side." On the count of three, they rolled her to her back. Quickly, Mickey assessed her condition. Gently palpating Mother's abdomen, her heart stopped for a second.

"It feels as if she's bleeding internally, maybe with damage to the liver and the spleen." Thinking quickly, she muttered, "We don't have time to call an ambulance - it would take too long to get here and then get her to Millvale." She looked up at the others. "Who can drive?"

"I can," Sister Mary David volunteered.

"Good, get the abbey's station wagon, put the back seat down and..." She saw the outdoor entrance - the one she had come through on that windy day she had first met Sister Anselma - and said, "Back up to that door."

To Sister Paula, she said, "Go get Father Andrew. Tell him to bring everything he'll need for... for the worst." Sister Paula put her hand to her mouth, but Mickey barked, "GO!"

She looked at the others. "We need a board of some type that we can use as a stretcher."

Sister Catherine brought a layout board made of plywood. "Will this do?"

Together, they rolled Mother Theodora to one side and slid the board under her. In just a few minutes that felt like twenty, Sister Mary David was back with the station wagon. They picked the board up and carried Mother Theodora to the car, sliding her in through the tailgate. As they got her positioned, Father Andrew came running up. Mickey and Sister Anselma climbed in the back. Mickey instructed her in how to stabilize Mother's head. Father Andrew knelt on the passenger seat, facing backwards and administered the sacrament while Sister Mary David drove as quickly and as carefully as she could. Mickey monitored Mother's heartbeat and respiration. And prayed.

☨ ☨ ☨

Fortunately, someone had thought to call the hospital and tell the ER they were coming. The station wagon pulled into the ER drop-off fifty minutes after leaving St. Bridget's. Nurses came running out with a gurney. They laid the board on the gurney and wheeled Mother Theodora inside and into a cubicle.

"She's bleeding internally," Mickey said authoritatively as she accompanied the gurney into the cubicle. "We need a surgeon right away – it's already been over an hour."

The nurses looked at each other.

"What?" Mickey snapped.

"We only have an orthopedic surgeon on call this weekend," one of the nurses explained. "The only other doctor we have is Dr. Allenby, and he's a GP."

Just then, a tall, thin man came into the cubicle. "What's the situation?"

Mickey looked at him. "Greg?"

He stared back for a moment, then his eyes widened in surprise. "Dr. Stewart? Is that you?"

"It's me. Listen, Mother Theodora is – how old?" she turned to Sister Mary David, suddenly realizing she had no idea of Mother's age.

"Seventy-two."

"She fell down some steps, internal injuries," Mickey continued. "Haven't been able to get a BP, pulse is one thirty-four and weak, no idea yet if there are any fractures. I understand there's only ortho on call. Can we get a Medivac out here?"

He shook his head. "I just heard them on the scanner. They got called out to a multi-car pileup on I-90."

"God help us," she groaned. "Think…" she muttered to herself.

"Dr. Stewart," Greg said hesitantly, "I don't think we have a choice. You're the only one here who can do this."

She stared at the floor. "Will you assist?" she asked at last, looking up at him.

He nodded. She turned to the nurses. "Lori, Cindy," she said, looking at their name tags, "I'll need one of you to scrub in also. Has someone called the anesthesiologist?"

There was a tremendous amount of activity as everyone went into motion. Mickey gave orders for Mother Theodora to be prepped for surgery and the nuns and priest were politely ushered out of the cubicle. Mickey came out to where they were waiting.

"This could take several hours," she told them. "I don't know if you want to wait here or back at the abbey."

"We'll wait here," they replied in unison.

She glanced at Sister Anselma, then quickly looked away, certain that her fear and uncertainty must be showing in her eyes. Never a good sign in a surgeon about to operate on someone. *How many times did I tell my residents that?* She turned to go.

"Sister?" Sister Anselma's voice stopped her. "Could we pray before you go?"

She took Mickey's hands in hers. Father Andrew placed a hand on one shoulder and Sister Mary David the other. "Father," Sister Anselma prayed, "guide these hands in their work. If it is your will, please allow them to heal our dear Mother and return her to us. Amen."

Mickey couldn't respond. Her throat was suddenly too tight. She squeezed Sister Anselma's hands with one last look and left them.

Lori showed her to the women's locker room. "Here are some scrubs, Doctor... I mean Sister..." she stumbled, not sure how to address her.

Mickey smiled. "Just call me Mickey." Sitting alone in the locker room, Sister Anselma's words kept running through her head. "If it is your will..." Mickey had never prayed like that when she was practicing, had never thought in those terms. She hadn't been praying for Danielle Wilson like that, even now. It was her will that every patient would live. She had never considered that it might be God's will that some would not. Quickly, she changed, hanging her habit in a locker. She pulled on shoe covers, and tied on a cap and mask. Exiting the other end of the locker room, Mickey joined Greg at the scrub sink. Cindy was already in the OR, laying out instruments.

"So, what are you doing here, Greg?" Mickey asked as she began scrubbing.

"Well, I'm from the Rochester area, so when I finished my residency in family medicine, I came back up here. I fill in here at the ER every now and then." He scrubbed. "Um, what about you?"

Mickey smiled. "You mean, what is one of your old professors doing in a nun's habit?"

He grinned. "Yeah, kind of."

"I left Hopkins over two years ago to do this. I didn't plan to be operating again."

"I can't think of anyone better," he said sincerely.

She took a deep breath. "Ready?"

Five hours later, Greg found Father Andrew, Sister Mary David and Sister Anselma praying in the hospital's tiny chapel. Anxiously, they looked up as he entered. He looked exhausted.

"She's stable for now," he told them as he collapsed into a pew. "Dr. Stewart had to remove her spleen – it was ruptured. The liver had to be repaired and there were some intestinal bleeds as well. We don't have an ICU here, so we're going to keep her in the recovery room where we can monitor her."

At the looks of relief on their faces, he hastened to caution them, "She's not out of danger yet. She may very well need more than one surgery to fix all the damage, and even then..."

Father Andrew said, "Thank you, Doctor. Why don't we go back to St. Bridget's and update the community?" He glanced at his watch. "It's nearly midnight, but I imagine everyone will be up."

"I'd like to stay," Sister Anselma said.

Sister Mary David nodded. "We'll be back tomorrow to see how she is."

When they had gone, Greg leaned his elbows on his knees, his head resting in his hands.

"Are you all right?" Sister Anselma asked solicitously.

He sat up. "I'm fine. Just tired." He looked at her. "I did one of my surgical rotations with her, but I never saw anything like this."

She frowned. "What do you mean?"

He shook his head. "There was so much blood, I couldn't tell where it was coming from. Her hands, they moved so fast, so certainly. She'd get one bleed under control, and find two more. She was amazing. I can't believe she's not doing this anymore." He looked at Sister Anselma quickly. "Sorry, I didn't mean to imply -"

"It's all right," she assured him.

"Would you like to see them?" he asked.

"Yes, if I may," Sister Anselma answered in surprise.

He smiled. "Sure, come with me."

He led her down a corridor, her eyes squinting a bit from the harsh fluorescent lighting. He propped open the door of the recovery room for her. Mother Theodora was the only patient, a whole host of monitors standing like sentinels around her bed. A bag of blood hung from a pole at the head of the bed. Mickey was standing on the far side of the bed, checking a monitor. She had removed her mask, but still had her cap and scrubs on. She looked up as Sister Anselma entered, and came around the bed.

"Hey there," she said, but then suddenly looked concerned. "Are you okay? You looked flushed."

"No, I'm fine," Sister Anselma hastily reassured her. "It's just that..." she looked over at Mother Theodora lying in the bed.

"I know. It's hard."

Sister Anselma nodded, keeping her eyes on Mother.

"Come and sit," Mickey insisted, indicating a chair next to Mother's bed. She pulled another up for herself.

"Dr. Allenby said she's stable," Sister Anselma said quietly.

"For now. The problem with internal injuries is it's so easy to miss something, or new bleeds can develop as the inflammation worsens, or the whole abdomen can become septic if there's even the tiniest nick in the intestines." She watched Mother's pasty, greyish-white face. "There's just so much that can go wrong."

"She looks so frail."

"I know, but she is a very tough woman," Mickey said.

"And how are you?" Sister Anselma glanced at Mickey.

Mickey expelled a deep breath. "I'm okay. I had to stay focused on the details and not think about who the patient was, or I'm not sure I could have done it."

"Yes, you could have. I had complete faith in you," Sister Anselma said seriously.

Mickey looked at her quizzically. "Why would you say that?"

Sister Anselma looked at her as if this should be obvious. "Because you're you, Michele."

Mickey couldn't meet her gaze anymore. She got up and went to the other side of the bed, busying herself checking monitors and lines. Nurses came and went as they continued their vigil. Greg came to say goodnight.

"The nurses have my phone number if anything happens and you need me."

"Thanks so much for everything," Mickey said appreciatively.

He grinned at her. "Just a little payback for all the extra time you spent teaching me surgical technique."

As the night crept by, Sister Anselma began nodding off. Her head jerked a couple of times, and Mickey went to her, laying a gentle hand on her shoulder. "Why don't you lie down in this next bed?"

Sister Anselma protested, angry at herself for having fallen asleep. "It's all right. I'll wake you if I need anything. This is going to be a long night," Mickey promised her.

Mickey sat between them, two women who had become such an

integral part of her life. She watched Mother Theodora closely for any change in her condition, but her gaze kept wandering to Sister Anselma as she lay sleeping. She had never seen her face this unguarded, and she watched, transfixed, aware of a familiar, unwelcome stirring of her heart as she did.

Sister Anselma was startled awake by monitor alarms going off and urgent voices.

"BP is dropping."

"Call Dr. Allenby and the anesthesiologist immediately."

"Let's go everybody."

Sister Anselma leapt out of the bed, trying to stay out of the way. She saw Mickey helping to push Mother's bed back into the OR. She looked at a clock on the wall, and saw that it was just after four a.m.

Unsure where to wait, she went back to the chapel, praying fervently, "please, please, please… don't take her," but she knew she was praying just as hard for Michele's sake as she was for Mother's. After a long time without word, she went outside for some fresh air. Dawn was just beginning to break. It was too cold to stay outside for long, and as she came back in she saw that it was almost seven. She went back to the recovery room and peered through the window in the door. She saw Mother Theodora there with Dr. Allenby and several nurses. She went to the chapel, and found Mickey standing in front of the altar, her head bowed, one hand covering her face. Sister Anselma went to her and placed a hand on her shoulder. Startled, Mickey turned. Her cheeks were wet.

"We almost lost her," she whispered.

Sister Anselma guided her to a pew and they sat. "What happened?"

Mickey wiped her cheeks. "She developed a bleed in the superior mesen – it doesn't matter which artery. It was bad. She actually flatlined on the table, but we were able to get her pressure stabilized."

Mickey closed her eyes and bowed her head again, shaking it. "I don't know what brought her back, but it wasn't me." She clenched her hands together in her lap. All the adrenaline of the last hours had left her shaky and weak. She didn't want Sister Anselma to see her hands trembling, but she wasn't really surprised to feel Sister Anselma's hand reach over to hers. "You've never been able to hide anything from her," she chided herself, "why would you think you can hide this?" She clasped the offered hand tightly.

"Michele," Sister Anselma said in her calm, comforting voice, "don't you understand by now that you are the prayer? Whatever you do, whether it's surgery or making a tapestry or doing the laundry, if you do it with love and reverence, then you and the prayer are indistinguishable."

They sat in silence like that for several minutes. At last, Mickey released her hand and stood, saying, "Let's go see how Mother is doing."

Chapter 24

David Farley found Mickey in the doctors' lounge. "Hey, Mick, can I speak with you for a moment?"

"Sure," she replied, grabbing her coffee cup and following him into a consultation room where a few medical students sat, going over some x-rays.

"Guys, could you give us a minute?" he asked.

They got up and left the room as David tapped computer keys, bringing a series of MRI images up on a large screen mounted on the wall. Mickey stepped closer to look at the images.

"Holy cow, David. Look at the extent of that spinal tumor. And look here," she pointed, "it's already spread into the lungs, the liver..."

Her eyes flicked to the corner of the monitor where the patient's name was printed. Her coffee cup crashed to the floor, and she felt the room spin. David grabbed her and helped her into a chair.

"I'm so sorry, Mickey," he said in a low voice. "I should have ordered an MRI right away."

Her white face was expressionless. "A few weeks wouldn't have mattered," she waved her hand toward the images, "not with all that."

He sat miserably, not sure what to say next.

"Have you told her?" Mickey asked.

"No," his voice cracked, "not yet."

She got up and walked over to the telephone on the wall. She punched the numbers and waited. "Alice? Can you meet me at the office?"

Chapter 25

When Mother Theodora finally regained consciousness, Mickey was hovering. "You look terrible," Mother said in a weak voice.

Mickey smiled in relief. "You've looked better yourself."

When Father Andrew and Sister Mary David had returned to the hospital the day after the accident, they brought Sister Scholastica with them. Mickey had permitted them to come into the recovery room, but warned them that Mother was not yet conscious.

"I'll stay until she is out of danger," she said firmly, knowing full well that she was speaking to the acting Abbess, and that she should have asked permission. It barely registered that Sister Scholastica didn't chastise her.

When they left, Sister Anselma returned to the abbey with them, leaving Mickey to her solitary vigil. She stayed in the recovery room, sleeping fifteen to twenty minutes at a time in the next bed before starting awake and rushing over to check on her patient.

When she was finally stable, Mother was transferred to a regular room. Greg Allenby stopped by two or three times a day and someone from the abbey, usually Father Andrew, came daily to check on Mother and provide updates to the community where, Mickey was certain, a round the clock vigil had been held, the nuns rotating through shifts in an unceasing prayer for Mother's recovery – "and for you," they would tell Mickey later. Greg introduced Mickey to Ian Zakovski, a general surgeon in practice in Millvale. They discussed Mother Theodora's continued care, and finally, five days after the fall, Mickey felt comfortable leaving her. She called the abbey to ask for a ride home.

Sister Scholastica came with Sister Mary David to the hospital. They visited Mother briefly, reassuring her all was well at St. Bridget's and conferring with her as to her instructions for the abbey during her absence. By the time they left her room, Mickey had changed back into her habit and was waiting for them.

She sat silently in the back seat of the station wagon. Sister Mary David watched her worriedly in the rear-view mirror. Mickey looked gaunt, and there were dark circles under her eyes. The habit hid much, but Sister Mary David was sure Mickey had hardly eaten. "Mother said you are to go to bed for the rest of the day, and tomorrow you are not to work or attend classes. You may stay in your cell all day if you wish," she said to Mickey's reflection. Mickey nodded but still said nothing.

When they got back to the abbey, Sister Scholastica pulled her aside. "Sister Michele, you have done an immeasurable service for the community." Her sharp, hawkish features softened a little. "I... I would like to apologize for my earlier hostility."

Mickey looked at her tiredly. "Sister, your hostility was based on what you learned about my past. That hasn't changed. I'm the same person I was then. The only thing that has changed is now I'm a lesbian who operated on someone important to you. I will accept your apology for the sake of the community, but unless it's based on a change of heart, it doesn't mean much." And with that she went to her cell where she undressed, fell into bed and slept for over twenty-four hours.

☩ ☩ ☩

Two weeks from the day of her fall, Mother Theodora was released from the hospital, but "what a weird two weeks," Mickey would tell her later.

She encountered Father Andrew in the garden a couple of days after she got back, where he was rebuilding a trellis that had partially collapsed the previous winter under a heavy snow.

"I didn't know you were a carpenter," she said.

He looked down at her from his ladder. "I didn't know you were a surgeon." He climbed down and surveyed his work. "I've discovered it helps to stay busy."

"So, you're doing okay?" Mickey asked tentatively. "You haven't...?"

"Fallen off the wagon?" he finished for her. "No. I can't say this accident of Mother's didn't shake me up. It would have been so easy to... but, I can't do that to her. She trusted me, argued with the abbot that I should be allowed to stay here, even if it means having to have a permanent roommate. I can't betray her by drinking again."

He looked at her. "How about you?"

Mickey gave a half-laugh as she looked around at the garden in early bloom. "It's been almost as strange as it was during the Wendy and Abigail fiasco. People avoided me then because they were afraid of being found guilty by association, but now... it's almost as if they're afraid to come near me out of deference or awe."

He nodded. "It can be lonely, being singled out, left to yourself. It should get back to normal, assuming you don't have to save lives too often," he smiled.

Frowning, Mickey asked, "Why were you assigned here? I mean, did you want it? Isn't it lonelier than being at St. Dominic's?"

He bent over, picking up another handful of nails. "I didn't want it at first. I was pissed when Abbot Daniel assigned me here, but..." He looked around the garden and up at the stone bell tower. "There's something about this place, something that's not present at St. Dominic's."

"Women, maybe?" Mickey grinned.

He laughed and Mickey wondered if she had ever heard him laugh before. "Maybe that's it. There's a gentleness and peace that's just not there in a monastery full of men. I love arguing philosophy with Sister Stephen – who has read Plato and Socrates in the original

Greek, by the way – and the day to day conversations I used to have with Sister Linus, about homely things, nothing important. It's like living in a family where I have seventy-five sisters instead of the five I grew up with. Maybe that's part of it."

Mickey laughed. "I only had one brother. And every now and again, having seventy-five sisters feels a little crowded."

"So," he held his hands out, "enjoy this time where they're leaving you alone."

When Mother Theodora got back to St. Bridget's, one of the first things she did was summon Mickey to her room. Mickey had never been to Mother's private room which was actually three rooms: a larger bedroom than a typical cell, a sitting room with a desk and, tucked into its own alcove, a small chapel with a prie-dieu. She found Mother Theodora sitting up in a chair, in her nightgown with a blanket on her lap and a short veil on her head. She still looked frail, and suddenly seemed much older to Mickey than she had ever seemed before.

Mickey knelt beside her chair, taking Mother's hand in both of hers. "How are you feeling, Mother?"

"I am being compliant with my doctor's orders," she replied with a wan smile.

"Then it's worse than I thought," Mickey grinned.

"Sit. And stop taking my pulse!"

Mickey laughed and pulled a second chair closer.

Mother Theodora shifted, wincing in obvious discomfort. "I don't know how to adequately thank you," she said. "Not only for what you did in the operating room, although I understand that was quite remarkable, but for being willing to take the risk of failing." She looked kindly into Mickey's eyes. "There really is a light that beckons."

In a rush of emotion, Mickey fell to her knees again, pressing her forehead against Mother Theodora's knee and clutching the blanket. "I could feel you," she whispered, "I knew you were on the cusp of making that choice. I was so terrified you would leave." She felt Mother's hand on her head.

"I know you were, child," Mother said softly. "I couldn't do that to you, although I was quite willing to go." She grasped Mickey's shoulders. "Please sit, Mickey. I want to know how things have been for you since you got back."

Mickey resumed her seat, wiping her eyes. "It's been... strange. Sister Scholastica apologized to me, but I'm afraid I wasn't very gracious about it. I basically told her it was meaningless unless it was prompted by a change of heart."

Mother's eyes narrowed as she considered her next words. "Sister Scholastica very nearly became Abbess when Mother Benedicta died. It took eleven votes before I was elected, and I think she was truly crushed not to have been chosen, although why anyone would ask for this is beyond me. She has always felt that I am too liberal, and she feels the need to be vigilant to safeguard the abbey. It may be small comfort to you, but I believe she truly thought, probably still thinks, that you represent a threat to religious life." Mickey nodded resignedly. "How about the others?"

Mickey shrugged. "They're behaving a little oddly, but..."

Mother smiled. "Things will return to normal."

"That's what Father Andrew said."

"On a different note, have you been contacted by Millvale General's administrator?"

Mickey laughed. "Oh, yes. He was hovering around the recovery room waiting to talk to me, but Greg wouldn't let him come in and disturb you. He is so afraid you may sue them for permitting an unlicensed, out-of-state surgeon to operate on you. I told him he should be more worried about being sued over not having the ER adequately staffed."

Mother smiled. "Yes, he sent flowers. He has been very solicitous. Poor man. It must be terrible to live in such a constant state of distrust."

Mother shifted again with a grimace of pain, and Mickey insisted she get back in bed and rest. She helped get her settled as comfortably as possible, and left as Sister Mary David came in to check on her. As she walked down the corridor, back toward the Chapel,

Mickey paused to look out a window. The trees were just beginning to bud, waving tiny leaves in the spring breeze.

Even Sister Anselma was different, although Mickey suspected it wasn't for the same reasons as everyone else. Every time she looked at Mickey since her return, she seemed to get the same flush to her cheeks she'd had in the hospital. For her own part, Mickey had found that she was disturbingly aware of how beautiful Sister Anselma was.

She shook herself from these thoughts. "Mother is right," she told herself, "this will pass. Things will return to normal."

☩ ☩ ☩

Greg Allenby began making weekly trips to St. Bridget's. He brought medical supplies to Sister Mary David, including things he knew Mickey could administer, such as suture kits and IV bags of saline. He began seeing some of the sisters as patients for minor injuries and check-ups. He usually found time to visit with Mickey, and she got the feeling he was enjoying his role as the abbey's physician. He also took over Mother Theodora's post-operative care, which Mickey welcomed now that Mother was out of danger. It had been difficult being a very junior subordinate of the Abbess one minute and her physician the next. Every time Mother Theodora tried to talk to Greg about payment, he would laugh and tell her he was putting it on account. "Who knows?" he would say, "I might need to make a withdrawal someday."

Things did begin to return to normal for Mickey as predicted. The most notable exception was the three new novices; though they had been open and talkative in their first weeks in the Novitiate with Mickey and the others, now they just couldn't seem to get past their intimidation whenever they were asked to participate in group discussions in front of Mickey. "This is getting us nowhere," Sister Josephine said in frustration, but she couldn't find anything that would prompt them to speak up.

In June, Sister Regina needed their help again with the first hay cutting. The six novices and two new postulants all went out to stack and store the bales. Mickey and Sister Kathleen were on the wagon stacking the bales as they were tossed up by the others. Sister Kathleen was a tiny woman, maybe five feet tall and Mickey guessed about ninety pounds. This was hard work, but she wasn't complaining. They wore gloves to protect their hands as they grasped the bales by the binding wires on either side and, together, tossed them into position. Sister Kathleen had grabbed her side of a bale and, as she and Mickey tossed it on top of the stack, her glove got caught on the wire. The weight and momentum of the hay pulled her over.

"Oh my gosh! Are you all right?" Mickey asked, rushing over to see if she was okay and help her untangle herself.

"I'm fine," Sister Kathleen said, brushing herself off.

"I wish we had a video of that," Mickey laughed. She stood up and was just starting to turn back to Jessica and the others on the ground when a bale hit her in the chest, knocking her backwards. She tripped over the bale behind her and fell head over heels, landing with her legs sticking straight up in the air, her skirts around her waist.

Sister Kathleen was laughing so hard, she had to sit down on another bale. "No, I wish we had a video of that!" she giggled.

In a few seconds, all the others were doubled over with laughter also. Sister Regina turned around on St. Jude and saw a trail of bales behind her, still on the ground as the juniors wiped tears off their faces. Mickey was laughing, too, still sitting with her butt stuck between bales.

"Well, I never!" Sister Regina exclaimed indignantly. This just make them laugh all the harder.

The next day, they were still giggling about how ridiculous Mickey had looked. After that, getting them to talk in Sister Josephine's discussions was not a problem.

What was a problem was Tanya. Mickey had been so pre-occupied with Mother Theodora's accident that she had forgotten about whatever was bothering Tanya, so it had been with some surprise that she saw how Tanya's surliness had increased while she was away. During their discussions of vows with Sister Josephine, she was stubbornly silent. Finally, even Sister Josephine was at her wit's end. She asked Jessica and Mickey to speak with her. "I just can't get through to her," she said in frustration, "but you three are closer than most after all you've been through together. Please try."

Mickey and Jessica walked Tanya up to the cemetery one afternoon so they could talk privately.

"Won't you tell us what's wrong?" Jessica asked.

Tanya stared at the ground, refusing to look at either of them. Jessica started to reach her arm out around Tanya's shoulders, but Tanya quickly pulled away. "Don't touch me!" she snapped.

Jessica jerked her arm back as if burned. Tanya quickly apologized. "It's not you..." She let out an exasperated breath. "I need a good fuck!"

Jessica put a hand to her mouth in genuine shock at this outburst. Mickey coughed as she choked in her surprise.

"How old are you now, Tanya?" she asked.

"Twenty-eight. I'll be twenty-nine in October," she answered sullenly, mashing an acorn under her heel.

"Just a guess," Mickey said, "but are you wondering if you wouldn't rather be married, raising a family?"

Tanya surprised them again by bursting into tears. They let her cry, guiding her to a bench and sitting with her.

"You know, there's nothing wrong with that," Mickey said softly.

"But," Tanya hiccupped, "I've wanted to be a nun all my life." She sniffled a few times. "And Wendy and Abigail –"

"– were jerks," Mickey finished for her. "No one was upset because they left. It was the way they left and what they tried to do after."

Jessica bravely reached out to Tanya again, and this time Tanya let her. "No one will think anything bad about you if this isn't where you feel you're supposed to be," Jessica said gently.

"But I'd miss you two so much," Tanya protested weakly.

"We'd miss you, too. But that would be eased by knowing you're happy," Mickey pointed out. "And you've got to talk with Sister Josephine."

Tanya nodded, sniffing. "I know. I've been horrible to her."

"She's worried about you."

Tanya pulled them both to her for a group hug, and they walked back down the hill. As they walked, Mickey caught Jessica's eye and she knew they were thinking the same thing: their group of five looked as if it might soon be whittled down to two.

Chapter 26

"Would you mind if we went home for Dad's birthday?" Alice had asked. Charles and Edna Worthington still lived in the family home in Orange, Virginia. Alice and her seven siblings and the spouses and children of those who were married all came home for that birthday. No one said it out loud, but they all knew it would probably be the last time they would all be together.

Alice hadn't complained once, so Mickey had taken to asking her frequently if she was in pain. By choosing not to have chemotherapy, Alice hadn't gotten really sick, though the cancer was wasting her physically. She had had enough energy to visit friends and places that were special to them. But Mickey could tell the pain was getting worse, despite Alice's constant good mood.

Mickey had hastily arranged for an extended leave from teaching and from the practice after Alice's diagnosis. She knew it was a matter of weeks. She watched Alice laughing and talking with her mother as they iced Charles's birthday cake. Unexpected tears sprang to her eyes, and she had to go outside for a few minutes to get her emotions under control.

Jennifer followed her. She didn't say anything, just slipped her hand into Mickey's and walked with her. Mickey felt, had always felt, that Alice's family had embraced her as one of their own. She'd known Jennifer for more than half of Jennifer's young life.

"How would you like to come to Maine with us next week?" Mickey's asked when she could trust her voice.

"Really?" Jennifer's face glowed for a moment, but then she frowned. "But, don't you want to be alone?"

"Jennifer," Mickey looked over at her. "I don't have to be alone with Alice to love her. Besides, you're one of the reasons I love her – she brought you into my life," she said with a smile.

Chapter 27

"You did this for others for years," Mickey heard Jessica say to tiny Sister Angelica who was apologizing for needing help.

In late August, Sister Scholastica, still filling in for Mother who was only just resuming some of her responsibilities, read out the reassignment of duties – "it feels a bit like a lottery, doesn't it?" said Sister Kathleen.

"A scary lottery, when it's Sister Scholastica," Mickey muttered to Jessica.

Mickey and Jessica had been assigned to the infirmary, an assignment Mickey hadn't been thrilled with, though she tried to hide her dismay as she could feel Sister Josephine's gaze on her, gauging her reaction. "I don't want to get stuck there," but she knew better than to say it aloud. "Stuck?" Sister Mary David would have bristled if she had known how Mickey felt. "It is a privilege and a blessing to take care of these sisters." To Mickey's surprise, she found her medical background was not needed as much as a lot of patience and a strong back. The infirmary rarely had a truly ill or injured person in it. Mostly, it had a few of the elderly, infirm nuns in need of care. Bathing, dressing, changing linens was all hard work.

As physically hard as it was, Mickey admired Jessica's gentle, kind care, even when dealing with some of the more unpleasant tasks such as changing diapers. "However unpleasant it is for us, the humiliation has to be worse for them," Jessica shrugged philosophically.

"No one here has ever had a bedsore," Sister Mary David had told them during their orientation to the infirmary. "And we will keep it that way. If we are diligent in our duty, they need never suffer that additional pain."

Now, Jessica was smoothing lotion on Sister Angelica's papery skin. Sister Angelica had been the infirmarian for forty years prior to Sister Mary David. "Someday, it will be my turn to need someone's help," Jessica smiled.

Occasionally, someone did have to spend a day or two in the infirmary. Sister Regina sprained her knee badly when she slipped off St. Jude's large rear tire one day, and should have stayed off that leg. She refused to remain in bed, insisting, "there's nothing wrong with the rest of me," but she did return to the infirmary three times a day to apply ice to her swollen knee.

Sister Helen was still working in the infirmary. Since the proceedings with Father Thomas, she and Mickey had been able to resume a more genial relationship, with none of the tension that had been there previously. "See?" Mickey smiled as she pictured Sister Rosaria saying, "Good can come from even the worst things."

One of them was always on duty, day and night. They rotated nights and were excused from the lesser hours and one work session the next day to catch up on sleep. Mickey found the nights to be peaceful times. She wrote letters or read. Sometimes, one of the old sisters would be restless, unable to sleep and would welcome some company and perhaps a little conversation. Mickey knew she wasn't supposed to break Silence, but she couldn't see that anyone would begrudge these gentle souls whatever comfort they wanted after all their years of service.

One night in late September, Mickey had the night shift. Everyone was sleeping and she had some uninterrupted time to write letters. Tanya had returned home to Minnesota, but wrote to Mickey and Jessica every couple of weeks. She was finding life outside the abbey difficult to adjust to - "televisions and radios and phones everywhere," she wrote. "It all seems so purposeless." She had started to date an old high-school boyfriend who still lived in her hometown, and she was hopeful things might work out with him. Mickey wrote a letter to her mother and lastly, she wrote to Jennifer who was in Lyon, France, doing an internship at a textile museum there. Apparently, Lyon has a long history of producing exquisite silks, a fact Mickey had been unaware of. Jennifer was due to return to New York later in the fall. Ironically, as Mickey wrote Jennifer's letter, the clock struck midnight, and she realized it was the fifth anniversary of Alice's death. "I've found a kind of peace and happiness here I never thought I'd know again," she wrote, "and it occurs to me, as I read your letter and think about all the people who have cycled back into my life since I ostensibly withdrew from the world to live in this small spot in the middle of nowhere, that my world is bigger now than it ever has been."

☤☤☤

October was unusually cold and wet, with almost twenty days in a row of damp, rainy weather. An atmosphere of gloom seemed to have settled over the abbey and tempers ran a bit short with everyone stuck inside for so long. Those who did have to work outside such as Sister Regina and the nuns currently working with her on the farm were so chilled when they came back inside that they felt they couldn't get warm. Mother Theodora ordered the furnace to be turned on earlier than normal – over Sister Scholastica's objections – and asked Sister Cecilia to have hot tea and coffee available during Recreation.

Just when it seemed it couldn't get any gloomier, an outbreak of flu hit the abbey, brought by a delivery man who was very ill, coughing and sneezing. To make the situation worse, he also seemed to have brought an intestinal virus which caused severe bouts of diarrhea. The bugs spread like wildfire through the abbey, as the nuns were usually isolated from outsiders. Most of the nuns caught one or the other, but a few unfortunate souls got sick with both. Most of the respiratory cases involved a low-grade fever and a cough, with some of the more serious cases turning into bronchitis and pneumonia.

The infirmary staff was inundated with almost more than they could handle. Mickey was very grateful for all the saline Greg had brought them as several nuns became dangerously dehydrated. He made several trips to the abbey to bring antibiotics for the worst respiratory cases. So far, Mickey had felt fine, but she caught Mother Theodora on her way to the infirmary to visit some of the ill sisters and pleaded with her to stay away.

"Forgive me, Mother, but you are not yet strong enough to get through this easily if you do catch it." Mother Theodora acquiesced, and sent cards instead.

Sister Mary David had a high flush to her cheeks after a few days, and Mickey knew she must have been running a fever, but she refused to rest.

One morning, Sister Catherine came to the infirmary, coughing. Sister Helen tried to usher her to a chair, but, "It's not me," she said. "Sister Anselma has been sick, but refused to come see you. She hasn't come out of her cell today, and she doesn't answer a knock." None of the infirmary staff had been to the Chapel or refectory for nearly a week. They had lost touch with how the community as a whole was functioning. They had taken their meals in the infirmary and had even been napping there whenever they could.

"Go," Sister Mary David said to Mickey and Sister Helen.

They hurried up to the third floor. Knocking loudly on the cell door, Mickey called, "Sister Anselma?" Getting no response, she opened the door a crack and looked in. Sister Anselma was lying on her bed, the covers thrown off. Mickey and Sister Helen went in to her. She was dangerously hot, but was not sweating at all. Sister Helen tried to help her sit up, but she was too weak.

"I think I can carry her," Mickey said, wrapping her in a blanket and gathering her up in her arms. Sister Helen ran ahead, opening doors.

"She's very dehydrated," Mickey gasped as she laid Sister Anselma gently on one of the beds in the infirmary. Sister Helen brought an IV bag and Mickey got it started, although she had difficulty finding a vein to get the needle in. Mickey asked for a stethoscope and listened to

Sister Anselma's lungs; they were full of fluid. She added a bag of antibiotic to the IV line and asked Jessica to keep cool cloths on her forehead and neck. Later in the day, after a couple of bags of saline, Sister Anselma began to sweat with her fever. She woke a few times, but slept most of the day. Mickey had never seen her hair, and was surprised at how blond she was. She brushed strands of gold off Sister Anselma's forehead as she gently bathed her face and neck with a fresh cool cloth.

Sister Mary David was scheduled for the night watch, but she looked so ill that Mickey insisted she go to her cell for a full night's sleep. She knew Sister Mary David must have been feeling bad when she agreed.

As evening fell, Mickey lowered the lights. Everyone was finally resting peacefully. She could hear the soft sounds of Compline coming from the choir. She pulled a chair up next to Sister Anselma's bed. Her breathing was still very shallow, with an audible rattle. Her fair cheeks were flushed with her fever and she was still shivering. Mickey covered her with another blanket. Her mind drifted back to when it was Alice's bed she sat beside. Sometimes, it seemed only a few weeks ago, not five years.

"Am I dying?"

Mickey was startled out of her reverie by Sister Anselma's whisper. She realized her cheeks were wet with tears. Brushing them away with the back of her hand, she leaned forward and smiled. "I don't think so, but you probably feel like it."

"My chest feels like someone is sitting on it. I can't take a deep breath."

"That's because you have pneumonia. You shouldn't have gone so long without coming to us," Mickey chided gently.

Sister Anselma's eyes burned as she watched Mickey's face. "I didn't want to be a bother when you were all so busy with everyone else."

Mickey raised one eyebrow. "Good plan. A little while longer, and we wouldn't have been bothered by you at all, except for your funeral."

"Am I that sick?"

Mickey's face became serious. She reached out and brushed silky blond hair from Sister Anselma's forehead. "Yes," she said tenderly. "You are that sick. Another few hours, and... promise me you won't do that again."

Sister Anselma looked at her for several seconds before whispering, "I promise."

Someone in a nearby bed began coughing and Mickey went to look after her. When she looked back over, Sister Anselma had drifted off to sleep again. Mickey was kept busy administering the next round of cough medicine and antibiotics to those who needed them. When she was done, she sat in the rocking chair they kept in the infirmary for the long night vigils when someone was seriously ill or dying. "We don't fear death," Sister Mary David had told them, "but we try to make sure no one passes into our Lord's care alone."

She must have dozed off because she was jerked awake by the sound of violent coughing. Sister Anselma was sitting up, coughing so hard she began retching. Mickey had kept a basin by her bed for this.

"Cough it up," she urged as she held the basin and supported Sister Anselma's shoulders. "You've got to get that fluid out of your lungs."

When the coughing spell subsided, Mickey gave her a glass of water to rinse her mouth, and helped her sit propped against the head of her bed.

"Here's some fresh water, drink." Mickey handed her a new glass which she accepted with a trembling hand.

"That was awful," Sister Anselma said shakily. "I felt like I was choking."

"I know, but it's necessary. You've got to clear your lungs. I'm afraid this is just the beginning," Mickey warned. "You need a little nourishment. How about some soup or broth?"

Sister Anselma made a face. "Some broth I guess, but I don't feel like putting anything in my stomach."

Mickey smiled. "This is going to take a long time to get over, but you'll feel so much better in about twenty-four hours." She brought Sister Anselma a cup of Sister Cecilia's chicken broth from a large crock pot they had set up in the infirmary so that the nuns too sick to go back to their cells could eat whenever they needed to.

Sister Fiona, who had been hit hard by the intestinal bug, needed to go the bathroom, but almost fell over as she got out of bed. Mickey rushed over to assist her and stayed near the bathroom door until she came out.

"You wouldn't believe how many people we've picked up off the bathroom floor," she joked as she helped Sister Fiona back into bed. "I don't know if I should be more scared of telling Sister Mary David they cracked their head or telling Sister Scholastica they cracked the sink."

Sister Fiona wrapped her arms around her ribs. "Don't make me laugh," she groaned. "It hurts too much."

It seemed Sister Fiona's activity triggered the need for several others to use the bathroom or get something to drink. Mickey finally got everyone settled and looked over to see Sister Anselma lying on her side, watching.

Mickey hurried over and knelt by the bed. "Are you all right? Do you need anything?" she asked as she laid her hand gently on Sister Anselma's cheek. "You are still very feverish."

Sister Anselma laid her hand over top of Mickey's. "You are so gentle, Michele. I've never..." she stopped, her eyes filling with tears, "I've never felt this way..."

Mickey's heart was thumping so loudly she was sure Sister Anselma could hear it. Reluctantly, she pulled her hand away and forced herself to smile. "I think you must be delirious."

The tears spilled from Sister Anselma's eyes. "I wish I were," she whispered, and she rolled over to face the wall.

Mickey went back to the rocking chair, her heart still racing. "God, please don't let this be happening," she prayed. She knew for herself, it was a bit too late for that prayer. She cursed herself for not keeping her guard up. *I, of all people, should have seen this coming,* she thought. *And after everything that happened before, no one would believe I didn't try to make this happen.* She rocked agitatedly. *Did I?* She was the one who laid her hand on Sister Anselma's cheek, the one who brushed her hair off her face. She was mortified at the thought that she might have invited all this. She glanced over at Sister Anselma who still lay with her back to Mickey. *Maybe, if she remembers any of this, it will all seem like a bizarre dream.*

It was nearly Thanksgiving before the choir was back at full voice. None of the senior nuns could remember such a devastating illness running through the entire community.

Mickey was one of the few to have come through it unscathed. "Physically, maybe," she would have said. Sister Anselma had been the most critically ill. She had stayed in the infirmary for five days. After that first night, any time Mickey had come to bring her food or medicine, their eye contact had been brief and neutral, and Mickey honestly couldn't tell how much Sister Anselma remembered.

As the infirmary emptied and the work load returned to normal, Mickey and Jessica resumed their classes with Sister Stephen and Sister Josephine. Mother Theodora asked to see both of them. Jessica had only been to Mother Theodora's office once, during one of her visits to the abbey with her family when she was a candidate.

"Sister Mary David has told me how enormously helpful you both were," Mother Theodora said once they were seated. She looked at Mickey. "And she told me how many night shifts you worked for the others."

Mickey shook her head. "Everyone else got sick and tried to keep working, but they had to get some rest or I would have been on my own." She shrugged. "So it was actually a selfish ploy on my part to make sure they didn't bail out on me entirely."

Mother Theodora smiled and said, "Well, I wish I had some way of expressing my gratitude to you both."

"That's not necessary, Mother," Jessica said shyly. "Any of the other sisters would have done what we did."

"Nevertheless, I am going to give you Christmas Eve and Christmas Day off – no obligations other than Mass. You may visit with family if they are coming, stay in bed, whatever you wish."

"Thank you, Mother," they both replied.

The juniors once again helped Sister Teresa decorate the Chapel for Advent and Christmas – "but it was easier when there were more of us," Jessica lamented. They also reprised an Advent activity the abbey hadn't participated in for years. They made small cards, one for each member of the community. On one side, painstakingly written in gold ink, was *Quomodo Veniet?* How will He come? On the reverse was a phrase, taken from Scripture, of how Christ might manifest himself in their meditations. Mickey's was *Solatium Nostrum*, Our Solace. Mother Theodora's was, appropriately, *Pastor Nostrum*, Our Shepherd.

"It's kind of like a religious fortune cookie," Sister Linus joked as she reached into the jar.

Mickey kept her card propped on the desk in her cell. She wasn't sure she needed solace, but as she sat to write Danielle a Christmas card, she prayed that the Wilsons would find solace this Christmas. In the year since their surprise visit, Danielle had had two of the three lobes of her right lung removed and was undergoing a new round of chemotherapy and radiation for the spinal tumor. Mickey had kept Danielle's prayer card on the board and she knew that many of the community kept the Wilsons in their prayers. "We will keep praying," she wrote to them, "and you keep hoping."

A couple of weeks before Christmas, Mickey and Jessica were carrying a small Christmas tree to the infirmary for the older nuns as Sister Mary David followed them with a box of ornaments. They ran into Sister Anselma.

"Would you like to join us?" Jessica asked enthusiastically.

Sister Anselma's face showed no expression at all as she replied, "I have to get back to the vestment room, but thank you for asking."

"The wall of ice is back up," Sister Mary David muttered as Sister Anselma walked away.

"What?" Jessica asked.

"Nothing."

Mickey planned to spend most of her Christmas Eve holiday in an extended visit with Jamie. Natalie was staying in Florida for Christmas this year, but had sent cases of oranges and grapefruit to the abbey again. When Jamie arrived, they went for a walk through the abbey's front grounds as he excitedly told her about his recent gallery show in New York. The air was sharp and cold under a cloudless December sky and they were soon chilled through, despite the sunshine.

"Brrr," Mickey said, "let's go back in and get some hot tea."

They were walking back up the abbey's long drive when a familiar blue Ford passed them on its way to the parking lot. As they approached the front doors, they saw Jennifer standing there.

"You're back!" Mickey exclaimed, giving her a tight hug.

"Just got back a couple of weeks ago," Jennifer said. "Is it okay to come for a visit?"

"Yes. We were just going in to get warm," Mickey said. "You remember my brother?"

"Boy, have you grown up!" Jamie exclaimed.

Jennifer blushed. "You haven't changed at all."

Mickey ushered them into one of the parlours and went to get a tray of hot tea.

"Here," said Sister Cecilia, putting a plate of freshly baked orange cranberry muffins on the tray.

"Well, tell us all about your trip to France," Mickey demanded when she returned to the parlour.

Jennifer had brought photos of the countryside around Lyon as well as of the tapestries and silks she had studied while she was there. "The patterns are so intricate," she explained, "no machine could do this. They still do it all by hand, the way they have since the Middle Ages."

"You know," Mickey mused as she looked at the photos, "I'm no expert, but these look a lot like the vestments and cloths the abbey produces."

"Really?" Jennifer looked over Mickey's shoulder. "Like this? I'd love to see some of the work sometime."

Mickey turned to Jamie. "Did you bring any pictures from your gallery show?"

Jennifer eagerly leaned in for a closer look as Jamie pulled out several newspaper clippings and photos. Mickey sat back as they talked art and New York.

"Where are you staying tonight?" Jamie asked as the parlour began to darken by late afternoon.

"I got a hotel room," Jennifer said.

"You can use Mickey's old room at my place, if you like," he offered. "It's sitting empty. We can get some dinner and be back tonight for Midnight Mass."

"Are you sure?" Jennifer asked. "That sounds much better than a hotel."

They gathered up their coats to leave.

"Would you wait for me just a minute?" Jennifer asked. "I need to speak to Mickey alone real quickly."

"Take your time," he smiled.

"What's up?" Mickey asked after Jamie left to wait by the front door.

Jennifer opened her purse, frowning. "I don't know if you even remember, but after we got back from that trip to Maine, you gave me Alice's luggage set. I haven't used it until this trip, and... I found this in one of the pockets."

She held out an envelope. On the front, in Alice's beautiful handwriting, was Mickey's name. Mickey took it and stared at it. When she looked up, Jennifer had tears in her eyes. She quickly gave Mickey a hug and a kiss on the cheek. "See you tonight," she said, and left.

Mickey tucked the envelope into the inside pocket of her yoke, and went to dinner. As in years past, the nuns were dismissed after dinner to get some rest before Midnight Mass. Mickey sat on her bed, holding the envelope. She couldn't bring herself to open it. She placed the envelope on her desk and undressed to try and get some sleep, but every time she closed her eyes, there was Alice - "you two go," she had insisted, watching and waving from the rocky beach as

Mickey and Jennifer sailed a little sailboat not far from shore, tacking back and forth, or "you go, I'll wait for you here," pushing them out for bike rides she no longer had the stamina for. She had spent much of that trip sleeping, but Mickey supposed she must have written during one of those outings.

Mickey had not cried during Alice's brief illness. She had not cried at the funeral or after. It had felt like, if she allowed herself to start, she would never, ever stop - she would find herself drowning in an abyss of misery and grief.

She had felt herself floundering in that abyss during her retreat, but Sister Anselma had been there to buoy her up, pull her out....

At last, she fell into a fitful sleep and didn't feel rested at all when it was time to rise. Even the beauty of the Mass couldn't bring her solace as she tried to sing. She suddenly remembered the little card sitting on her desk. *Solatium Nostrum.* She closed her eyes. *How do you always know?* When she opened her eyes, she saw Sister Anselma on the other side of the choir, watching her as if she could feel Mickey's turmoil.

When Mass was over, she had another brief visit with Jamie and Jennifer. Jamie obviously knew now about the letter because he asked with concern, "Are you okay?"

"I'm fine," she assured him, "I'll see you both tomorrow."

The nuns went to the refectory for tea and cookies. Not in the mood to be social, Mickey forced herself to go to be polite. She looked out the tall windows and saw that a full moon was shining outside.

"Something tells me you're not with us tonight."

Startled, Mickey turned to find Mother Theodora beside her. "No," she smiled, "I guess I'm not."

"Is anything wrong, Sister?"

"I guess my visit with my family stirred up a lot of memories." She supposed this was close enough to the truth.

"Understandable. This time of year, as joyous as it is, can be hard at times." Mother gave Mickey's arm a squeeze and moved on. Mickey saw Sister Anselma watching her from near the tables. It only lasted a second, but the look in her eyes was so tender, so unguarded – and then it was gone, and she turned away.

Mickey suddenly felt as if the women around her were pressing closer and closer, leaving her no room to breathe... she had to get out. She slipped quietly out of the refectory and went to her cell. There, she tucked the letter back inside her pocket and went to get her heavy winter cloak. Once outside, the air was cold and crisp and she felt could breathe again. It hadn't yet snowed that winter, but the frozen grass crunched as she walked through the enclosure and let herself through the gate. The moon was so bright, it was almost like daylight. She found herself heading toward the barn. She slid the heavy door open just enough to let herself in and closed it behind her. A few of the cows shuffled at the disturbance. She spoke to them in a low, soothing voice. At the rear of the barn was a small room which had a cot for Sister Regina during calf season. She clicked on the light and took off her cloak. Sitting on the cot, she pulled the envelope from her pocket. She stared at Alice's handwriting, tracing a fingertip gently over the swirls of ink. This was probably the last thing Alice had written. At last, she turned the envelope over and carefully pried the flap loose. Her hands were trembling as she pulled out the paper inside and unfolded it.

My beloved Mickey,
    By the time you read this, I should be gone. I know it's melodramatic and clichéd to leave an 'after I've died note', but there are a few things I want to say to you.
    The most critical is that I know you're blaming yourself – that we didn't catch this sooner, that there wasn't anything you could do – a whole host of recriminations. I want you to forgive yourself because there is nothing to feel guilty about. As a matter of fact, it's a little egotistical of you to think you personally should be able to undo what God has allowed to transpire. I don't know Her reasons, but I believe with all my heart that there are reasons for all this. Someday we will understand them.

Mickey paused to smile and wipe tears from her eyes. Damn, why hadn't she brought tissues? It was so like Alice to find a way, even after she'd died, to keep Mickey grounded.

> I'm not going to write about how much I love you, because if I didn't show you that while I was alive, it's too late now. What I do want to say is, I know you well enough to know that right now, you are keeping your emotions under control. You will have to allow yourself to deal with this at some point. I hope, when you let that happen, you will heal. As you heal, I hope you will allow love to come back into your life. I know you won't go looking for it, but I also know it will come to you. You are such an incredibly good, pure soul that people cannot help but be drawn to you. When it does come, don't turn away. It isn't a betrayal of the love we had for you to love someone else – just the opposite; it would belittle our love if you could never love again. And remember, love comes in many forms.
>
> It really is much easier to be the one leaving rather than the one left behind. I will be waiting for you in a place where time doesn't exist, and where our love continues undiminished.
>
> Alice

Mickey was crying so hard by the time she finished that she could scarcely breathe. Like that night during her retreat, her grief and pain and loneliness seemed bottomless. Eventually, she cried herself to sleep.

At five that morning, Sister Regina found her on the cot with three of the barn cats curled up around her, her cloak sliding off her shoulders. The letter lay on the floor where it had fallen from her hand. Sister Regina folded the letter and placed it on the cot next to Mickey, and then covered her again with her cloak. Quietly, she fed the cows and began milking, humming Christmas carols. If a stable was good enough for Jesus, she saw no reason why it shouldn't be just fine for one of them.

Chapter 28

"I don't want it," Alice protested. "It'll just make me sleep, and I don't want to sleep the days away."
"I know you don't," Mickey assured her. "We'll try to find the minimal dosage to take the edge off, okay?"

Even Alice could no longer hide the pain she was in, and Mickey gently insisted on adequate pain control. By the time they returned from Maine, Alice was getting weak. Jennifer stayed with them and helped look after Alice so Mickey could do things like the grocery shopping. "I want to take care of her myself," she said when hospice called. Friends stepped in to bring meals - "they know how pathetic you are in the kitchen," Alice joked weakly.

Christopher came by often, bringing Alice Communion and bags of letters and cards from the youth group and other parish members. When she asked, he heard her confession, and blessed her, dipping his thumb into the container of holy oil and anointing her forehead with a cross "in the name of the Creator, and of the Redeemer, and of the Consoler."

Mickey called Edna and Charles to tell them it was time. Alice died with her family gathered around her, held propped against Mickey as she took her last ragged breaths. The next days were a blur of activity. Mickey was overwhelmed by the number of people who came to the funeral home and then the funeral. St. Matthew's was packed with many of the parishioners as well as teachers and administrators, parents of Alice's students past and present, several former students, most of whom were now parents themselves, plus Alice and Mickey's wide circle of friends. And then there were Mickey's colleagues and students, even patients who had heard or read about Alice's passing. It was ironic that, not until then, had Mickey realized how wide Alice's circle of influence had been. More than one young adult told Mickey that he or she had become a teacher because of Alice's example.

Jennifer, Edna and Charles were the last ones to leave a couple of weeks later. They helped Mickey write thank you notes to everyone who sent cards. Together, they went through Alice's closet and dressers - "Are you sure you're ready to do this now?" Edna asked, but "I have to," Mickey said. She had encouraged Alice's family to let her know if there were specific items they wanted - jewelry, clothing, whatever. The rest would be distributed among the church's thrift shop and women's shelters.

"You will be with us for Thanksgiving," Edna ordered as she gave Mickey a hug.

"I'll be there," Mickey smiled. She waved them off, and went back inside the house. Standing with her back against the door, she suddenly felt suffocated by the emptiness, as if the house had become a vacuum. Clutching at her chest, she tried to slow her breathing and stop the tears that threatened to drown her. When she could breathe, she stood in the living room, looking around.

"Now what?"

Chapter 29

Mickey woke, drenched in a cold sweat. Gasping, she sat up, clutching the edge of her thin mattress. These dreams were becoming unbearable – such realistic, erotic dreams involving bizarre mixes of Alice and Sister Anselma. They made her dread going to sleep so much that she wasn't sleeping most nights, choosing instead to spend many of those long, night-time hours in her choir stall, praying, begging for release.

She was surprised at how many people came to the Chapel through those dark hours – several nuns each night, slipping quietly into their stalls to spend thirty minutes or an hour, even Mother who went to an ordinary stall, not hers at the head of the choir – "I miss being out here, in my old stall," she would say long after when Mickey asked her. If they noticed her there, night after night, at all hours, they said nothing, leaving to her to battle her demons – "The way we all must," the nuns could have told her. "Nights are always the worst. The devils come out then." The doubts, the physical urges, the bottomless melancholy – all were worse in the dark, when it seemed morning would never come. "Not like this," Mickey would have said, but "you'd be surprised," they would have replied sagely.

Alice's letter, five years late, had dredged Mickey's grief to the surface, making the loss feel brand new. She was constantly on the verge of tears, and could only maintain control by keeping everyone at a distance.

"Was that really necessary?" Sister Josephine rebuked her sharply one afternoon when Mickey's sarcasm had caused Sister Alison to stomp off angrily.

Only Jessica was brave enough to attempt penetrating Mickey's caustic defenses, but when she approached, asking what was wrong, Mickey could feel herself choking up. "I can't," she mumbled before walking away. There was only one person she could have talked to about all that she was feeling, but Sister Anselma was maintaining a careful distance. Sometimes, when Mickey looked across the aisle in choir, she thought she saw Sister Anselma's eyes leaving her, but she couldn't be sure.

In January, Mickey and Jessica had been required to do another inventory of possessions, but "this one must include not just what you brought with you to St. Bridget's," explained Sister Bernice, the abbey's cellarer, "but everything you own in the world. Once you take your vows in April, you cannot own any physical property, no investments, no animals or cars if someone was keeping them for you, nothing."

Nothing.

Mickey's list included, presumably for the last time, a house and a storage facility of furniture and other items which would all have to be sold if she were to take vows. Nearly every night, she sat at her desk, staring at the list, knowing she should have contacted a realtor long ago if she intended to stay. She wasn't required to give the money to St. Bridget's, but "any money you do offer will be kept in an escrow account, not to be touched, until you take your solemn vows," Sister Bernice told them.

All around Mickey, the life of the abbey continued, like a river whose waters are briefly churned by one boulder causing turbulence, then calming again downstream from the disturbance, but "just because we go on, doesn't mean we don't notice."

Up in the infirmary, "Are you ill?" Sister Angelica asked one day as Mickey bathed her and changed her nightgown. "I may be old, but I can see that something is troubling you, dear."

Behind her, Mickey could tell Sister Mary David and Jessica had become still. Unwilling to lie, Mickey said, "I'm not ill, Sister."

"But something is troubling you."

Mickey looked into her concerned eyes, remembering that she had been the healer here for decades. "Yes," she said simply.

Sister Angelica nodded. "I'll pray for you," she said, patting Mickey's arm.

Mickey's throat tightened. "Thank you."

"What the hell is wrong with you?" she asked herself one bitterly cold night when she had abandoned her choir stall to pace the paths of the enclosure, her heavy winter cloak drawn tightly under her chin. "Why can you not just make a decision and live with it?"

As she came back around to the door into the cloister corridor, Sister Anselma was standing there. Startled, Mickey stopped and stared at her.

What was she doing here? They weren't supposed to break Silence.

"Come," was all Sister Anselma said. She led Mickey to the same study they had used on previous occasions. "Sit down," she said as she turned on a lamp and closed the door. Mickey took off her cloak and sat tensely on the edge of a chair, staring at the floor.

Sister Anselma sat also. "Michele, I don't mean to invade your privacy or presume that you would want to talk to me, but... I don't think we can go on like this." Mickey forced herself to meet Sister Anselma's gaze. "You have seemed so unhappy lately, and I can't help but feel at least partially responsible for that." Sister Anselma could no longer look Mickey in the eye. "I must apologize for the things I said when I was in the infirmary –"

"No," Mickey cut in. "It's not that. It's not your fault. I... read this." She pulled Alice's letter from the pocket where she kept it most of the time lately. As she read, Sister Anselma's pale cheeks burned scarlet and she had to wipe her eyes.

Mickey began pacing again, and her voice when she spoke quavered. "I got that letter at Christmas. It had been tucked away and just recently found. I feel like I've lost her all over again." She clasped her hands together inside her sleeves to stop their trembling.

"I don't know what to do about vows, but I can't imagine leaving this place I've come to love so much." She paused and turned to look at Sister Anselma with tortured eyes, knowing if she spoke now, there was no turning back. "And I don't know what to do about how very much I love you." She put her hands over her face. "I feel like I'm losing my mind," she choked as her shoulders shook.

Sister Anselma came to her and held her tightly. Mickey wrapped her arms around Sister Anselma in return, clutching at the fabric of her habit. They stood like that for a long time, then Sister Anselma led Mickey to the sofa where they sat side by side.

"There are some things you must understand," Sister Anselma said in a very quiet voice. "I told you before that my family was dysfunctional. I had never truly loved anyone in my life - not my family, not people I went to school with, no one - not until I met Mother Theodora. My love for her is a love born of respect and gratitude for all she's done for me. But I have lived my life here coldly, in isolation. The solitude of monastic life has never been a problem for me. Mother told me when I was newly professed that I should expect religious life to become difficult at some point, but it never has - until now."

She looked so frightened at that admission that Mickey asked, "Have I done anything - or said anything to -?"

"No," Sister Anselma insisted, looking helplessly at Mickey. "You haven't done anything - except to be you. Alice was right. I can't help but be drawn to you, for so many reasons. You were so trusting of me during your retreat; I've watched the joy and laughter that follow you, with Sister Linus and Jessica; at the hospital, you were so sure, and so kind and so gentle as you cared for Mother, and then in the infirmary... Every time I turn around, you've broken through my defenses. You touch me in ways no one ever has before - and I find I don't want to push you away." She looked down at her hands. "I know loving you is wrong, at least within these walls, but loving you has made me a better person, a better nun. How ironic is that?"

Mickey pulled some tissues from the box on the end table. "Vows are coming up in a couple of months," she reminded both of them again as she blew her nose.

"If not for this," Sister Anselma asked, "would you be questioning your vows? Would you be happy here?"

"I still have a house and all my furniture to sell, and I have to admit that's a scary leap to make, but yes, I would do it if not for this."

Sister Anselma turned to face her. "I know it's selfish, but I don't want you to go. We've acknowledged our feelings; there's nothing we can do about the fact that we feel this way, but we can control what we do about it. The feelings may pass in time."

Mickey looked at her dubiously. "Can you be content, living with me here and being faithful to our vows? Because we cannot betray Mother's trust in us."

"You forget who you're talking to," Sister Anselma replied as her face hardened into the mask it so often wore. "I'm the ice queen, remember?"

Mickey smiled tenderly. In the only physical expression of her feelings she would permit herself, she gently laid her hand on Sister Anselma's cheek. "You have never been that to me," she murmured. She picked up her cloak and Alice's letter and left without looking back.

☩ ☩ ☩

That night with Sister Anselma felt a bit like an exorcism for Mickey. Having finally been able to admit her feelings, they seemed easier to control. She was able to sleep most nights, and felt like she was back on solid ground emotionally. She wrote to Carol Barnes, her realtor in Baltimore, asking her to put the house on the market. When she mentioned all of this to Jamie, he surprised her by asking her to hold off selling her furniture. "I always liked the way you and Alice furnished the house. I might be interested in buying it," he said vaguely.

Mickey and Sister Anselma both exercised stringent self-control and discipline, refusing to seek each other out at Recreation or to glance in each other's direction in choir. Sister Josephine had told the novices about the old custom of "custody of the eyes," used by monks and nuns to avoid eye contact with one another in an age of strict discipline. It seemed so extreme, the novices had laughed at it, but "I'm not laughing now," Mickey said to herself.

A heavy snow fell across the region in early February. The juniors were asked to shovel the paths throughout the enclosure. Mickey shoveled the snow from around the enclosure gate and opened it to find Father Andrew shoveling the porch and walk of his residence. Together, they cleared the walk, their breath hanging in vapory clouds as they puffed with their exertions. When their shoveled paths met in the middle, they paused, catching their breath.

"Thanks," he gasped.

Mickey looked up at him. "Are you okay?" she asked.

"Just out of shape," he smiled. He eyed her more closely. "How about you?"

"Oh," she said, scraping her shovel against an icy spot on the walk. "Um..."

"I know a little bit about sleepless nights," he said. She looked up at him, wondering how many of her sleepless nights he had noticed and why he'd been up. "It's okay," he said, anticipating her reaction. "I'm not drinking. I just hope things are better."

"Things are better, now, thanks," she said.

She kept repeating that to herself as she paced in the corridor outside Mother's office later in February. She and Jessica were each required to meet with her prior to taking vows, but Mickey had never felt so anxious at the prospect of talking to her. She had never lied to Mother Theodora and desperately hoped she would not be asked any questions she could not answer honestly. "Just remember, things are better now," she said to herself one more time as she took a deep breath and knocked.

"*Venite*," came the expected response.

"*Pax tecum*," Mickey replied as she entered.

"*Et cum spiritu tuo*, my child. Come in, Mickey, sit."

Mickey sat, as she had so many times before, in the chair facing Mother Theodora's desk.

"How are you?" Mother Theodora's dark eyes were probing. "You seem to have been struggling lately."

"I have been," Mickey admitted. "But... it's getting better."

"Do you feel prepared to take your vows?"

"Mostly."

Mother smiled. "But you still have reservations?"

"I wish I could say no."

"An honest response." Mother Theodora continued to study Mickey's face as she asked, "Is there any reason you should not proceed with your simple vows?"

Mickey paused for several seconds before answering. "No, Mother," she said pensively, "but if circumstances became such that I felt I should not remain here any longer, I would come to you."

Mother Theodora didn't break her gaze. "I hope that will not be necessary, Sister," she said quietly. "You have made a very real contribution to our community, and I would not like to see you leave, so long as you are confident it is God's will that you be here."

Once again, the community was asked to vote on the candidates for the novitiate and for simple vows. If Mickey thought she was nervous the last time her future at St. Bridget's hung on a vote, it was nothing to the nerves she felt this time. She'd now been at St. Bridget's for three years. Going back to the outside world would be very difficult, but so much had happened over the past two years, bad and good - the accusations from Wendy and Abigail, Mother's accident and surgery - that she honestly couldn't tell how the balance of those things might affect the vote.

The meeting with the Council went smoothly enough, although Mickey found it difficult to look Sister Scholastica in the eye. There were what she supposed were the standard questions: "Do you understand the gravity of the vows you will make?" "Are you prepared to live in accordance with your vows and the Rule of this abbey?" "Do you see any reason why you should not proceed in your vocation?" Mickey was very glad Sister Scholastica couldn't read minds as she answered this last question, trying to maintain a neutral expression. When she received word this time that she had been accepted, she went to her choir stall and prayed fervently, "Please let me be worthy of their confidence."

On Holy Thursday, Jessica and Mickey were again part of the foot-washing. Mother Theodora couldn't help a quiet grunt as she lowered herself to her knees - "your abdominal muscles will never be as strong again," Mickey had warned her after her surgery - and it took all of Mickey's self-control not to assist Mother to her feet after she had washed the last woman's feet. As always following the Mass, the Eucharist was temporarily removed from the main Chapel, but this year the common room was to be used as the choir and chapel for the next two days. The altar in the main Chapel was closed from view by a floor to ceiling drape. Mother Theodora would only say that the Chapel was being remodeled. The nuns could hear workers on the other side of the drape.

As the Easter Vigil Mass began Saturday night, back in the main Chapel, a partial drape was still in place above the altar. Mickey glanced into the public chapel and was surprised to see Jamie and Jennifer sitting there. She had been expecting them for Easter Sunday, but neither had said anything about being there that night. Communion was distributed, and as the Recessional music began with the organ reverberating and voices joyfully proclaiming, "*Exsultet iam angelica turba caelorum exsultent divina mysteriosa...*", the drape was released, falling dramatically to the floor. Mickey gasped and forgot to sing. Behind the altar, seemingly suspended in mid-air, was a larger-than-life sculpture of Jesus, arms raised overhead, body arched. It was simultaneously the posture of the crucifixion and an expression of triumph. She turned to Jamie who was smiling proudly.

Mickey got to speak to him only briefly through the grille following Mass. "It's absolutely beautiful," she said, her eyes shining. "I am so proud of you."

"Thanks," he said, taking her hand through the grille.

Mickey glanced at Jennifer and was shocked to see her looking at Jamie with a radiant expression. "I want to talk to you tomorrow," she said to him with the twin look.

Bishop Marcus returned to the abbey the next day for the profession of Jessica and Mickey into simple vows. Together, they sang the Magnificat as they approached the altar where the Bishop and Mother awaited them. Bishop Marcus gave Mickey a small nod of recognition.

Lying facedown on the floor, Jessica and Mickey made their vows, signed the agreement and received the plain silver bands signifying this stage of religious life. Mickey choked up as she felt the weight of the band where Alice's ring used to be. After their short, white veils were exchanged for long, black ones in the side chamber where they had first received the habit, they went to their choir stalls while the two postulants were Clothed. Mickey was barely aware of what was happening to them. Though the Clothing was a much more elaborate ceremony, this one – this simple exchange of promises and veils felt so much more profound. "Well, it would be after all the drama you created to go with it," she reminded herself. "Why do you always have to make everything so hard?"

When Mass was over, the two newly professed nuns and two new novices went through the traditional receiving line, ending with the Abbess. As they had when Mickey and the others had been Clothed, many of the hugs were accompanied by wishes of encouragement, "I'm so glad, Sister," or "God bless you, Sister." Sister Josephine's green eyes twinkled with a smile as she said, "You've aged me ten years in the last few months. I didn't think you'd make it this far."

Mickey laughed. "For a while, I wasn't sure either. Thank you for everything," she said sincerely as she gave Sister Josephine a hug.

When she got to Sister Anselma, neither trusted herself to speak. For a couple of seconds, they allowed themselves to let down their guard as they looked into each other's eyes. Their embrace was the only touch they'd shared since admitting their feelings to one another. Reluctantly, they released each other and Mickey moved on.

Mother Theodora gave Mickey a tight hug, whispering, "My prayer for you is that you find peace, Mickey." Mickey noticed she didn't say "find peace here," but "you're just being paranoid," she told herself.

There was a reception in the refectory for the families of the four women celebrating the day. Mother Theodora introduced Jamie as the sculptor of the figure hanging in the Chapel. He received an enthusiastic round of applause. Mickey had to wait for the crowd around him to disperse before she could talk to him.

"Jamie," she beamed as she hugged him tightly. "Why in the world didn't you tell me? It's incredible!"

He smiled, still red-faced from all the attention. "Thanks. I've been working on it for the past year. Mother Theodora asked me to come up with some sketches, and we worked out the design. She asked me not to say anything to you; she wanted it to be a surprise for the community."

"Isn't it wonderful?" Jennifer appeared at Mickey's side and hugged her also. "I've seen some of his other work at galleries in New York, but there's something special about this piece."

Her dark eyes focused intently on Mickey. "How are you? The letter…?"

"It was rough for a while," Mickey admitted. "It was like hearing her talk to me five years after she'd gone… but it's better now," she smiled. *Keep saying it and someday you'll believe it.*

"You look wonderful," Jennifer said. "I can't believe I'm saying that about one of these." She made a face as she tugged at the sleeve of Mickey's habit.

Mickey laughed and caught Sister Anselma's eye. Beckoning her over, she introduced Jamie and Jennifer. "Sister Anselma is in charge of the vestment room."

Jennifer's interest was piqued. "Really? Could we… I mean, I don't mean to impose, but I would love to see some of your work."

Sister Anselma smiled curiously. "Why is that?"

"Well, I'm an assistant curator of cloth art for a museum, and I've been studying Renaissance and medieval ecclesiastical vestments, and I would love to see a modern example of that type of work."

Sister Anselma nodded. "We will need to ask Mother's permission first."

Jennifer and Sister Anselma went to find Mother Theodora. Mickey turned to Jamie. "Well?"

"Well, what?" he countered, but he was turning red.

"You and Jennifer," she said with mock sternness. "You know exactly what I mean."

He grinned and scratched the back of his head. "We've stayed in touch since Christmas." He looked seriously at Mickey. "She's really special, Mick, but if this is too weird for you, we'll stop."

She looked into his earnest blue eyes. "Do you love her?"

"I think it's going in that direction."

"Jamie," she said, laying a hand on his arm, "you and Jennifer are two of the people I love most in this world. I would be thrilled if you fell in love."

He let out the breath he had been holding. "I was hoping you'd say that."

A short while later, Jennifer and Sister Anselma returned to the reception. Jennifer was gushing, "I can't believe I never knew you were here! Your work is exquisite! And the techniques you use are just like it was done hundreds of years ago." Her face lit up as another thought occurred to her. "Would you consider taking on some restoration work? It pays very well." She clapped a hand to her mouth. "Is it okay to talk to a nun about money?"

Sister Anselma smiled again. "You would need to discuss that with Mother Theodora." She looked around and spied Mother across the room. "She's over there."

"Come on," Jamie said, taking Jennifer's elbow, "Let's see if she'll schedule a meeting."

"She certainly is enthusiastic," Sister Anselma said to Mickey after they left. "Is she your brother's girlfriend?"

Mickey's eyebrows went up. "Apparently she is. She's also Alice's baby sister." Sister Anselma looked at Mickey in surprise, and then back over to Jennifer and Jamie. "That's almost exactly what Alice looked like when we met. The resemblance between them is remarkable."

"She's beautiful," Sister Anselma murmured, studying Jennifer with greater curiosity. She turned to Mickey. "Are you all right, being around such a strong reminder of Alice?"

Mickey smiled. "I have to admit, the first time she came to visit me, it was like seeing a ghost. It took me a few minutes to collect myself." She looked over at Sister Anselma. Here, in the midst of the celebration, it seemed safe to talk. "How are you?"

Sister Anselma looked down at the floor, rather than at Mickey. "About as you'd expect. For over sixteen years I've never doubted being here, never was unhappy, never struggled with anything. Nothing feels the same anymore."

Mickey didn't know what to say, but Sister Anselma seemed to sense her guilt. "This is not your fault," she insisted quietly.

Mickey nodded, but didn't trust herself to look at Sister Anselma again. Further conversation was cut off by Jamie and Jennifer coming back over to say good-bye. Jennifer promised Sister Anselma she would follow up on the restoration work as Mickey walked them to the entrance.

Jamie paused and looked at Mickey. "What is it?" he asked, placing a hand on her shoulder.

She knew better than to lie to him. Neither of them could fool the other, and the truth always came out eventually. Instead, "It'll be okay," she reassured him.

As she watched them drive away in her old SUV, the realization struck that there were no more classes or ceremonies to distract her. Now, there was only the daily life of the abbey stretching out before her without interruption. For a few seconds, Mickey almost ran down the drive after them, begging them to take her with them. She got her panic under control. *Damn*, she thought, with another quick thought that she really should stop swearing, *that was almost the shortest vows on record.*

Chapter 30

Mickey unlocked her front door, balancing her Chinese take-out in one hand and carrying a large bundle of mail under her arm as she let herself in. She tossed the mail on the kitchen island and went to get something to drink. Opening the refrigerator, she stared at the nearly empty interior. With a sigh, she got a glass and filled it with cold water from the tap.

She stood at the island, eating out of the cardboard food containers as she sorted through the mail, tossing most of it into a pile to be recycled. She almost threw out a personally addressed envelope. Looking closely at the return address, she smiled when she saw that it was from Jennifer. Mickey hadn't seen her since Christmas at the Worthingtons', but Jennifer and her parents had written every couple of weeks, just cards and brief notes. It helped to come home to them.

She pried open the envelope and read the note inside as she pushed the play button on her answering machine. Multiple messages played: one from Christopher, "Mickey, we miss seeing you at Mass. Everyone asks about you. Please, come back soon." Three were from other friends and two from Jamie, asking her to call.

Mickey wandered back to the master bedroom where the bed lay undisturbed, the spread neatly pulled up, pillow shams in place the way Alice liked them. She pulled clean underwear and pj's from the dresser drawer and went to shower. The phone rang as she got dressed. She looked at the caller ID before answering.

"Mickey?" Jamie's voice came over the line. "I can't believe I got you. If I hadn't reached you tonight, I was ready to come down there in person."

"I'm sorry," she said. "I've been getting in late."

"Liar. I've called late. And I've left five messages on your cell phone. Remember who you're talking to," he scolded gently. "You haven't been coming home at all, have you? You've probably been sleeping at the office." He took her silence as acknowledgement that he was right. "Anyway, I was calling to see if you can take some time off and come up for a visit?"

"Oh, I don't know," she hemmed, "I'm really busy right now."

"I know you are," he agreed. "I'm sure you've taken on extra cases to keep yourself busy, but spring break is coming up in March, isn't it? So there'll be a week with no teaching. How about then? Please?"

She smiled. "I'll see what I can do."

"You'd better. Talk to you soon."

"Jamie?"

"Yeah?"

"Thanks."

She placed the phone back on the charger and went down the hall to the guest room where the bedclothes were crumpled, the bed unmade. She crawled in, pulling the covers over her and turned out the light.

Chapter 31

Mickey yawned as she walked to the barn. She and Claire Decault, one of the new Novices, had been working with Sister Regina on the farm for the past few weeks. Though Mickey had made peace with being assigned to the infirmary, things had quieted there and when Sister Regina asked for volunteers to help with the extra work load that came with spring, Mickey jumped at the opportunity. She breathed deeply, enjoying this beautiful April morning, the sun not yet up, misty patches of fog lying in the low areas of the fields as they walked through the dewy grass. She could hear deep moos coming from the cows, and the higher pitched bawling of the calves in a farther pasture. All spring, as calves were born at a rate of two or three a day, milking had been suspended so they could nurse. Most of the nuns had found excuses to come out and laugh as the calves ran and played, cavorting clumsily on their wobbly legs. Now, most of the calves were old enough to be weaned and nobody was happy about it. They had to coax the cows into the barn and into the milking stanchions. Talking in low voices, they gave the cows some feed to calm them. Pulling stools up beside the cows, they washed the udders and began milking. Claire had grown up on a farm in Québec province, but Mickey had never stood next to a cow before. "They're huge!" she exclaimed in surprise her first day. "They are," Sister Regina admitted fondly, patting a Guernsey on her broad face, "but you'll learn," and she had learned how to handle them and was getting the hang of milking. Claire liked to talk to them in French as she milked, and was almost as fast as Sister Regina. Mickey had been a little tentative at first – *you'd think handling an udder would come more naturally*, she thought with a wry smile at what Alice would say to the comparison. She finished milking her first cow, and moved on to a young cow named Fuzzy who had had her first calf that season. She was agitated, kicking at her uncomfortably full udder as Mickey washed her and sat down on her stool.

"Quiet down," Mickey crooned, trying to soothe her as she began pulling on the teats. Fuzzy seemed to be settling down as the milking eased her discomfort, and she ate a bit.

"SHIT!"

Sister Regina and Claire looked up just in time to see Fuzzy swinging her hindquarters into Mickey, knocking her off the stool and kicking over the milk bucket. Mickey stood up with one side of her face plastered with wet manure from Fuzzy's tail and her habit drenched with milk.

"Yes," said Sister Regina calmly, looking at Mickey's red face. "It's shit."

Claire started giggling. "In French, it is *merde*," she laughed.

Mickey stood with her arms out, looking down at the mess. "Oh well," she shrugged, using her sleeve to wipe the worst of the manure off her face. She cleaned her bucket and moved on to the next cow.

When they were done milking and had mucked the stalls, Mickey went in to wash up before breakfast. She attracted several curious, amused stares as she walked through the cloister to the stairs. As she could have predicted, she passed Mother Theodora and Sister Anselma who were conferring in the hallway. They stopped talking and turned in her direction.

"Don't even ask," Mickey muttered as she hurried past. She could hear stifled laughter behind her. She hurriedly cleaned up and changed into her spare habit and went down to breakfast. Nervously, she got through the morning, keeping an eye out for Sister Lucille.

"You haven't kept an eye on the housing market in Baltimore, have you?" her realtor, Carol, had asked over the telephone when she called a few days ago to confirm an offer on Mickey's house. She had predicted it would sell quickly, but "how much did you say?" Mickey asked weakly.

All the paperwork requiring her signature was being brought to New York by Susan Harris - "are you sure Susan volunteered to come up here?" Mickey asked incredulously when Carol told her.

"Yes, why?"

"Nothing," said Mickey. "Nothing except the last time I saw her, she screamed at me and walked out and I haven't heard from her in three years," but she didn't say that.

When Sister Lucille came for her, Mickey almost ran to the parlour, pausing to brace herself before going in. Susan's mouth hung open as she looked Mickey up and down.

"Hi," Mickey said a little uncertainly.

"Oh my God," Susan said weakly, collapsing onto the sofa. "I knew this would be a shock, but... I just can't believe this is you."

"It's me," Mickey grinned. She sat next to Susan. "Are you okay? Can I get you anything?"

"No," Susan replied brusquely, seeming to regain her composure. "Here are the contracts," she said, pulling papers out of a legal-sized folder.

"We can do this later. Tell me how you've been," Mickey asked anxiously.

Susan frowned down at the papers. "No, we'd better take care of this first, before I forget all the places Carol said you have to sign."

Puzzled, Mickey gave in and signed everywhere Susan indicated. When they were done, and Susan had put everything back in the folder, Mickey laid her hand on Susan's arm. "I've known you for a very long time," she said quietly. "Please tell me what's going on."

Susan looked at Mickey, her eyes hard. "It's no big deal. Christie left."

The words hung in the air. "What do you mean she left?" Mickey asked incredulously. "You two have been together for ten years!"

Susan smiled bitterly. "You'd think that would count for something, wouldn't you?"

Mickey searched Susan's face. "Why did she leave? Is there someone else?"

Susan looked away.

"Susan?"

"I have breast cancer."

Mickey closed her eyes. "Christie's mother."

Susan swallowed. "She said she can't go through that again." Susan's bravado suddenly crumbled and she burst into tears. "I'm so scared."

Mickey held her tightly. "I know... I know." She held Susan until she calmed down, and then wanted to know the facts.

"I'm having a mastectomy in two weeks," Susan said. "They don't know yet if the lymph nodes are involved."

Mickey advised her on what questions to ask her doctors. "Where is Christie now?"

Susan blew her nose. "She's staying with Julie and Sharon until she figures out what she's going to do."

"Would you mind if I write to her?"

"I was hoping you would." Susan's chin began to quiver again. "You were so good with her when her mother was dying."

"What about you?" Mickey watched her closely. "Do you have anyone to talk to?" Susan shook her head. Mickey scribbled a name and phone number on the outside of the folder. "I want you to call this counselor. You need help in getting through this – all of this. She'll get you in touch with a support group." Susan made a face and started to protest. "I know you think you're John Wayne, but you can't deal with this alone."

Susan laughed for a moment and then looked at Mickey, embarrassed. "I feel like such a hypocrite – I mean, I was so angry and felt so betrayed when you told me about this... I wasn't there for you during what must have been a tough decision... would you... could you... pray for me?" she asked as her eyes filled with tears again.

"Of course I will pray for you," Mickey said earnestly. She took Susan's hand and held it tightly. "Everyone here will pray for you. It is so much more powerful than anything I could have done before."

"You really believe that?" Susan's eyes probed Mickey's, demanding the truth.

Mickey squeezed Susan's hand. "I really believe it."

※ ※ ※

Mickey stood at the top of the steps into the vestment room, the first time she had been there since the day Mother Theodora fell. Sister Catherine saw her and beckoned her in welcome. Sister Anselma was working at her loom and didn't look up.

"A little calmer than the last time you were here, isn't it?" Sister Catherine smiled. She gave Mickey a tour, showing her around the various work stations, some for weaving, some for embroidery, some for cutting and finish work.

Mickey hadn't known how to react when, in June, Mother Theodora had given Jessica and her their new, more or less permanent assignments, Jessica to the library - Mickey had enviously watched the rapturous expression on Jessica's face - while Mickey was assigned to the vestment room. This was Sister Anselma's realm, the place where she excelled according to Jennifer, and, "I don't want to be in your way," she would say to Sister Anselma later.

Sister Catherine asked Mickey to begin by working with Sister Madeline who was transferring designs from paper to fabric for later embroidery. Sister Madeline was the next most junior nun here in the vestment room. She showed Mickey how to use different symbols to indicate specific details and colors for the embroiderers later. Mickey looked up once to see Sister Anselma watching them.

Over the next few days, Mickey was introduced to the different work stations and shown what each involved. Most of the nuns let her try her hand at the work, but she soon realized how quickly she could ruin hours of their labor in her beginner's clumsiness, and she would turn the task back over, preferring to observe. Finally, she was observing with Sister Anselma at her loom and had an opportunity to speak with her alone.

"Are you all right with this?" she asked anxiously. "I had no idea Mother would assign me to work here."

Sister Anselma smiled at Mickey. "It's all right. I admit I was startled when she suggested it..." she paused to change to a shuttle with a different color thread, "but I saw no reason not to give it a try."

Mickey could think of plenty of reasons as her heart thumped at being so near Sister Anselma, but she told herself if Sister Anselma could accept this invasion of her territory, then "I'd better find a way to deal with it."

The following few weeks passed quickly for Mickey with the stimulation of the training she was receiving. In addition to the actual weaving and embroidery, the nuns often dyed their own thread when a specific color was needed that couldn't quite be matched commercially. Age-old dye recipes reproduced true, accurate colors just as monasteries would have produced centuries ago, "well, almost," Sister Catherine explained. "We now know some of the old ingredients were toxic, so we've had to make some modern substitutions."

Mickey quickly reached a level of competence where she was responsible for transferring designs by herself. She was carrying a piece of pale yellow silk on which she had just finished marking a design over to Sisters Catherine and Paula who were both working on embroidering a very large, intricate scene adapted from an illuminated text. Sister Paula was having trouble getting some of the detail in the face of the monk in the design. Watching her, Mickey had an idea. She went to her cell and brought a pair of hemostats back to the vestment room. Using pliers and a hammer to bend a needle, she asked Sister Paula if she could try her idea. She sat down and used the hemostats to guide the needle in and out of the cloth. It was like surgery. She got lost in the work, looking from design to cloth and, with tiny stitches, produced a face almost more detailed than the drawing. She sat back to get a better look, and was startled to realize all the others had gathered round to watch. She had been so absorbed in what she was doing that she hadn't noticed. Her face burned as she looked up at Sister Anselma who was looking back with an expression of such intensity that it felt to Mickey like a caress.

"I think," Sister Anselma said, turning back to her loom, "that we need to set up another embroidery station."

They bent more needles and experimented with different stitches and techniques. Mickey showed the other nuns surgical knots and stitches, and they showed her more traditional stitches; by combining them, they improved the level of detail considerably, although it slowed the work somewhat.

Sister Anselma called Mickey over one day to begin teaching her how to weave. They spent an hour setting a loom for a small practice piece for Mickey to learn on. She sat next to Sister Anselma, transfixed at the speed and delicacy of her work. Her hands were beautiful - long-fingered and deft. Alice had always laughed at Mickey's obsession with hands, but Mickey stubbornly insisted hands said as much about someone as their eyes. "Concentrate, you idiot," Mickey chided herself when she realized she hadn't been listening to a word Sister Anselma was saying to her. It was embarrassing and humbling to try and work the loom and the shuttle herself; she felt so clumsy and awkward in comparison to Sister Anselma's grace.

"How did you learn this?" Mickey asked in awe after Sister Anselma patiently pulled out the third mistake Mickey had made in the pattern.

Sister Anselma smiled. "When I was newly professed, I was sent here to work under old Sister Basil. She taught me everything she knew, gave me a wonderful foundation."

Mickey watched her face as she spoke. "But you're miles beyond what Sister Basil taught you, aren't you?"

Sister Anselma blushed and kept her eyes on her work. "I discovered what I have a gift for. This is my prayer."

"Sister Anselma?"

They turned to find tiny Sister Lucille standing in the doorway at the top of the steps.

"Yes, Sister?"

"You have visitors."

Sister Anselma frowned a little at the interruption. "I'm not expecting anyone and we don't have any deliveries ready to go out. Did you get a name?"

"I asked, but they wouldn't say," Sister Lucille sniffed, clearly not impressed with the visitors' manners. "They would only say they were here to see Lauren Thackeray."

Sister Anselma's face turned to stone, and she closed her eyes. "Keep going with this pattern," she said to Mickey as she rose.

Everyone else resumed their work, but Mickey found it difficult to concentrate, which was unfortunate as she ended up pulling more threads out than she actually wove. Lauren Thackeray. She could never admit it to anyone, especially Sister Anselma, but in her brief fantasies of what it would be like to live with her outside the abbey, one awkward point had been her name. Being named for a rather obscure Italian saint was fine in here, but plain "Anselma" just didn't sound the same. Lauren suited her.

When the bell rang for Vespers, Sister Anselma had not returned to the vestment room. As Mickey took her seat in Chapel, she saw that Sister Anselma was already in her choir stall, her eyes downcast and her face almost as white as her wimple.

Mickey's weaving lessons did not resume. Sister Anselma was quite distant with everyone, remaining at her loom most of the time, working on an intricate pattern for several days. Mickey assisted Sister Catherine with an ornate altar cloth, glancing frequently in Sister Anselma's direction, hoping to catch her eye, but Sister Anselma concentrated only on her work.

Leaving the refectory after lunch one afternoon, Mickey was caught by Sister Lucille who asked her if she would take a bolt of cloth to the vestment room. "They brought it to the front door by mistake again," Sister Lucille explained apologetically, trying to hold the bulky roll.

Mickey gathered the large paper-wrapped bundle in her arms and made her way through the corridors, remembering the first time she did this – the day she had met Sister Anselma and caused such havoc in the vestment room. Chuckling, she thought, *now I know why she was so pissed. If someone did that to me now...* She backed through the door to the vestment room, and as she started down the wooden steps, she was startled to realize Sister Anselma was there, working at her loom.

"Didn't you eat lunch?" she asked as she set her bundle down on a worktable.

"I wasn't hungry," Sister Anselma answered, not interrupting her rhythm.

Mickey wavered a few seconds, then went to sit next to Sister Anselma at the loom. "Won't you tell me what's troubling you?"

Sister Anselma stopped the action of the loom, but her hands maintained a tight hold on the shuttle wound with the deep purple thread she'd been weaving. "My visitors the other day were my sister and two of my mother's attorneys," she said. She shook her head. "Even from her grave, my mother is still finding ways to manipulate us all."

She looked at Mickey with eyes the color of steel. "In her will, she divided her estate in half - one half to my sister, and the other half to me."

Mickey frowned. "I thought you had other family - your father and a brother?"

Sister Anselma laughed bitterly. "Oh, I do. That's the beauty of my mother's plan. I can only claim my half if I renounce my vows and leave the abbey. If I don't, everything goes to my sister. She's crueler than my mother, if that's possible. If she's in charge of the entire estate, my father will be lucky if she lets him stay in the house. As for my brother, well... he's an alcoholic. He's burned a lot of bridges. My sister would like nothing better than to see him cut off completely."

"How much money are we talking about?"

Sister Anselma hesitated as if it were distasteful to even say it out loud. "Something like twenty million."

Mickey choked out a half laugh. "Your half is twenty million dollars?" she asked weakly.

Sister Anselma nodded.

Mickey thought for a minute. "What did you say?"

Sister Anselma shrugged. "I didn't know what to say. The will stipulates that if I haven't left and claimed my portion within five years of my mother's death, it all goes to my sister anyway."

Mickey stared at her. "But that means two years have already gone by. I don't understand why you're just now hearing about this."

"I guess my sister has been trying to see if there was any way to break the will. Apparently there isn't, or she wouldn't have come." She looked at Mickey again, but this time the hardness was gone from her eyes. Instead, there was only doubt and vulnerability. "Can you believe the irony of her timing? Before you, I would have said no without a second thought. But now..." she looked down again, "I can't help but think about the possibility of leaving."

Without thinking, Mickey reached out and took her hand. Sister Anselma's fingers wrapped tightly around hers. "I can't deny I've thought about it, too," Mickey said in a soft voice, "but whatever we decide has to be based on... on other things. I wouldn't want one cent of your mother's money to taint our lives. You are all –" She stopped and withdrew her hand.

Sister Anselma lifted her face. "What were you going to say?"

Mickey met her eyes, frightened at where they were going. "You are all that I would need."

They stared at one another for several seconds. Sister Anselma's eyes filled with tears. "God help me, I love you so much, sometimes it is physically painful."

Mickey stood abruptly. "I am so sorry," she whispered. "I never meant for this to happen." She spent the remainder of Recreation in her choir stall, praying, "Oh, God, you brought us together, probably the only other woman I could love this much. Please, please help us through this."

☩ ☩ ☩

By unspoken agreement, Mickey and Sister Anselma avoided any situation which might have left them alone together. The other nuns in the vestment room were unwitting buffers in this dance. Despite her efforts at self-control, Mickey felt like anyone who really looked at her would see the truth. She felt raw and chafed, beat up by the tumult of emotions churning within her. Her only balm was the Divine Office. For brief moments, the beauty of the chant and the ancient Latin words would transport her to a place of calm, a place where "I could remember why I had chosen this life," she would explain to Jamie much later. But ever since Sister Anselma had admitted to thinking about leaving, that possibility had been gnawing at her. Images would pop into her head of their life together, although she often had to smile as she had difficulty picturing Sister Anselma in anything other than a habit.

The nuns in the vestment room were startled one afternoon by the arrival of Mother Theodora, Sister Scholastica and the rest of the Council. Sister Anselma and the others all ceased their work and looked questioningly at one another.

"May we speak to all of you, please?" Mother Theodora asked. They gathered round and Mother continued, "As I'm sure you know, we have received a proposal from the Mannheim Museum to do some of their restoration work on tapestries, vestments and other cloth art they acquire. This has been initiated by a very persistent young woman who is an old friend of Sister Michele's." She looked at Mickey with a droll smile.

Mother Theodora glanced around at the excited faces of the nuns. "The idea holds tremendous promise for the financial security of the abbey, however, our ability to take on this work is based almost completely on Sister Anselma's expertise. Despite the fact that all of you contribute to our finished product, it is under her direction and artistic guidance that the abbey's work has become so well-known. If we are to consider taking on the additional work, it would mean assigning more sisters to the vestment room, and it would necessitate more training for all of you. In addition, we would have to update the physical layout of this area to meet the museum's insurance requirements. Our old knob and tube electrical wiring would all have to be replaced, and the air-conditioning would have to be upgraded to control the environment more precisely."

Sister Scholastica spoke up. "Our concern is that we will spend so much money in renovating this space and become so preoccupied with productivity in here that we might become a tapestry factory instead of an abbey." She glanced at Mother Theodora with what Mickey thought was a disapproving look. "If we agree to take on this… project," - Mickey had the distinct impression "travesty" might have been her preferred word - "it must be with the firm understanding that the Divine Office is our highest priority, and the restoration work may take longer than they would like."

"So," Mother Theodora said, looking around at all of them, "our questions to you: is it feasible to take on more work, and are you willing to undertake the additional training and study it would require, not only for you, but for the extra sisters I would assume would be needed to meet the demand?"

Sister Anselma frowned a little as she considered. "I don't think we could take on any additional work now, with just the five of us. I think we would need to bring other sisters in and train them first, then we could decide who would continue with our current work and who would do the restoration work. A small team would probably be best for the museum work. I assume the museum will assign a curator to work with us?"

Mother Theodora nodded. "Jennifer Worthington would work closely with us."

"Do we have enough sisters to assign more here without compromising other areas within the monastery?" Mickey asked.

Sister Bernice responded, "We have averaged two to three new entrants a year for the past several years, so, yes, we could assign five to ten sisters to the vestment room without leaving other parts of the abbey short-staffed."

There was a long pause as the five current vestment workers considered the impact of this change.

"Mother," Sister Anselma said, glancing at the others, "I believe I speak for all of us - we are willing to take on this new challenge. Realistically, we're going to need at least six months to train new workers in here and to study enough to be ready for the restoration work."

The Council members looked pleased, with the exception of Sister Scholastica.

"My only other concern," Sister Anselma added with some hesitation, "is that this assignment may be looked upon as more desirable or prestigious than other work within the abbey. But the training is so intense that it really isn't practical to rotate these positions on a regular basis."

Mother Theodora looked at Sister Anselma appraisingly. "I appreciate your sensitivity to that issue, Sister. I agree, this has the potential to turn into a competition, and we must handle it carefully so that those who are not chosen do not feel slighted. After all, entering religious life does not mean that we checked our egos at the door."

Chapter 32

"Am I interrupting?"

Mickey looked up from the table in her office where she was poring over medical references, researching a rare cancer which had been newly diagnosed in one of her patients. "No... well, yes, but it's a welcome interruption," she said, rubbing her eyes tiredly. "What can I do for you, Kara?"

Kara Anderson was one of the best surgical residents Mickey had ever worked with. She would never say this to anyone else, but Kara reminded her of herself, "professionally," she would have clarified if she had said it out loud to someone. She was extremely intelligent, learned quickly and exhibited tremendous skill in the OR. Physically, Kara was slender and blond and gorgeous. In the women's locker room, she was not shy at all about walking around naked after showering, showing off her triathlete's body. Mickey, to her embarrassment, had been caught looking a few times.

"Well, I've been wanting to talk to you," Kara said as she closed the office door and came to sit next to Mickey at the table. "About a few things actually." She looked at Mickey with eyes that were a beautiful chocolate brown. Her gaze moved to the books on the table. "Oh, yes, I was researching this case earlier today, also." Mickey could smell Kara's perfume as she leaned near to look at one of the open texts. Kara had a disconcerting habit of positioning herself so near to Mickey during rounds and consults that their elbows or shoulders often were in contact. She looked back up at Mickey. "I wanted to ask you how you're doing," she said, laying a hand on Mickey's forearm. "I know these last few months have been difficult for you, but you're always so busy looking after the patients and us - I don't know how many people are looking after you."

Mickey could feel her heart beating faster. She had to avert her gaze. "I'm managing," she murmured. "Work has helped to keep me focused."

"I worry about you," Kara said, increasing the pressure of her hand on Mickey's arm. "I see the lights on in here at all hours. I have a feeling you're avoiding going home."

Mickey turned away, but didn't pull her arm away. "I've had plenty of family and friends checking up on me."

"But," Kara boldly moved her hand to Mickey's cheek and made Mickey face her again, "is there anyone taking care of you?" She leaned dangerously close. "Because there should be," she whispered, gently pulling Mickey to her for a kiss.

Mickey resisted for a few seconds... Kara's lips were so close, Mickey could feel the warmth of her breath, she could see the variations of the colors of her irises... as Kara's lips touched hers, she gave in to the closeness, the softness. She stood, pulling Kara up with her and pressed her against the table, one of Kara's thighs between hers. She kissed Kara hungrily, probing deeply with her tongue, her fingers digging so roughly into Kara's shoulders that she make her gasp. Kara pulled Mickey's hips more forcefully against her thigh. She returned the kiss just as hard, catching Mickey's lip against her teeth and nicking it. Mickey opened her eyes as she tasted blood. Suddenly, she pulled away, her eyes having trouble focusing on Kara's face.

"Go," she said in a strangled whisper, her breathing rapid and harsh.

"Don't," Kara protested, "please don't -"

"Please... just go," Mickey repeated, releasing Kara and backing away.

"Don't push me away," Kara pleaded, reaching a hand out to Mickey's shoulder.

"Get out!"

Kara brushed tears from her cheeks as she crossed the room. Closing the door as she exited the office, she touched a finger to her lips and looked at the drop of blood there. She jumped at the impact of something shattering against the other side of the door.

Chapter 33

Over the next few months, there was a flurry of activity, but "in monastic life, what counts as a 'flurry' would probably not even make a ripple in secular life," Mickey wrote to Christie who was back home with Susan, going to counseling with her and learning to deal with her mother's death and Susan's illness.

Professed nuns who had an interest in learning more about the work in the vestment room were rotated through in two week shifts so that they could receive some introductory training, and mutual compatibility could be assessed. "I never realized this work was so detailed and so... tedius," more than one nun said, and most realized they weren't suited for the concentration required to spend weeks or often months working on the same piece.

"I wish I could give it a go," said Sister Linus to Mickey one day as they sat under the cherry tree. "But ninety-five-year-old eyes and these hands –" She held up her gnarled hands, reddened from working in the laundry just that morning. "Oh, well," she sighed. "That's for the younger ones."

"It doesn't mean you can't come see what we're working on," Mickey suggested.

Jennifer began coming to the abbey once a week for a series of lectures on the history of weaving and cloth art, and to discuss some of the issues that went into deciding whether or not to restore a piece.

These lectures were open to anyone who wished to come, and Mother Theodora was pleased to see nearly the entire community in attendance. Mickey felt a warm flush of pride every time Jennifer gave one of these lectures. She was very well-spoken and more knowledgeable than Mickey had realized. Sometimes, she could still see Alice in Jennifer and her mind would wander… "I can't seem to help wondering, 'what if'," she would admit to Mother later, but invariably, she would come back to the moment to see Sister Anselma glancing at her, as if she could feel Mickey slipping away, and was trying to guide her back.

These lectures, which were Sister Anselma's idea, had the hoped-for effect of uniting the community in the endeavor they were about to undertake. Whether they worked in the vestment room or not, the monastic contribution to the history of European cloth art was something they could all take pride in and had become a frequent topic of conversation during meals and Recreation – "tapestry factory," Sister Scholastica scowled.

"You are creating the pieces that someone like me will be lecturing on two or three hundred years from now," Jennifer told the nuns one afternoon as she reverently held a sixteenth century altar cloth she had brought as an example next to an elaborately embroidered chasuble Sisters Catherine and Paula had just completed.

Mother Theodora noted the murmur of approval that rippled around the room at Jennifer's comment. "You are as good at public relations as you are in your area of expertise," she said to Jennifer at the end of the lecture. Jennifer just laughed.

Much of the "flurry" involved the abbey's need to upgrade the electrical and air-conditioning systems in the vestment room. The high, beamed ceiling was stripped of its old knob and tube wires, while new wires were run, looking like stark white strands of spider web against the dark beams and stone walls, all springing from a large box of circuit breakers attached to the back wall.

It was rumored that the Council, spurred by Sister Scholastica, had rejected higher bids from electrical contractors who proposed more aesthetic solutions for hiding the wiring and the box in favor of keeping expenses to a minimum.

"It's so ugly," Sister Madeline complained, looking at the grey metal box stuck on the stone wall. "It's like a pimple on a beautiful face."

Mickey laughed. "But it's practical and it's a lot safer than what we had before."

By October, seven new nuns were working in the vestment area, with the emphasis on trying to get caught up on old orders before they began any of the restoration work. The new nuns were learning quickly, but Sister Anselma looked exhausted. Mickey was still learning much of the work herself and could not do much of the training. Sisters Catherine, Paula and Madeline did as much as they could, but not even they had realized how much they relied upon Sister Anselma for the final word on almost every aspect of their work.

One afternoon, when she was interrupted for the fifth time while working on a particularly complex weaving on the loom, Sister Anselma lost her temper.

"What is it now?" she snapped angrily.

Sister Stephanie, one of the new nuns assigned to the vestment room, was the unfortunate one who had interrupted her. She backed away, apologizing. Sister Anselma was immediately on her feet, reaching for Sister Stephanie's arm.

"Sister, please forgive me. I had no right to speak to you so harshly."

Sister Stephanie, still red-faced, murmured that it was all right.

"No, it isn't," Sister Anselma insisted. "Would all of you come here for a moment, please?"

When they were gathered round, she said, "We need to make some changes in here. I'm not sure how it happened, but somehow, it seems the work we produce is seen as my work, with all of you assisting me. I'm ashamed to say even I have thought that way at times." Mickey saw Sisters Paula and Catherine exchange knowing glances. Sister Anselma continued. "It can't be like that. The vestments and cloths we produce are St. Bridget's work, all of us contributing anonymously. If something happened to me, this work would go on. I am your teacher, not your boss. As you learn in here, you must also feel free to create. Let's agree that we will speak up if anything we produce is unacceptable as a reflection on the abbey, but otherwise, small differences in how we do things are part of the art."

She hesitated, looking down at her hands. "I will try to be less controlling. Please let me know if I slip back into my old habits."

There was an uncomfortable silence. Looking around, Mickey realized no one there would tell Sister Anselma any such thing. "I get it," she quipped, "old habits, nun humor."

Sister Anselma shook her head and smiled, breaking the tension, and the others laughed. As they all went back to their work, Sister Anselma gave Mickey a look of such tenderness and gratitude that it put a smile on Mickey's face for the remainder of the afternoon.

☩ ☩ ☩

Mickey hurried past the common room and heard the juniors rehearsing for their Christmas concert for the community. Sometimes, it still seemed strange - "and a little sad," she would have admitted - that she wasn't doing those things anymore. Mother Theodora had asked to see her, their first private conversation since before Mickey took her vows.

Mickey knocked impatiently, waiting for, "*Venite.*"

"*Pax tecum*, Mother. Are you all right?"

"*Et cum spiritu tuo.*" Mother Theodora came from behind her desk to greet Mickey with a hug. "I am fine, Mickey. That is not why I sent for you. I know I shouldn't keep calling you Mickey, but somehow, it just suits you, even in a habit," she said with a smile. She joined Mickey, taking the other chair in front of her desk.

Clasping her hands together, Mother Theodora looked at Mickey with a serious expression. "I asked to see you because I have heard from Abigail Morgan. She's asking to re-enter St. Bridget's."

Mickey stared at Mother Theodora, certain this must be some kind of bad joke, only Mother wasn't smiling. She felt as if someone had knocked the wind out of her. "What about Wendy?" she finally asked.

"She claims she and Wendy parted company soon after the affair with the attorney. She seems to be deeply penitent about her role in that matter." Mickey got up and went to the window as Mother Theodora continued. "She realizes that she was partly to blame for causing you a great deal of humiliation and possibly ending your time with us."

"What did you tell her?" Mickey asked from where she stood, looking out at the grounds and trying to control the angry retorts that leapt to her tongue.

"I told her that the legal matter had affected more than you, that it had embroiled the entire community in an atmosphere of distrust and paranoia. I told her that, of course, I would need to speak with you, but that it would also be necessary to ask the entire community for a vote on whether to accept her back here."

"Why here?" Mickey asked in frustration, turning to look at Mother Theodora. "Why doesn't she just start over somewhere else?"

"I asked her that, too. She said if she is to pursue her vocation, she needs to face her mistakes and be accountable for them."

Mickey returned slowly to her chair and stared down at her clasped hands. "How do you feel about this, Mother?"

Mother Theodora sighed. "I am of a mixed mind. On one hand, we, in theory, should be able to forgive if we are convinced that someone's remorse is genuine. In this case, I think that is a great deal to ask," she added sympathetically. "On the other hand, if she does return, I fear Abigail would be a target of excessive scrutiny and unrealistically stringent expectations."

Mickey pulled absently at a hangnail on her thumb, frowning as she considered. "I wish I were a big enough person to say I'm ready to forgive her and move on." She glanced up at Mother Theodora. "May I take a couple of days to think about it?"

Mother Theodora nodded. "Of course. I would like to discuss this with the entire community later this week so I can give Abigail an answer. Do you think you could be ready to participate in a discussion of the matter by, say, Friday? And I want you to be candid, Mickey. Whatever we decide must be based on an honest dialogue."

"I understand."

As the nuns gathered in the common room Friday evening after Compline, Mickey guessed she was the only one who knew why they were meeting. She sat, a queer sick feeling in her gut, while all around her were curious whispers speculating as to why they had been called together. She had suspected all along that Wendy was mostly responsible for the legal blackmail, but that didn't excuse Abigail of her involvement. No matter what had led to their split-up, she couldn't help feeling resentful at this intrusion into her world. "I earned the right to be here!" Mickey wanted to shout, but she knew that wasn't true. "None of us has earned any special favor as far as our Lord is concerned," she could hear any number of the nuns say, and furthermore, she knew if it hadn't been for Mother Theodora's trust and support, she herself would never have been given the chance to test her vocation within these walls.

"Sisters." Mother Theodora's voice immediately quieted the room. "I have called you together, ironically, to discuss another chapter in the same matter we met about the last time I called you together like this. Abigail Morgan, one of the two young women who falsely accused Sister Michele two years ago, has contacted me, asking to be re-admitted to St. Bridget's as a postulant. She deeply regrets her involvement in the previous incident. We do not normally meet like this to discuss a candidate's request for admission, but due to Abigail's history with us, and the fact that it involved the entire community, I told her it would have to be a community-wide decision." She paused for a moment to let her news sink in. Mickey saw several heads turn in her direction, including Sister Anselma's. "We will open the floor for comments or questions."

There was a stunned silence for a few seconds and then Sister Scholastica stood. "I think the entire idea is preposterous," she huffed indignantly. "An abbey is no place for a woman who..." She paused with a quick glance in Mickey's direction and Mickey had the feeling she was weighing her indignation over Abigail's request against her reluctance to champion Mickey in any way. "For a woman of her character."

"I disagree," Sister Cecilia said, standing also. "None of us were saints when we entered, and the last time I looked, none of us are yet." There was some laughter at this. "Isn't the point of religious life to try and overcome the faults and temptations that would pull us away from God - whatever form they take?"

"Mother, do you feel Abigail is truly sorry for what she did?" someone asked from the back of the room.

"I do," Mother Theodora responded.

"I'd like to know what Sister Michele has to say about this," someone else said.

Mickey took a deep breath and stood, her cheeks hot and flushed as all eyes focused on her. "Mother told me of Abigail's request a few days ago," she began. "I've been wrestling with the issue since then, and I confess I've felt more anger than forgiveness, but -" She paused. "When I was nineteen or twenty, I went through a period where I was so extremely self-centered that I did and said a lot of things that were cruel and hurtful to people around me. For a long time afterward, I wished I could undo those things, but as I got older, I realized that, as humiliating and regrettable as it is to think that I left such a trail of hurt feelings and that those people will always remember me like that, the lessons I learned during that period were largely responsible for making me the woman I eventually became. To undo those events would be like," she glanced at Sister Anselma who was watching her closely, "like pulling apart the tapestry of my life. With the perspective of time, I would not now choose to change my past, but I also would not want to be forever judged by who I was then."

She lifted her head and looked at Mother Theodora as she continued. "If we decide to accept Abigail back among us, and I am willing to do so, we have to let her start fresh. As Sister Cecilia said, there are no saints here yet. Abigail has some apologies to make, but... if she's humble enough and brave enough to return here, knowing what we all know, I believe she should be given the chance."

There was not a sound as Mickey sat.

Mother Theodora let the silence stretch on for a minute or two that felt like an eternity. "Are we ready to vote then?"

Later, as the nuns dispersed, Sister Linus waited for Mickey.

Leading her off to one side, she peered up into Mickey's face. "I'm not sure we're not making a mistake," she said, "letting her back in. I think I agree with Sister Scholastica - ha! There's a first." Mickey smiled. "But, I figure you're the only one with any real right to complain, and if you're willing to give her another chance, who are we to stand in her way?"

Sister Anselma approached. "Sister Linus is right," she said. "With one word, you could have ignited the righteous indignation of nearly everyone in that room, and no one would have blamed you if you had. Instead, you gave us an example of forgiveness and generosity of spirit no one could argue with. Sister Scholastica looked as if someone had slapped her."

Sister Linus chuckled. "Something I've wanted to do many times over the years."

Mickey shook her head. "All I did was remember that nearly all of us have done regrettable things, sometimes horrible things, in our youth. No one should be judged by that for the rest of her life." She glanced from one to the other. "And I keep reminding myself I haven't been face to face with Abigail yet. What if I lose my temper and punch her in the face? What will you two think of me then?"

Chapter 34

"Hey, sis," said a male voice behind Mickey as she sat for one of Jennifer's lectures.

"Jamie! What are you doing here? And what are you doing *here*?" she asked in surprise.

He laughed. "It's all right. I got permission from Mother Theodora and drove up with Jen this morning."

"You survived Mom's Christmas visit? How was she with Jennifer?"

"She was... okay. She was civil."

"That's more than she ever was with Alice," Mickey said with a trace of bitterness.

"You just have to ignore some of the things she says, not take them personally," he said sympathetically.

Mickey made a grimace. "You're a better person than I am."

Jamie stood suddenly. "Hello, Mother Theodora," he said, extending a hand. "Thank you again for granting me permission to sit in on this lecture."

"Of course, James," she smiled. "I'll talk to you later."

Jennifer was set to begin, and the lights were dimmed for her slides. This was the first lecture since before Christmas. She was talking today about Chinese weaving and tapestries - "some, like this one," she said, holding up a piece of what looked at first like solid amber silk until she moved it in the light, "were woven for meditation, with only subtle, abstract variations in the weave, while these," she held up a tapestry depicting a battle, "are as intricately woven and embroidered as anything produced in Europe."

An hour later, as the nuns filed out, Mickey and Jamie stayed to help her pack up her materials.

"Uh, Mickey," Jamie said with a quick glance at Jennifer, "could we talk to you for a minute?"

They pulled three chairs aside and sat, Mickey waiting expectantly.

"What is it?" Mickey asked when neither of them seemed able to start.

"We," Jennifer stumbled, "we wanted to talk to you, to tell you that... uh..."

"We'd like to get married," Jamie finished.

"Married?" Mickey sat stunned for several seconds. "Are you asking my permission?" she asked finally.

"Yes, actually," Jamie answered, blushing furiously.

"You are so important to both of us," Jennifer said, reaching for both Mickey's and Jamie's hands. "We want to be sure you're okay with this."

"Of course I'm okay," Mickey said, pulling both of them to her for a hug. "I think it's wonderful!"

"There's one other thing," Jamie added, "We'd like to be married here at St. Bridget's."

"You're kidding!"

"No, we're serious," Jennifer said. "We feel like the abbey, and you, are so much a part of what brought us together. We can't think of any place else that would mean as much to us."

"Do you think Mother Theodora would give her consent?" Jamie asked.

"I think she might," said Mother Theodora from the doorway, making them all jump. She smiled as she came in. "St. Bridget's would be honored to host the wedding of two people who have contributed so much to our community. Did you have a date in mind?"

Jennifer looked over at Jamie. "We thought May might be a good time. The abbey will be done with the Easter Clothing and vow ceremonies, and it seemed like it would be relatively quiet."

"That's not far away. Didn't your sisters need something like a year or more to plan their weddings?" Mickey asked.

Jennifer laughed. "All we want is family and a few close friends. No bridesmaids, no groomsmen, just us and all of you."

Mother joined them as they made tentative plans, and then Jamie and Jennifer took their leave.

"How do you feel about this?" Mother Theodora asked Mickey as they walked down the corridor toward the Chapel.

"I really am delighted for them. I hope they'll be as happy as Alice and I were."

Mother Theodora stopped outside the Chapel and looked at Mickey quizzically. "And are you happy here?"

Mickey thought for a moment before answering. "It's different from the happiness of sharing your life with someone who loves you… but, yes, I am happy here."

"Is this life as satisfying as your old life?"

Mickey paused. "That's difficult to answer. There are many things I miss, but there are a lot of trivial, meaningless things that can consume you in secular life if you let them. This life can be lonely at times, but it feels full. Every moment seems to matter more somehow. Each life has rewards the other can't offer, and each would be a sacrifice to leave. Why do you ask?"

"I was just curious," Mother answered with an expression Mickey couldn't interpret.

By the time Jennifer returned the following week, most of the community had heard about the wedding plans. She received numerous congratulations.

"Where's your engagement ring?" Sister Anselma asked after the lecture as they helped Jennifer fold up the samples she had brought with her.

"Don't have one. I told Jamie I didn't need for him to make a downpayment on me as if I were a car. As far as I'm concerned, buying

Mickey's old furniture and a new washer and dryer is all the declaration I need of his intentions."

"This is going to be an interesting marriage," Mickey laughed.

"I hope it'll be as good as yours was," Jennifer said sincerely.

Mickey blushed deeply, and Sister Anselma looked at her with an amused expression.

"Oh, shit," Jennifer gasped, "I forgot, I mean, I figured, oh shit..." she repeated with her hand over her eyes.

"It's okay, Jen. Sister Anselma knows about Alice," Mickey reassured her.

Jennifer looked with relief from one to the other. "Good." She gathered up her bags. "Mickey, could you give me a hand with this stuff?" Mickey helped Jennifer carry her things to the car. Closing the trunk, Jennifer turned to Mickey and asked, "Does she know?"

Mickey's eyebrows raised in surprise. "Well, yes, I told you inside that she knows about Alice."

"No," Jennifer chided, laying a hand on Mickey's arm. "Does she know that you're in love with her?"

Mickey leaned against the car, suddenly feeling dizzy and nauseous. "How did you know?" she asked weakly.

"I've wondered for a while. Actually, Jamie noticed first. The way you look at her when you're not aware. But just now, when we were inside, you were so embarrassed... she knows, doesn't she?"

Mickey nodded, looking at the ground.

"And she feels the same way." This was a statement, not a question. Mickey nodded again. "Oh, Mick, what are you going to do?"

"I don't know, Jen," she answered quietly. She looked up suddenly. "Are you okay? I mean, I don't want –"

"Mickey," Jennifer interrupted, "this isn't about Alice or me. It's been years. Alice would have wanted you to be happy. I just don't know how you're going to find happiness in this situation."

"Neither do I."

Chapter 35

"Damn," Mickey cussed under her breath. She squinted again at the topographic map she pulled from her fishing vest, trying to identify some feature that would tell her where she was. Four hours ago, she had left her SUV parked alongside a dirt logging road, and started following the stream adjacent to it, but along the way, she had cut across a ridge to get around a section of the stream swollen with run-off from the spring thaw, and now she had no idea which way the logging road was.

Jamie would be getting worried if she wasn't back soon. The most frustrating part was, she knew the reason she'd gotten lost in the first place was because she'd only half been paying attention as she wandered away from the main trail - "you know better. What the hell were you thinking?" she muttered as she looked around for some identifying landmark. "Concentrate." But that was the problem. She'd arrived at Jamie's two days ago, and had found that, without the focus and concentration required by her work, she couldn't keep her mind from drifting to thoughts of Alice. "And Kara," she reminded herself angrily. In all her years of teaching, she had never crossed the line with a student or resident. Her face burned with guilt every time she thought about it.

"Come on, you idiot," she chastised herself, "there's got to be something here."

The deep toll of a bell broke through her self-recrimination. She looked around to figure out which direction the sound was coming from, and began picking her way through the woods toward the bell. It stopped ringing, but she hoped she was still going in the right direction. She had to stop several times as her fly rod got tangled in bushes and undergrowth, but finally, she saw a stone belltower rising from an enclosed cluster of buildings in the next valley.

Curious, she made her way down the ridge toward a drive. *St. Bridget's Abbey*, spelled the bronze letters over the entry. She heard singing. Not sure if she was even permitted on the premises, she walked up the drive to what she guessed was the entrance to the church. She leaned her fly rod against the wall outside, and carefully opened the door, stepping into the dim interior. The singing she'd heard from outside filled the Chapel. She sat in one of the back pews, transfixed as she listened to the nuns singing on the other side of the iron grille. She felt a keen disappointment as the chant faded away several minutes later. For a little while, there had been no empty feeling in her chest - a sensation that had been a constant since Alice's death.

She remained seated as the nuns rose and left the Chapel quietly. She was surprised and a little alarmed when one of them let herself through the grille and came to her. She stood, not sure what to say.

"Hello," said the nun, extending a hand in greeting, "I'm Mother Theodora, Abbess of St. Bridget's."

"I'm Mickey Stewart," Mickey said uncertainly as she shook the offered hand. "I didn't mean to intrude."

"Not at all," Mother Theodora assured her, gesturing with her hand toward the pew and sitting next to Mickey. "We get many visitors, but..." her eyes twinkled with a smile, "I think I can honestly say that no one has come to us in fishing waders before."

Chapter 36

In March, Jennifer brought the first tapestries from the museum. "Wait till you see," she said excitedly as she gently unrolled a large, canvas-wrapped bundle. "They were discovered in a secret room in a Belgian manor. We think they were hidden during World War II to protect the family's treasures from the Nazis. There were all kinds of things squirreled away – dishes, jewels, some furniture. We put in a bid and got everything." Inside the canvas, the tapestries were rolled around a hard cardboard tube. "You can see where they were folded before," she explained, indicating deep creases in the material.

The largest tapestry was very elaborate, depicting a boar hunt. It was marred by soot and several singe marks. "This one dates back to the mid eighteenth century. It was probably hung near some torches or lanterns which burned it," she said. The nuns in the vestment room gathered round for their first glimpse of their new project.

"These," Jennifer said, laying out two smaller tapestries of garden scenes, "were most likely hung in ladies' chambers." She pointed to the damage on the lower portions of each. "It looks like these sustained water damage, so we're guessing they were used as window hangings."

The entire community was invited to come by the vestment room and see them.

"Doesn't altering them decrease the value?" Sister Bernice asked, leaning over for a closer look.

"Generally, yes, that's true," Jennifer acknowledged. "If the damage were minor, we would not do anything except, perhaps, clean them. But these have been so heavily damaged that restoring them is the only way to let people see what they might have been like originally. And believe me, they're still very valuable," she smiled.

Jennifer stayed at Jamie's house for a couple of nights so that she could come to the abbey each day and be on hand to discuss the best approach to undoing the damage to these three tapestries. Mickey and the others continued their work while Jennifer and Sister Anselma matched thread colors and decided how much to alter. At one point, Mickey looked up and, for an instant, was startled at what looked like Alice and Sister Anselma standing side by side.

"Boy, that was weird," she whispered to herself.

They were engrossed in their work when the bell rang for Sext and Sister Anselma stood.

"Where are you going?" Jennifer asked in frustration. "We only had two hours this morning and two this afternoon."

"This will not happen quickly," Sister Anselma reminded her as the other nuns headed for the Chapel. "You're operating on monastic time."

After three days, Jennifer returned to the museum, leaving the restoration work totally in Sister Anselma's hands. It was decided to focus initially on the largest tapestry. Sister Anselma assembled a team of Sister Paula, Sister Madeline and Mickey to help her while Sister Catherine took the lead on their other projects. The restoration team began by creating a very detailed drawing of the pattern and then began to carefully remove the singed portions and begin working in new threads, dyed to match the originals as closely as possible. It was tedious, painstaking work and "I can't take any more of this right now," Sister Anselma said, standing to stretch her back and rub her eyes tiredly. "We're going to have to take breaks," and the others nodded gratefully.

Sister Anselma went to work at her loom where she could lose herself for a while in the hypnotic movements. Mickey, who had been accustomed to spending hours over an OR table attending to tiny details, could usually stay at it for the entire work period, but the others quickly found that, although the restoration work was interesting, they could only stay focused for limited periods of time before they needed to rest their eyes and do something that didn't require as much concentration.

"Sister Michele?" Sister Lucille called from the doorway one day and Mickey turned to her.

"Yes?"

"You have a telephone call."

Mickey quickly followed Sister Lucille to the message room near the abbey's entrance. Mother Theodora had telephone extensions in her office and bedroom in the event of anything urgent, but the only other telephone in the abbey was this one. She could hear a little static as she held the heavy, old-fashioned handset to her ear.

"Hello?"

"Sister Michele," came Greg Allenby's voice. It had taken him a long time to call her that. "I didn't know who else to call," he said, sounding dazed.

"Greg, what's wrong?" Mickey asked.

She could hear him breathing for a few seconds. "My wife and daughter were in a car accident," he finally said. "They're in Rochester..." His voice trailed off.

"Greg," Mickey said firmly, trying to keep him focused, "what's their condition?"

"They're both critical," he answered, starting to cry.

"Are you on your cell phone? Are you driving?" she demanded.

"Yes."

"Then you have got to keep yourself together. You'll be of no use to them if you get in an accident also," she said in her best professor voice.

He cleared his throat. "You're right."

"Do you know any more at this point?"

"No. That's all they would tell me," he said shakily.

"Then get yourself to Rochester safely. Call me when you have an update. And keep praying, Greg. You know you'll have our prayers, too."

"Thanks." He paused for a second. "Tell Mother Theodora I'm cashing in on my account."

The entire community started a round-the-clock prayer vigil. Greg's wife had sustained a severe head injury and several broken bones when a sleepy truck driver drifted into her lane, pushing her over a guardrail on the interstate down into a ravine below, he told Mickey when he called back. Their five-year-old daughter had serious internal injuries and some broken bones as well. Greg continued to call regularly with updates. Mother Theodora spoke with him often, trying to offer reassurance.

"It's so hard, feeling this helpless," Mickey lamented after hanging up with Greg on the fourth day with no real change in his wife's condition.

Mother Theodora looked at her thoughtfully. "Would you be any less helpless in the hospital?"

"No, but you can fool yourself into feeling less helpless because you're doing things," Mickey blushed, sheepishly realizing that Mother Theodora had again caught her underestimating the value of prayer.

"Then do something – pray harder."

✟ ✟ ✟

For Mickey, this Lent – in addition to the worry about Greg and his family – bore the additional burden of Abigail's impending return to the abbey after Easter. "You agreed to this," she kept reminding herself. But no matter how much she tried to reconcile herself to it, she found herself feeling increasingly resentful and bitter.

"What now?" she grumbled in exasperation one morning as the task light over her embroidery station flickered on and off a couple of times before going out.

Sister Catherine glanced up from where she was setting a new piece, winding the warp threads through the tension rollers on her loom. "Check the breaker. I've had to re-set the breaker for my lights at least a dozen times."

"How many times has the electrician been asked to come back and fix this?" Sister Paula asked of no one in particular.

"At least five," Sister Anselma answered absently, her nose inches away from the tapestry. "He says he'll come back out in between his other jobs, but he won't say when."

They all jumped at the simultaneous sounds of Mickey cussing and a loud pop. Sister Anselma looked up to see Mickey at the breaker box shaking her hand in pain. "What happened?" she asked as she went to her.

"It shocked me!" Mickey exclaimed. "I just flipped the breaker off and back on, and it shocked me."

"It also burst the bulb," Sister Stephanie remarked as she inspected the task light which was still smoking, stepping gingerly as she heard glass crunching underfoot.

"Are you okay?" Sister Madeline asked. "Did it burn you?"

"No," Mickey replied sheepishly. "I think it just scared me more than anything."

"Let me help you clean this up," Sister Anselma said, coming over to inspect the embroidery which was now covered by fine shards of glass. As the others returned to their work, Mickey and Sister Anselma shook off the glass they could and began picking the remaining pieces off with tweezers.

"Are you all right?" Sister Anselma asked quietly.

Mickey kept her eyes on her work. "I'm fine," she replied. "Why?"

"Oh, you've just been a little short-tempered," Sister Anselma said with a shrug. "Either my mean nature is rubbing off on you," she said, noting that she'd elicited a small smile from Mickey, "or something is bothering you. Abigail maybe?"

Mickey's shoulders slumped a little. "I'm ashamed of myself."

"For what? Being human?" Sister Anselma looked up at her. "One thing I know is that you will find the grace to deal with this."

Mickey met her gaze, her own eyes filled with doubt. "I hope you're right."

Greg came to the abbey a few days later to give them an update in person. "Melinda has been moved out of the pediatric ICU," he told them happily. "She's doing really well."

"And your wife?" Mother asked.

His smile became a bit more forced. "Well, Judy's brain injury is responding more slowly. But she's stable."

He was so relieved and so happy at their improvement that Mickey couldn't bring herself to ask about his wife's long-term prognosis. After he was gone, Mickey asked Mother Theodora to encourage the nuns to keep praying for as full a recovery as possible.

"It's always the same," she said to Mother Theodora. "At first, it's just 'please let her live.' Then, when you're left with the reality of a body that's alive, but a brain that's not functioning normally, everything changes."

☩☩☩

The week after Easter, the new postulants were to be admitted. "Abigail has asked to see you privately beforehand," Mother told Mickey. "She'll be here on Thursday during Recreation." She reached a hand out to squeeze Mickey's shoulder. "Be gentle."

Startled, Mickey looked at her. "With her?"

"With both of you."

On Thursday, Mickey paused in the foyer, her clammy hands concealed inside her sleeves. Bracing herself, she went to the appointed parlour to find Abigail sitting there. She jumped up immediately when Mickey entered.

"Sit down," Mickey invited, taking one chair as Abigail sat tensely on the edge of another.

"I... I wanted to see you, alone," said Abigail.

"Why?" Mickey asked more calmly than she felt inside.

"I will apologize to you publicly, in front of the whole community, tomorrow, Abigail said in a small voice, "but I wanted to apologize to you privately first."

Mickey gazed searchingly at Abigail, and she realized how much older she looked. Her eyes were the eyes of someone much more mature than her twenty-five years. All the youthful brashness was gone and she seemed – "diminished, somehow," Mickey would realize later.

"We have to let it go," was what Mickey meant to say, but "Why did you do it?" was what came out instead.

She couldn't hide the bitterness in her voice or her eyes as she looked to Abigail for an explanation.

Abigail's face blanched like it had that day she cut her finger. "I don't know," she whispered. "I was so in love, but I know now, it was not a healthy kind of love… I let her control me, control everything." Her chin quivered. "It's not an excuse, I know that. I tried to talk her out of it, but she hated you so much. She said you were jealous of her, of us, and I believed her back then." A blotchy flush crept up her neck to replace the pallor in her cheeks. "I know better than that now, but…" Tears filled her eyes and spilled down her face.

Mickey's jaw tightened at the sight of the tears. "Why did you break up?"

Abigail's eyes closed and more tears leaked out. "She lied to me. She didn't tell me about the other woman, in the convent in Philadelphia. When I found out, it was like I saw her differently than before. She's… she's not the person I thought she was, and… I started to feel horrible… about the lawyer, about leaving St. Bridget's, about turning my back on God and my vocation."

This last was nearly lost in her sobs. She covered her face with her hands and her shoulders shook as she cried. Mickey's face turned to stone as she stared at the floor, letting Abigail cry, coldly refusing to comfort her. She stood abruptly. "I'll see you tomorrow."

Abigail and three other women were presented to the community during Mass the next day. Mickey, who had spent a nearly sleepless night, was so agitated that she actually felt nauseous. "I can't do this," she had breathed in the darkness of her cell. "I don't forgive her. I can't. How can I face her in front of everyone?" She briefly considered going to the infirmary to avoid having to face Abigail again, but knew that she was only putting off the inevitable. Later that day, during lunch, Mother Theodora called for silence.

Abigail came around to where Mickey was sitting and said, loudly enough for all to hear, "Sister Michele, two years ago, I... I was involved in a plan to embarrass you in front of the community." Abigail's face burned that splotchy red, and her voice quavered, but she continued, "I'm very sorry for what I did, and I want to ask you now for your forgiveness."

Mickey briefly fantasized about turning back to her plate with a "No", but Abigail looked so miserable, standing there, humiliated, with everyone watching... Mickey stood up. "I forgive you," she heard herself say, reaching her arms out to embrace Abigail.

"Thank you," Abigail whispered. Mickey could feel her trembling uncontrollably.

As Sister Anselma had predicted, Mickey felt herself unexpectedly swept away in one of those moments of grace – "more like a tsunami," Mickey would have said, as all the anger, bordering on hatred, she had been harboring toward Wendy and Abigail dissolved in that moment, leaving her feeling exposed and vulnerable. To her intense embarrassment, as she held Abigail in her arms, she was on the verge of weeping in front of everyone. "I was not prepared for the power of those three words," she told Mother Theodora afterward. "Few are," Mother responded.

Later, as she took her dishes to the kitchen pass-through, Mickey passed Sister Anselma who stopped her by laying a hand on her arm. In her eyes, Mickey could see that she knew exactly what had happened. Suddenly feeling like she could cry again, Mickey blinked hard and looked away. "Don't be so cocky," she muttered, "I still may punch her."

Chapter 37

The Saturday of the wedding dawned clear and warm – a perfect May day. Sister Teresa had beautifully decorated the Chapel with understated arrangements of flowers from the nuns' garden. Mother Theodora had declared the day a holiday, with no obligations other than the wedding Mass.

Mickey got up at the normal time, and went to help Sister Regina. The cows still had to be milked, holiday or not. *Besides, it'll give me something to do while I wait,* she thought anxiously as she walked through the dewy grass to the barn. Today, she would see Alice's family for the first time since the Christmas after her death. She had written to Edna and Charles several times, but she wasn't sure how awkward it would feel to see them again – in a monastery, in a habit....

She was on hand to greet them all when they arrived. As expected, there were lots of shocked faces and good-natured teasing about the change in Mickey's appearance since they had seen her last. There were several new grandchildren to introduce. It felt like a family reunion. Most of the nuns were delighted to have an opportunity to interact with the babies and children, holding them and keeping them entertained. It was much as Mickey remembered – the Worthington clan truly seemed to enjoy being together. "Are they always like this?" Mother Theodora asked with a smile as she watched them. "Yes," Mickey grinned. "They became my family when Alice and I were together."

"And it was a good thing," she sighed, looking over at Natalie, who, along with Mickey, was the only other guest on Jamie's side, sitting stiffly in a chair in the corner of the common room where everyone had been given permission to gather. Mickey went to sit beside her.

"Mom, have you said hello to Edna and Charles? They always ask about you."

"We spoke," Natalie answered. "They said they were happy to welcome my other child into their family also." She glanced at Mickey out of the corner of her eye. "I... I suppose I ought to apologize for not being more accepting of you... before," she said as if the words were being dragged out of her.

Mickey stared at her, feeling a poison rising in her like bile. "Don't you dare," she breathed. "Don't you dare apologize to me now... after you ignored Alice for twelve years." Natalie looked around, afraid that someone might overhear. "Not once did you acknowledge her when she was alive," Mickey continued, unable to stop now she was started, "and now, because Jamie is getting married, the good son, doing what I couldn't with this Church-sanctioned ritual, you're suddenly feeling magnanimous enough to apologize?"

She stalked away, oblivious to who might have heard. She got as far as the enclosure garden before she was aware of footsteps behind her. It was Jennifer, already changed into her simple long, white dress.

Filled with shame, Mickey sat on Sister Linus' bench under the cherry tree, covering her eyes with her hand. Jennifer followed silently. "Jen, I am so sorry," Mickey said softly. "Of all the days for me to have a meltdown..."

"I've been expecting it," Jennifer said, slipping her arm through Mickey's.

Mickey looked up at her. "What do you mean?"

"Mickey, I know you love Jamie and me, and that you're happy for us, but you'd have to be a saint not to feel at least a little angry and hurt and jealous about all this fuss when you and Alice loved each other so much with no real - I don't know what word to use... validation, I guess, of your relationship."

"We didn't need that," Mickey protested.

Jennifer looked at her tenderly. "It's a lot easier to not need it when it's a choice to have it or not. I know you could have been married now, but it wasn't an option then."

They sat silently for a bit. "Do you realize," Jennifer continued, looking out at the garden, "that you and Alice are the model Jamie and I hold up for what we want our marriage to be like? Not my parents, or yours," she said pointedly, and Mickey couldn't help but smile, "or any of my other brothers or sisters. The two people in our lives who could never be married gave us the best example of how to build a life together as completely equal partners. You're why I'm not being walked down the aisle by Dad - I'm not a piece of property being transferred from one man to another. You're why I don't need an engagement ring or a huge wedding or gifts. All I need is Jamie and the things we learned from you and Alice."

Mickey's throat was tight as she hugged Jennifer and said, "My brother had better treat you like the treasure you are."

Jennifer kissed her on the cheek and said with absolute faith, "He will."

The wedding was simple and beautiful. Sister Margaret had chosen works by Bach and Handel for the Mass, and she had rehearsed a small, chosen choir to sing harmony as the community sang the melody. The doors of the grille had been opened so that the wedding guests could come to the altar for Communion.

After the Mass, in lieu of receiving gifts - "you've already given us so much" - Jamie and Jennifer gave the abbey a set of the twelve Stations of the Cross. Jennifer had found them in a church in France that was being remodeled, and Jamie had restored and then bronzed them so that they could be placed around the enclosure as places of meditation.

An extra table had been set up in the refectory so that everyone could eat together. Edna and Charles had arranged to have the meal catered so that no one had to cook or clean up. Sister Cecilia kept looking anxiously at her kitchen every time one of the servers came through.

Late in the afternoon, when everyone was finally gone, the abbey settled once more into its quiet routine. Jamie and Jennifer, who were scheduled to leave for England the next day on their honeymoon, were hosting as many people as Jamie's little house would accommodate, and the others were staying at inns in Millvale. "How romantic," Jennifer's family had teased at hearing that they would be spending their wedding night in a house full of relatives, but "it's romantic enough for us," Jamie and Jennifer insisted.

Mickey restlessly waited until nearly midnight before she went to the orchard. It was a night very like the last May night she'd come out here - a warm breeze was blowing, stirring Mickey's soul with a yearning, an emptiness so deep she felt she would never be whole.

Mickey hadn't been out there long when she heard, "I knew you'd be here." Sister Anselma sat beside her on the hill where they'd talked before.

"And I knew you would come." Mickey looked at her in the moonlight, feeling reckless and breathless at how near she was.

"It was a beautiful ceremony."

Mickey smiled. "Yes, it was. It was the only wedding I can truly say I enjoyed."

"You know, it occurred to me, Jamie is your twin, and you said Jennifer looks almost exactly like Alice - if they have children, they'll be as close as you and Alice could have come to having children of your own."

"I know. Alice and I thought about it. We even asked Jamie once if he'd be a sperm donor - artificially," she added quickly, "I not that open-minded."

Sister Anselma laughed, something she did more frequently now, Mickey realized as she listened.

"But when we really thought it through, my schedule was so erratic, and Alice worked with children all day - it just didn't seem fair to have her come home to be a single parent most of the time."

She looked at Sister Anselma. "Does it bother you to talk about Alice so much?"

Sister Anselma smiled and shook her head. "I feel like she's a part of our history together."

Giving in to her feeling of recklessness, Mickey reached over and took Sister Anselma's hand. Their fingers intertwined, then pulled apart, only to rejoin in a sensuous dance. For a long time, there was only this forbidden contact, setting every nerve ending in Mickey's body on fire. "Do we have a history together?" she asked softly. "What about a future?"

Sister Anselma looked at her, and whispered, "Do you want a future with me?"

Mickey didn't answer directly. "Most of the time I'm okay as we are, but sometimes..." Gently she pulled Sister Anselma to her, haltingly, slowly. Their lips touched in a kiss, feather-light, exquisitely soft. Abruptly, they both pulled away.

"We can't," Mickey groaned.

"I know," Sister Anselma murmured. "And this is not the right time to be making decisions about anything – with the wedding, and all the emotions it stirred up."

"You're right," Mickey agreed. "I'm sorry."

"I know I should be," Sister Anselma said, "but I'm not."

☨ ☨ ☨

Life settled back into a more normal rhythm over the next few weeks. Most of the weaned calves were sold, and Mr. Henderson took a few cows at a time to neighboring farms to "visit the boys." The abbey always gave the farmers a few calves in payment for the bulls' services. The hay was growing tall. The enclosure was bursting with color as dogwood, crabapple and cherry trees all bloomed at once. The bronze Stations of the Cross were positioned around the periphery of the enclosure and small flower beds were planted at each one: hydrangeas, roses, azaleas and lilies. The plants were chosen so that there would be something flowering almost continuously through October. Life seemed idyllic. *I should have known better,* Mickey thought later when she looked back.

The restoration of the largest tapestry was coming along. The smaller tapestries, ironically, were proving to be harder to work on as nearly the entire bottom third of each had to be carefully pulled out after the design was painstakingly drawn. Then new threads had to be worked in without looking like new threads. They were using a tea dye to age the newer threads.

Jamie and Jennifer were splitting their time between his house outside Millvale and her apartment in New York. They came out to St. Bridget's when they got back from England to visit and allow Jennifer an opportunity to check on the tapestries. "I think we'll have the largest one done by Christmas," Sister Anselma told her as she brought Jennifer over to where Mickey was carefully working in new threads in one section depicting a hunter on a horse. Mickey felt a tingle run through her body as Sister Anselma's shoulder grazed hers.

"Excuse me," Mickey murmured, forcing herself to move away.

Ever since the wedding, Mickey had felt acutely aware of Sister Anselma's every movement. She had no idea if Sister Anselma was feeling the same way or not, but Mickey was also feeling the strain of constant physical desires. It wasn't just sexual – "although that part is pretty damn strong," she would have said – it was the longing to hold her, touch her, kiss her. She couldn't believe how much she missed just being touched.

Mickey coped with her excess energy by continuing to help Sister Regina with as many farm tasks as she could. She worked her required hours in the vestment room, but she spent her Recreation time weeding the vegetables, cleaning the barn, helping with maintenance on St. Jude – anything physical to take her mind off Sister Anselma. She'd had to reassure Sister Regina that this really was how she wanted to use Recreation. And she prayed. When it didn't seem to help, she prayed harder as Mother Theodora had suggested. But she had a guilty feeling that maybe the reason prayer wasn't helping was because part of her didn't really want these feelings to go away. "I like being in love again," she finally admitted, but only to herself – having someone to dream about as she drifted off to sleep at night, someone to think about while she did all this extra work in an effort not to think, only to realize that she was humming and smiling as she labored.

And yet, "Being true to your vows is much more than just living them superficially," Sister Josephine had told the novices more times than Mickey could count. "It requires a whole-hearted commitment to the spirit of your vows, to the call that brought you here in the first place."

"Where is that call?" Mickey asked Mickey. "Have you forgotten it?"

"No, I haven't," she replied. "It's still there. It's just..."

"Just what?"

There was no answer to that.

"Off to the farm again?"

Mickey snapped to at the sound of Father Andrew's voice. He was coming from the direction of the orchard, carrying a small sack.

Mickey nodded. "Getting ready for the first hay cutting. We need to make sure the trailer is ready to go." She nodded toward the sack. "Hunting?"

"Kind of," he grinned. "Sour apples. I like them early before they're ripe." He fell in step with her. "You've been going out to the farm almost every day. I thought you had been rotated elsewhere."

"I was, but I like the farm work," she said. "Makes me feel more productive than whiling away my Recreation time doing nothing."

"Hmmm," he intoned. "And it has nothing to do with... say, needing to tire yourself out or distract yourself from anything?"

Startled, Mickey halted. "Why would you say that?"

He looked at her. "You forget. You're talking to an expert at denial and running from personal demons. I recognize the signs." He smiled when Mickey just stared at the ground. "It's okay. We all go through this."

"Do we?" but she didn't say it aloud. Instead, she said, "I really should go. Sister Regina is waiting for me."

"All right," he said, turning back toward the abbey. "But if you ever need to talk..."

Mickey didn't look back as she descended the knoll separating the abbey from the farm buildings. "Damn," she muttered as she walked. If others were noticing... *maybe I should request to be transferred from the vestment room,* she worried as she neared the barn.

"Oh, there you are," Sister Regina said. She already had the rear-end of the trailer up on jackstands, both wheels off so they could get to the rear axle. "We need to re-pack these bearings with grease," she said, holding a can out to Mickey. "Roll up your sleeves. This is a messy job."

An hour later, the wheels were back on and the trailer pronounced fit to go. "Thank you so much," said Sister Regina gratefully. "This would have taken me an extra day or two on my own."

"You're welcome," Mickey said, using a rag to wipe her hands clean of excess grease.

The bell rang for None. "We'd better get back," Sister Regina said, pulling a tarp over the trailer.

Together, they walked back to the abbey. They topped the knoll and their eyes were caught by movement below. Black smoke was billowing into the sky from the roof of the vestment wing.

"Call the fire department," Mickey shouted over her shoulder as she took off in a sprint down the hill. She went to the back entrance to the vestment room and wrenched the door open to find the interior already filled with thick, black, choking smoke. She could see flames against the far wall, running vertically up to the roof timbers where more flames blazed. The wiring. She took as deep a breath as she could and ran to the circuit box on the wall. Sparks kept bursting from the overhead lights, raining down and starting smaller fires below as cloth and fibers were set ablaze. When she got to the electrical box, some of the breakers had actually melted. She grabbed a wooden shuttle from the nearest loom, and used it to whack the main breaker to the off position. Coughing and choking, she made her way back to the door and slammed it shut to find Mother Theodora and several others hurrying over.

"Has the fire department been called?" she gasped.

"Yes," said Mother. "What happened?"

"I don't know," Mickey answered, still coughing. "I think that bad wiring may have started it. Is the rest of the abbey safe?"

"For now," said Mother. They were both thinking the same thing – it would take the engines over fifty minutes to get out to the abbey.

Suddenly, Sister Catherine ran up to them, crying, "Where's Sister Anselma?"

"What do you mean, where is she?" Mother Theodora demanded.

"When she heard about the fire, she said she was going to get the tapestries. She never came back up the stairs. I thought she must have come out this entrance."

"God, no," Mickey groaned. She pulled loose from Mother Theodora's restraining grasp and ran back in, ignoring the shouts behind her. She immediately realized she couldn't breathe and wouldn't last more than a minute or two. Dropping to her hands and knees, she scrambled to the dye sink where she tore her veil off, soaked it in water and wrapped it over her face to better filter her air. Staying close to the floor, she crawled to the work table where the large tapestry had been. She couldn't see more than about two feet in front of her. Squinting through tears caused by the acrid smoke, her hands felt Sister Anselma's limp body before her eyes recognized the black form.

Mickey transferred her wet veil to Sister Anselma, quickly wrapping it around her head. As she grabbed Sister Anselma under the armpits and began dragging her toward the door, she could hear timbers groaning and cracking overhead. Showers of embers rained down through the smoke and hit them, smoldering and burning through the cloth of their habits. Mickey felt like she was drowning – each breath she took seared her lungs. "Help me," she prayed desperately, tugging, stumbling backwards, hoping to God she was going in the right direction. Everything looked different as she fought to keep from panicking. Where was the door? The smoke was so thick she couldn't see any hint of daylight, but she should be near it by now. An enormous crack sounded overhead. Mickey heaved with the last of her strength, throwing Sister Anselma's body as hard as she could, just before a heavy burning timber crushed her to the floor. The last thing she remembered was black skirts coming out of the smoke, pulling Sister Anselma away.

Chapter 38

"Why won't you tell me where you're going?" Mickey looked over at Susan as she brought her suitcase out to the living room.

"I did tell you," Mickey reminded her. "I'm going to visit Jamie."

"Uh huh." Susan clearly didn't believe her. "You've visited Jamie more this year than in all the years I've known you put together."

It was true. Mickey had been going up to New York for weekend visits every month or two. What no one, not even Jamie, knew was that she was going to visit with Mother Theodora. Jamie thought she was off fishing. Mickey just wasn't ready to tell anyone else about the abbey yet - she wasn't even sure what all these visits were leading to.

"And what about all the other strange things you've been doing lately? Going back to that church? Selling the house on the bay? Getting rid of Alice's car?"

"I don't need two cars," Mickey explained patiently, "and Jennifer's had broken down for the fourth time. The church, I go to mainly for Christopher - he always made us feel welcome. As for the house, I haven't been there since - in months. Why hang onto it?"

She had been slowly selling off extra things. Without Alice to go to the bay with, she had felt absolutely no desire to be there. It actually felt good to be "lightening up her life," as she had come to think of it. She had asked her financial advisor to invest the money from Alice's life insurance and the sale of the bay house for her.

"Are you seeing someone?" Susan was like a terrier.

Mickey laughed. "I promise you, if I ever start seeing someone, I'll let you know." She looked into her friend's knowing eyes. "I've just needed to get away - away from this house, away from work. These visits have been good for me."

She was telling the truth. Mother Theodora was very skilled at drawing her out of herself while seeming to be carrying on casual conversation. Slowly, Mickey had discovered - "no, re-discovered," Mother Theodora would have pointed out to her - that what seemed to be missing from her life, now that Alice was gone, was some kind of spiritual anchor, something to ground her.

"I don't think I could talk about this to my brother or my friends," Mickey had said to Mother at their last visit. "Not yet."

Mother shrugged. "If you did, they would all try to help, and in the clamor, it might be hard to hear the whispers."

"Whispers?"

Mother Theodora smiled. "Sometimes God knocks us off our feet with something dramatic, but, in my experience, more often, he simply whispers and waits for us to be quiet enough to hear."

Chapter 39

"How are her vitals?"
"We need to change the dressing."
"Mother, may I have permission to stay?"
Snatches of conversation filtered through the haze. Accompanying them were other sounds: beeps, rhythmic wheezing, bed rails being raised and lowered. Vaguely, Mickey felt like she could come up out of the haze if she wanted to, like choosing to wake up from a dream, but it was comfortable in the haze, and so she chose to sink back in whenever she got too near the surface.

Some of the voices were familiar – Jamie, Mother Theodora. She thought she heard Alice's voice sometimes. "Take me with you, I'm ready," she tried to say to her.

Then, in her ear, was Sister Anselma's voice. "Michele, please don't leave me." She didn't respond at first... not until that plea was repeated, and then reluctantly, she broke through the surface into harsh light.

Blinking, her eyes had difficulty focusing. Sister Anselma's face was the first thing she recognized. She tried to speak but couldn't. Sister Anselma saw the fear in her eyes and said in a calming voice, "Don't try to talk. You're hooked up to a ventilator." Slowly, Mickey realized the ventilator tube was inserted into her trachea with a feeding tube running through her nose as she lay on her side.

Sister Anselma smoothed Mickey's hair. "I can't believe you're awake," she murmured, her eyes filling with tears. "I was so afraid you wouldn't wake up."

Mickey tried to lift her hand, but couldn't. Again, her eyes widened in fear. Sister Anselma held her hand, saying, "They have you restrained. They were afraid you might panic when you woke and start pulling at tubes."

Mickey saw then that her hands were tied to the bedrail by soft, padded straps. She mouthed words, hoping Sister Anselma would be able to read her lips.

"How long?" Sister Anselma interpreted. "Six days. Do you remember what happened?"

Mickey frowned. "Some," she mouthed.

"You came to rescue me from the fire. When you got me near the door, a roof timber fell on you. Some of the sisters carried me out while others got the timber off you and pulled you free." Her voice cracked as she tried to continue. "Your spine was... your spine was broken in several places and you have serious burns on your back." She was crying so hard she had to stop. Frustrated by her own inability to communicate, all Mickey could do was squeeze her hand. When Sister Anselma could speak again, she said, "You've had two surgeries to fuse your spine, although the doctors argued over whether to do it now because of your burns and the risk of infection."

Mickey pointed to the ventilator tube.

"Your lungs and airways were damaged by the heat and smoke."

For a moment, the only sound was the asthmatic pumping of the ventilator. Mickey mouthed more words.

"How am I?" Sister Anselma's eyes filled with tears again as she laid a gentle hand on Mickey's cheek. "I'm all right. I was in the hospital for a couple of days for smoke inhalation and a few small burns, but I'm fine. You saved my life," she finished in a whisper in between ventilator gasps.

Just then a nurse saw that Mickey was awake and called for a doctor.

"Would you wait outside?" said a sixtyish man in a white coat as he entered the room accompanied by three younger men, also in white coats, in addition to the nurse. Pushing their way to the bed, the oldest man said in an overloud voice, "I'm Dr. Atwood. You've been injured in a fire and we have you on a breathing machine."

"She's a physician," Sister Anselma said from behind him.

"What?" he asked, irritated that she was still there.

"She's a physician," she repeated. "You don't have to speak to her as if she were an imbecile. And you don't have to shout at her," she added with clear disdain.

The medical students smirked at each other as Dr. Atwood responded with a lame, "Oh." Raising his bushy eyebrows, he said, "Well then, Doctor, you suffered severe respiratory damage from the fire as well as comminuted fractures of T10 to L5. We've done two procedures to internally fixate the fractures and stabilize your spine. We don't yet know the extent of the neurological damage."

He moved to the foot of the bed where Mickey could no longer see him. "Can you move your toes?" She wiggled them. "Did you hear me? Move your toes," he repeated. Angrily, she wiggled them again.

"Well," he said, more to the students than to her, "it's very early. We'll have to wait and see."

The rhythmic wheeze of the ventilator was the only sound in the room as they left. Sister Anselma came back to the bed and gently wiped away the tear rolling from the corner of Mickey's eye.

� ☦ ☦

"I'm sorry to interrupt, but we need to do a dressing change," said a pleasant-looking nurse as she brought a tray of supplies into Mickey's hospital room.

Jamie and Jennifer had come for a visit, along with Mother Theodora, Sister Mary David and Sister Anselma who had been making the trip to Syracuse from the abbey two or three times a week for the past month.

"May I assist?" Sister Mary David offered. "I'm the abbey's infirmarian, and I may be doing these dressing changes when Sister Michele returns to St. Bridget's."

"We'll wait outside," Mother Theodora said.

"When did they start the grafts?" Jamie asked as they walked down the hall to the solarium.

"Just last week," Mother replied. "They wanted to start them earlier, but the doctors had to be sure she wasn't going to need any further surgeries on her spine first. It's a slow process. Apparently, they can only do small areas at a time, as new skin grows back to take for the grafts. Harvesting, they call it."

Jennifer shuddered. "That sounds painful."

Jamie paced in the solarium. "Why is the ventilator back in her room?" he asked, pausing to look worriedly back down the corridor toward Mickey's room. "She was being taken off it the last time we were here."

"They did take her off," Sister Anselma said, "but then she got pneumonia and had to be put back on for several days. She just got off it two days ago."

A half-hour later, Sister Mary David found them in the solarium.

"Are you all right?" Jennifer asked when she saw Sister Mary David's ashen face.

Sister Mary David sat, raising a trembling hand to her mouth.

"Sister?" Mother Theodora put a hand on her shoulder.

"Forgive me, Mother," Sister Mary David said in a hushed voice. "I wasn't prepared... I've never seen anything like that." She looked up at Mother Theodora, a horrified expression on her face. "Her entire back, her buttocks, her thighs... what isn't burned is raw and bloody from taking skin for the grafts. The pain of removing the gauze to clean the wounds..." She squeezed her eyes tightly shut, as if shutting out the image. "I don't think I can do that to her two or three times a day..."

"Does she feel it?" Jamie asked, his face pale also. "Aren't they giving her pain medication?"

"Yes, but... I don't think any pain medication is strong enough to... The only sound she made was one whimper..." Sister Mary David reached for a tissue to dry her eyes.

"She hasn't said a thing," Jennifer whispered.

Sister Anselma stood abruptly and left the solarium. Jennifer followed.

"Let's go for a walk," Jennifer suggested when she caught up. Sister Anselma didn't say anything as Jennifer slipped an arm through hers and steered her out to the landscaped grounds.

Outside, they found an empty bench in the shade of a large oak tree. They sat in silence for a while. Jennifer watched a bumblebee lazily drifting from flower to flower in a nearby flower bed before finally asking, "How are you doing?"

"What possible difference could that make after what we just heard?" Sister Anselma sat stiffly, staring at her hands which were clenched in her lap.

"It matters a great deal." Jennifer watched Sister Anselma's face carefully as she continued. "Sister Anselma, I don't know if Mickey told you, but I confronted her a while ago about her feelings for you. She admitted that she's in love with you, and… she said you love her, too."

Sister Anselma's only reaction was to clench her hands more tightly.

"I think I have a better understanding now of how careful and guarded you've both been," Jennifer continued, choosing her words with care, "so I would imagine you have had no one you can talk to. We've all been worried to death about Mickey, but what about you?"

Sister Anselma's stiff, upright posture crumpled and her head bowed.

"I feel so incredibly guilty," she admitted in a voice that was barely a whisper.

"Don't you think that's a natural reaction?" Jennifer asked. "But this is Mickey."

"What do you mean?"

Jennifer turned to look at her. "I've known Mickey most of my life, and I know how devoted she was to my sister," she said. "If she loves you as much as she loved Alice, she would rather have died trying to get you out than to have left you in that fire alone." Jennifer paused for a moment, then said, "Forgive my prying, but I can't help but feel a little protective of her. Do you love her that much in return?"

For the first time, Sister Anselma looked Jennifer in the eye. "Yes."

"Enough to leave St. Bridget's to be with her?"

"It's not that simple," Sister Anselma struggled to explain. "Both of us felt called to monastic life for reasons that we would each need to address first. That is bigger than this - for both of us. I won't be responsible for pulling her away from her vocation, and I know she feels the same. And then there is the issue of my vows - vows I intended to abide by for the rest of my life. If I can be swayed to ask for dispensation from those now, after all these years, how can I trust myself to make a lifetime commitment to Michele?"

Jennifer digested these words. "Is there no one in the abbey who can help you work through this? Mother Theodora seems like a very open-minded woman."

Sister Anselma closed her eyes and sighed. "Perhaps it is time to be honest with Mother. If she hadn't guessed about us before, she certainly has by now."

Chapter 40

"Dr. Stewart, we're going to offer a settlement."

Mickey stared at the insurance representative, not sure she had heard correctly. "You can't be serious," she said in disbelief.

"This is not an admission of guilt," he protested.

"The hell it isn't!" she retorted angrily. She leaned forward and stared at him. "I stayed by that kid's bed for five days, operated three times. What did they want - a miracle?"

For the first time, this balding fortyish-looking man looked directly at her through his thick glasses, an empathetic expression on his face. "Probably."

This had been a horrible trauma case. An eleven-year-old hit by a car while riding his bicycle. The internal damage had been extensive: heart, lungs, viscera.

"You've got to see how this would look to a jury. You've got a dead child, grieving parents. It's not likely they would see you as a bad doctor, but they won't want to send these parents away with nothing. It's just the way these cases work. They don't see the money as coming from you, and they sure don't care about making an insurance company pay. It's a matter of minimizing costs."

An hour later, Mickey was walking aimlessly. In nearly a decade of medical practice, this was her first malpractice case. Rationally, she knew it was just the way the system worked, but she had poured her heart and soul into that child's care. "I don't care what the damned lawyers say, this is personal," she fumed.

Suddenly she stopped. This was it. She had been going through the necessary steps to apply for entrance into St. Bridget's: a detailed physical, copies of her certificates of birth and baptism, letters from Christopher corroborating Mickey's status as a member of his church – he'd been very happy for her when she finally told him about St. Bridget's. But still she had been holding back on making the actual decision, waiting for... what? God's whisper? The one Mother had talked about? "Please give me some kind of sign," Mickey had prayed so many times over recent months, "something to let me know where you want me to be." This lawsuit definitely felt like the thing she had been waiting for – a shout more than a whisper. It was time to go.

Chapter 41

After nearly ten weeks in the hospital, Mickey was considered stable enough to be transferred to a rehab center to continue her wound care and begin the process of trying to walk again. Her spinal cord had been compressed by the timber that fell on her, but it hadn't been severed. As a result, the damage to the nerves was intermittent – "Medically, it's considered an incomplete spinal cord injury," she had explained to Jamie. "Some of the nerves are normal, some are partially firing and some aren't working at all. The trick will be to strengthen the muscles that still receive innervation and see if enough of them are working to hold me up."

For Mickey, the process was complicated by her lungs and her burns. She required daily sessions with a nebulizer for her respiratory system, but still her ability to breathe deeply was impaired, which left her gasping during her strenuous exercise sessions. Her burns and grafts required ongoing care for application of dressings and creams, and inspections of any areas that might begin breaking down or become infected. To control scarring, she had to be helped into a skin-tight garment that fit like a corset to maintain constant pressure over the grafts.

The day after Mickey was transferred to the rehab center, Jennifer brought a collection of sweatpants, t-shirts and underwear plus a pair of tennis shoes.

"Keep going," Jennifer smiled as Mickey pulled the clothes out of the bag in her lap.

In the bottom of the bag was a portable CD player with earphones and a small collection of CDs. "Gregorian chants?" Mickey grinned as she leafed through the discs.

"I thought you might be feeling homesick for St. Bridget's," Jennifer said. "And for Sister Anselma?"

"Oh, Jen," Mickey sighed, slumping back against her wheelchair, "I miss... everything so much. That's the hardest part, harder than any of the physical things."

Jennifer's expression became serious. "Mickey, I've always admired you, and even," her face turned a deep red, "had a bit of a crush on you, but... everything before pales in comparison to the awe I feel at how brave you've been through all of this."

Mickey grimaced and shook her head. "Not so brave. I have never felt so close to panic in my life as I did in that fire and again when I first woke up – with the ventilator and the restraints, unable to move or breathe on my own. It was terrifying to be so completely helpless when the ventilator would clog up and the alarm would go off – it was like everyone was moving in slow motion before I could breathe again. And when the grafts started," she shuddered, closing her eyes, "the only thing that kept me from screaming was reminding myself over and over why I did it."

"I told her that," Jennifer said softly. "She feels so guilty, Mickey. I told her you would rather have died with her than to have left her in there." Jennifer bit her lip. "To tell you the truth, I feel kind of guilty myself."

"You? Why?" Mickey asked in surprise.

"None of this would have happened if I hadn't interfered. The whole idea of the abbey doing the restorations was my idea. That prompted the re-wiring, and all my big talk about how valuable the tapestries were..."

"Jen, that's crazy. You opened a whole new world for the community. Nothing that happened is your fault." A thought occurred to her. "How are the tapestries anyway?"

"Believe it or not, they didn't burn," Jennifer said in bewilderment. "They're almost the only things in there that didn't. Mostly smoke and water damage. We're having them cleaned, and they should be fine."

"Hey, while you're here, would you help me with one more thing?" Mickey reached over to a table and held up a set of electric clippers. "Shave my head?"

Jennifer looked shocked. "What? No, Mickey."

"Look, I haven't had to worry about anything as meaningless as my hair for a long time. It's amazing how functional a habit is in freeing you from having to even think about what to wear or what to do with your hair, but I can't wear a veil here, and I can't pay for haircuts. I don't want to have to worry about this. Shaving my head is the simplest solution." Mickey held out the clippers. "I will if you don't, but it'll look a lot better if you do it."

A few days later, when Mother Theodora and Sister Anselma arrived for a visit, neither of them hid her surprise very well.

"Well, it's simple, it's cool and it solves a problem," Mickey defended herself with a grin, running her hand over the soft, red bristles.

"How are you adapting to being here?" Mother Theodora asked. "It seems a fine facility."

"It is. The therapy is strenuous and tiring," Mickey admitted. "I can't believe how weak I've become. But the noise: telephones, televisions, visitors – I miss the quiet of the abbey. Jennifer brought me these," she said, showing them the CDs.

"I need to speak with the billing department about the abbey's insurance," Mother Theodora said. "May I suggest some outdoor air might be good for you? It's a beautiful day."

Mickey transferred herself to the wheelchair next to her bed, and insisted on wheeling herself as she and Sister Anselma went outside. The rehab center had beautifully landscaped grounds and gardens with wheelchair paths criss-crossing the property. They made their way to a remote corner where they could talk without being overheard. Mickey angled her wheelchair so that she could face Sister Anselma as she took a seat on a bench.

"How are you really?" Sister Anselma asked.

"Okay," Mickey answered vaguely. "I feel better physically now, but it's harder being away from St. Bridget's, and away from you," she added. Looking intently at Sister Anselma, she asked, "What about you?"

Sister Anselma's grey eyes focused on her for several seconds before she responded, "Not so well. When you were in the hospital, when we didn't know if you were going to live…" She had to stop for a second, diverting her gaze to a nearby clump of azaleas. Mickey waited. "Nothing felt the same. Even after you were past the worst danger, there was no joy, no sense of purpose in being at the abbey without you." She looked down at the ground. "I hope you will understand, but I've been talking with Mother."

"It was time to be honest with her," Mickey admitted. "What was her reaction?"

"She guessed of course," Sister Anselma said with a wan smile. "She's been very supportive, trying to help me discern what it is that keeps me at St. Bridget's versus the things that might prompt me to leave."

"Have you reached any conclusions?" Mickey asked, her mouth dry and her heart suddenly hammering.

"The only conclusion I've reached is that we both have to decide independently whether we are still being called to religious life or not. I've decided to go on a retreat to help me figure that out. I'll be leaving this week for St. Anne's near Buffalo."

"When will I see you again?" Mickey knew full well that the fact that she asked that question indicated where her heart truly was.

"I don't know," Sister Anselma said softly.

Tears sprang to Mickey's eyes before she could stop them. Sister Anselma shifted on the bench so that she could pull Mickey to her. Resting her cheek against the soft fuzz on Mickey's head, she whispered, "I love you as I have never loved anyone, but we can't go on as we have been."

Mickey was still crying when Sister Anselma, steeling herself, left to go find Mother Theodora. All the physical pain, all the surgeries, all the fear of what the future would bring in her compromised condition felt as nothing compared to the despair and anguish she felt at the thought that, when she finally got back to St. Bridget's, Sister Anselma might not be there to come home to.

╬ ╬ ╬

A cold November breeze stirred the few remaining leaves on the trees as Mickey waited. Ignoring the curious stares of other patients and visitors, she self-consciously rubbed the sleeve of her new habit. Sitting beside her chair in the lobby was a small suitcase, crutches and a lightweight wheelchair. Father Andrew was due any minute to bring her at long last back to the abbey.

He had taken to coming to the rehab center every Saturday for the past three months to visit, occasionally with Mother or Sister Mary David or Jessica in tow. He brought her Communion each week and, together, they wandered the grounds in good weather, Mickey taking her first tentative steps without a therapist at her side while he pushed the wheelchair until she dropped into it, exhausted. Week by week, her endurance had improved – "let's try to make it to that next tree up there," he would encourage as she clopped along clumsily with her crutches. He brought her updates on the abbey and the nuns, but never any mention of Sister Anselma – "and I can't bring myself to ask," Mickey said to herself nearly every Saturday evening after he was gone.

One week, he surprised her by bringing Sister Linus. "She insisted," he said with a bemused smile.

"So how are you?" Sister Linus asked, her sharp eyes probing as she looked Mickey over, taking in every detail.

"I'm doing all right," Mickey said noncommittally.

"No, you're not," said Sister Linus. "And you shouldn't be. Not yet. Not after what you've been through. But you will get through this."

Mickey's eyes hardened. She was getting sick and tired of everyone telling her it would all be fine, everything would be okay – her therapists, her doctor, even the rehab center's psychologist. "How the hell would you know?" she wanted to rage because no one knew, no one could know....

Sister Linus looked at her as if she could read her mind and was almost daring her to say aloud what she was thinking. When Mickey remained stubbornly silent, Sister Linus held out her hand. "I wanted to give you this." She dropped a delicate white mother-of-pearl rosary into Mickey's palm. "It was given to me on my first Communion."

Mickey stared open-mouthed at the polished beads puddled in her hand. "I can't accept this," she protested.

"Of course you can," Sister Linus snapped. "It's helped me through some rough times. I expect it can help you now."

"Thank you," Mickey said humbly.

The next week, when Father Andrew came out, he looked haggard. "What's wrong?" Mickey asked.

"I have some news," he said reluctantly, as if he dreaded being the bearer of any more bad tidings. "Sister Linus passed away this week."

"What?" Mickey asked, startled, reaching into the pocket of her sweatpants where the rosary was safely tucked, with her constantly since Sister Linus had given it to her.

He shook his head. "Her heart just gave out. She... she must have known."

Mickey stared at the iridescent white beads, the engraving on the silver cross nearly worn off from decades of Sister Linus's fingers praying with it – "... *ora pro nobis peccatoribus, nunc, et in hora mortis nostrae...*" – but her eyes remained dry. There had been no more tears since that day with Sister Anselma. No tears, no happiness, no anything....

When the abbey's stationwagon pulled up to the front door, Mickey slipped the cuffs of her crutches around her forearms inside her sleeves and stood. To her surprise, it was Mother Theodora who got out of the car. Mother smiled when she entered and saw Mickey waiting for her, and came over to embrace her tightly.

"I wasn't expecting you," Mickey said.

"I thought this would give us some uninterrupted time to talk," Mother Theodora responded. "Is this everything?" She wheeled the chair and suitcase to the tailgate of the stationwagon and placed them in the back. Mickey noticed gratefully that Mother allowed her to make her own way to the passenger seat, not rushing to open doors for her.

"You look thin," Mother Theodora commented as they got underway. "Did they not feed you?"

"They fed me as much as I wanted," Mickey replied. "I guess it's all the exercise."

"You seem to be walking better than the last time I saw you. How do you feel?"

Mickey glanced at her. "It's like walking through mud. Each leg feels as if it weighs a hundred pounds."

"And your wounds?"

Mickey looked out the car window and didn't answer immediately.

"The physical ones, to start with," Mother Theodora clarified.

"They're healing," Mickey answered. "The scar tissue tears easily and the grafted skin doesn't have any functional oil or sweat glands, so it still requires care. But because of the location…" Her hand clenched tightly on the door handle of the car.

"You have to depend on others to do it for you," Mother Theodora finished for her. "Yes, Sister Mary David explained that to me. And what about your spiritual wounds?" When Mickey didn't respond, she said, "I don't know if he said anything to you, but your doctor called me several times. He was concerned that you seemed to be depressed. He had noticed that you didn't laugh or smile or interact with the staff or other patients, and wondered if that was typical of you. I assured him it was not, but felt it was understandable, given the circumstances. He was afraid your mental state might impede your physical progress. Father Andrew confirmed that you were quieter than normal, but he felt you were making good progress from what he could see during his visits with you."

Mickey looked back out the car window and stated in a flat voice, "There wasn't anything to laugh or smile at. I was there to accomplish specific physical goals, and I think I worked toward those to the best of my ability."

"Have you been able to pray?"

"I've done nothing but pray." Mickey replied, biting the words off angrily.

There was silence for a few minutes.

"Do you have any regrets?" Mother Theodora asked at last.

"About going back in to get her?" Their first reference to Sister Anselma. Mickey had wondered how it would happen. "Never." She looked over at Mother Theodora. "Does she think that I blame her, or that I wish I hadn't done it?"

"Have the two of you communicated?"

Mickey shook her head. "Not since that day in August when you both came to see me."

"She loves you very much," Mother Theodora said gently. "That is something I doubted I would ever say about Sister Anselma."

Mickey felt her face get hot and said in a gentler voice, "And I love her. But you already know that. I should have seen it coming, should have been able to prevent it, but by the time I realized what was happening, it was too late. We tried to keep our feelings under control, and for the most part were able to. But the day of the fire, I would have done anything to get her out." She looked down at her hands. "We never meant to deceive you. And I want you to know that nothing... inappropriate happened."

"I never questioned that, Mickey. You are both too honorable for that. Do you remember my telling you on the day you entered that, in the monastery, the true you would be magnified?" Mickey nodded. "When you entered, your grief for Alice was like a shade pulled down over your soul. As you healed, the light of your presence began to shine more brightly, and it was inevitable that others would be drawn to you. Like Sister Helen. I thought it ironic that the one most strongly drawn to you was Sister Anselma. In an effort to protect herself from anyone else ever hurting her as her mother had, she erected walls no one had ever been able to breach. Until you. As stoic and self-possessed as she has always been, she was completely unprepared for you."

A few miles rolled by in silence.

"What now?" Mickey finally asked.

"What indeed?" Mother Theodora sighed. She glanced over at Mickey. "If you have not communicated with Sister Anselma since August, you probably don't know that when she came back from her retreat, she requested a dispensation from her vows. She has left St. Bridget's," she finished quietly.

Mickey closed her eyes. All during the months at rehab, all the weeks she hadn't been able to bring herself to ask Father Andrew, she had clung to the hope that Sister Anselma would be there when she got back, not wanting to hear anything to the contrary. When she could talk, she asked, "Do you know where she is?"

"In San Francisco, dealing with her family. She writes often. I've kept her up to date on your progress." Mother glanced over. "She has wanted to write you –"

"She won't." Blinking back tears as she looked out the window again, Mickey said in a strangled voice, "She told me in August we each had to decide separately where our hearts lay."

"And where does your heart lie?"

Mickey's throat burned. "I've agonized over this. I love her, and I love the abbey." She looked over at Mother Theodora. "And I love and revere you." She squeezed her thighs with her hands. "This is probably as good as it's going to get. In the back of the car is a wheelchair that I have to use when I get too fatigued. I'm forty-one now, and as I get older, I'll probably have to rely on it more and more. My cell is on the third floor. The vestment room is fifteen steps down. The whole abbey is laid out in such a way that I don't know how fully I can contribute." She paused. "But it's safe there. I'm ashamed to admit it, but the thought of facing the outside world again like this is terrifying," she confessed. "All these conflicting thoughts and emotions have been battling within me for months." She hesitated again. "It hasn't felt like a decision I could really make without having been at St. Bridget's for the past six months."

"I agree that you need to be back at the abbey for a while before you make that decision," Mother Theodora concurred. "But I would have asked you to come back for at least a few months anyway, Mickey. St. Bridget's needs you. There has been a pall hanging over us ever since the fire. The physical damage to the building felt devastating to many, but more important has been your absence. The gravity of your injuries, followed by such a lengthy convalescence, has left many of us feeling almost as if there had been a death. And with Sister Anselma's departure… We need you, at least for a while, so we can heal. As for your feelings of doubt about being able to contribute, if you decided to stay, I assure you, you would continue to be an integral member of the community. We have actually had an elevator installed as part of the rebuilding process – you are not the only one having difficulty with the stairs," she smiled.

"If I decided to stay, how would you feel? Knowing about Sister Anselma and me…"

"Unlike my predecessors, I do not feel that situations like this automatically require expulsion or exile to another abbey. Your situation is already altered by the fact that Sister Anselma has chosen to leave." She paused for a few seconds as she negotiated a sharp curve in the road. "My viewpoint, I'm sure, is influenced by the fact that I lived through a similar situation. Except that I have never revealed it to anyone – until now."

Humbled by Mother Theodora's trust in telling her that, Mickey waited.

"For now, I would ask that you return to work in the vestment room for one work period a day, and for the other, I would like for you to go to Sister Mary David to have your wounds tended and work on your exercises."

They were getting near the abbey by now. "I don't know how to thank you, Mother, for your understanding and guidance through all this," Mickey murmured.

Mother Theodora reached over to squeeze Mickey's arm. "You can thank me best by promising me that you will be as open as you can to where God leads you, even if it is not where you would wish to go."

Chapter 42

Mickey sat in her choir stall – a new one at the end so that she didn't have to clumsily try to climb over others to get to her old stall in the middle of the row. If she'd wondered how she would know which was hers, she needn't have worried – the stall was layered with cards of welcome, as her cell had been. When Sister Lucille had greeted her the day she arrived home with Mother, she carried Mickey's suitcase and led her to her cell where nearly her entire bed was festooned with notes and homemade cards all welcoming her back. In a vase on her desk sat a small arrangement of holly leaves with a cluster of brilliant red berries.

"You were missed, my dear," Sister Lucille said with a smile, leaving her to rest.

There, on her pillow, was the one note she had been certain would be there.

My dear Michele,
There are no words to express my gratitude for your act of unbelievable selflessness and bravery.
Much has happened that I will tell you about someday, but for now, the most immediate thing is that I have decided to leave St. Bridget's. I think you know me well enough to know what a heartwrenching decision that was for me.

My biggest regret in making that decision while you were gone is that I will not be here to welcome you home. However, it will allow you the opportunity to make your own decisions without unnecessary distractions.

Please know how fervently I pray for you, and that I will see you one day soon.

Lauren

Mickey had read it over and over, and then, placed it in her Bible with Alice's letter.

Moving about the abbey, Mickey had quickly realized how noisy and conspicuous she was, with her crutches and awkward gait. She'd made a habit of trying to get to the Chapel early, and, as she sat now, a bell sounded above her and soon the Chapel was filled with the quiet shuffling of feet and the creaking of wood as the nuns filed in for Vespers. Once the organ sounded and the voices rose, the music of the Office enfolded her, transported her, as it had since the first day she had wandered in in her fishing waders, to a place where her pain was "not gone, but lessened," she would have said. Closing her eyes, she tried to absorb and memorize every scent – incense, flowers, the lemon wax Sister Fiona preferred for polishing the walnut choir stalls. But when she opened her eyes, it was a harsh jolt to see Sister Anselma's empty choir stall.

When she arrived at the vestment room for the first time, her heart was pounding, "and not from the exertion of walking." There was still a very faint smell of smoke, but visually, it looked almost as if nothing had happened. "I'm not sure what I expected," she would say to Jamie much later. "I knew it would be repaired, but...", "But it felt like nothing had happened, like they moved on without you," he guessed. New timbers criss-crossed the vaulted space high above, supporting the new roof; the stone walls had been scrubbed clean and new windows had been installed. She was standing at the top of the stairs when the others saw her. Awkwardly, she descended the wooden steps and made her way toward them.

"Welcome back," Sister Caroline said solemnly, giving Mickey a hug. As the most senior nun there, with the longest tenure working under Sister Anselma's guidance, she had taken charge of the vestment room and the work they were doing. Sister Paula, Sister Madeline and the others also came over to greet her.

"Where would you like me to work?" Mickey asked.

"Would you mind helping at this embroidery station?" Sister Catherine asked. "We're trying to get caught up on the work that was lost in the fire. We don't know when or if we'll resume any restoration work for the museum."

Mickey suspected Mother Theodora had already explained Mickey's physical limitations to Sister Catherine as this embroidery station was one where she could remain seated. To her surprise, there was a small basket with an arrangement of pine greens and dried baby's breath sitting on a table next to her embroidery frame. Shrugging, she studied the pattern marked on the silk, and threaded a needle.

In the corner, untouched, was Sister Anselma's loom. The half-finished vestment on it was pockmarked with burns and water stains. It sat there, almost a presence in the room, catching Mickey's eye at unexpected moments when she glanced up or spoke to someone in passing. It was a couple of weeks before Mickey could bring herself to approach it, arriving early one day so that she was the only one in the vestment room. As she neared the loom, she could see the tonal pattern that Sister Anselma had been weaving into the cobalt-blue silk. She swallowed the lump in her throat as she stared at the only visible reminder of the fire - *well, almost the only,* she thought as she turned and clomped back to her work station.

☊ ☊ ☊

Mickey lay naked on her stomach, covered only by a sheet, as Sister Mary David came in and secured the curtain around the bed. She pulled aside the sheet and carefully removed the gauze still covering the few open, bleeding areas on Mickey's back, tugging gently to loosen it where it was stuck. The first time Mickey had come to the infirmary for this treatment, she'd been able to feel the trembling of Sister Mary David's hands.

"Sister, what is it?" Mickey had asked, struggling to sit, wrapping the sheet around herself. "Is this too difficult, too disturbing? We could ask Mother –"

"No, Sister Michele, it's not that!" Sister Mary David insisted. She looked as if she were ready to cry. "It's just... every time I remember that day in the hospital, and everything you've endured, I'm so ashamed. I cannot begin to fathom how much pain you were in, but the fortitude you showed... and I was too weak and cowardly to watch and help. I'm so afraid of hurting you."

To Sister Mary David's alarm, Mickey laughed – an angry, bitter laugh. "You can't hurt me, not compared to –" She pressed her fingers to her eyes, and said more gently, "Believe me, I understand. I hated getting burn cases when I was practicing. As for my so-called bravery, I absolutely dreaded those sessions. The medications couldn't touch the pain. It was often more than I could take. I just prayed for release, and on the good days, I passed out." She laid a reassuring hand on Sister Mary David's arm. "I promise I will tell you if I need you to do anything differently, okay?"

Thus reassured, Sister Mary David had quickly became more comfortable doing Mickey's burn care, cleaning the dried blood and applying an emollient to keep the scarred skin supple and soft. Sister Mary David finished this step now, saying, "All done. I'll be back in a moment."

Mickey quickly dressed in t-shirt and sweatpants for their exercise session. This, too, had been difficult at first, as Sister Mary David gave only tentative resistance to work Mickey's legs. "Harder," Mickey had urged until Sister Mary David learned how to judge Mickey's strength and how much to push.

"Come on, you wimp," Sister Mary David said now. "You can do better than that."

Mickey's face was scrunched and red with her effort. "It's a shame," she panted, "that you're not as timid about this as you were about looking at my butt."

Sister Mary David was so shocked and surprised that she dropped Mickey's leg. In a few seconds, both of them were laughing so hard they had tears running down their faces. Neither of them was aware that, on the other side of the curtain, Mother Theodora had come into the infirmary to see how the exercise sessions were going. She held a finger to her lips when Sister Helen saw her and smiled as she listened to this exchange, and then realized that the sounds had changed. Mickey was crying. Mother could hear Sister Mary David murmuring to her. Silently, Mother Theodora left the infirmary.

☩ ☩ ☩

Mickey sat at her work station, hemostats in hand as she worked a needle in and out of the cloth. As she worked, she could smell the faint scent of the dried roses sitting at her work station. The mysterious floral arrangements had continued to appear every few days in her cell or the vestment room. No one seemed to know who was bringing them. The juniors had just performed their Christmas concert for the community. Unconsciously, Mickey began humming the *Coventry Carol*. She was so absorbed in the detailed stitches she was making that she didn't see Sister Paula and Sister Stephanie exchange smiles as they heard her.

"It's nice to see you laugh and smile again," Sister Helen said one afternoon. She was cleaning the infirmary windows as Mickey was finishing her exercise session with Sister Mary David, telling a story about how she broke her arm when she was a child, climbing onto the garage roof to retrieve Jamie's Frisbee.

Mickey glanced up at her in surprise. "Have I been that bad?"

"Yes," Sister Mary David interjected. "You have. But I don't think many could have come through everything you have without being a little bitter. It is nice to see you melting - like Sister Anselma did during your retreat," she added with a cryptic smile.

"Good God," Mickey said to herself, "does the whole damned community know?"

Christmas was three days away when Mickey got one of her best presents in the mail. Danielle Wilson sent a Christmas card with her senior picture in it. She was graduating a year late because of all the time she'd spent in the hospital, but her cancer was completely gone, something her doctors couldn't explain, "but I can," Danielle wrote. She had already been accepted at the University of Maryland as a pre-med student. Mickey shared the news with the entire community.

As if in answer to a Christmas prayer, the abbey was covered in about eight inches of snow on December 24th. Although it was beautiful, Mickey stood looking out the cloister windows, realizing it would be nearly impossible for her to walk through it for more than a few feet. Over the past few weeks, it had become clear that her part of the abbey had become very small, limited mainly to the enclosure garden. Sometimes at night, she dreamed about running through the orchard, but when she woke, she knew the only way she would ever get back out to the orchard or the farm would be in her wheelchair.

On her way to the vestment room that morning, Mickey saw the juniors outside shoveling and sweeping the walks of the enclosure to create clear paths. A thought occurred to her, and before she could talk herself out of it, she went outside, dropped her crutches and eased herself backward into the snow. Waving her arms and legs, she made a snow angel. The juniors all looked at each other for a moment, clearly not sure what to think. Then Abigail dropped into the snow also. In a few seconds, the enclosure was peppered with supine figures waving arms and legs, making snow angels and giggling like kids. Faces appeared in windows, laughing and pointing. Sister Josephine came rushing outside, an expression of consternation on her face. The juniors all sat up, waiting to be reprimanded.

Looking around, she spied Mickey. "I knew it was you!" she scolded.

"I've wanted to do this since I was a postulant," Mickey grinned. "Here, help me up."

Sister Josephine reached for her hand and yelped as Mickey pulled her down into the cold, dry snow. "C'mon, you know you want to!" Mickey laughed, falling back into the snow again.

All the juniors watched Sister Josephine a little apprehensively and were shocked when she fell backward into the snow and made her own snow angel. Laughing again, several of them moved to fresh snow to make more angels.

"How appropriate."

Everyone stopped and sat up. Mother Theodora was standing there, looking very dignified with her hands tucked inside her sleeves.

"The last bit of decorating for Christmas, I presume?" she asked, looking around, her eyebrows raised.

"Wouldn't you like to make one of your own, Mother?" Mickey asked, looking at her mischievously as if daring her.

Mother Theodora's eyes twinkled. "I believe I will."

And to everyone's surprise, she walked out to an undisturbed patch of snow and, lowering herself to the ground a little more carefully than the youngsters, made a snow angel. When she sat up, Mickey and the juniors cheered and clapped.

"Now," Mother said, "if some of you will be kind enough to help an old lady to her feet, I'm going to change into a dry habit."

They all got to their feet and brushed each other's backsides off. The juniors resumed their shoveling, still laughing and chattering.

Mother Theodora slipped an arm through Mickey's as Mickey got her crutches back in position. Walking together toward the cloister, Mother said, "Thank you, Mickey."

"For what?" Mickey asked. "Getting you all wet and snowy?"

Mother Theodora smiled. "For reminding us that religious life, all life, is meant to be lived joyfully. This is why we needed you back among us for a while." She stopped and looked at Mickey as they entered the corridor. "I pray this is a very blessed Christmas for you," she said seriously. Then she kissed Mickey on the cheek and left her.

Mickey kept playing Mother's words through her head. She wasn't sure exactly when or how, but she had decided. As strongly as she had felt pulled to the monastery to re-establish a deeper spiritual life and learn to how to live with things she had no control over, she now felt she was being pulled back to the outside world. This would be her last Christmas as a nun at St. Bridget's. She had a feeling Mother Theodora knew it as well.

Chapter 43

"You understand that I will not be able to return to take care of repairs or other issues," Mickey said to Carol Barnes, the realtor who would be acting as property manager for the rental of Mickey's house in Baltimore. "I've put together a list of the purchase dates of all appliances and mechanical systems in the house. Some are still under warranty. And here is a list of all the tradesmen who have worked here and know the systems."

Carol blinked. "I wish all my clients were this organized," she smiled, flipping through the notebook Mickey handed her. "And you're going where, again?"

Mickey's acceptance into St. Bridget's had been finalized two months ago. There were so many loose ends to tie up: the house, her leave of absence from the practice and the university, finances. She'd forwarded five thousand dollars to St. Bridget's to cover her rent during her postulant and novice years. "No one is turned away if they don't have the money," Sister Bernice had written, "but it helps tremendously to offset our expenses." Mickey was also keeping active checking and savings accounts to cover any expenses related to the house. She'd considered selling it, but, "I just can't. Not yet."

"I'll be on temporary assignment in central New York," she said to Carol. "Here's the address. I've given your name and telephone number to the housing office at Hopkins. You should have no trouble limiting renters to medical residents or doctors coming for fellowship training. My furniture will all be in storage by next week."

Telling people about this decision had been harder than she expected. Almost universally, the reaction - after the initial shock - had been that she was wasting her medical training and that she was doing this as a reaction to Alice's death. Jamie, of course, had understood.

"I didn't think you were really coming up here just to see me, or to go fishing," he teased. He put his arm around her shoulders as they walked. "I'm happy for you, Mick. You have seemed more at peace with yourself the past few months than you have since you lost Alice."

The most shocking reaction had been Susan's. "This is a joke, right?" she asked at first. As it sank in that Mickey was serious, the anger had surfaced. "You know, I've understood you going to the church here because that priest is so open-minded, but to go to a goddamned convent, putting yourself under the authority of one of the most repressive churches on the planet - it's turning your back on everything we've fought for all these years - wait..." She stood there, breathing hard. "Don't even tell me that you're going to make some apology for being gay, or that you're claiming to be cured like those asshole fundamentalists preach."

Mickey was taken aback - she hadn't anticipated such a vehement reaction. "No! I'm not denying who I am," she protested. "I think I can pursue this call without getting all tied up in the politics of the Church."

Susan shook her head. "I don't even know you anymore." And she walked out. Mickey hadn't heard from her since.

Now, the house looked bare. Mickey had packed a trunk with her favorite books, and the items on the abbey's list. Most of her clothing had been given away; she'd packed one suitcase of clothes to keep in case she left the abbey, "or they kick me out," she joked. All of their photo albums had been packed away - she wasn't prepared to let those go yet. Most of the knick-knack things had gone to the thrift store. It was amazing to her how much stuff she owned that she had to figure out what to do with: kitchen stuff, bathroom stuff, all the stuff in the attic. It seemed never-ending. Finally, though, all that was left was to get the furniture into storage.

"This nun thing better work out," she grumbled to Jamie over the phone. "If it doesn't, it's going to cost me a fortune to replace all this crap."

Chapter 44

"Maybe snow angels weren't such a good idea," Mickey groaned as she got up the day after Christmas. She had a bad cold and had hardly slept at all due to her congestion and sneezing.

Christmas had arrived with an unexpected visit from Natalie who came with Jamie and Jennifer to the abbey. It was the first time she and Mickey had seen or talked to one another since the wedding.

"That is not our mother," Mickey insisted as she blew her nose, watching Natalie interacting with Mother Theodora. "She hugged me and wished me a Merry Christmas. She's a pod person."

"Jamie said the same thing," Jennifer giggled.

"What happened to her?" Mickey asked, eyeing Jamie suspiciously.

"The day of the wedding, while you and Jen were talking, she came to me all weepy and complaining about how cruel and unfair you'd been when she was making an effort."

"And?" Mickey asked menacingly, knowing how manipulative their mother could be.

"And I told her she had deserved everything you said and more for a long time."

Mickey looked at him with her mouth open.

"That's what Mom looked like," he grinned. "I told her she'd elevated being miserable to an art form, and that if she wanted to be happy, she had to learn to make the choice to be happy – it wouldn't just bite her in the butt."

"Wow." It was all Mickey could think of to say.

"What about Sister Anselma?" Jennifer changed the subject. "Have you heard from her?"

Mickey shook her head. "I haven't expected to. She's leaving me alone to decide where I should be without any distractions from her."

"And have you decided?"

Mickey looked from one to the other. "I've decided to leave," she said quietly.

Jennifer glanced at Jamie before asking, "Are you sure?"

Mickey looked at Jamie. "Do you remember how many times you asked me that when I told you I was entering? It hasn't been easy." She looked around at all the familiar figures. "You know, when I first came here, everyone looked the same to me – just a habit. But now, I can identify almost everyone, just watching posture and movements. It will break my heart to leave. I don't know how Sister – Lauren did it after almost twenty years. It's going to take a while to get used to the change in names."

"I asked her about that once," Jennifer recalled, "because all of you kept your given names as your religious names. I assumed she wasn't always Anselma."

Mickey was curious since that was something she had wondered about. "What did she say?"

"Only that when she entered, she didn't want any connection to her past. She wanted to start fresh, so she requested a new name."

"What about her?" Jamie asked. "After you leave I mean?"

Mickey shrugged. "I don't know. She's also dealing with a lot in regard to her family. I know she and Mother communicate. I'm just holding tight to the belief that she'll find me."

Now, fighting this cold, it was all Mickey could do to drag herself around on her crutches.

"This is not a good idea today." Sister Mary David had completed the care for Mickey's burns and was trying to take her through her exercises. "You're weak and you can't breathe. You need rest more than you need to exercise."

"I think you're right," Mickey agreed. "I'm going to go to my cell and sleep."

"Do you want to use the wheelchair?" Sister Mary David asked as Mickey struggled to her feet. Mickey glowered at her. "All right," Sister Mary David laughed. "Be stubborn. I'll let Mother know where you are."

Mickey limped to her cell and fell asleep almost immediately. She wasn't sure what time it was when she awakened in the dark, barely able to breathe. She struggled to a sitting position, but still could take only shallow breaths. There was no way she could walk. She reached for a crutch and banged on the wall she shared with Jessica. When there was no response, she banged again. A moment later, there was a soft knock and the door opened.

"Michele?" Jessica whispered.

"On the bed," Mickey gasped. Jessica came to her. "Pneumonia - need to get to hospital."

Jessica quickly woke Sister Kathleen on the other side of her own cell. She sent her to get Sister Mary David and Mother Theodora. "And tell Sister Mary David to bring the wheelchair. Hurry!"

Coming back into Mickey's cell, she turned on the lamp and calmly helped Mickey put on a robe. "It's too snowy for slippers," she said matter-of-factly as she brought shoes and socks and put them on Mickey's feet. Then she sat next to Mickey on the bed, supporting her with an arm around her shoulders. She could hear the rattle as Mickey tried to breathe. "We'll get you to the hospital as quickly as we can."

By the time they pulled into the ER, Mickey's lips and fingernails were blue and she was unresponsive. The ER physician was able to get a ventilator tube down her throat while IV lines were started. Mother Theodora, Sister Mary David and Jessica prayed in the waiting room.

"She's beginning to respond," the doctor told them a couple of hours later. "The secretions in her lungs are much thicker than normal, and only a portion of her lungs are functioning anyway. She cannot treat colds and flu casually anymore."

Sister Mary David looked stricken. "It's my fault. I checked on her last night, but she was sleeping so soundly I didn't check more closely. I should have been more observant."

"You had no way of knowing," the doctor said kindly. "This is her first cold season since her injuries." He turned to Mother Theodora. "She will have to stay in the hospital for a few days."

Mickey was able to be removed from the ventilator after two days, but had to stay on oxygen and nebulizer treatments for a few more days. Greg Allenby came by to see her. He hadn't been to the abbey in weeks.

"Greg, what is it?" she asked in alarm when she saw him. He looked terrible, with dark circles under his eyes.

He ran a hand over his face. "It's Judy. I've been racking my brain to figure out what I can do to keep the practice going and be able to spend more time with her. She still needs therapy three or four times a week, and I've only been able to find part-time help at home."

Mickey bit her lip. "Have you considered bringing in another doctor part-time?"

He threw up his hands. "Who? I don't know anyone who only wants part-time work."

"Well, actually you do," she said. "You have to keep this quiet. I still need to talk to Mother, but... I'll be leaving St. Bridget's soon, and I was wondering what this crippled, ex-nun might do for work."

He looked at her earnestly. "Maybe go into practice with a former student?"

"Are you sure?"

"This could be the answer to both our prayers if you're really interested."

Mickey laughed and immediately choked, triggering a fit of coughing. "Yes," she gasped when she could breathe again. "I'm interested."

His expression brightened. "I'll come see you at St. Bridget's soon and we can start working out some details."

When Mickey did return to the abbey, Sister Mary David anxiously asked her to stay in the infirmary for a couple of days. "At least spend a few nights here," she pleaded, "or I am going to camp outside your cell." Mickey acquiesced when Sister Mary David said seriously, "I would never forgive myself if anything happened again during the night."

Mickey requested a private meeting with Mother Theodora, and told her of her decision to leave as well as Greg's proposed partnership.

"I hope you don't think I just used the abbey as an escape for a while," Mickey said.

"Not at all," Mother Theodora assured her. "As a matter of fact, I think your time with us has allowed you to find an important part of yourself. And I know we benefited from your presence."

Mickey blushed as she said, "Well, I don't know about that, but things around here should be calmer without me. I seem to create more drama than everyone else combined."

Mother Theodora smiled. "Life has definitely been more interesting with you around," she mused.

"I've found the perfect house!" Jamie told Mickey excitedly. "Okay, maybe not perfect in every way – it's going to need a ground floor addition for your bedroom and bath, and some ramps may have to be added, but," he grinned, obviously very pleased with himself, "it's perfect in other ways. You just have to trust me."

"Okay," she laughed, "I trust you."

"Good," he said, pulling out some rolled-up blueprints and spreading them out on the table in the parlour, "because I've already asked an architect to draw up some plans for the changes. Look these over and see if there's anything you want added or moved or whatever."

The plans depicted a two-story house, about eighteen hundred square feet. The three existing bedrooms and bathroom were on the second floor. A ground floor addition had been drawn up to include a bedroom large enough to allow wheelchair access all around the bed. The bathroom was also completely wheelchair accessible, with a shower but no tub, and a free-standing sink attached to the wall on a hydraulic slide that would allow it to be raised and lowered to accommodate someone standing or sitting. There were separate built-in closets and cupboards for storage. A laundry room and garage were also included, built with no stairs or thresholds to obstruct a wheelchair.

"This looks wonderful," Mickey murmured, looking the plans over.

"Jen has been working hard on this, trying to think of everything you might need eventually," Jamie said. "The kitchen will be redesigned so the appliances will all be in locations where you can easily get to them sitting or standing."

Mickey sat back and looked at him fondly. "Thank you both so much for all of your help with this."

"No problem" he smiled. "It's been kind of fun. We're actually thinking about changes we want to make to our house – like a nursery."

It took Mickey a moment to process what he'd said. Her mouth dropped open. "You're kidding!"

His face couldn't have smiled any bigger. "About eight weeks, we think. She goes to the doctor next week. I can't believe it," he said, running his hands through his hair. "Life is really going to change."

"You and Jen will be wonderful parents," Mickey said, laying a hand on his arm. "And I can't wait to be an aunt!"

She pulled out some papers. "Here is the new account my funds have been transferred to," she said, handing him a statement. "I've named you as co-holder of the account so you can access it to pay anything that may come due over the next month."

Jamie's eyes popped as he looked at the statement. "Wow," he breathed, "I've never seen so much money in one place – that I could get to," he added with a sly grin.

"Don't get too excited," she warned him. "It's the money from my old practice, both houses and Alice's life insurance. And it's all been invested for most of the last six years, but I'm probably uninsurable now, and I'll be buying into a share of Greg's practice. And this," she indicated the blueprints, "will make a dent also. A few more incidents like my trip to the hospital at Christmas, and this could go faster than you think."

He looked at her sympathetically. "I guess you're right. Do you want your old furniture back?"

She laughed. "No, I'll start fresh." She frowned at the blueprints. "But I do have a few extras I'd like to add to the house."

☦ ☦ ☦

"I don't know how to say good-bye," Mickey said with tears in her eyes. She was in Mother Theodora's office, wearing khakis and a sweater for the first time in five years.

"Then don't," Mother Theodora admonished. "Simply tell me that you'll see me soon."

"I will," Mickey promised. "I'll call and arrange a time with Sister Mary David in the next two or three weeks to begin medical visits."

"It's very generous of you to offer your services to the community, Mickey. I wish you would allow us to pay you something. I still feel we owe you some compensation for your injuries."

"That's not necessary," Mickey insisted. "This arrangement allows me to feel that I'm giving something back to the abbey for all it's given me, and selfishly, still allows me to feel a connection to this place. But please emphasize that my feelings will not be hurt at all if any of the sisters prefers to see another doctor, or Greg. As I'm sure you can attest, it isn't always easy having a personal relationship with your doctor."

Mother Theodora smiled. "Personally, I count myself blessed to have such a dear friend as my physician."

Mickey's throat suddenly felt too tight for a response. The telephone on Mother's desk rang. She answered and then said as she hung up, "James is here."

Mickey stood with her crutches, and then braced herself on one so that she could embrace Mother Theodora as she came around her desk.

"I will miss you very much," Mickey managed to say.

"And I you, Mickey."

Together, they walked down the corridor to the entry where Jamie already had Mickey's trunk and wheelchair loaded into the back of the SUV. Mickey was not prepared for most of the community to be assembled to see her off. She had said private farewells to many of them over the past few weeks: to Sisters Catherine, Paula and Madeline who had taught her so much; to Sister Stephen who confided that Mickey had been one of the best Latin students she had ever taught; to Sister Regina who had provided perhaps the best example of how to balance prayer and work; to Abigail from whom she elicited a promise not to betray Mother Theodora's trust. To Sister Mary David, "There aren't words enough to thank you for all you've done for me," she had said, with a promise to call soon.

One person she'd known wouldn't be here was Father Andrew. She'd gone to see him immediately after her meeting with Mother. He must have heard the click of her crutches coming up the walk to his house, because he opened the door as she raised a hand to knock.

He stepped back to let her in, and went to clear a place at the dining table for her.

"Raymond is a scholar, but a messy one," he said apologetically, as he shoved books and papers aside and pulled out a chair.

"I wanted to talk to you," Mickey huffed, winded by the walk to the chaplain's house.

"You're leaving," Father Andrew said, taking an adjacent chair. "What is there to talk about?"

Mickey looked at him in surprise. "Did Mother –?" she began, wondering how he could have heard so quickly.

He shook his head. "No. You told me." He looked into her eyes. "In bits and pieces, over the past three or four months. I could hear it in the things you said, and in the things you didn't say."

Mickey digested this. "Are you disappointed?" she asked.

"In you?" He shook his head and leaned toward her. "No. Never in you." He paused and absent-mindedly folded over a corner of one of the papers lying on the table. "And just in case you're wondering if you've made any kind of difference around here... you have." He cleared his throat and sat back. "I'm sober because of you."

"Because I threatened to turn you in, you mean," she reminded him.

"Same difference," he insisted. "You had the guts - the fortitude, the sisters would say - to act on what you knew was right. You've done that again and again while you've been here." He waved his hand. "I know you'll continue to do it out there."

Mickey nodded and gathered her crutches to stand. Father Andrew walked her to the door.

"Just so you know," he said, "I'm not good at good-byes."

Mickey looked up at him, swallowing all the words lying unspoken between them. She nodded again and turned to make her clumsy way back to the abbey.

Many of the nuns, the ones who didn't know Mickey well, made an effort to wish her well over her last days. Perhaps the greatest surprise had been Sister Scholastica, who had stopped Mickey in a corridor a few days before she was scheduled to leave. "Sister," she began hesitantly. She didn't seem to know where to look - she couldn't meet Mickey's gaze, nor could she seem to bring herself to look down at Mickey's crutches. She averted her eyes to the adjacent wall as she struggled with what she wanted to say. "I wanted to speak with you... I wanted to tell you that the abbey will be the poorer for your absence." Her jaw worked back and forth as she raised her gaze as high as Mickey's cheek, but still not quite to her eyes. "I wish you well in your new venture," she added before turning to walk away.

She stopped abruptly as Mickey said gently, "I hope you know that none of this is your fault."

Sister Scholastica stood rigidly, her veil obscuring her face from view.

"And thank you for the flowers."

With a barely perceptible nod of her head, Sister Scholastica continued on her way.

Lastly had been Jessica, to whom Mickey had said, "You have

been my rock. I wouldn't have lasted this long without you." And Jessica, in her typical, unflappable way, had replied, "You'll be nearby, and will be out here weekly, so we'll still have each other to talk to. This is not good-bye."

Mickey's eyes ran now along the line of figures, all dressed alike in black and white, yet so different. And so familiar. Not trusting herself to say anything more, she walked out the door and climbed awkwardly into the SUV. Jamie placed her crutches in the back seat. As he pulled out of St. Bridget's drive onto the main road, Jamie said, "I would've bet I'd be coming back to get you after five weeks, not five years."

Mickey nodded and blinked back tears as she looked back through the trees at the abbey. "I would have made the same bet."

Jamie drove her to the new house, her first actual view of the clapboard and stone bungalow in the midst of renovations. The drive and yard were dotted with mature trees and construction trucks. Workers were framing the roof of the addition which extended from the rear of the house. They looked over toward the old detached garage where heat and air-conditioning were being installed.

"The new garage will come directly into the utility room over there," Jamie said, walking her in that direction.

Mickey looked around and sighed. "It's beautiful. You were right –"

"Wait," Jamie cut her off, glancing at his watch and holding up a finger.

Mickey stood there, not sure what they were waiting for when she heard it. The bell for None was ringing from somewhere behind the house.

She looked unbelievingly at Jamie who beamed. "Your property butts up against the abbey's farm land," he pointed, "just over that ridge. If you walk to the top, you can see the roof of the abbey and the bell tower."

She hugged him tightly. He laughed, picking her up and swinging her around, her crutches flying. "I told you it was perfect!"

Chapter 45

The windows were all open, letting a wonderful early summer breeze blow through the house. Mickey peeled off her chambray shirt and stood balanced against the kitchen island in jeans and a t-shirt, making a salad.

"It's beautiful," Jennifer called admiringly as she came back downstairs, looking around the living room.

"It won't win any design contests."

"I don't know," Jennifer disagreed. "It's austere – nothing on the walls, no frills, but every piece you've picked is beautifully made, functional. The hardwood floors are in beautiful condition. I like the sage and beige you've picked for the walls. It's clean and... meditative."

Mickey grinned. "Think maybe my taste has been influenced by five years in a monastery?"

"Undoubtedly." Jennifer looked around. "Including no television, I see."

"Too much noise," Mickey wrinkled her nose. "I prefer the quiet. Speaking of which, I can't tell you how much I appreciate you and Jamie allowing me to stay at your house the last few weeks while the work here was being completed. The commotion of all the construction workers was unbelievable."

"Well, it's not like your presence inconvenienced us in any way," Jennifer replied, pausing to peruse the books on the built-in shelves.

"We were both stuck in the city for the past month. Jamie's latest commission was very well received, and he got two more as a result. That's where he is now." Jennifer stopped in front of the only photo on display – it was one taken about a year before Alice got sick. Mickey was sandwiched in between Alice and Jennifer, all of them laughing hysterically at something – Jen couldn't remember what.

"Dinner is almost ready," Mickey said. "Any chance Jamie'll be joining us?"

"I'm really not sure. You know what he's like when he gets working," Jennifer shrugged. "He may be there all night long." Jennifer pulled a book out and flipped through the pages. "I noticed there's one furnished room upstairs," she said nonchalantly.

"Very subtle," Mickey observed sarcastically. "I'll furnish the other rooms as I find decent stuff at moving sales and antique shops, but… I wanted one room ready for her in case she wants her own space."

Jennifer turned from the bookshelf. "You said in her letters that she never comes out and says if or when she'll be back. It's been months. Do you really still believe she'll come to you after all this time?" she asked dubiously.

Mickey didn't answer immediately. Her crutches clicked metallically as she moved over to the stove to stir the chicken simmering in a pan. "I have to," she said quietly. "Could you set the table?"

"Sure," Jennifer said.

"Mickey!" she exclaimed, stopping in her tracks as she entered the kitchen.

"What?" Mickey jumped, looking around to see what had startled Jennifer.

"Look at you! I haven't seen you in anything but a habit or a sweater for ages. I didn't realize you were this lean, and look at your arms!"

Mickey laughed as she spooned rice into a bowl. "I can't afford to carry any extra weight anymore. Hauling my ass around on these," she nodded toward the crutches propped against the countertop, "for the past year has been like a daily weight workout."

"Well, you look fantastic," Jennifer said, giving Mickey's butt a pat on her way to the cupboard to get plates. "If I weren't married..."

"To my brother."

"Well..."

"And pregnant."

"Oh. Yeah."

"You are rotten," Mickey scolded, but she smiled as she added, "But thanks anyway." She put the bowls of food on a rolling cart and pushed it all out to the table, using her hips and crutches to steer it.

"What a great idea," Jennifer said as she set the bowls on the table.

"Well, it's noisy, but I'm learning to make as few trips as possible," Mickey said as she sat.

"Ummm, this smells great. Alice would be so proud of you," Jennifer said as she passed the chicken to Mickey.

"No," Mickey laughed, "she'd be pissed that I could have learned to do this a long time ago, and didn't."

Just as they began dishing food onto their plates, the doorbell rang.

"Come in!" Mickey called out, salad tongs in hand. "You're just in t–"

Jennifer grabbed her arm. Mickey looked at Jennifer and then followed her gaze to the door. It took her a few seconds to recognize the woman standing there beside Jamie.

"Look who turned up at our house," he said.

Lauren was wearing corduroy slacks and a light turtleneck, and her blond hair was long enough to be pulled back into a loose braid, but the eyes, Mickey would have known those eyes anywhere.

Mickey sat back weakly in her chair, still holding the salad tongs. "We were just talking about you," was all she could think of to say.

"Am I interrupting?" Lauren asked uncertainly.

"Of course not," Jennifer said, jumping up to give her a hug. "Come in and sit down," she insisted as she led Lauren and Jamie to the table.

Jamie held back. "We should go."

"Don't be silly," Mickey chided, collecting herself. "Let's say grace and eat."

They clasped hands and Mickey prayed, "We thank you for all the blessings you have given us, for the food we are about to receive, but mostly," she squeezed Lauren's hand, "we thank you for allowing us all to be together again. Amen."

As they began eating, Jennifer excitedly asked Lauren to tell them what she'd been doing.

"I've been in San Francisco," Lauren answered. "Dealing with my mother's will. Did Michele tell you anything about that?" When Jennifer and Jamie shook their heads no, Lauren continued, "Well, it's been a nightmare. I was finally able to buy my sister's share of the house and give my father the deed. I convinced her to contribute to a trust fund for him, and I got my brother set up with a trust fund also, which will only pay him the interest. If he finds a way to go through the principle, he's on his own."

She ate a few bites, not saying anything more until Mickey asked uncomfortably, "What about the rest?"

Lauren looked at her with a smile and said, "That's the best part. After all my mother did to try and sever my connection to St. Bridget's, I've given the abbey the rest of her money."

Mickey stared at her for a moment, then threw her head back and laughed.

"It took a while to set it up in such a way that the diocese can't touch it. It all goes to the abbey," Lauren said happily. "I'd give a lot to see my mother's reaction to that."

Jennifer looked confused. "How much?" she asked innocently.

"Just over fifteen million."

Jamie dropped his fork. "Fifteen million dollars? You gave up fifteen million dollars? You didn't keep any of it?" he asked as if he was having trouble comprehending this notion.

"I've never wanted my mother's money." Lauren looked down at her plate, pushing her food around with her fork. "I kept a few thousand, enough to set up a new life somewhere..." she looked up at Mickey uncertainly.

"Here? I hope," Mickey said, her eyes shining.

Lauren's face was radiant as she smiled back at Mickey. After a few seconds, she turned to Jennifer. "Tell me about you and Jamie, and the museum's restoration work."

Jennifer chatted happily as they finished their meal, filling Lauren in on Jamie's latest work. The tapestries they had nearly finished before the fire were now on display at the Mannheim, but, "Mother Theodora hasn't been able to tell me whether or not the abbey will be able to resume any restoration work for us," she said as she rose to carry some plates into the kitchen.

"You're forgetting something," Mickey said as she caught Jennifer, wrapping her arm around Jennifer's waist. "We're pregnant," she announced, patting Jennifer's abdomen.

Lauren looked from Jamie to Jennifer and back to Mickey. Smiling, she asked uncertainly, "'We' are?"

"Yes," Jamie replied, grinning. "We are."

"You and I are going to be aunts!" Mickey said happily.

"And when are we due?" Lauren played along.

"In September," Jennifer answered. "And I'm going to remind all of you of the 'we' part when it comes time for labor!"

Mickey struggled to her feet, getting her crutches in position, and began walking into the kitchen.

"Michele!" Lauren exclaimed, her hands pressed to her chest. "I didn't realize - the last time I saw you, you weren't walking."

Mickey burned a deep red. "I don't know if you can call this walking, but it keeps me out of a wheelchair."

She stood propped at the sink to rinse the dishes as Jamie loaded the dishwasher and Jennifer and Lauren put away the leftovers.

"And now we are going home," Jamie announced as he put the last plate in the dishwasher. Mickey walked them to the door. "Call us when you're ready for company," he whispered as he gave Mickey a kiss on the cheek.

Mickey closed the door and turned to Lauren. She suddenly felt very self-conscious now that they were alone. "Let me show you around?" she suggested, turning to the stairs. She led the way up, showing Lauren the layout of the rooms up there. In the furnished bedroom, she explained awkwardly, "This room, this whole floor can be yours, if you want." She stared at the floor, blushing again. "I didn't know... I didn't want to assume..."

Lauren stepped close and took Mickey's face in her hands. Mickey felt she was drowning in those soft, grey eyes. Wordlessly, she brought Mickey's mouth to hers. The softness of her lips stunned Mickey who had almost forgotten what a kiss felt like. "That's not fair," Mickey whispered, resting her forehead in the crook of Lauren's neck when they parted. Lauren wrapped her arms around Mickey in a strong embrace. "I'm already weak in the knees."

Lauren pressed her soft cheek against Mickey's and murmured, "Why don't you show me to our room?"

Mutely, Mickey led the way back down the stairs. Suddenly, several thoughts occurred to her. "How did you get here? Do you have any luggage? And how did you find the house?"

Lauren smiled. "I flew into Syracuse and rented a car. I found Jamie and Jennifer's house, and Jamie drove with me here. I'm sure he and Jennifer will have an interesting conversation tonight. I'll go get my bag." She was back in a moment and followed Mickey through the family room into the new master bedroom.

"That dresser can be yours," Mickey pointed. "There are clean towels, t-shirts, robe - anything you need. I'll let you wash up while I go lock up the house."

She took her time locking the doors and windows. When she got back, Lauren was just coming out of the bathroom, wearing a sleeveless night shirt.

"I'll just be a minute," Mickey said. She quickly showered and brushed her teeth. Her heart was hammering as she buttoned up her pajama shirt. She braced her hands on the sink, inspecting her reflection in the mirror. She could see the shadow of the agitated pulse beating in her neck. Taking a deep breath, she reached for her crutches. When she emerged from the bathroom, the bed was turned down, and the bedside lamps were on their lowest setting. Lauren was sitting on the side of the bed, her blond hair falling loose down to her shoulders.

"It looked like this might be your side of the bed," Lauren said shyly as Mickey sat beside her, laying her crutches within reach on the floor. She reached up to run her fingers through Mickey's red hair. "I see you've kept it short."

"I always liked it better that way," Mickey said. She took Lauren's hand in hers, gently intertwining their fingers. "I can't believe you're finally here."

"I feel like I've been in purgatory, just waiting to be able to come to you. I'm sorry it took me so long," Lauren said sincerely. "I wanted to come immediately when Mother wrote that you had left, but every time it seemed I might be able to leave, my sister pulled some new legal trick to drag things out. I'm so sorry I was never able to give you a date, but I was afraid of saying I'd come and then not be able to. I had to be sure she couldn't undo everything I'd been working on."

"I've missed you so much," Mickey murmured.

Lauren traced her fingers over the contours of Mickey's face. "And I've missed you, more than I would have believed possible." A smile flickered across her face. "But you were waiting for me? You had a room ready for me? You trusted me that much, even after so long?"

Mickey looked at her, all the love she was feeling leaving her totally defenseless. "Yes."

Lauren again pressed her lips to Mickey's, but this time Mickey was ready, her lips parting, tongue gently exploring, asking Lauren to respond which she did.

Mickey pulled away after a moment and said softly, "I haven't done this in a very long time."

Lauren blushed. "It's been even longer for me, and I've never... with a woman..."

"But," Mickey said nervously, "now... some things are working, some things aren't... I don't know..."

Lauren brought her lips to Mickey's cheek and murmured reassuringly in her ear, "We'll figure it out together." She remained there for a few seconds, breathing in Mickey's ear. "Would you let me see your back?" she whispered.

Mickey nodded and let Lauren unbutton her pajama top. She slid it off Mickey's shoulders, her eyes admiring Mickey's muscular arms and shoulders, her small breasts. Mickey stretched out across the bed on her stomach. She understood. Lauren was as scarred by everything that had happened as Mickey was, only her healing had been put on hold while she was gone. The healing she needed to do had to be done together. Lauren pulled her night shirt off and lay gently next to Mickey. Mickey's skin still had large areas that were numb, but she could feel Lauren's fingers as they gently probed and caressed the scars and ridges on her back. Lauren shifted so that she was partially lying on top of Mickey, the soft pressure of her breasts and stomach warm against Mickey's skin. She could feel Lauren's hair and her breath and her lips as she tenderly kissed Mickey's back, and she could feel her tears.

"I never dreamed anyone could love me this much," Lauren whispered.

Mickey rolled over and wrapped her arms around Lauren, pulling her close. "I love you so much more than that," she said fervently. Everything else that needed to be said was said with her kiss.

⚜ ⚜ ⚜

Mickey woke with her cheek nestled against Lauren's shoulder, her arm rising and falling with Lauren's breathing as it lay draped over her chest. She shifted her hand to feel Lauren's heartbeat. Closing her eyes, she smiled. She had always felt blessed beyond reason to have the love of a woman as genuine and good as Alice, but she never expected to experience that kind of joy again. And yet, lying here, warm and soft, was a woman she would love, and who would love her in return, for the rest of her life. She glanced at the bedside clock, and woke Lauren with a kiss on the cheek.

"Good morning," she smiled. "I want to show you something. Let's get dressed." Mickey slid out from under the covers, and reached for her crutches. "Oh my gosh!" she yelped as the cold metal brushed her naked hips. In a few minutes, they had brushed their teeth, dressed and were going out the kitchen door.

"Where are we going?" Lauren yawned, pulling the collar of her jacket more tightly around her neck to ward off the pre-dawn chill.

"You'll see," Mickey told her excitedly. "This was the one extravagance I allowed myself."

They were walking along a six-foot wide pathway built of decking boards. Benches were positioned every hundred yards or so, and the walk was lit, dimly now as dawn approached, by a series of solar lights. Even though it was chilly, Mickey was soon panting and sweating with the effort of the steady uphill climb.

"Why don't we sit and rest?" Lauren asked worriedly.

"I'm fine," Mickey insisted breathlessly. "We're almost there."

With one final climb up some steps, the path ended at a screened-in gazebo with two chairs facing to the west. Behind them, the eastern sky was just beginning to lighten.

"Wait," Mickey gasped as they sat in the chairs.

Lauren sat beside her, patiently waiting for a moment, and then she heard it. The bell for Lauds was ringing. She turned to Mickey in the rosy light, an expression of amazement on her face, and reached for her hand.

"Listen," Mickey whispered. Faintly, they could hear singing. When it ended nearly forty minutes later, Lauren wiped tears from her cheeks. "You can only hear the singing for Lauds and Prime most days," Mickey said, "and sometimes in the evening the voices will carry over here from Matins, but you can hear the bells all day long."

"I can't believe it," Lauren said, still weeping. "I've been so cut off from everything I've cherished – the abbey, you – it felt like I've been exiled or imprisoned somewhere I didn't want to be."

"You've given up so much," Mickey said guiltily.

Lauren looked over at her. "I didn't give it up for you, but I gave it up because of you." She clasped Mickey's hand more tightly. "You have opened my heart to a world where love and joy and trust are simply there – without any games or deceit. Believe me, after spending the last several months in a place where none of those things exists, it reminded me how rare and precious you are. And last night," she closed her eyes, remembering. "I confess, I've struggled a bit. Not with the fact that I love you, but our love has been so esoteric, so spiritual that part of me worried whether giving in to the sexual desire I feel for you would ruin things somehow, leave us feeling empty and lost once that part was satisfied. But last night... last night felt holy to me. I never knew what it could feel like to be so connected to another person, body and soul."

Mickey kissed Lauren's hand. "I love you so very much."

A bell rang in the distance and they could hear voices again, singing the hour of Prime. They sat side by side, holding hands, lost in the music as the dawn grew brighter around them.

"That's the last we'll be able to hear until maybe the evening," Mickey sighed when the singing faded. "I guess the air currents change as the day warms up." She reached for her crutches. "There's something else I want to show you."

"There's more?" Lauren laughed as they started back down the path.

"Jamie found this place and convinced me to buy it sight unseen," Mickey explained on the way back toward the house. "The original garage was too far from the house to be practical for me, but it was perfect for something else." When they got to the garage, she opened the door and flipped on the lights.

"Oh, Michele," Lauren breathed, bracing herself against the wall. "I can't believe this."

There was a floor loom, empty, waiting. To one side was a large work table and embroidery frames of various sizes. Along the wall were three utility sinks with drying racks attached to the wall.

"I didn't know if you would want to start working on your own creations, or maybe take on some restoration work. From what Jennifer says, even if St. Bridget's resumes some, there's a lot more waiting, even from other museums that have contacted her." She looked anxiously over at Lauren. "If anything isn't the way you want it, we can change it. I'd be willing to help. Just tell me –"

Her words were cut off by Lauren's kiss – a deep, passionate kiss as her arms held Mickey strongly against her. Lauren pulled away, holding Mickey's face in her hands and looking at her with a gaze that was hungry, almost angry, in its intensity. "Come back to bed with me," she said.

Inside, Lauren knelt and undressed Mickey as she sat on the side of the bed, caressing and kissing her as she did, and then undressed herself and lay down on top of Mickey. Remembering which areas had seemed the most sensitive the night before, Lauren touched and kissed and teased until Mickey was on the edge of orgasm and then positioned herself so that Mickey could touch her also. Together they came in a tumultuous climax that left them both trembling.

Lauren propped herself up on an elbow and tenderly ran her fingertips over Mickey's lips. "That was unexpected," Mickey gasped, still catching her breath. "This part of you is unexpected."

Lauren smiled uncertainly. "Is that good?" she asked.

"It's very good," Mickey laughed.

"I think I'd better get you some breakfast or you'll never have enough stamina for our first day together."

"If it's going to be more of this, it had better be a really big breakfast."

Chapter 46

"Thank you, everyone," Mickey said, looking around at the nurses and anesthesiologist as they continued counting instruments and cleaning up the surgical debris after the patient was wheeled into the recovery room.

Mickey stepped off the draped apparatus she'd been standing on to perform a hernia repair, a relatively simple forty-five minute procedure, but one she couldn't have done two weeks ago.

"I can stand upright without my crutches if I can brace my hips against something," she had told Greg as they had a late lunch at the hospital one day. The small cafeteria was nearly empty except for a few visitors and a maintenance man who was replacing an overhead light fixture. "But in the OR, I've got to be able to lean over the table and stay there at least a half hour, up to who knows how long? My muscles just won't hold me in that position, and I can't take the risk of endangering a patient by starting a procedure and having to stop in the middle of it to rest." She rested her forehead on her other hand as she poked at her chicken with her fork. "I don't think I'll be able to do this," she said quietly.

As she had expected, Mickey's first few weeks in Greg's practice were slow – two or three patients a day during her two days a week in the office. "It'll get busier once they get to know you," he assured her. She had been talking to the hospital administrators about operating there one day per week, but those talks had stalled when her physical limitations were brought up. She was surprised at how many of the hospital staff remembered her from Mother Theodora's accident. Several people asked about Mother, and she assured them Mother was doing well. If they were also curious about why she was no longer a nun, they didn't ask.

A few days after her conversation with Greg, Mickey was at the hospital, visiting a patient who had been admitted for a knee replacement, when she heard her name. She turned to see one of the hospital's maintenance men. He ran his hand nervously through his blond crew cut as he approached her.

"You were working in the cafeteria the other day," she recalled.

He grinned and nodded. "I'm Hank Matthews." He was caught off-guard when Mickey let go of her crutch and extended her hand to him. Hesitantly, he reached out and shook it. She could feel the calluses on his large hand.

"What can I do for you, Hank?"

"Well, I hope you won't think I was listening on purpose, but I heard you talking to Dr. Allenby that day in the cafeteria, and..." He gestured down the corridor in the direction from which he had come. "I've got something to show you, if you have a few minutes."

Puzzled, Mickey accompanied him to a maintenance workshop she'd never noticed.

"I may need to change some things," Hank said as he led Mickey to a tilted wooden platform, fitted with pads covered with vinyl upholstery. "Get on," he prompted when Mickey looked at him. She saw there was a foot plate to support her feet as she leaned her knees and hips against the pads. The pads supported her perfectly. "My wife is about your height, so I asked her to keep trying it out to get the pads right," he said modestly. "I didn't know how high to build it," he said, getting more excited, "so I made the upper part removable." He showed Mickey how the chest piece could be slid out of the main body of the platform. "But in case you do need this part, I cut the edges in so you can move your arms." He indicated the curved sides of the chest piece. "Is the angle all right? To hold you over an operating table? I could adjust it..."

His voice faltered as Mickey got off the platform and turned away. She swiped her hand across her cheeks and coughed to clear her throat. "Hank, why in the world would you go to all this trouble?" she asked, her back still to him.

"My wife remembers you when the Mother Superior was in the hospital," he answered, almost reverently. "She said you wouldn't leave her bedside, and you hardly ate anything –"

"Tammy?" Mickey recalled, turning to face him. "Tammy Matthews is your wife – from dietary?" He nodded. Mickey laughed a little. "I remember – she kept bringing me different things, trying to get me to eat."

"Well then," he stammered, getting red in the face, "we all heard about the fire, and how you got hurt pulling one of the other nuns out. Kenny, the guy who did the electrical work out there, used to work here with us." He looked down at his dusty workboots. "He was fired because he did such sloppy work." He scuffed one boot against a small pile of sawdust on the concrete floor. "Anyway, when I heard you saying how you couldn't lean over the operating table now, I got to thinking, and..." he waved a hand at the platform. "If it's not gonna work, you don't have to –"

"Are you kidding?" Mickey laughed. "Can we go try it out?"

Now, after her first successful surgery on Hank's tilted platform, Mickey checked on the hernia patient one last time, then she changed and was walking toward the staff exit to the parking lot. The metallic click of her crutches echoed a little in the tiled corridor.

"Dr. Stewart?"

She turned to see Tammy and Hank Matthews coming toward her. Hank was holding an envelope in his hands. "Dr. Stewart, we can't accept this," he said as they got near.

"Why not?" Mickey asked, afraid she had offended them somehow.

"It's too much," said Tammy.

Mickey smiled. "It's one weekend away, just the two of you, at an inn at the Finger Lakes. You probably haven't done anything for yourselves in ages." She laid a hand on Hank's shoulder. "You literally saved my career. Please let me do this one small thing for you."

They looked at each other and eventually nodded.

"Good!" Mickey said. "I want to hear all about it when you get back... well, maybe not everything," she added impishly as they both blushed.

☩ ☩ ☩

"Is that everyone?" Mickey asked Sister Mary David as she began packing up her stethoscope and unused gloves.

Her visits to the abbey had been well-received by the community. Over the past few weeks, she had treated several of the sisters for a variety of conditions. Some were as benign as hay allergies in one of the new postulants, but some situations were more serious. Sister Cecilia had finally admitted to having chest pain with the exertion of carrying some of the heavier pots in the kitchen. Mickey was ordering a cardiac catheterization for her as soon as it could be scheduled.

"I believe so," Sister Mary David replied, pulling aside the curtain they used to give Mickey a private exam space within the infirmary. "Sister Scholastica," she said in surprise. "I didn't realize you were here."

Mickey wheeled around on the stool she used to maneuver within the infirmary.

"I don't... I shouldn't..." Sister Scholastica stuttered. She started to turn around, but Sister Mary David deftly blocked her exit.

"You're here now," she said calmingly, taking her elbow and steering her toward the exam cubicle. "I'll leave you to talk to Dr. Stewart privately," she said as she pulled the curtain closed.

Mickey looked up at Sister Scholastica who still stood, her hands tucked into her sleeves. "Please, sit down," she gestured to the chair opposite.

Sister Scholastica sat on the edge of the seat, stiff and tense, staring at the floor. Her face was pale, except for a red blotch on each cheek.

"What is it, Sister?" Mickey asked gently.

When Sister Scholastica raised her gaze, Mickey was startled to see the fear there - "I've seen many emotions in those eyes, but I never thought I'd see fear," was Mickey's immediate reaction.

"Sister?" Mickey prompted again.

"I... I have a lump in my breast that probably should be examined."

Mickey opened and closed her mouth a couple of times. "How long ago did you find it?" she asked at last.

"I don't remember exactly," Sister Scholastica responded. "Probably three or four months ago."

Mickey quickly decided against lecturing her about the folly of waiting so long. "Has it gotten bigger?"

Sister Scholastica nodded and said in a matter-of-fact voice, "My mother and grandmother both died of breast cancer."

Mickey felt the goosebumps as a chill settled over her – the same chill she always got when she knew a bad diagnosis ahead of time. "Are you sure you're comfortable with me examining you?" she asked even more gently. "I could arrange –"

"No," Sister Scholastica interrupted. "No, Sister – I mean Doctor." She raised her gaze to Mickey's again. "I trust you."

Mickey bowed her head. "All right. I'll have you change into a gown," she said as she gathered her crutches and struggled to her feet. "I'll return when you're ready."

Outside the cubicle, she found Sister Mary David waiting for her. "I'm going to need you," she said quietly.

When Sister Scholastica was ready, they entered the cubicle together. With Sister Scholastica lying on the bed there, Mickey scooted her stool near and carefully pulled aside the gown to expose only as much as she needed for her exam. As she feared, the lump was large, and felt as if it extended deep into the breast tissue.

"I'm going to order a mammogram and an ultrasound to be done this week," Mickey said as she covered Sister Scholastica again. "I can't be certain without those results, but this is most likely going to require a mastectomy. Probably both sides with your family history."

Sister Scholastica nodded stoically. "You'll do it?"

Mickey searched her face. Sister Scholastica's features were still sharp, hawkish, but there was an expression of trust in her eyes that Mickey had never seen before. "I will if that's what you want."

"I do." Sister Scholastica sat up. "This will remain confidential?" she asked, sounding much more like her usual self.

"Except for Mother," Mickey replied. "She should be told."

Sister Scholastica nodded. "Yes. I'll go to her at once."

After Sister Scholastica had left, Sister Mary David said, "I've been infirmarian for over ten years, and that is the first time she has ever sought medical care at all that I know of. She always has some excuse for avoiding check-ups."

"I can't believe she came to me, of all people," Mickey said wonderingly. "After everything that happened before... it seems like a miracle."

Sister Mary David smiled. "Miracles happen all around us if we just take the time to see them. You should know that."

Chapter 47

Jamie looked out the kitchen window at the sound of tires skidding on the gravel driveway. "We don't need a doorbell to know you've arrived," he teased as Mickey and Lauren came in. Lauren carried a bowl of tomato salad into the kitchen and put it in the refrigerator.

"Sorry," Mickey grinned. "I'm still getting used to the hand controls. Whatever is grilling outside smells fantastic."

"Thanks. I'm cooking chicken and steaks. They've been marinating since last night. Hope you like the taste."

"Hi," Jennifer said as she came down the stairs. "I thought I heard Speed Racer arrive," she smiled, coming over to hug both of them.

"Did you just get in?" Lauren asked as she and Mickey seated themselves on the sofa.

"Yes, about an hour ago," replied Jennifer. "The train is working out really well. And my boss has been very understanding about letting me work from home. Luckily a lot of my research can be done on the internet. I've only had to go in one or two days a week. I brought home some pieces to show you. Fourteenth century Italian and we think tenth century Irish."

"Really?" Lauren's face lit up.

"After dinner," Jamie commanded. "Otherwise you two will disappear for hours."

"And I'm hungry," Mickey chimed in.

"You're always hungry," Lauren laughed.

"Well, I've been working up an appetite," Mickey defended herself.

"Oh?" Jennifer responded in an innocent tone, but with a wicked gleam in her eyes as she looked from Mickey to Lauren.

Jamie snorted with laughter as Mickey's face turned scarlet and Lauren sat back with her arms folded, eyebrows raised.

"I meant because I'm getting busier at work," Mickey tried to extricate herself.

Jennifer came around the sofa and hugged Mickey from behind on her way to the kitchen. "You don't have to explain. We're happy for you no matter where your appetite is coming from."

"I'll go turn the meat," Jamie said, still laughing as he went out to the grill.

"Sorry," Mickey murmured when they had both left. "I can't help that reaction. And I'm a horrible liar."

"I'll remember that," Lauren said, sliding closer to Mickey on the couch. "Actually, I'm not as uncomfortable as I thought I'd be. They're so easy to be around." She reached over for Mickey's hand. "I like not having to hide."

As if to prove her point, Lauren surprised Mickey by remaining where she was when Jamie came back inside.

"Everything should be ready soon," he announced.

"I'll set the table," Lauren volunteered.

Within a few minutes, they were all seated at the table.

"How was the doctor's appointment last week?" Mickey asked as she cut her steak.

"She said everything looks good," Jennifer answered, passing the salad bowl to Jamie. "The ultrasound was fine, and I've only gained five pounds since my last appointment."

"And you still don't know if it's a boy or girl?" Lauren asked.

"No," Jamie smiled. "We want to be surprised." He turned to Mickey. "We're turning your old room into the nursery for now."

"What about the addition?" Mickey looked up from her plate.

"We decided to wait. If we started now, we'd still be in the middle of all the construction mess when we bring the baby home."

"Any decisions on names?" Mickey asked.

Jamie and Jennifer looked at each other with expressions equal parts amusement and exasperation. "It's an ongoing discussion," Jennifer said diplomatically.

Deciding it was a good time to change the subject, Jamie turned to Mickey. "How have your visits to the abbey been going?"

"Really well. It's strange to be back there. I wasn't sure what kind of reception to expect," she said. Remembering her visit with Sister Scholastica, she added, "but I feel like I'm meant to be there in this role."

Jennifer looked at Lauren. "Have you been back yet?" She thought she saw a shadow pass over Mickey's face, but it was just a flicker and then it was gone.

"I have an appointment to see Mother Theodora next Tuesday," Lauren replied. "It's been nearly a year since I last saw her. I have to admit I'm a little nervous. There are a few details of my gift to the abbey that we need to talk about."

After dinner, Mickey and Jamie went out to the barn to see his latest sculpture while Jennifer and Lauren went upstairs to look at the vestments Jennifer had brought home.

"Oh, Jennifer," Lauren breathed in awe, "these are exquisite."

"Aren't they?" Jennifer smiled. "All most people see is the damage, but I knew you would appreciate the workmanship. We think this Italian piece may have traveled to Avignon with one of the popes during that period. And this Irish vestment," she held up a much less ornate and more fragile piece of embroidered linen, "was found not too long ago in the cellar of an Irish monastery. Are you interested in restoring them?"

"Absolutely." Lauren bent to get a closer look at the fine stitches still visible through centuries of dirt and water damage.

Jennifer watched Lauren's skillful hands as they gently probed some of the broken threads. "I don't mean to pry," she said hesitantly, "but is Mickey upset or worried about your visit with Mother Theodora next week?"

Lauren sat back in her chair and looked at Jennifer. "You picked up on that?"

Jennifer nodded.

Lauren frowned a little. "I think part of her still worries that she pulled me away from my vocation."

Jennifer looked puzzled. "She's afraid you'll want to go back to St. Bridget's?"

"It's the opposite of being afraid I'll leave her; she's afraid I won't. She thinks I feel so guilty about her injuries that I wouldn't be open to hearing that call if it were still there."

Jennifer's protective instinct prompted her to ask, "Is she right?"

Lauren looked past Jennifer, considering her response. "I don't know if I can explain it in a way that anyone else can understand. If I had never met her, I could easily have lived the rest of my life at the abbey. St. Bridget's, and Mother Theodora, gave me the chance to rebuild a shattered life into one with meaning, and I was content there." She shifted her gaze back, and Jennifer was struck by the hypnotic quality of those grey eyes. "But when I met Michele, my entire world changed. She's not good in a saintly way, not like Mother. She got into trouble, she swore and was very unmonastic at times," Lauren remembered with a tender smile, "but underneath that is a person of such incredible goodness that my heart could burst trying to contain all the love I feel for her."

Lauren was usually so reticent in discussing anything personal that Jennifer was unprepared for this unabashed outpouring of emotion.

Lauren continued, "She forgave horrible wrongs aimed at her, more than once, giving even the holiest women in the abbey an example they would have a hard time emulating. She sacrificed herself for days when Mother had her accident and again when we were all ill. She nearly gave her life saving mine, and it didn't have to be me – she would have done it for any of the others. She gives of herself more completely than anyone I have ever known." Lauren seemed to have a little trouble continuing as her voice cracked slightly. "I don't know what I ever did to deserve to be the next one she loved after your sister, but... I adore her. I will not feel called back to St. Bridget's because the contentment I knew there pales in comparison to the joy I feel at being around her. How do I tell her that just being with her is the greatest blessing I have ever known?"

Lauren and Jennifer both jumped at the sound of Mickey's crutches in the hallway. Jamie was standing at the door, looking in the direction of the stairs where they could hear Mickey's uneven footsteps as she descended.

"I think you just did," Jamie said quietly.

⚜⚜⚜

Lauren was at her loom when she heard Mickey's car pull into the new garage. A few minutes later, the door to the workshop opened, and Mickey came in.

"Hi," Lauren smiled as she looked up. "How was your day?"

"It was good," Mickey replied, coming over to sit next to Lauren like she used to at St. Bridget's. "We did a double mastectomy on… a patient with breast cancer, and I think we got everything," she said as her eyes tried to follow the rapid movements of Lauren's hands.

"I've been meaning to ask you," Lauren glanced at her curiously, "when you operate now, is it any different from the way you used to? Before the abbey?"

Mickey reached up to run her hand over Lauren's blond hair. "I always remember the way you prayed before Mother's operation, and now I say a similar prayer before every procedure." She paused. "I never make the mistake any more of thinking I'm in charge. What are you making?"

"I thought I'd make some drapes for the house," Lauren answered. "The simplicity of the furnishings you chose would be nicely complemented by a rich silk brocade. Each panel will be half of an adaptation of a Renaissance design of the Tree of Life," she explained. "Do you like it?"

"It'll be beautiful," Mickey said appreciatively. "Please tell me if there is anything you ever want to add or change. This is our house, not mine."

Lauren paused the loom and turned to Mickey. "I love you very much," she said sincerely. "I've never lived with just one other person. I didn't know what to expect, but you are so easy to live with."

Mickey kissed her, savoring the moist softness of her lips. "I'll get dinner started," she said. She struggled to her feet, groaning a little.

"Michele! What happened?" Lauren cried in alarm as Mickey turned toward the door.

"What?"

"Your back is bleeding," Lauren said, coming over to inspect a large patch of blood which had soaked into Mickey's shirt.

"Damn," Mickey muttered, craning her neck, trying to see the spot herself. "I tripped on a curb – didn't pick my foot up high enough, and fell onto the stupid crutch." Now Lauren noticed her right forearm was also scraped and bloodied where the cuff of her crutch had been caught when she fell.

"Come inside," Lauren insisted. "We'll take a look."

In the bathroom, Mickey sat on the toilet lid and removed her shirt and bra to reveal a long gash across her ribs where the impact of the crutch had split open a grafted area. As gently as she could, Lauren bathed the wound with a warm washcloth, cleaning up the dried blood which had dripped down Mickey's back. Mickey didn't complain, but a sharp intake of breath let Lauren know how painful it was.

"Are you sure you didn't break any ribs?" she asked, worried. "You have bruises starting to show." The black and blue imprint of the crutch could be traced along Mickey's ribs now that the blood was cleaned off.

"I don't think so," Mickey assured her. She instructed Lauren how to dress the gash with ointment and gauze.

As she knelt and finished applying tape to hold the gauze in place, Lauren wrapped her arms around Mickey, holding her tightly and kissing her shoulder. Mickey let herself lean back into Lauren's embrace. "Thank you," she said. She placed her hands over top of Lauren's and moved them up to her breasts.

Lauren could feel Mickey's nipples harden under her fingers. "Aren't you hungry?" she asked softly, kissing Mickey's ear.

"Yes," Mickey whispered, "but not for food. Let's move to the bed."

"Are you sure? This won't hurt you more?"

"I'm sure."

Over at the bed, Mickey unbuttoned Lauren's blouse. She pushed it off her shoulders and unfastened her bra. Barely touching her, Mickey ran her fingertips over Lauren's skin, smiling at the goosebumps that followed. Gently, she pushed Lauren back on the bed and bent to take a nipple in her mouth before she slid Lauren's pants and underwear over her hips. "I will never tire of looking at you," Mickey murmured, bracing herself on one arm and running her free hand over Lauren's velvety stomach and the curve of her hips. "You are so beautiful."

"So are you," Lauren said, sliding her hand up Mickey's arm, feeling the contour of the firm muscles.

Mickey abruptly sat up and turned her face away. "Don't," she said, a trace of bitterness in her voice. "I know better."

Lauren sat up and placed a hand on Mickey's shoulder. "Why? Because of your scars? Your crutches? They could never be ugly to me," she said reverently, "They remind me how much you love me and what you were willing to do for me. But no matter how you got them, no physical scar could detract from how beautiful you are inside."

When Mickey didn't respond, Lauren placed a hand on her cheek, compelling her to turn and face her. Looking into Mickey's eyes, Lauren was shocked at the doubt, the vulnerability she saw there. "I am so sorry I never said this to you before," she whispered, "I thought you knew." She pressed Mickey back to the mattress, kissing her, softly at first, and then with more passion as she shifted so that she was lying on top of Mickey, the warmth of their breasts pressing against each other. Lauren kissed her way along Mickey's neck, down to her breasts, feeling Mickey's excitement mount with her own. She moved back up and looked into Mickey's eyes. "How could you not know how beautiful you are?"

⹋⹋⹋

The next morning, Lauren carried two mugs of coffee up to the gazebo. They had kept the monastic habit of rising early, climbing up to the gazebo most mornings to start the day with a silent period of prayer and reflection as they listened to the faint voices in the pre-dawn quiet. Mickey was more winded than usual when she got to the gazebo.

"Your ribs?" Lauren asked worriedly when she saw Mickey wince as she lowered herself into her chair.

"Yeah. Just stiff and sore from the fall," Mickey said as she accepted a hot mug from Lauren.

In silence, they sipped their coffee, waiting for the bell to signal the start of Lauds. Lauren noticed that Mickey's breathing was not slowing down as quickly as it normally did. The bell rang and distant voices were carried to them in the still morning air. When Lauds and Prime were over, Lauren turned to Mickey.

"Michele, are you certain you are comfortable with my visit to Mother this morning?"

Mickey reached for her hand. They hadn't discussed the overheard conversation with Jennifer. "Yes," she responded softly. "I just needed to be sure you weren't ignoring a call back to religious life." She kissed Lauren's hand tenderly. "I'm sure now," she said with a smile.

Lauren leaned over to kiss her. "I'm going to shower and then I'll start breakfast."

"I'll be down soon."

Back at the house, Lauren stood under a hot shower until the chill was gone from her bones, then toweled off and dried her hair. She pulled her jeans and sweatshirt back on and went to the kitchen.

"Michele?" she called, peering into the living room. Puzzled, she went to the kitchen window and looked up toward the gazebo. The morning was light enough now to make out the path. She saw no sign of Mickey. She went out the back door and called. There was no answer. Feeling uneasy, she started back up the hill. Halfway up, there was a limp form lying in the grass. She ran to Mickey, kicking the crutches out of the way.

"Michele!" she cried, turning Mickey over. "Oh God, no," she moaned, panicking. Mickey was lying in a pool of blood she apparently had coughed up. There were frothy red bubbles on her lips and blood running down her cheek. "I'll go call for help," she said desperately.

"No," Mickey whispered with more bubbles. "Don't go." Her hands grabbed tightly to Lauren's arms. "Just hold me," she insisted, her voice sounding like someone talking underwater. Lauren could hear a wet rattle with every shallow breath.

"Michele," she said in an urgent voice, "please don't leave me." But she knew better.

Calmly, Mickey looked at her and whispered, "I'm sorry."

Lauren brushed the bloody bubbles away and kissed her softly. "I love you."

Mickey smiled. "I know." Her chest heaved once in a reflexive attempt to pull in more air, and then she was still.

⌁⌁⌁

Lauren was still sitting on the hill, holding Mickey when Jamie and Jennifer arrived nearly half an hour later. She heard tires squeal to a halt in the driveway and could hear their voices calling out as they searched the house and workshop. She tried to call to them, but no sound would come from her throat. Eventually, they came up the pathway, Jamie breaking into a run when he spied Lauren and Mickey. He dropped to his knees, his face a stark white.

He raised his eyes questioningly to Lauren's. "She's gone," she whispered.

Lovingly, he took Mickey's limp body in his arms and held her to him as he sobbed. Jennifer knelt beside him, crying also as she wrapped her arms around both of them.

It wouldn't occur to Lauren until hours later to ask Jennifer what made them come. "Jamie knew," Jennifer told her. "He knew something had happened. He came to get me and told me we had to get over here right away."

Lauren sat with them for a while, and then went down to the house to call Greg. She told him what had happened. "I wasn't sure who to call," she said in a dazed, emotionless voice.

It took a few seconds before he could speak. "I'll take care of it," he finally said. "It sounds as if she had a pulmonary hemorrhage, but an autopsy will probably be ordered to be sure."

Lauren went back up the hill to sit with Jennifer and Jamie until an ambulance arrived for Mickey's body. The three of them accompanied the gurney back down the hill, answering questions for the paramedics' report.

"What now?" Jennifer asked when the ambulance had left and they were seated around the kitchen table.

Lauren looked around blankly. "I guess we'll have to contact a funeral home... I should let Mother Theodora and the community know what happened. I'll ask if the funeral can be held at St. Bridget's."

"Can she be buried there?" Jennifer asked, as her eyes filled with tears again.

Lauren shook her head. "Only the nuns can be buried in that cemetery. But... if Michele were cremated, we might be able to disperse her ashes there."

Jennifer smiled through her tears. "I think she'd like that."

Lauren looked at the clock. It seemed impossible that it was only nine thirty. This day already felt a lifetime long. She stood up. "I'm going to change," she said, looking down at the blood on her sweatshirt and jeans. "I'll keep my appointment with Mother Theodora." She turned toward the bedroom, but stopped. "Would the two of you go to the funeral home with me later?"

Jamie used his sleeves to dry his cheeks. "Yes. We'll call the relatives. Why don't you come to the house when you leave the abbey, and we'll go together to make the funeral arrangements."

When Lauren got to St. Bridget's, she paused in front of the oak doors. For most of the past year, she had imagined what it would be like to come back. When she was in California, she'd thought she might feel a little homesick, maybe a little awkward, but the past six weeks with Mickey had changed everything. Life after the abbey had been more than she'd ever dreamed it could be, until this morning....

She knocked. It took Sister Lucille several seconds to recognize her. "Sister Anselma!" she exclaimed happily, giving Lauren a hug.

"It's Lauren now, Sister," Lauren reminded her, returning the embrace, though Sister Lucille's head only came up to her shoulders.

"Of course, my dear. Mother is waiting for you. You remember the way."

"*Venite.*"

"*Pax tecum*, Mother."

"*Et cum spiritu tuo*, Lauren," Mother Theodora replied with a smile as she rose from her desk to greet Lauren with an embrace. She stopped as she drew near, her sharp eyes boring into Lauren's. "What is it? What's wrong?"

Lauren hadn't cried a single tear all morning, but now she crumpled into Mother Theodora's arms, sobbing. Mother Theodora guided her to a chair, and sat next to her, holding her closely and praying as she feared the worst. She waited patiently until Lauren could gasp, "Michele... died this morning..."

Mother Theodora closed her eyes and let her own tears flow. "I am so sorry, my child," she murmured as she rocked Lauren. When they both were able to talk, Lauren told her what had happened and Greg's guess as to the cause.

"I don't know how long an autopsy will take, but would it be permissible to hold her funeral here?"

Mother Theodora nodded. "We would be honored to be part of the celebration of Mickey's passing into our Lord's hands." She took Lauren's hand. "What about you? Is there anything you need?"

Lauren closed her eyes and shook her head. "A short while ago, I wouldn't have known it was possible to hurt this much, but... I think maybe this is the price I had to be prepared to pay in order to know the joy of loving her. She gave me more happiness in the time we had together than I had known in my entire life previously."

"I think we will find that that happiness is the legacy she gave to most who knew her," Mother Theodora mused.

Chapter 48

No one was prepared for the outpouring of sympathy as word got around. Most of the cards, telephone calls and flowers were directed to the abbey, as most of the people who knew Mickey still associated her with St. Bridget's. Sister Lucille and Sister Teresa recruited the juniors to help carry the seemingly endless procession of flower arrangements into the Chapel. Mother Theodora herself gathered the cards together in a bundle for Lauren.

Jennifer had contacted Susan and Christie who quickly spread the news of Mickey's death among their friends and Mickey's former colleagues at Hopkins. They put an obituary in the Baltimore Sun, and arranged a caravan for those who could make the trip to New York. Christopher and what seemed like half the congregation of St. Matthew's made plans to drive up. Natalie flew up from Florida, and the entire Worthington family made the trip. Danielle Wilson and her parents came as well.

The day of the funeral dawned clear and cool for late July. Sister Teresa came to Mother Theodora in a panic. "Mother, the funeral Mass won't even begin for another hour, but the public Chapel is already packed, with people standing outside who can't fit into the Chapel."

Mother Theodora came to see for herself. It was like a party. Many of the people in attendance seemed to know one another, and were catching up with each other and exchanging stories about how they knew Mickey. She recognized several people from Millvale's hospital. "Let's open the doors to the Chapel, and gather as many chairs as we can - from the refectory, the common room, wherever we can find them."

The nuns scurried like ants, creating an outdoor seating area. "They won't be able to see, but at least they'll be able to hear," Mother Theodora said.

And what they heard sounded like angels singing, Lauren thought from where she sat in the front pew with Jamie and Jennifer and their parents. Mickey's plain, wooden casket was covered with a white cloth that Lauren had woven, working almost twenty-four hours without resting to have it finished in time. Sister Teresa had artfully placed some of the flower arrangements around the casket where it rested in between the two tiers of choir stalls.

Father Andrew asked Christopher to co-celebrate the Mass with him, which proved to be a blessing as both men choked up at different times, leaving the other to carry on for a minute or two alone. Together, they stood below the stained glass window, both of them wearing joyful, jewel-colored vestments as the nuns sang, "*Recordare Iesu pie, quod sum causa tuae viae...*"

The entire community seemed to stretch the volume and the enunciation of the Latin just a bit so that the sound absolutely filled the stone-vaulted space of the Chapel, spilling through the open doors in waves to those listening outside.

As there was no cemetery procession, most of the guests gathered outside following Mass, visiting, reminiscing, crying and holding one another, some of them laughing as they told stories about Mickey. Mother Theodora gave permission for those nuns who wished to do so to go out front and join them. Jessica, Sister Mary David and the nuns from the vestment room were among those who went.

From where she stood with Jamie and Natalie, Jennifer watched all the nuns make a point of seeking Lauren out for an embrace and promises of continued prayers on her behalf. When Sister Mary David left her with a kiss on the cheek and whispered words, Jennifer came over to Lauren and asked, "How much do you think they know?"

"Before today, I wouldn't have known how to answer that," Lauren replied in bewilderment, "but now, I'd say they all know – all the ones who really knew us."

As people said tearful good-byes and the crowd dwindled, Jamie came over to them. "I've asked your folks to take Mom back to our house with any of your family who can stay," he said to Jennifer. They exchanged a meaningful glance, then Jamie turned to Lauren. "Let us drive you home."

As they pulled out of the abbey's drive, Jennifer struggled to turn in her seat so she could talk to Lauren. "I can't wait till this baby is born," she grumbled, trying to readjust the seatbelt. "Lauren," she began hesitantly, "we've invited some of Mickey and Alice's old friends back to your house. Mickey was especially close to one woman, Susan Harris, and her partner, Christie. Mickey had written of you to Susan, and they asked if they could meet you." Jennifer could see the old wall come down over Lauren's features and she hastily continued, "They will only be here overnight, and most of them are staying at the hotel in town."

"Why would you do this?" Lauren asked angrily. "I don't want company, and I don't want to talk to strangers."

"Lauren," Jamie cut in, "they weren't strangers to Mickey." All she could see of his face were his eyes in the rearview mirror, and for a moment, it was as if Michele's eyes were looking at her. "They could be a support system for you if you'll let them. You've told us how you isolated yourself at St. Bridget's. Do you want to go back to living like that?"

All of Lauren's consternation and indignation dissolved. "You're right... it's just that I won't know what to say to them."

"We know this will be difficult," Jennifer said gently. "That's why we wanted to be there with you."

Apparently, Susan and the others were following Jamie's car to the house. When they arrived, a couple of strange cars pulling into the driveway behind them, Jamie said, "We'll give you a few minutes alone before we bring them in."

Lauren's heart was pounding as she walked through the house into the bedroom. The only thing she had in common with these women was Michele. "No, not Michele. Mickey," she corrected herself. Pre-monastic Mickey, people who knew her from a life Lauren hadn't been a part of – that had been Alice's role. She sat in a chair where her blood-stained sweatshirt and jeans were still draped over the back. Clutching the sweatshirt to her, she whispered, "Oh, Michele... I don't know how to do this without you." She could hear voices out in the kitchen. Bracing herself, she wiped her eyes on the sweatshirt and went out to join them.

"Lauren," Jennifer said, coming to take her by the hand while Jamie made coffee, "come and meet some of Mickey and Alice's old friends from Baltimore."

"Watch that 'old' stuff, Junior, or we'll tell Jamie stories from when you were thirteen," said one woman who came forward immediately, extending a hand to Lauren. "Hello, Lauren. I'm Susan." She reached her other hand out to the woman next to her. "And this is my partner, Christie. We were so sorry to hear about Mickey. I know how much St. Bridget's meant to her, and how hard it was for her to leave. I was so very glad to hear that she had found someone to love again."

Susan introduced the others, perhaps six or seven. Lauren lost track of the names.

"Come have some coffee," Jennifer said, inviting everyone to sit in the living room with a few extra chairs pulled from the dining room.

"The house is beautiful," Christie said admiringly as she looked around.

"It's all Michele's doing," Lauren replied with a proud smile. "She remodeled the house, with Jamie and Jennifer's help," she added as the two of them sat on either side of her. "I wasn't able to join her until a short time ago."

"How tragic," said one of the women whose name Lauren couldn't recall.

Lauren looked at her. "In what way?"

The woman shifted a little uncomfortably under that intense gaze. "Well, you both gave up everything, as nuns I mean, to be together, and then to only have a couple of months together..."

Lauren's countenance changed, and it seemed a light emanated from her. "You're wrong," she said quietly. "Religious life, and the intimacy of a close relationship with God, can be sublime - so much so that no human love could approach it. I was never fortunate enough to experience that state of grace as a nun. Meeting Michele opened my eyes and my heart to what a real relationship should feel like. For me, I would rather have had one night in her arms, one day basking in the happiness she gave me than a lifetime as I was. The tragedy would have been never to have known her at all."

Chapter 49

"Hi!" Jennifer said excitedly as Lauren knocked and entered the house. She came over to give her a hug and asked, "When did you get back?"

"Just last night," Lauren responded. "I'm not interrupting your morning, am I?"

"No," Jennifer laughed, pouring a cup of coffee for Lauren and joining her at the table. "There's no such thing as sleeping in anymore." She tilted her head to one side. "Come to think of it, there's no such thing as a schedule, either."

"How is Jamie adjusting?"

Jennifer's eyes widened as she expressed her surprise. "He has been wonderful. I honestly didn't know what to expect from him, but he's been incredible."

As if on cue, Jamie came downstairs, carrying the baby. His face lit up when he saw Lauren. "Hey, how was the trip?" he asked as he gave her a kiss on the cheek.

"It was really good," she answered, accepting the baby from him. "Thank you both for pushing me to go. Susan and Christie were very hospitable. They took me to some of the Baltimore museums, and then we went to D.C. and took in parts of the Corcoran and the National Gallery. It's overwhelming. I could live there for years, and never get through all the exhibits." As Lauren talked, the baby's eyes never left her face. Lauren stared back into eyes that were a lighter blue than Jamie's, looking at Lauren as if recognizing an old friend.

"Where are they now?" Jennifer asked.

"I left them sleeping at the house." She smiled. "I tend to forget that the rest of the world doesn't get up at four thirty." She looked up at both of them. "I'll go back to get them and we'll meet you at the abbey." She suddenly seemed to remember something, and looked around the house. "Where are your relatives?"

"Mom and Dad rented a vacation house not far away so that we could have some peace and quiet here," Jennifer explained.

"And they took our mother with them," Jamie said with a big grin. No one had pointed out to him that he frequently used plural pronouns as if Mickey were still with him.

Later that morning, a caravan of cars drove up to the abbey where the large Worthington family, along with Lauren, Susan and Christie, converged once again upon St. Bridget's, disrupting the quiet, meditative atmosphere.

Mother Theodora greeted them in the Chapel, explaining the procedure for the day's ceremony. "We don't do this too often. In fact," she corrected herself, laughing, "I don't believe we've ever done this."

Leaving the grille opened, she returned to her chair at the head of the choir. Within a few minutes the nuns filed in, singing a processional chant. Father Andrew began the Mass, and after the reading of the Gospel, summoned Jennifer, Jamie and Lauren to the altar with the baby.

Mother Theodora held a large silver basin in lieu of a baptismal font, as the abbey did not have a permanent one. Lauren took the baby in her arms as Father Andrew asked, "Who stands with the parents in raising this child as a child of God?"

"I do," Lauren replied, but her voice was drowned out as nearly the entire community stood and said with her, "I do."

Father Andrew was clearly not expecting this, nor were Lauren, Jamie and Jennifer. Jennifer grasped Jamie's arm and pressed her face against his shoulder as he squeezed her hand. Lauren blinked back tears as she turned back to Father Andrew whose eyes were also shining.

"What name has been chosen for this infant?" he asked, his voice cracking a little.

Lauren gazed lovingly down at the small bundle in her arms. "Michele Alice Stewart," she answered clearly.

"Michele Alice Stewart," Father Andrew said, sprinkling the baby's head with holy water as Lauren held her over the basin, "*Te baptizo in nomine Patris, et Filii, et Spiritus Sancti.*"

The baby didn't make a sound, but grasped Lauren's finger tightly and held on as she watched Mother Theodora who stared back, entranced.

Following the Mass was a brief reception during which baby Michele was unquestionably the center of attention. She calmly allowed herself to be passed from nun to nun.

"She's the most unusual baby I've ever seen," Mother Theodora said to Lauren. "I'm not a believer in reincarnation, but I would have sworn when she was looking at me, that she knew me."

"I know what you mean," Lauren smiled. "She's been like that from the day she was born. I've never heard her cry. She seems ancient and wise. When I look into her eyes, she calms me." She turned to Mother Theodora with a curious expression. "What prompted the community's response today?"

Mother Theodora sighed with a small smile. "I think it was a combination of things. Most of the members of the community saw this as an opportunity to honor Mickey's memory, and I think many of us feel a certain sense that we, or I should say St. Bridget's, served as the epicenter of the events that brought this new life into the world." She glanced over to where Sister Scholastica, still recovering from her mastectomy, was now holding the baby. "We don't usually get to experience this."

Lauren smiled back. "Michele often said the abbey – this small, insignificant spot she called it – felt like the center of the world to her. She was amazed at how many people it had helped to bring together."

Mother Theodora slipped an arm through Lauren's and guided

her to an empty sofa in the corner of the common room. "I also believe one other reason for the community's decision to offer our support as the extended family of this baby is that many have guessed where the gift to the abbey came from." At Lauren's frown, Mother Theodora hastily added, "I have honored your request of anonymity, but most of the sisters believe it came from Michele or you, or both of you. I confess to being greatly surprised at the tolerance and acceptance I've heard expressed. I'm sure that attitude is not universal, but those people are keeping their opinions to themselves. In my early talks with Mickey, one of her biggest concerns about entering was the fear that she was turning her back on everything she and Alice had worked for in regard to changing people's fear and bigotry toward gay people."

Lauren looked down at the floor, blinking rapidly. "She's been gone for over two months, and she's still touching people, changing people. Including me." She took a deep breath. "I think it's time."

"Are you sure you want to do this alone?" Mother asked, laying a hand on Lauren's shoulder.

Lauren glanced over to where Jennifer and Jamie were talking with Sister Catherine. She caught Jamie's eye. He smiled and nodded. "Yes, if I may," she replied, turning back to Mother Theodora.

She slipped away from the common room, and retrieved a small wooden box she had left in Sister Lucille's office near the entryway. She moved quietly through the abbey into the enclosure garden and let herself out through the gate. The October sun felt warm on her face as she walked out to the orchard. A cool autumn breeze danced along with her, blowing leaves off trees and swirling them in tiny vortices on the ground. In the orchard, the apple trees stood like ugly gnomes, with their squat trunks and twisted, gnarled limbs, a few apples still clinging to the highest branches.

Lauren walked to the hill where Mickey had found her so long ago. Sitting, she cradled the wooden box in her lap. For a long time, she stared at the box, tracing her finger along the woodgrain of the top. "I know you're not in here," she murmured, "I don't know why this is so hard."

Suddenly, a warm pocket of air enfolded her, like a warm breath. Inhaling sharply, her entire body felt as if it were wrapped in an embrace more intimate, more erotic, more rapturous than any sensation she had ever experienced, leaving not only her body tingling, but feeling as if it reached all the way to her soul. She had no idea how long she sat there, but slowly the warmth dissipated, and she became aware once again of the normal sensations of the sun's warmth contrasted by cool air touching her skin.

"Thank you," she whispered, wiping away tears she hadn't realized she was crying.

She stood and opened the wooden box, tipping it to let the ashes within float away on the breeze. She walked slowly back to the abbey, still filled with the presence she had felt in the orchard.

When she returned to the common room, Jennifer and Jamie were waiting for her. "Is everything okay?" Jennifer asked, studying Lauren's face carefully. "You look... are you all right?"

Lauren reached out to take the baby from Jamie's arms. Even if she'd wanted to, how could she explain what had happened? Little Michele looked at her and broke into a smile. Lauren pressed the baby's cheek against hers and said, "I will be."

The End

About the Author

Caren was raised in Ohio, the oldest of four children. Much of her childhood was spent reading Nancy Drew and Black Stallion books, and crafting her own stories. She completed a degree in foreign languages and later another degree in physical therapy where for many years, her only writing was research-based, including a therapeutic exercise textbook. She has lived in Virginia for over twenty years where she practices physical therapy, teaches anatomy and lives with her partner and their canine fur-children. She began writing creatively again several years ago. She is the author of GCLS Award winner *Looking Through Windows* and *Miserere*. *In This Small Spot* is her third novel.